PRAISE FOR **IN THE FABLED EAST**

"Blends compelling realism with a naturalistic approach
to myth and magic realism... A novel that, while rich in
echoes of works like *Heart of Darkness* and *Lost Horizon*,
is breathtakingly original and shockingly powerful...
Simply put, *In the Fabled East*, is a winner, drawing on
disparate elements to create a singular, stunning whole."
Vancouver Sun

"No other writer gets the heat, the chaos, the shimmering
otherness of the East quite like Penticton's Adam Lewis
Schroeder... A witty romp through colonial Indochina...
the dimensions of which can only be imagined within the
pages of this marvelous and compelling tale."
Toronto Star

"An unforgettable tour of colonial Vietnam, connecting
characters and storylines from 1870s France to the after-
math of Dien Bien Phu with skill and authority, moving
with insight and wit from the ordinary to the mythologi-
cal without a seam. A fabulous piece of writing."
KARL MARLANTES, author of *Matterhorn*

"A novel of profound intelligence and wit, deftly
weaving history and myth, male and female, East
and West, agony and splendour... A stunning book."
ANNABEL LYON, author of *The Golden Mean*

"An enjoyable novel."
Globe and Mail

"A sublime and often hilarious travel adventure."
Toro magazine

"Schroeder deliciously conjures the mad, hot, stinking confusion that is Indochine ... A book to read, a writer to watch."
Telegraph-Journal

"[A] funny, profound and stunningly intelligent book. *In the Fabled East* is a madcap adventure, a sly, gregarious novel that tempts us, passionately, into the invisible realms."
MADELEINE THIEN, author of *Certainty*

"A risky literary enterprise well worth the journey ... You'll get so immersed in the world [Schroeder] creates that it might take some time to emerge from it."
BC BookWorld

"The 'fabled' in the title is a meaningful indicator ... the characters fashioned out of varying cultural interpretations of the East in their time periods ... But as historical fiction, the novel isn't really a critique of that era as much as it is of that era."
Vancouver Review

ADAM LEWIS SCHROEDER

IN THE

FABLED

EAST

A NOVEL

Douglas & McIntyre
D&M PUBLISHERS INC.
Vancouver/Toronto/Berkeley

Douglas & McIntyre
An imprint of D&M Publishers Inc.
2323 Quebec Street, Suite 201
Vancouver BC Canada V5T 4S7
www.douglas-mcintyre.com

Cataloguing data available from Library and Archives Canada
ISBN 978-1-55365-464-3 (cloth)
ISBN 978-1-55365-812-2 (pbk.)
ISBN 978-1-55365-615-9 (ebook)

Editing by Barbara Berson
Cover and text design by Jessica Sullivan
Cover image by Peter Lilja/Stone/Getty Images
Printed and bound in Canada by Friesens
Text printed on acid-free paper
Distributed in the U.S. by Publishers Group West

We gratefully acknowledge the financial support of the
Canada Council for the Arts, the British Columbia Arts Council,
the Province of British Columbia through the Book Publishing
Tax Credit and the Government of Canada through the
Canada Book Fund for our publishing activities.

For my parents.

CHINA

BURMA

DIEN BIEN PHU

HANOI

LUANG~
PRABANG

INDOCHINE

Gulf of
Tonkin

HAINAN

L
A
O
S

Mekong

SAVANNAKET

HUÉ

Kemmarat
Rapids

SIAM

BANKOK

KHÔNE

River

FRANÇAIS

PNOM-PENH

SAIGON

MY THO

Bay of Bengal

Gulf of Siam

Mer de Chine

MALAYA

INDOCHINE

0   100   200   300 mi.

0   200   400 Km.

THE FABLE OF THE
SPRING OF IMMORTALITY

as told by the Sadet.

ONCE a rich man was so miserly that he chose to live in the forest apart from other families. Leaving on a hunt, he told his son, "Watch over my jar while I am away, for it is our family's wealth." But the son fell ill with fever so that monkeys were able to enter the house and take great sport in rolling the precious jar out the door.

Because he was blustering and loud the rich man was a poor hunter and caught nothing, and so returned home in a rage, and was so angry when he discovered the jar stolen that he dragged his poor son into the forest and raised his knife. Because he was pure of heart the boy's last words were not "I do not wish to die" but "I wish that no one would die." Then his father left the little body unburned and unburied so that wild beasts would devour it. But instead the Spirit of the Water caused a spring to gush from the boy's mouth.

That night the rich man's relations, hurrying to invite him to a feast, took their rest beside the spring. They were surprised, for in all their years of travel they had never seen one in that place. They were no less surprised when they stumbled across the murdered boy as they made camp. They could no longer recognize him as their nephew, so they agreed that they would make no funeral but simply burn the little body in the morning.

They boiled water from the spring. They threw in their dried fish, and then the most surprising event of all occurred: live fishes leaped from the kettle! The water of the spring, the relatives suspected, was rife with spirits. They splashed water on the murdered boy and he sat up and through his mutilated lips described what his father had done.

The enraged travellers raced through the night to find the rich man. Hearing their cries, he ran out of his house—but because he was blustering and loud, he blundered into a tiger's jaws, and afterward this tiger suffered incurable diarrhea.

Meanwhile the son discovered the jar where the monkeys had abandoned it, and with this recovered wealth he founded a village below the spring. Of course the rich man should have known that a family's wealth is not its jars but its children.

MARSEILLES CUTTHROATS

Pierre Lazarie.

WHITE PEOPLE do not travel to Indo-China for their health, nor for prestige nor even for anything so straightforward as happiness; men come to make their fortunes.

Wishing to amass capital both intellectual and monetary, I arranged to sail in January 1936 from Marseilles for Saigon. Standing at the rail of the *Felix Roussel* on the morning of departure, I watched the crane swing a pallet of luggage aboard, the blue-sweatered men on our afterdeck holding up gloved hands to intercept it. I watched with some anxiety, really, since the pallet likely contained the trunk that itself contained the nine linen suits that had unburdened me of my governmental allowance at a stroke. Circling seagulls squawked as though the pallet were made of herring.

—Your mother insisted, Marguerite said, that you planned this trip even before it all happened!

My fiancée wore the tight-fitting green jacket she'd bought especially for the jaunt, its collar so liberally ruffled that her head looked as though it were emerging from the maw of a carnivorous plant. But the colour did complement her red hair rather nicely, and I noticed a number of men look up from their cabin assignments to assess her calves at the very least. Myself, I still wore the brown serge suit of my recently passed student days, as Marseilles' climate in January is less than tropical.

—I started dreaming of it five years ago! I said. That's no great revelation.

—She said *their* lives are different enough, with the housekeeper and the rest all gone, but *you* carry on unperturbed. Is there really no money?

—What does that matter? I'm going to make enough.

—Well, in her opinion you're so naive you're as likely to be knifed by a busboy at a cafeteria as you are to find these battlefields you go on about.

—Do we have to discuss my mother? I sail in five minutes.

—She says your head's so far in the ether you'll address all your letters to your father—but this legal business has unbalanced her. Hadn't you at least imagined travelling in First Class?

Upon my father's death we'd learned that he'd sired another family long before meeting Maman, and the legal business had upset her and my sisters to near-hysteria. Marguerite too, apparently, though she'd said nothing on the train down from Paris.

—Until the will was read, yes, I said. I thought I'd be going First Class.

She put a gentle hand on mine. She wore the same white gloves she'd bought the previous winter, though the material was beginning to pill; I'd mail her a new pair for her birthday in April. I flickered my eyelashes at her until she threw her arms around my neck.

—You looked so handsome when you tried on that white suit. I meant to ask, do they drive on the same side of the road as here?

—It's not a *British* colony!

—I just worry you'll look the wrong way and get run down. I'm not the one worried about the busboy at the cafeteria! But when you put on one of those suits you'll get your confidence, I know it. When does everybody change clothes?

—Once we're into the Indian Ocean, I expect.

The crane had finished its work and the blue-sweatered men hurried down the gangway. The ship's whistle sounded. We told each other again that we'd write every day, that it would seem as though we weren't apart at all, then we kissed again and again. She tasted saltier in Marseilles and I wondered if I did too.

—Another year or two, I said, and you'll be Madame Lazarie.

Her eyes were quite red.

—Give the tigers a pat on the head, she whispered.

I squeezed her hand once more, kissed her, then turned and walked toward the bow. The deck was so rife with breathless embraces one might've thought it was New Year's Eve at a honeymoon resort. A biting wind rose off the water so I fastened the top button of my jacket. I would not look back at Marguerite; I would have a drink. The ship's whistle sounded again and all around me ruddy-cheeked women sobbed afresh.

I strode into the Second Class saloon to discover a quartet of cadaverous card-sharps already resplendent in white suits, their broad white sun helmets shimmering on the benches. Already! In my brown serge I'd stand out like a chimney sweep at a garden party, so I sought out the barman.

—Where is the chief steward? I asked.

—Just now he could be anywhere.

—I need the trunk I sent below!

—I don't imagine you'll be able to get near that until we're well underway, sir.

A man in pinstripes nudged my elbow.

—Ridiculous, he said.

His blond moustache was bedecked with beer foam. With a wayward eyebrow he indicated the quartet in white as they smugly studied their cards.

—It certainly is uncouth to play with unescorted women still aboard, I agreed.

—It's those *get-ups* that are ridiculous—ten-to-one they took their quinine as though we were already at Colombo! Newcomer yourself? I'll let you in on a secret: those are their *only* suits, and the families pawned the silver services to be rid of them.

—They're not old China hands? I took them for game hunters!

—They're Marseilles cutthroats hired to ride herd over the coolies—rubber or coffee or tea or timber, coolies are all the

5

same stripe. And even if they were sunburnt and coughing betel nut I'd certify these ones had never set foot in Saigon, son, for we *know* each other there, and by way of example—if I'm not boring you?

—No, no. And another for my friend, I told the barman.

—Much obliged. In the corner, with his hand on that fellow's neck? He was up in the First Class saloon the last time out but, ah, there were inquiries into expenses, that's all a conscientious man ever hears these days, so he's gone from secretary at the Regency of Indo-China to *under*-secretary at the *Vice*-Regency of *Cochin*-China, you see the distinction, yes?

—What's he, then, a sort of copyist?

—A white man for a copyist—that is extremely funny, son, considering that the Yellows throttle each other for a post like that. But now that I look around—ah, that's refreshing, and you ought to have one yourself while the barrel's fresh—now, excepting those louts I can say that I'm acquainted with every man here. Starting at the back, there's Public Works, Court of Appeal, Chamber of Commerce, Commercial Port with the scar on the forehead, Bank of Indo-China, Military Port, Bank of Indo-China again—those boys with magazines are all Bank of Indo-China, and at the long table they're all from the consulates. That Dane, the little fellow, I swear every fever makes him an inch shorter, it's quite hilarious!

—And yourself?

He raised his eyebrows over the rim of his glass then came up with a snort, wiping his moustache clean with his bottom lip.

—I keep books at the opium factory on rue Paul-Blanchy!

He said it as though I'd be able to see in my mind's eye this undreamt-of thoroughfare some ten thousand kilometres distant. He hunted through his pockets.

—My name's Pierre Lazarie, I told him.

—Marcel Coderre. Delightful to meet you.

I swallowed the anxious saliva pooling beneath my tongue.

—Monsieur Coderre, well, I'd like to be prepared, mentally speaking. Might you give me some idea how many tigers I'm likely to come across, say, in the first month?

He looked up from his pocket watch with a slack-jawed smile.

—In Saigon?

—Certainly, yes, in Saigon.

—Be serious, how could each of these fellows get to their bank each morning if the streets were full of *tigers*? We're underway now, you see, the pilings are going past, so it's time to put stories for boys away!

—Ah! I must have imagined the protectorates less developed! I see, yes.

I gulped the rest of my beer.

—Even in the wilderness they never appear during the *day*, that's scientific fact!

Yet even as he chastised me my belly felt warmer, my head lighter, and generally speaking I was feeling extremely comfortable in the Second Class saloon.

—What's your line, anyway? he was saying. Write for a magazine?

—Oriental Studies, I said. Just received my baccalaureate! You must have seen the Colonial Exhibition in Paris in '31?

His foamy moustache shook dismissively.

—That *is* a shame, I said, because once I cast eyes on those stones from Angkor my heart was no longer my own. Our field doesn't much concern itself with the present-day Orient, of course, so much as with the old cultures, the Khmer, Cham, even the Moï and all the rest who're still up in the hills. I'm preparing a book on Annamese generals prior to French involvement, specifically the Tay Son brothers' capture of Saigon in 1776, though in the meantime, and provided I like the office work well enough, I'll draw my pay from the Immigration Department. But perhaps a modern study of Ly Thuong Kiet and the rest has already appeared in your part of the world?

—Look me in the eye, will you? No, I suppose not. Still, you talk as though you'd had eleven pipes already!

Evening found me still in the saloon, though I'd moved to the card table where I persisted in educating myself, though my every question—where does one do one's marketing? take one's collars to be starched?—was met with dumbfounded looks, as though I'd asked whether the bakery were the place to find bread or the cathedral communion. My friend of rue Paul-Blanchy dropped his cards abruptly upon their faces and I dragged the pot into my pile—a chap who, prior to the voyage, had only played Mouche on weekends with his grandparents!

—Now I'm not so green as to imagine your opium to be *illegal* out there, I said, but considering the civilizing mission we've officially undertaken, isn't it counterintuitive to happily *manufacture* the stuff?

Coderre wet the end of his cigar.

—Well, despite what you may have read in your tour brochure, son, Indo-China is not a church fête. We are not interested in *playing* with these people. The colony exists to turn a profit, yes? The colony exists so that the government at home can turn a profit and any business concern with a government contract can turn a profit and the government can make still more off the taxes those concerns pay. There's more dosh to be made out of taxing the stuff my outfit makes than there is from selling it wholesale, see, so why not give *me* the baccalaureate in Oriental Studies?

The quartet in white, bound for tellers' windows at the Indian & Australian Chartered Bank, chuckled and shifted cigarettes between their yellow knuckles. A steward on the dawn watch came around with a siphon and whisky.

—Exactly, I said. Most people hear the word "academia" and imagine we wear white gloves whether it's chemistry we're researching or the *Song of Roland*, refinement at the expense of reality—well, I intend to change that. I want the story of Indo-China from the mouths of its people, not from dusty manuscripts penned by dusty old men! It was dust that brought my father to his end, you know, even if the doctors disagreed.

—How's that? asked the commercial traveller who'd gone bust an hour before.

—Trigonometry professor. Used to climb a ladder, his equations were so long, and all that chalk dust! Came down with a fever, wasted away in front of us, which his doctor said was consistent with tuberculosis but where was the blood, then, the hemorrhaging? I knew it wasn't TB, I knew that as a result of his career his lungs were blocks of calcite.

—They do call it the White Death, smiled Coderre. *Chalk-white!*

—Call what? asked the commercial traveller.

—Let the detective explain!

—But even if my researches prove fruitless, I'm committed to earn some of this money you mention. Before she went ashore my fiancée advised me to do so in no uncertain terms. Mercenary, wasn't she? No, I cannot claim to "care for others first and enjoy happiness after," as Nguyen Trai suggested—

—Get your fiancée to do that for you, purred one of the quartet.

—Perhaps, I blustered, but it brings us to my *real* philosophy!

—At last, muttered Coderre. The wait was killing me.

—My ambition, my friends, is to love. Certainly, yes, I *am* a baccalaureate in Oriental Studies, a discipline which consumes me night and day, true; but it is also a means to an end—to win a reputation as well as a nest egg despite these lean economic times, and return before very long to my girl. For as Le Quy Don so aptly put it, "Verdant spring passes quickly, man ages rapidly like a bamboo shoot, and one should marry in good time."

—Your wedding night might be a good time, said the commercial traveller, if she could shut you up for ten minutes!

—"Fiancée"? asked another of the quartet. Which one of the pigeons was that?

—Was she that redhead? asked his crony.

—She *may* have been the redhead, I murmured. But I'd prefer not to say, for that way you're left with a mystery which will linger in your mind decades longer than any acknowledged fact. Yes, as a gift, I leave you the mystery.

Then we stared *en masse* at the high-chignoned cameos that lined the walls. My lecture, I admit, had been piloted by the seeming-lucidity of exhaustion, and when Coderre suddenly shuffled the deck we all blinked as one body.

—And did this redhead imagine, he asked, that any one of us had come aboard for his *health*?

Which brings me back neatly to my initial point.

MONSIEUR
HENRI LEDALLIC

Pierre Lazarie.

THE DOCK AT Saigon! My professors had tried to impart some idea of the scene: the tattered sails of the sampans plying the black river; the thatch-roofed native neighbourhoods; the pier crowded with French colonials, and the rickshaw and bullock-cart drivers jockeying for position under the trees beyond; the half-naked coolies, in hats shaped like candle-extinguishers, streaming up the gangway to carry off great steamer trunks in the hope of receiving a few pennies. As Parisian rain lashed at our windows I'd imagined this panorama so feverishly that each lithe and leathery coolie had become a sacred object in my mind, choristers all in an eternal opera, and as they rushed aboard the *Felix Roussel* each one was just as poignantly emaciated as in my dreams. Yet I was not prepared for every second coolie to be rheumy-eyed and sniffling, yawning into the back of his hand.

Neither had my teachers advised me that the colonial crowd would not be entirely male, clad in sun helmets and white tunics buttoned painfully at the throat as depicted in lithographs on our departmental walls, but would instead wear red ties, grey suits and fedoras, alongside a female population well-represented by curly-headed beauties peering up from beneath parasols and bedecked in the very styles worn at that moment in Marseilles—indeed, I spotted a septuagenarian flaunting

Marguerite's outrageously ruffled jacket. Nor had they described how richly yellow the flag of the Indo-Chinese Union would look as it snapped from every conceivable lamppost and house-top—an exhilarating sight for the newcomer, if perplexing, for to this day the significance of its colour alludes me. Yellow fever? Gold in the Mekong? Yellow men?

Three weeks out of Marseilles I'd been handed a shore-to-ship telegram from the Immigration Department for the Colony of Cochin-China. "Monsieur Henri LeDallic will greet you at the wharf," it had advised, information which had caused me to yawn abruptly before I'd returned my gaze to the cards in my hand and, just beyond those lovely jacks and nines, the fellows who'd been sitting opposite me for the previous sixteen hours. I was a chap fortunate enough to have a true love, an intellectual mission *and* six thousand francs on the table, so who was this "LeDallic" to me?

A steward took responsibility for seeing my trunk to cus-toms—those inopportune white suits!—so I could join the passengers streaming down the gangway while the coolies slipped past us as lithely as fish swimming upstream. The cash in my pocket caused my jacket to slope perceptibly while my mind turned over the fact that six thousand francs was the exact amount a classmate had paid to a private hospital for his girl-friend to have an abortion. Only as I scanned the hundreds of upraised white faces did I try to imagine this Henri LeDallic—a boy, a twisted old cripple? The crowd shouted names, certain women scrutinized each arriving face, and pairs of arms held up placards—*M. Ramèges, M. Martin, du Fresne*—but I failed to see my own name.

Men stood chatting without turning so much as an eye toward the *Felix Roussel,* like football spectators who care only to be part of the throng, while others, winking from beneath their hat-brims, seemed to have come solely to see the pencilled eyebrows and tailored waists of the womenfolk. A middle-aged couple in the crowd pushed unsteadily past a pink-cheeked, yawning man in a Panama hat. The couple waved and a passenger behind me shouted and jostled my arm. I gazed down at the crowd again to see the pink-cheeked man staring me in the face.

—Pierre Lazarie? he called.

I raised my eyebrows and nodded to him but at that instant, there upon the dock at Saigon, the crowning moment of my fledgling career, my colleague's name went clean from my mind. Nonetheless, the pink-cheeked man set a boot upon the sandbags at the foot of the gangway while all about him sobbing wives collapsed into husbands' arms. I stepped down and he took my fingers in his meaty hand.

—Lazarie? he asked again.

—Delighted to meet you, I whispered. You must be ... Henri LeDallic?

—In the flesh! They've picked out a desk for you across from mine. Here, mind these syphilitic Malays!

Bent double under steel trunks that must have outweighed them twice over, the coolies hurried past with every tendon of their arms and legs straining at the skin. Where were the hydraulic cranes used for such tasks in Marseilles? Stewards from Messageries Maritimes tried to clear a path for the poor men while my colleague took my arm.

—I know what's in your mind, but in this country labour will always be cheaper than equipment. And do you see how none of the faces are spotty here? Exhaustive sweating clears the pores. How different my young life might've been with exhaustive sweating! Here, come into the shade.

—Shouldn't I show my passport to someone?

He scratched at a rash on the inside of his wrist.

—Such things are for lesser men, firstly, they really are. Secondly, I completed your forms a week ago, in triplicate, no less, though you'll learn that's nothing special.

We leaned against a shed reeking of hemp rope and tar. Smells, colours, the palpable heat—every impression of Saigon was more visceral than my senses could fairly take on, as though Mother France, a vivid enough place to most observers, had been anemic to the point of death.

—Henri! called a man with a pipe. Funny seeing you outside the Continental!

—Don't give him the wrong idea, said LeDallic. You'll make my protégé swallow his gum!

Even beside the river there was no breeze, and my pores were clearing wonderfully. LeDallic seemed to be studying the white faces filing down the gangway.

—If we're waiting for another passenger, I—

—I was here only a week ago to see my friend Beyle aboard the *Yang Tse*. He still hadn't made up his mind whether he'd be glad to see home or not. I got fifteen years of dominoes out of him and now for a solid week I've gone without. Every outgoing ship of the Messageries Maritimes is packed to the beams with men who on paper have elected to retire but in practice are going home to die. These are men of thirty-five!

—I do appreciate—

—As to the causes of their ruined health, I could go into a lengthy diatribe concerning humidity, microbes, drinking water and once more humidity, but it will suffice to explain that the sun shines too hot here and every other ill stems from it.

—We needn't wait for my trunk, I said. It's being delivered to the office.

—*Our* office? Not on your life—if the porter's not off his head he'll trade it for a few pipes, otherwise he'll relieve himself all over your delicates. That's what you have to look forward to. We'll wait, and you'll thank me, and depending on the volume of work they shovel over us tomorrow we'll have dominoes.

—You mean opium, that's his trouble? I have heard about that.

—Well, if you've *heard of opium* then there's precious little else I can teach you about the East, is there? What else was on your cv, "Sculptural Innovations of the Vanished Khmer"? That will prove useful in our line of work, certainly!

With his hat-brim hiding his brow my colleague looked remarkably like the villainous Max Dalban in the picture Marguerite and I had watched in Marseilles.

—If you *are* such an ardent anthropologist, he went on, why not clerk for the Indo-China Society or, the, what, Institute of Eastern...? Oh, the name eludes me.

—I assure you, Monsieur LeDallic, that I would have been—

—No, "Henri," I insist. If Nguyen calls me "Henri" you had better as well.

—I assure you, I would have been overjoyed to pool minds with such learned men, but the understanding in Paris is that there isn't a place in the world with a thriving economy just now and so the various protectorates ought to be made to pull their weight.

—In short, none of our vaunted philanthropic bodies were hiring so it's the Immigration Department for you.

—Yes. Though if that's my biography in one line it's rather uninspiring.

The ship's captain strode down the bucking gangway, smiling benignly beneath his great brown moustache. He met with a hundred handshakes, even from a clutch of straight-backed natives in fedoras.

—Here, don't let it upset you, said Henri. It's for greater men than us to inspire through *biography*, and they have to wear great heavy hats, those men, and carry sceptres, and I understand they're dead tired. Speaking of which, shall we go for a drink?

—Once we collect the trunks?

—Then or now, whichever suits you. I'm infinitely yielding.

The middle-aged couple passed us, a crate-bearing coolie following at their heels, but in all of an instant this unfortunate lost his footing in a tangles of ropes and fell heavily against me. The crate slipped from his back while he and I dropped together into a pile of chicken baskets whose occupants produced blood-curdling shrieks as our party scattered across the pavement. As I landed on my back I heard the slap of much shoe-leather and a rush of worried voices, but if meant for me the concern was unfounded for I hadn't had so much as the wind knocked from me. The luckless coolie lifted his head from my chest and blinked. I felt his haunches shift as he prepared to spring away.

—Get off him, get off! hissed Henri.

A rigid brown shape arced through the air, and the next instant the coolie was flattened against me, incisors digging into my shirt front. LeDallic had struck him with an oar! My colleague lifted it again but the coolie rolled away to disappear behind the row of fawn suits, the welt across his back so vivid it might've been painted on.

—There! smiled Henri, dropping the instrument with a clatter. Done and done!

The middle-aged couple had not reappeared; two new coolies lifted the crate. I took Henri's arm to regain my feet. As junior partner in our relationship I knew it was neither the time nor place to take my colleague to task, but that time would come. The most violent act I'd ever witnessed!

—Still in one piece? he asked. Then no harm done to anyone.

THE UBIQUITOUS TENNIS RACKET, I decided, would serve as a title for the slim volume detailing my initial impressions of Indo-China; once I was outside the bustling and piquant port district, every white person I saw was carrying one. I'd also observed that every wizened native woman of advanced years, when seen without her conical hat, was largely bald, but I couldn't see how any turn of phrase describing that fact could serve as a sale-able title.

Tennis skirts were worn shorter than at home and, despite Henri's comments regarding climate, the tanned, muscular calves of the young ladies spoke of nothing but good health. Behind bottles of lemonade they sat at streetside cafés, plastic straws resting against their lips. Though Marguerite did not care for tennis, her legs were remarkable. If my career in Indo-China gained too much momentum to be interrupted, I wondered, would I be able to cajole her east?

Our rickshaws rolled down quiet streets cut with long shadows from stately tamarind trees and mustard-coloured villas lolling behind steel fences. A clutch of coolies dozed in their rickshaws outside every gate, awaiting the windfall of a fare, and it struck me that the number of rickshaws in the city was entirely out of proportion to the prospective number of riders, unless these same rickshaw coolies completed their workday only to promptly hail rickshaws themselves. I envisioned an article, "The Oversaturation of Rickshaws in Saigon and Environs," which might interest the popular as well as academic press provided I could make it sufficiently lively. We circled a group of cone-hatted natives squatted like a crop of mushrooms around a soup- or tea- or toasted-rice-husk-coffee-vendor, and I noted the intersection so I could return and find out which. For each drink had its ancient origin; indeed, rice-husk coffee has been traced to the Cham empire of a thousand years ago. Might make a fine letter to Marguerite!

The trio of rickshaws rolled to a stop in front of a gabled two-storey house dozing behind its wrought-iron fence. The place had a homier aspect than most, for instead of a circular driveway, it had a narrow gate and paved walkway, grass sprouting eagerly between the stones. Henri stepped over the rickshaw's yoke and directed the coolies with furious hand signals as they wrestled my trunk from the third vehicle.

—Careful, you apes, careful! Here's the communal manse, Lazarie. Thought I'd have to take my shoes off the first time I went in, they keep it neater than a damn pagoda. Don't slam it down, that's the lad's whole world in there! Here, let's be rid of these red marks in the register. Yellow marks rather. Oh, my wit's worn out, Lazarie, I hope you've brought something new with you. Nonsense, I'll have the department reimburse me, put it away. Now where's that rat of a porter? Our Malay's at dinner—pull the bell.

—Must we? I asked. I'd rather not disturb anyone at table.

Gloom descended on the street—trees and buildings reduced to a palette of blues and greys—and I realized this must be the nationally agreed-upon dinner hour, for excepting a chicken stalking across the top of a wall there was not a creature in evidence. My colleague doffed his hat to swab the top of his head with a tartan handkerchief. Rat-tails of black hair lay across his bald pate and twinkling beads of perspiration dripped from his cheeks to his collar, though it was markedly cooler under the trees than it had been beside the glare of the river. He caught my gaze and jammed the sodden handkerchief into his pocket.

—Two hours outdoors is too long in this place, let me tell you.

—How long *have* you been East, might I ask?

—Well, how old am I? Forty-four. That makes twenty-five years. If they could admit it's a prison they'd have paroled me by now.

—What, have you never had leave? I was assured that after three years we spent six months at home!

—If they can spare you, yes. But as you might well imagine I can't be spared.

The dismissed rickshaws turned onto the main road, the coolies' feet padding tirelessly across their native soil just as the ancient Khmer had jogged between their temples at dusk, water buckets balanced across lean shoulders.

—We can at least take it into the foyer, I said. Can you manage that end?

Henri rubbed his jaw then extricated himself—with eleven or twelve heartfelt grunts—from his sweat-stained tunic. Beneath the garment he wore a thin grey shirt with a yellow stain down one side reminiscent of a burst appendix. I heard a metallic jangle as he hung the tunic over a loop in the fence and I guessed that a rail had come loose, but as he turned I noticed, to my amazement, a half-dozen copper bangles bunched on his forearm. He bent and seized the leather handle. In unison we lifted the trunk and as I backed up the walk streams of perspiration immediately ran down my arms and dripped from between my fingers. We carried it fifteen steps, twenty, then my colleague abruptly dropped his end—the steel corners sparked as they struck the paving stone.

—Whatever's the matter? I asked.

Biting his lip, he clapped his right hand over his left shoulder.

—I'd hoped it'd be all right, but the thing won't be rid of me!

He retreated, and pulled a cord at the gate. A bell clanged in the villa behind me.

—But what's happened? I asked.

He gingerly draped his tunic over the stricken arm then resumed massaging the shoulder, his bangles jangling sympathetically.

—My old tiger bite, he said. No harm done.

—"Tiger"? Come, I may be just off the boat, but—

—This is enough excitement for me, he murmured. I'll be in the courtyard.

He slipped out the gate. The street had turned quite black and his white form turned insubstantial as he hurried past the fence. I realized that cicadas were shrieking from the trees, the grass, and every centimetre of space, and in that moment I formed an opinion of Indo-China that has never changed: too shrill, too hot, too utterly baffling.

—At the Continental! called Henri's disembodied voice.

Bare feet hurried down the steps behind me; an impeccable little native couple, both in crisp white shirts, he in blue corduroy trousers and she in a print sarong, came nodding and smiling past me to take up the handles of the waiting trunk.

—*Chao ong*, I grinned. *Cam on ni-yoh.*

This meant "hello" and "thank you." I expected a quick "don't mention it" in response, *kong co chi*—a drill I'd performed countless times in language class—but instead they stared at me quizzically. The man whispered a single syllable and together they lifted my trunk up the stairs. I wished I might have asked what they thought of the Tay Son brothers' capture of Saigon in 1776.

HER
PHOTOGRAPH

Pierre Lazarie.

SLEPT LIKE a stone until four o'clock in the morning, when I discovered that in the Far East even a well-tended urban villa can have chickens roosting beneath its eaves. At dawn the yawning porter set a pitcher of cold water on my dressing table, and after washing I made a compromise between reality and my expectations by dressing in brown serge trousers and a white linen jacket. I resembled the comic relief in an American film.

Then, to begin my employment. As Henri had not come home I shared a rickshaw into the centre with a garrulous housemate, his neck awash in acne scars, who informed me in the most solemn tones that a native prostitute who is as tall as a white girl can write her own ticket and therefore demand a commitment of two nights.

—And not only will she want boiled eggs, he said, but mayonnaise to dip them in!

—Grateful for your advice, I said.

More fodder for my letter to Marguerite; I pictured her lips parting in wonder as she read. The muscles in our coolie's back shifted subtly as he hurried over the pavement in that soft morning light—the city seemed to be all in blues and yellows—past terrace cafés where a hundred men read newspapers, then on into the still-softer shadows beneath the trees. No white women were apparent, as though Saigon were an Alpine resort where they slept while the men set out hiking. The air smelled of mould.

The porter at the *Vice*-Regency on rue Lagrandiere did not appear in any way to be an opium addict bent on soiling the contents of my trunk. Rather he was an immaculate young Vietnamese in blue suit and black necktie.

—LeDallic? he asked. Oh, yes, these stairs here. All the way to the top.

—*Cam on ni-yoh,* I said.

He grinned slyly while regarding my jacket and trousers; a tennis racket would've complemented the ensemble neatly.

A half-dozen electric fans busied themselves on the ceiling of our third-storey office, yet the moment I was through the door I could smell Henri—a sweetness like cherries. He sat with elbows on his knees, a pen between his teeth and a swaying tower of documents on the desk before him. For a moment he regarded me from beneath heavy lids then glanced across to the only other desk, untenanted except by a comparable tower.

—They've been expecting you, he said.

My desk chair's wheels must have been freshly oiled, for it darted away into the corner. As I led it like an unruly colt to its stall I reassured myself that I'd slip away just as easily—I might visit the Far East Institute on my coffee break.

—The unsightly Madame Louvain brought up a telegram, said LeDallic.

A yellow envelope lay in the shadow of my tower of documents, and as I extricated the slip of paper I guessed at its import: that I ought not to make myself comfortable with Immigration, as my professors had arranged a lucrative research position. The sender's line, though, made no mention of the University of Paris—the telegram had been sent by Marguerite Gély.

REGRET TO INFORM YOU, it read, THAT I HAVE MARRIED ALDO MASSON. WISH YOU WELL.

From what I knew of Aldo Masson he was not a bad chap. But it was not the vagaries of his character that dropped my chin to my chest or turned my knees elastic.

—You've won the Bavarian sweepstakes, suggested Henri.

I lay the paper on my desk and looked across at him. At his sweat-beaded temples. And then, rather than rereading the telegram, as I'd planned, I wrenched my arms free from that idiotic linen jacket and stuffed it into a desk drawer. I would never wear the thing again, for at the sight of it I'd recall the pallid creature I'd been at that moment and have to choke back a quantity of bile. That task accomplished, I crumpled the telegram and lobbed it into the Saigon morning before slamming down the window and fastening the latch behind. I turned to find LeDallic suddenly on his feet.

—Keep your personal interests in your trousers, yes? That is your seat, do you see it? Take your seat.

—You now have my full attention, I replied.

In the February heat my mistakes in India ink couldn't be blotted out for love nor money, and indeed my blunders with the rubber stamps couldn't be blotted out at all. The labels for both "Cancelled" and "To Be Filed" had been eradicated by the acidity of innumerable palms, and in my distress I hazarded to *guess* which was which.

—They may not drive the economy entirely, Henri shouted, but entry fees are more than enough to pay our wages, my friend, more than enough, so when certain Shanghai businessmen—how many, *fifteen* of them?—apply to be ordinary residents and—what else—to bring in a half-*million* piastres' worth of machine parts, I suggest you not reach for your "Cancelled" stamp, you understand me?

—Did I really? I must apologize, I can't seem to—

—There's a notch out of the wood on that one, take a goddamn bite out of it if you can't tell the difference, they . . . is this the *top* carbon you stamped?

I allowed a pencil to roll from my desk, and in bending to retrieve it spent a tranquil moment studying the geometric flowers in the red linoleum and wondering whether there might be positions with the Indian & Australian Chartered Bank.

—The entire carbon, when I said very plainly the *third*? Three-quarters of an hour 'til lunch—has the clock stopped? I have to take a walk or I'll vomit. Good God, *now* what are you doing?

—Filing them as approved for ordinary residence permits.

—No, no! Give them privileged!

—But they don't want more than three years, look, they have the departure—

—Give them privileged and charge them each the extra hundred piastres, they're rich men and won't know the difference, and we can report that this office has floated its own barge well and truly! Yes, and now the third page, "To Be Filed," yes, exactly, I can see what made you such a hit at the Sorbonne. But now what to do with the "Cancelled" on every page, eh?

Junior Chief Clerk Dubois bustled in, knocking a sheaf of papers off the filing cabinet but catching it deftly behind his back as though it had happened a hundred times before. Short, rather young, with an alabaster forehead and close-cropped hair, he wore his jacket and collar while LeDallic and I were both now in shirt sleeves. Dubois stood beside my desk, for there was nowhere else to stand, lit a cigarette, then tapped one of my ledgers.

—You can't make money in the service here, not like in China. A white man needs to be the only white man if he wants to make any real money. Consider it.

The longer he stood there, the larger the notch I'd gouged into the "Cancelled" stamp seemed to loom. I tucked it under an empty folder.

—The *Felix Roussel*'s just come in, he muttered.

—*Yesterday* it came in, said Henri. Where'd you think I found this reprobate?

—An army captain came off the *Felix Roussel*. He's in with Frémont. Agitated.

—Frémont? With the stacks of files he ladled over us it's *we* who ought to be agitated, and Lazarie here has—

—Frémont wants the two of you to talk to this army captain.

—After lunch might be all right, said Henri. Half-past three? Time permitting afterward we'll get some dominoes.

Dubois' gaze wandered over that disastrous multiple-party ordinary residence application—I deftly turned it over while replacing stamps on their carousel.

—But if you prefer, I said, we can come along and see him now.

—Bring a notebook of some kind, said Dubois. And put on jackets.

—Lazarie's promoting a jacketless initiative.

In the corridor Henri ran squarely into a native copyist in canary-yellow trousers, wavering beneath a stack of folders topped by a cast-iron embosser. As papers spilled from their folders like so many autumn leaves I gave the poor man my most sympathetic glance, but he never raised his eyes.

—Pick those up and quick! hissed Henri. You ought to staple those shut if you don't want trouble counter-filing—like it or not, it's the best system in the world!

—It's only that he's sober just now, murmured Dubois at my elbow. A few drinks with lunch and his mind will be agile. He'll be docile as a kitten.

The corridor's linoleum was a black square for every three of white. On the landing Dubois turned to LeDallic.

—Tremier is the captain's surname—that remind you of anyone?

—Who, a jockey? I don't know! Shall I guess again? Shall I hop on one foot?

—Frémont had thought you might have come across the name.

The ground floor corridor was of pink marble. As we hurried toward Frémont's office I was nearly blinded by the blaze of light emanating from between the slats in a colossal teak door. Dubois turned the pewter handle and we rushed after him into a wide room decorated with a massive desk, a few wicker chairs and a low table displaying trays of cigarettes and a bottle of whisky. Fully a dozen fans produced a breeze not unlike the seaside. A tall old man with spectacles rose from behind the desk and an equally tall man in a brass-buttoned khaki uniform shot up from one of the chairs. I felt an immediate kinship with him as his trousers looked as hot and uncomfortable as my own.

—LeDallic and Lazarie! announced Dubois.

—LeDallic has been here longer than anyone, said Frémont.

The room was lined with windows looking out over the trees and boulevards from an angle that somehow revealed no people at all. We newcomers threw ourselves into the creaking wicker chairs.

—How long have you been with Immigration? the captain asked me. You look to be the junior partner.

He couldn't have been past forty yet his broad forehead was deeply lined, with eyebrows set so far apart as to sit nearly on his temples. A physiognomist might've spent an entire semester on him. I tried unsuccessfully to meet his gaze and realized that his left eye was glass—it contemplated a potted fern in the corner.

—In truth, sir, I stammered, you find me on my first day at this—

—First *day*? the captain shouted at Dubois. Why'd you bring him into this?

—But you needn't worry! I said. If my colleague's expertise can't help, I happen to be a specialist in Vietnamese military history prior to European involvement!

The captain cracked his knuckles against the arm of his chair.

—When did *you* start here? he asked Henri.

—In 1911. I'd heard that girls in this country could be had for nothing.

—And can they?

—Yes.

—Captain Tremier, said Frémont, is hoping our records will lead him to locate his mother, a Madame Tremier, who landed in—which year? I can't read my own writing.

—October, 1909, answered Dubois.

—First name Adélie, the captain said. Adélie Tremier.

—Does that mean something to you, LeDallic? asked Frémont.

—Just that it's nearly lunch, said Henri.

—She'll celebrate her fifty-sixth birthday before long, said the captain, but the fact remains I haven't seen or heard from her in twenty-seven years. Now, I have confirmed that on August 29 of '09 she sailed from Marseilles for Saigon aboard the *Salazie*, and I trust you fellows will be able to do more with that information than I have. I've been trying to trace her since I was ten years old, but until recently the Messageries Maritimes had misplaced the relevant records.

—Typical of their inefficient practice back there, murmured Frémont.

—I did check the civil registers with the Ministry before coming to you, even the Saigon telephone directory for 1910, so if she did stay on here I—well, I can't imagine where! Forgive me. It's very seldom that I talk about her.

He massaged those distinctive brows. His unwavering glass eye was able to contain its emotion.

—The *Salazie* docked here in one piece? asked Henri.

—It was sunk in 1912. A cyclone off Madagascar.

—If it had gone down sooner that might have resolved your query.

At that Frémont fingered his pencil nervously. I fixed the captain's good eye with my most professional gaze.

—And she . . . she departed in good health, twenty-seven years ago?

—Ah, said the captain. On the contrary, she spent the year before she went away convalescing from tuberculosis.

—Odds are she died en route then, Henri said. They threw her over to Poseidon.

—The good captain, announced Frémont, leaves for Haiphong tomorrow to join his new battalion, so you and Laramie—

—Lazarie, I said.

—The matter is in your hands. Locate her arrivals ledger, see where it leads you.

Henri twisted a rat-tail of hair between his fingers.

—But, now, you see, Captain Fornier, you really must picture the stinking piles of work upon our desks. If the dear woman's indeed lost herself, surely the police, the secret police, will have—

—Henri, young Dubois said, this is the Department of Immigration for the Vice-Regency of Cochin-China—

—Yes, I've seen the letterhead, said Henri.

—And as we've told Captain Tremier, we have proved and will *continue* to prove ourselves capable regarding any matter called to our attention simply as a matter of pride. What's more—and this point should hardly concern the captain—Paris has lately discussed how best to make each department better accountable, not only in light of economic conditions—

—Discord, said Frémont. These people's laughable notion of self-government!

—Only a natural progression, said Dubois, as we shepherd the protectorate toward maturity. In coming months there will be audits at every level and, should we be found wanting, Paris of course has the power to ransack our funding, our staff, and apparently even our pensions.

—Our pensions! said Henri. Lazarie, you're done for!

—This "discord," is that these Bolshevists? the captain asked. I'm meant to ferret them out around Haiphong.

—Their political stripe is irrelevant, said Dubois. They're only youngsters looking for excitement.

—Same boys at home would be content to get drunk, said Frémont.

—To whom exactly are we referring? I asked. Is this some tribal group?

—Here's a useful professor! said Henri. Every idiot knows there are Bolshevik rats filling Paris, didn't they come fill your academic ears with all their talk of Indo-Chinese autonomy and a free drink special if ordered before five o'clock?

—Our faculty is aware that *something* is afoot, I said. But there's no way to make a study of a thing while it's still unfolding, is there? Perspective is required if we—

—I've met with the police about them any number of times, announced Frémont, and I do find the whole situation rather tiring. These are sons of rich men, landowners, these are native boys without a care in the world, yet they run their mouths about independence and they do it right in Paris, in the lion's den, because they know how soft the courts are back there—for a conversation that'd draw the death penalty here no one so much as blinks. Now any number of them are trying to sneak home and we're expected to catch them, despite their slipping in under assumed names and dressed as fishermen. And I *would* like to catch them! I shouldn't like to see what happens to my Michelin dividends if a lot of hoodlums burn a plantation down!

—The death penalty? I asked. For a conversation?

—Certainly! said Frémont. Hangings by the dozen.

—If we may return the topic to my mother, the captain said, I have an item which may prove useful.

From his breast pocket he drew a photograph in a small oval frame and leaned across to place it in my hand. No one spoke, though Henri's chair creaked peevishly. The picture showed a smiling couple and long-haired child in a white pinafore; the man appeared to be in the act of graduating from the Sorbonne.

—Look at the regalia, I said. Your father was an engineer! Around 1905, judging by her blouse—I've a picture of my mother in a number just like it. This *is* you, isn't it?

—I was the only child.

—It's not hard to see he's your father, with those eyes of his. Ah, and your mother, yes. Striking.

Henri rose to look over my shoulder: the future captain upon her knee, Adélie Tremier flashed white teeth at the camera while her masses of black hair gave the impression, even in that diminutive portrait, of a gale gusting around her. And there was a particular squint to her eyes that somehow spoke to me, despite every likelihood the woman had been dead two decades, of *lust*.

—Not hard by half, said Henri.

—My father was a professor of trigonometry, I said. And he'd drag me to these things—I've seen more convocations than I've had hot baths! Look how proud he is in that eight-sided tam. Now, does she have any particular interests, your mother?

—Charities. Had a particular interest in veterans and sick children.

—She'd fit in well around here! cried Frémont.

—"To care for others first and enjoy happiness after," I blurted. How old is she in this picture?

—Twenty-five.

Only two years my senior! I looked again and, honestly, the contrast of that ivory forehead framed by her black hair was so succulent that I imagined planting a row of kisses across her hairline. My wretched lips pressed together. Marguerite hadn't been able to hold out two months, yet Adélie Tremier had already waited twenty-seven years—here was a girl I could have for myself! Which made no sense, of course, as her brass-buttoned captain of a son stood there blowing his nose, but who in the world is such an authority that he might explain the behaviour of the heart under every conceivable circumstance? Never again Marguerite Gély, for my future lay with Adélie Tremier: the fact was as concrete as a lowland Lao whisky jar cast in bronze.

I was breathing too quickly. Frémont scratched his moustache and smiled across at the captain as Henri plucked the photograph from my hand and returned to his seat.

—And what if no results are forthcoming? he asked.

—Ah, to a resourceful man, Dubois said, this department can offer opportunities on the Cambodian frontier. You're fond of the countryside, aren't you, LeDallic?

—Captain, I said, if I may—it might aid in our inquiries for us to know exactly what you fear *may* have become of her.

—Perhaps sold into bondage of some sort, suggested Frémont.

Tremier rose and seized the photograph from Henri and then, unfolding his handkerchief, carefully wiped the glass and held the picture out to me. His mother smiled. I took it with a nod; he raised the handkerchief and blew his nose.

—You must forgive me.

—I'd like to go up to Haiphong myself, I said, and look into Le Loi's victory over the Ming in 1427. "If you want a thing done properly," I used to say, "give it to Le Loi!"

I followed my colleague back upstairs. With each landing the badly lubricated motor within his chest grew louder—groaning or growling, I couldn't say. He held the office door open for me then slammed it behind us, and I confess the rush of air was blessedly cool. He threw himself behind his desk, and his head onto his arms.

—Dubois has a cousin who wants my job. I saw the letter on his desk. And who do you suppose that captain really was? Some embezzler of public funds that they put up to it, all to be rid of me!

I stepped smartly to the window and looked out at the tree-tops of Saigon, each boulevard of them rolling down toward the river. How many of the city's doors would we knock upon in our investigation? I hoped it was five thousand. Every moment outside those four walls would be a windfall, until I glimpsed a woman in an enormous hat, the fashion of thirty years previous, the back of her white neck visible beneath of a swath of pinned black hair. I studied the picture again and yes, there really was something appealing in the carriage of Madame Tremier's head. I had not been wrong about her.

—Get that Malay bitch up here and pour us some coffee, said Henri.

I went to the door and grasped the glass knob but found I could go no further. My tongue fairly vibrated in my mouth.

—What ignorance could possibly prompt you to call these people "Malays"? They are Cochin-Chinese, the specific woman you refer to is Cochin-Chinese, or "Vietnamese," if you agree that they and the Tonkinese are the same race, as they themselves do—there really are several possible terms, but to call these people "Malay" is as correct as calling them Eskimo or German, can you understand that?

Henri bit down on his balled-up handkerchief.

—Do not try me just now, he finally said.

A BOY WITH
WATER IN HIS MOUTH

Mlle. Adélie Lissner, 1886.

IN TOUMBADOU she drew only shallow breaths as she sat near the tall window that looked down over the front door and the lilac trees and the town hall whose bell rang every hour, even in the middle of the night. "Keep well back," Maman said, "or you'll drop out of that window," and Adélie did not want to drop out, she liked the world as it was, so she drew only shallow breaths lest the force of the inhalations drag her out and dash her against the cobbles below.

In the window box the bees and the buzz of heat were as one, goose-egg and goose, she couldn't say which had made the other. She watched the flowers' buttery heads bend, and across the open blue shutters the shadows of butterflies flew so quick and skittish that the real ones vanished at the instant she looked for them, as though there were no such thing in the world as butterflies, but only shadows of butterflies. "They taste bitter," her little brother Georges announced, "horrible bitter." She stared up at the half-wagon-wheel above the window and at the painting on the wall of an old man in a boat with a broken mast in his hands—if only his face had showed some expression the picture would not have made her want to cry. The mystery of it.

Then it was noon, the white window frame so bright that she could only peer at it through a napkin until black-aproned Pilou closed the shutters. The neighbours whispered that Pilou had been born two days before the world, yet she was so strong she tugged the chickens' heads off each time she wrung their necks! "The triumph of a long life," said Pilou.

Boys were allowed out more often and even when he was five Georges knew more about the world. He said boys and girls were different underneath. He unabashedly pulled the cord on his wooden top in the town square. He sang in the front row of the choir, and on rehearsal nights his voice could be heard soaring like a kite into the backs of all the kitchens where mothers stored their sausage and dried wedding bouquets. Crouching beside the tall window, he told Adélie how the devil played violin on their bench below the flower box, alongside the eggshells and rinds that Maman dropped for Pilou.

At school they stood in a line and mouthed the French words, *Toumbadou was founded downstream from the waterfall where the young shepherd saw a vision of the Virgin and this same boy can be seen on our village fountain with the waters pouring from his mouth.* This was their father's language, not that of their mother who was true Provençal, but to tell about a boy who lived forever with that water in his mouth Adélie would have said the words in Silkworm or Donkey or even Greek.

ON THE WAY to Saturday market, Adélie and Maman and Georges stepped onto the new bridge that crossed the riffle far below; apples tumbled out of the market stalls but there was little water in the September streams. Nail heads glistened like buttons beneath their feet. Midway across the span the Old Soldier and a dozen boys laughed at the rail. Monsieur Montgaillard hobbled past with a turkey clutched to his chest, and Georges said *he* would see what they were doing and skipped toward the clutch of boys, his flapping jacket black as a crow. Adélie held her breath as they crept toward the Old Soldier for he always smelled like pee.

"Stay with us, Georges," murmured Maman, but she could not stop him, encumbered as she was with the basket and Adélie's flower-petal hand. Madame Sabatier and her crate of white ducks came abreast and the two women conferred beneath their bonnets. Madame Sabatier felt horrid selling birds that might go on laying for years, but all summer grown-ups had done nothing but complain, even swaying on the gravel with a silver *boule* in their hand, that there wasn't water for crops. Even her father, home from Aix, had only complained that there wasn't water in the stream to drown a kitten. Adélie pictured the bowlegged farmers who'd slurped up the water in the hills before it could tumble down to Toumbadou.

Ah, *now* she smelled the pee! The Old Solider did not look as they did in books—namely, with a musket and giant hat—for he wore a mildewed grey shirt, checked trousers and flap-soled boots, but Georges had explained that he was not a solider now but had merely gone to a war and come back dim. A war in "Prussia"—didn't that sound silly? He made *sous* for bread by scrubbing shop-windows with a bar of yellow soap, though after he'd leapt around the corner the shopkeepers would have to scrub the dreck away themselves.

Georges looked over the side and called to Adélie that there was no pool at all down there now. The big boy Antoine ran up with a stone the size of a bread loaf, his long-wristed arms thrusting it out over the rail, but droop-lipped Old Soldier snatched the rock so that he could drop it himself. After a long moment Adélie heard a weak splash, then the boys cheered and the Old Soldier turned from the rail like a picture-book Spanish dancer. Adélie couldn't hold her breath any longer and sucked in his goat-shed smell.

While they'd sat snapping beans she'd asked Pilou why the Old Soldier had gone away to a *war* because, like a jute mill, it was something Adélie couldn't picture. "He went for no reason," Pilou had said and thrust her chin out like a fist. "He'd have spared his mother months of worry if he'd stayed home and dashed his head against a rock."

At the rail the Old Soldier plucked Marcel's brown cap from his head and pitched it over the side, and the grown-ups grunted at that, mothers called to their boys, and straw-haired Marcel shoved the Old Soldier in the belly but the dimwit didn't mind, he laughed out his nose, grabbed one of Madame Sabatier's ducks by the neck and flung *it* over the rail. The bird's wings were bound so it dropped like a sack of sugar. The Old Soldier laughed out his nose again then bent and seized Georges by the shoulders.

Adélie tugged her fingers from her mother's grasp and struck the man in his shaggy eye with her fist, but the Old Soldier only gazed at her younger brother, as pleased as if he'd found a new sort of beetle. Adélie felt snot course from her nose. Some of the boys laughed so Georges laughed too, but Adélie kept hold of the man's wrist and kicked his shins to pulp with her twelve-button boots. Where she bit his arm it tasted like kerosene. Her brother could not get free—he looked at Adélie with an eye big as a cow's. At the last instant Maman tried to throw her arms around her son's waist, her fingertip catching his orange belt before the old smiling soldier lifted Georges and flung him into space.

The next day it was easy for Adélie to remember, thanks to her scratched face and the bruises down her legs, exactly how hard she had fought. But she could not recall, despite the next-door children's efforts to remind her, the cascade of adult kicks that had dropped the Old Soldier to the boards or the end of the story when Monsieur Sabatier hurried up with his shotgun. The children did not bother to tell her how Maman had scrambled down to the dry stream bed or how afterward she'd wandered the *cours*.

"I'll get 'em next time," Adélie muttered, picking scabs from her frail knuckles.

THE PEWS ALWAYS smelled like horse stalls. The priest stood in front of them and talked about Jesus-on-the-cross and Baby Jesus and Georges while Adélie thought how good it would be to bite into a piece of sausage. A moth flew past. Papa snatched it out of the air then opened his hand and stared at the black dust in his palm. Perhaps Georges was only a shadow across a river-bottom now. Bees floated on the hot breeze, she knew, but what kept she and Maman from falling to the ground from one moment to the next? A strong arm at the pump? Yes, and here was her evidence: a half-dozen women lifting Maman to her feet, for now she called for Georges and would not get up. One of Papa's thumbs was indigo and the other aquamarine, and when he went back to the dye-works in Aix they'd go with him. The dishes had been packed in cotton and crates hammered together in the very place the devil had been sitting.

Pilou took Adélie by the elbow and they stepped out of the church into the lane, blinking at the tablecloth of light that had been thrown over everything. The priest in his vestments spat and told the men that the pigs in those woods could hide as well as any beetle. The Virgin had blessed a sage bush for hiding her baby from Awful Herod, Adélie knew as much as that. Dry leaves from the plane trees rattled in the glittering dust and even the priest turned to watch, sweat dripping from his nose. The leaves rose in a column and swirled across the lane, scattering golden pebbles, swirling for the sake of it, alive as any little boy or as any wooden top dancing the Farandole once a boy had pulled its cord. Then the pebbles tumbled against each other amongst the stalks of yellow grass. Pilou led Adélie's elbow toward home—they would drink buttermilk instead of watching the burial. "Now I know," whispered Adélie, "that's what whirls inside me!"

Because a friendly gust of wind had become her breath when she'd been born, that explained everything, but with every new breath the gust lost its strength and the leaves whirling inside her would drop until only one hovered in the air and when that finally fell she would be as dead as the grey stones at the bottom of the waterfall where the rich family watered their horses.

Pilou blew her nose and told her not to cry, for heaven was here on earth and had no place for tears in it. "*This* can't be heaven," said Adélie, "Georges has left *here* to go to the better place." "Heaven is here on earth," Pilou said again. "We have only to look for it."

IN AIX EVERYONE spoke with an Aix accent and rode in a buggy with a pretty dog upon their knee or else sat upon the curb with a cap over their eyes and their arms blown off years before, Papa explained, in a war against the Prussians—as though she'd never heard of it!—but she needn't make a face for there'd never be a war like that again.

These things were all too new, they were meant to convince her that Georges had never been. While Pilou told her of an army defeated by a barrage of baked apples and of orphans in rags who went into the world to seek their fortunes, Adélie wondered if Georges might have just been a story too. What was the opposite of an orphan? Pilou peeled a beet in a long spiral and said she didn't know, but Maman said the opposite was a child who went on living happily with its parents, then Adélie wanted to know what a parent who'd lost its child was called, surely *that* was the opposite, and Maman said it was *survived by*, because that was how the newspapers put it.

Then Adélie wanted to know if it was worse to be an orphan or a *survived by*, and Maman spread out her knitting so it fell to her ankles and rolled across the floor so the cat got into it, and finally Maman said that an orphan had a sad past and bright future while a *survived by* had a bright past and a sad future, and which of those sounded better? "Oh," Adélie said, "to be an orphan must be a whole lot better!"

The copper pots from Toumbadou hung on the wall of the dark kitchen and on hot afternoons she would stroke them with the back of her hand. She asked again the name of the boy who finds the genie on the cover of the book and Pilou told her again it was Pati-Pati-Pati, though Adélie had hidden away in the linen cupboard and read for herself that it was Aladdin. "Well, whether or not she can read," Maman told her, "she looks after us very well." Pilou came in with a knife and cheese and apple on the board and said, "I beg your pardon, Mademoiselle, but at my age a person can learn and forget a thing like that a hundred times just as your genie forgets how often he's been out of the bottle."

A SAD PAST AND
A BRIGHT FUTURE

Mlle. Adélie Lissner.

SHE ATTENDED music recitals where the boys taught her card games between performances and tried to kiss her. Maman told her that if she was thought pretty she could thank her black hair and the Provençal arch of her eyebrows; Adélie looked in the mirror above the umbrella stand and touched those brows fleetingly, so as not to spoil them. Her father called from the other room that if he could make a black that shimmered so he would name it for her and fill the shops with it. Then her name would live on and on.

Her best friend then was Henriette, and not just because Adélie was elevated from "pretty" to "astonishingly beautiful" beside Henriette's pince-nez and pointed chin: in the entire school, none but they could write such scathing notes about the pug-nosed headmistress.

"Ah," said Henriette, "here is my fiancé right where he promised to be."

"You mustn't," Adélie whispered. "They say he's the only one from his company to not get killed!"

"Then I owe him a few kisses, don't I?"

A legless veteran leaned against the curb, his elbow on the sidewalk, an upturned regimental cap displaying a handful of *sous*—perhaps enough to make a single franc—and with a whirl of skirts Henriette took her place beside him. She smoothed her apron over her knees. The trouser-legs pinned over his stumps were filthy from constant dragging over the pavements, and except for his mouth and one bloodshot eye his entire head was swathed in bandages the colour of tea.

"But darling," she asked, "wherever shall I plant my kiss?"

The veteran's bloodshot eye blinked. His pink tongue appeared at the corner of his mouth and a sound like a distant mill rose in his throat.

"Henriette, you *must* leave him alone! Come away!"

"Ah, you're friends with the trooper as well?" asked a young man with scuffed shoes. "I thought I might be the only one—the flower of France in his day, wasn't he? With your help I can at least lift him out of the road. Take his arm, will you, please? I'm the assistant at the chemist's around the way and he used to send us endless notes asking for painkiller. He's given that up in recent years, though."

Adélie backed against the shop front as Henriette deftly wrapped her handkerchief around the veteran's sleeve to avoid touching him with bare hands. His red eye shot anxious looks as she and the chemist's assistant lifted him and set his bottom roughly on the sidewalk. He made a pained exhalation.

"Oh!" the young man shouted. "He's shit himself, poor man. You might wish to run along, ladies. I'll see what I can do for him."

"You don't mean—?" stammered Adélie.

Ashen-faced Henriette seized her by the wrist and began to run. As they rounded the corner Adélie dared to glance back: the regimental cap sat askew on the trooper's head as the young man strolled across the *cours*, jangling the handful of *sous* with studied nonchalance. He disappeared behind a baker's wagon.

"It's just as Napoleon said," choked Henriette, straining ever-forward. "'It takes more courage to suffer than to die!'"

"Wait here!" seethed Adélie.

Running into the alley that cut behind the shops, she leapt over a pile of barrel staves so that her skirts rose like an umbrella, then turned sharply to her right, interrupting two mongrels sniffing each other's bottoms, before sloshing through an ankle-deep puddle. Ahead she saw the purple rear door of the stationery shop once owned by a schoolmate's parents, and hoped that the new owners still left it unlocked. Ah! When she was three steps away the door opened and she bolted through. She did not see the boy of twelve standing in the gloomy entry-way under a stack of pink boxes.

"Sorry to leave you like that!" she addressed his prostrate form. "But I've a good reason!"

She passed through the shop, amidst a furious clicking of patrons' tongues, and out the front door. To her left she saw the yellow brick of the Oblates Chapel, and somewhere—oh, but if he'd turned off the *cours* he might be anywhere! She saw only bowler hats striding in one direction or another. What had the chemist's assistant worn upon his head? A green corduroy cap moved out of the crowd and by the gaiety of its owner's step she knew him to be her quarry, but he was about to pass beneath the trees onto Tournefort! Even as she ran she saw no way of stopping him, not a friend she could hail, only a jowly old man three metres ahead, leaning his cane against his hip while he adjusted the flower in his buttonhole. Heels clattering, she sprinted past, seizing the dark-red cane as she went.

"Sorry about this," she said, "but it's for a good reason!"

And with that she threw the cane like a spear across the square. It bounced once against the brown cobbles before catching between her quarry's ankles, and a half-step later the young man tumbled onto his head. She did not marvel at her feat but dashed after him before he could regain his legs. Her quarry was rolling onto his back, wiping the grit from his mouth, when she drove a knee into this chest and so pinned him. Panting like a hunting dog, she glared down at his astonished features—yes, thankfully, it *was* the chemist's assistant.

"To reduce a human being so!" she hissed.

"I assure you, lady," he gasped, "it's a gross misunder—"

"He was once a child in his mother's arms!"

"But what's happened, Mademoiselle?" asked a wire-thin old man—a retired schoolmaster, she guessed. "Has he accosted you?"

Which was quite funny, really, considering the young people's postures, but instead of laughing she explained to the gathering crowd that the recumbent scoundrel had robbed that legless old trooper by the Very Mossy Fountain of his last *sou*, and she'd continue to drive the breath from him until the money reappeared that she might return it. While a dozen people applauded, Adélie was asked to repeat herself. The young man did not stir; he crinkled his eyes and smiled up at everyone. Small boys hilariously re-enacted the manner in which the knave had embraced the pavement while a journalist from *L'Écho des Bouches-du-Rhone* scribbled on a notepad.

"Ought not to have *involved* herself," sighed one head-shaking matron to another.

"Ought to be in a jungle!" bleated the other.

Adélie was helped to her feet by several broad-shouldered gentlemen before the young man's pockets were turned out. The resulting coins—of a value nearing nine francs—were pressed reverently into Adélie's hands by the schoolmaster. The jowly old man bent to retrieve his cane and straightened to find that a crowd had gathered in hopes of shaking him by the hand.

She hurried back up the *cours* with the money cupped in her hands and a throng of boys at her heels. Sunlight passed through the branches of the plane trees to dapple the cobbles. She passed two fountains, now a third, their waters singing joyfully. Wasn't life a lovely thing, and didn't she wish that every person and dog and bumblebee could just go on and on without stopping?

The veteran had retreated to a doorway where he slumped as if asleep, the empty cap proffered between filthy knees. She poured in the several dozen coins. He did smell of shit. His eyelids flickered.

"What a life you'd have led otherwise," she whispered.

Henriette trotted from the corner, hands clenched before her chest.

"You got it back *yourself*?" she called. "Why didn't you go for a policeman?"

"Oh," Adélie said. "It never occurred to me."

An hour later the girls returned with Monsieur Lissner, a hamper of food and a washcloth—though where and how the veteran would wash himself remained to be seen—and though they searched within a radius of several blocks the poor man was nowhere to be found.

THE RUBBING
OF A LAMP

Mlle. Adélie Lissner.

F
EVER TRAVELLED through Aix like a yellow
cloth across a slate, wiping individual letters away, then entire words. The letters
that remained attempted to look as swaggering and cursive as
ever, but where once they'd been part of whole sentences there
were now only punctuation and swirls of chalk dust to hint at
what had been.

With Henriette she sat in the train station café, her head in
her hands. Henriette was the opposite of an orphan and would
go on living happily with her parents in spite of her pince-nez
and pointed chin. She told Adélie that women would not be
wearing such bright colours in Paris, so Adélie blew her nose
and asked Henriette what it would do to the Lissner name if her
father's surviving heir were to flap about black as a crow. She
was not a widow, after all—though was she much different? Papa
and Maman had sweated down to their very eyeballs, dwindled
to such meagre flames that before the end she saw them gutter
and nearly extinguish a dozen times.

"Let me have a little cure," her mother had murmured in
Provençal, as though caressed by the winds of an older earth
on a Toumbadou hillside, but the only cure Adélie knew was
for toothache, not fever. Nonetheless she had placed the olive
between Maman's molars and gently moved her jaw with her

hands, three times she had to bite it, that was gospel, before slipping it into an envelope for Pilou to fling into the river.

"Tell Georges to come upstairs," her mother had said.

A frequenter of the Lissner Boutiques, a doctor with lemon-yellow gloves, had come into the house and told Adélie specific medical facts that she wouldn't have wanted to hear even in idle conversation. Maman had sat up in the bed, her lips formed as ever to whisper his name, and seized her daughter's wrist like a great saucer-eyed vulture wrapped in bedclothes. Teeth shone like brass beneath her receded lip.

"You look after that little boy!" she'd hissed.

In the next bed Papa had stretched and dug his toenails into the mattress as a man in a desert might claw toward a puddle.

Then pine coffins in the lane, a cart, the horse twitching its ears, besieged with flies. Knowing the carter to be overworked Adélie had tipped him exorbitantly, and Pilou had loomed in the doorway with her carpetbag.

"Well?" Adélie had shrieked. "Is this the heaven you promised?"

"You're a perfectly capable girl"—and Pilou had *smiled*! "The most capable in the world, and heaven comes by putting others ahead of yourself, what do you think of that?"

She had not added, "Now I go to drown myself," or, "Now I go to nurse foundlings"; Pilou had simply marched down the lane as Adélie threw herself down in the dust. But Adélie had risen after an hour and picked the last of the tomatoes from the trellis, then fastened the noon shutters like an abbess alone in her convent.

"Oh, but to live as long as Pilou has," said Henriette, "a person must have a sense of self-preservation!"

"It was lovely that Papa and Maman could go away together," Adélie said in the train station café. "That's the marriage I should want to have—man and wife aren't meant to be apart. But I shall go mad without anyone to look after."

"But your grandparents—"

"How long can *they* last? I shall have to find someone else," said Adélie, as she raised her head from her hands. "That must be the whistle."

42

IN PARIS, SUNLIGHT shone through a jar of cloudy water. She passed intangible through the crowds, her cardinal sash and canary blouse secreted beneath a black cloak. She could walk all morning, cross every bridge she came to, ride an omnibus with soldiers in navy and charwomen in black, stroll through a department store, buy a scarf of Liberty silk or buy nothing at all and never see the same face twice. Only small boys ever met her eyes, boys with jam upon their collars—bright daubs in that sprawling city, its very air dank as dishwater. Of course, the eyes of small boys were the only ones she sought. She sometimes recognized the scowl Georges had been perfecting.

Her grandparents had once wheeled teal and scarlet samples of Lissner broadcloth from one department store to another, one month into the next, until they lacked the strength to return south. They were going blind and longed for smells. She lived with them inside a picture that every day she expected to step out of—the milk *tasted* of milk, but perhaps she'd only convinced herself of that fact.

She established a circuit of fifteen cafés far removed from one another, finding refuge in one after another over the course of an afternoon, sitting very straight to drink a demitasse of coffee and grin into the surrounding mirrors to see if her teeth had been stained brown. Such an asinine use for powers that she was certain could bring a wardful of lepers to their feet!

In the apartment she listened to Grandma talk of hard winters and brawls between vine-pruners, of the world they hoped to awaken to each morning, while tall-hatted men from department stores came to discuss the Lissner boutiques and lead Grandfather into his study. They always stepped out smiling, shaking his hand.

"Let me look after this business," Adélie told him.

"What business?" her grandfather asked.

She walked every evening beneath the gas lamps, crossing each bridge across the grey Seine, and more than once she broke up a group of boys who'd stopped to look over the parapet. She stood upon the pavement to study the men inside cafés. They sat with matchsticks between their fingers, planning. They laughed until Adélie saw their back teeth. They all had mistresses, she knew it. They all undressed their wives. She watched until they looked up and spied her, then she walked until she found another café. There could be no such year as 1898, she decided. It was the most obscene number imaginable.

AT THE MARKET at Les Halles, Grandmother had warned even from her deathbed, there were crayfish big as watermelons. Adélie watched men sell medicines and young women hawk flowers, but only old women could sell vegetables or crayfish or bushels of sage, and it seemed only old women in calico aprons, swathed under black shawls, were permitted to buy. Young people merely escorted their aunts and mothers, arrayed like gypsies' wagons with baskets, and secured the cab when Auntie complained of torpor. The smell of dry sage was the smell of Toumbadou and so the vast hall full of people became a pen of sour and dusty goats, jostling each other with hips like bare rafters.

"Black-pit herring, *chasse-marée*!" Adélie repeated.

The fishwives alone understood this language, far stranger than Provençal, churning from some undersea kingdom, and when the winds inside the fishwives subsided the unfortunate youngsters of the market would remain with the ocean's tang in their nostrils but no wit to purchase the wares. Buying a crab would become a lost art, like the minting of those Egyptian coins her grandfather had never failed to describe as she'd poured out his breakfast coffee.

"Black-pit herring! *Chasse-marée*!"

Pilou might have explained such talk. Meanwhile men in cloth caps pursed their lips as though sucking marbles, though a few in proper tall silk hats looked about as though searching for a bauble of unguessed power amidst the baby's breath and potatoes.

After her grandparents had died—one immediately following the other, as proper spouses ought to—the landlord had claimed their furniture for himself, and now she needed *something* in the apartment besides her clothes, especially now that the cat

had gone. And the coffee around the corner at Au Père Tranquille was exceptional, though the sale of the Lissner boutiques
had left her only enough to fill her demitasse for another month,
then—what? Go into the world to make her fortune. While on
each boulevard a Lissner shop went on selling chemises the
colour of her father's thumb.

The antiques men J. Quille Et Fils sold to old and young what
was once new, now old, and new again once sold. J. Quille
flourished his potato nose and moustache of baby's breath, and
shouted that the oil lamp she held was First Empire.

"Looks to me like it was cast on a hillside at the dawn of time!"
She sought desperately to make a joke. "Aha, ready? With the
rubbing of the lamp, I—"

She polished its tarnished lid with her cuff but it lifted away
and her elbow thumped back into what seemed a bag of flour.

"Right to the heart!" A tall man swayed behind her, massaging his breastbone. "You mean to lay me out, Mademoiselle!"

"Oh, I meant no offence," said Adélie, though it was not her
own voice she heard but that of a gasping carp upon a counter.
"If I've hurt you, I—"

"I invite you to repeat the performance whenever you like.
May I ask where you acquired such a charming manner of
speaking?"

"Oh . . . the South," the carp mouthed.

"A revelation." He stared at the surrounding faces as though
jealous of his prize. "It lifts me out of here and sets me down
somewhere sunny."

At first she'd thought him thirty, with his silk hat and irre-
proachable topcoat, but he was younger—pink cheeks beneath
his sandy moustache dimpled each time he smiled. Triangles of
eyebrow sat out on his temples so that no matter what he said he
looked as delighted as a lolling-tongued hunting dog rubbing its
snout against a baby's chest. An older man's spectacles wouldn't
have had frames so bright and golden; he lifted them to his forehead and squinted at the burnished wares along the edge of
J. Quille's table.

"If I watch Isabelle make her selections," he was saying, "I can plan with some exactness which nights this week to be home for supper, and Maman was about to have a lot of her old Grand Army cronies in for tea and I've heard enough about the leasing of Kwang-chau-wan to last a lifetime." His velvet pocket produced a gold cigarette case inscribed with a pair of bees. "Do you smoke?"

"No, sir, never."

"That's the best approach, even the doctors are saying so, but the smell in here does make me light-headed. We've blessed Asia and Africa with our cultural mastery when surely they had bad smells of their own already. Ah, Pasdeloup has the lobster for her—look at that beast! Do you suppose it will live until Friday? And what have *you* bought, may I ask? That was rude not to ask. You have your old woman with you?"

"No, sir, no. Only here to admire it all."

She gripped her cloak at the throat when it would have been better to tilt her head and look coquettish, but she wanted him to keep that expression of a new father raising a toast, though as far as she could tell it was his *only* expression, excepting that squint. His lips went on pronouncing words at the level of her eye, his pink tongue pressing against square teeth. She knew she stood upon the earth for she felt it rotate beneath her.

"I ought to have said my name is Nicolas Tremier. Our Isabelle would love to make your acquaintance if you have a moment— she's from down south as well."

Because dry sage was the smell of Toumbadou, every man and woman in the hall grasped handkerchiefs to dance the Farandole, wheeling about her and Nicolas Tremier in a long serpentine, skipping twice for every hop as the potato-nosed leader slipped beneath the swinging arms to pluck his followers from the spinning knot and each small boy with jam upon his collar touched the toe of his right foot to his left knee, pressed his tongue through the gap in his teeth and doffed his hat to Adélie Lissner. A cloth-capped hunchback with a turkey over his shoulder turned in a wondering circle and so mashed the sodden tail-feathers into the chest of her Nicolas, who picked the stuff from his coat with a smile and strode on. A rustic emperor flush with conversion. He led her toward an old woman with a shopping list crushed in her glove and the face of a storybook goose. Behind her Monsieur Pasdeloup was less a man than a bundle of rushes.

"Adélie Lissner," said Adélie.

She admitted to Aix rather than to sacred little Toumbadou, but it transpired that Isabelle's village was closer to the Atlantic than the Mediterranean.

"Your part of the country isn't so bad if one keeps an open mind," said Isabelle.

"Have you brought a carriage?" asked Nicolas Tremier. "If not, the lobster will gladly give up his seat."

"Only if it's no trouble," said Adélie. "Though perhaps we could step around to Au Père Tranquille, the coffee there—"

But Mauriac the bowler-hatted groom brought the carriage under the arch and across the cobbles. Nicolas Tremier sucked a purple thumbnail.

"Looks infected," said Adélie. "I'll bathe that in iodine."

In the afternoon sun his teeth were white as eggs.

"That would be most kind. And so long as we're all keeping company, Mademoiselle Lissner, wouldn't you care to christen our compatriot?"

Pasdeloup winked, his lower half in his master's shadow, his arid self steadily dampened by the *Le Journal*-wrapped lobster against his chest.

"I had a look, and he's a boy," Isabelle murmured.

"Must be an excellent swimmer," said Adélie. "So I'll make his name Georges."

A DETECTIVE
FOR THE REPUBLIC

Pierre Lazarie.

EVEN IN Saigon's eleven o'clock heat Henri
insisted on walking to the customs house
alongside the Chinese Canal, where the
congestion of sampans overloaded with crates and nets and barrels and barking dogs gave no indication of economic crisis. How
many dialects saw life on that black vein of water, what diverse
rituals and superstitions were observed, how much of the true
life of the country might be gleaned by a determined man with
a notebook, a box of linguistic dictionaries and an abundance of
time? *The "Arroyo Chinois" of Saigon,* I'd call the book, subti-
tled *Microcosm of the Fabled East.*

—Nearly, said Henri.

I spied our destination, an airy-looking villa poised at the
fork of the canal and Saigon River, just as Henri squeezed my
elbow and ducked under a café awning. The proprietor behind
the bar nodded to us, Henri fell into a chair and drummed his
fingers thunderously upon the table until the proprietor hurried
over, uncorking a bottle of Bordeaux in mid-stride; his mutton-
chop whiskers and starched white apron would have looked at
home in any café in France during any year of the 19th century.

—To your health, said the barman as he poured.

—It wavers, Louis, said Henri.

He seized the glass, drained it, then set it down. Louis
refilled. While he waited Henri breathed hard out his nose.

There was only the one glass so I sat with my chin in my hands, wondering whether our first step ought to be to seek out poor Adélie Tremier's name in a registry of cemeteries rather than to attempt to pinpoint the exact afternoon of her arrival. Henri actually sipped his third glass, arguing with Louis regarding a painting over the bar showing two women under a willow tree, apparently a copy from one of the Impressionists, though I wouldn't have known one from the other. From behind a curtain at the rear of the room a dark, hollow-eyed face appeared, retreating at a sharp word from the barman. I couldn't have said if it was male or female and I realized that the question scarcely mattered to anyone, that unless a Vietnamese was a prostitute—demanding mayonnaise, apparently—then as far as we colonials were concerned they had no gender, no family, no future or past. They were simply below us, as our aristocrats of 150 years before had regarded our peasantry, and it struck me that, despite fedoras and eyebrow pencils, the France we had diligently recreated in Indo-China was not that of our democratic present but of our inegalitarian past, so that every Frenchman east of the one-hundredth longitude, whether he had a plantation to his name or a wheelbarrow, could carry himself with lordly disdain. Did they not realize what had *become* of those aristocrats?

—Daydreaming? asked Henri as he climbed to his feet. We may be separated from our relevant work but I'm still your minder, and mental fatigue's the beginning of general fatigue, so have a care.

—Seen it a thousand times, said Louis.

Henri dropped a five-piastre bill on the table and Louis scooped it up just as an old woman rushed from behind the curtain, tucked the empty bottle into her armpit, lifted the empty glass and diligently wiped the tabletop though Henri had not misplaced a drop.

We crossed the canal via an ornate green bridge that would have looked at home in Venice; Henri rushed across, shouting like a carnival barker.

—I can't pretend Louis has Nguyen's style but in an emergency he's more proficient than an army surgeon—but what must the family make of this lacklustre position you've fallen into? Though as of an hour ago I can't put my finger on what that might be—"Detective for the Republic"?

I studied the canal below us. A pair of tawny hands protruded from beneath a rattan sail to arrange chipped flowerpots along a sampan's bow. I gasped, for exactly how old were those pots—and what time-lost detail of the Confucian system dictated their placement on the plank? I strove to bring scientific order to a reeking tangle.

—They expect, I said, that I should make a success of myself, despite my—despite my news of this morning. I do have money to wire home.

—You *arrived* with money? That isn't normal. How much have you got?

—I'd rather not say.

—How'd you come by it?

—Playing cards aboard ship.

—How much have you got?

—Six thousand francs.

—You *are* full of surprises, Professor!

We reached the southern bank of the canal where a clutch of waiting rickshaw men dogged our steps, clicking their tongues to attract patronage. We circled old women proffering pyramids of chili peppers and pungent dried fish.

—I do feel a little sentimental, Henri went on, observing your first day, en route to the customs house where I first came to work. Many a time at the Continental I've raised my head and looked about for that boy with his foolish string tie, airy ambitions and limitless time in which to realize them. But the heat forces a man to hydrate himself and the people are far too amenable—why, you shit-eating wretch!

A rickshaw coolie, crowded off the road by his fellows, had run a wooden wheel over the side of Henri's shoe, leaving a white scuff across the black leather. The clicking of tongues ceased. In light of the scene at the dock I felt beholden to intervene, but my hands were lumps of dough at my sides. The shit-eating wretch, too hemmed in to take even a step, gripped his shafts and held his stubbly head high; Henri's fist slammed into his cheek, knocking him into his rickshaw so that it over-turned on top of him. The other coolies immediately resumed beckoning while proclaiming in a nasal singsong—in French, I realized, and not a native dialect at all—that their benches were more comfortable than could rightly be believed. How this incident would factor into my "Oversaturation of Rickshaws in Saigon and Environs" I could not fathom.

Henri spat into his handkerchief and with a single stroke blotted the scuff from his shoe, then mopped his brow and resumed rushing over the pavement. The customs house was now only a hundred metres ahead and I ran to keep pace.

—I can't claim, he was saying, that it became an easy country, a friendly country overnight. But the work that's gone into it is no different than that of a father with his children. In the name of his love for them, you see, he may seem unnecessarily cruel.

—And what, I asked, makes *you* an expert on the raising of children?

—Why, nothing at all! Except that I've been one.

The blare of a band resonated to our right, then the deep into-nation of a ship's whistle—the *Felix Roussel* signalling its return to Europe. Marguerite and Aldo could kiss them all on the lips with my blessing. I felt the weight of the portrait in my pocket.

Bullock-cart drivers in blue tunics lounged beneath a spreading tree while sun-stricken colonials leaned against high cart-wheels, fanning themselves with sheaves of documents. At the brick gatehouse the white-jacketed guard merely winked as we hurried past onto the colonnaded veranda of the cus-toms house. Henri stopped and thrust his hand inside his jacket. On the river below a lighter crept toward shore, barely afloat beneath a pyramid of what might have been sandbags but was more likely rice. Had I been an economist seeking out the heart of the Orient, I need not have looked further.

—That damned visitor's pass from Frémont, said Henri. Here. You can see from that crowd, this is one place where simply being a white man does not write you a ticket. The guard knows me from Madame Shum's but the clerks upstairs, you know what the turnover is like. Appalling place, Madame Shum's. I put money on seven each time and reassure myself that with each failure my odds only improve.

The corridors were so narrow that we turned sideways to squeeze past a herd of portly officials laughing over a story one was recounting in a low voice. Henri muttered a greeting. They eyed him coldly.

The stairwell was lined with maps, each depicting with thick red lines the triumphant spread of our influence across Indo-China—telegraph lines erected, railways built, roads cut through swamps—though inland these networks appeared so tenuous that a hurricane or better-than-average rainy season might wipe them out completely. And where would that leave the telegraph operator in, say, Kratié, a pox-scarred orphan from Normandy who'd thought he was dying of loneliness even *before* his little machine had ceased to clatter? And how could a progressively minded researcher like myself gauge the after-effects of a telegraph line on the subsistence-farming natives of Kratié District if the line was there already and no control model ever established?

In an upstairs corridor of slatted wooden doors Henri turned a tarnished knob. Inside, the room's shutters were closed, but the light seeping in silhouetted a lone man on crutches, surrounded by crates beneath the ceiling fan.

—Is that LeDallic? he asked sharply.

—In the flesh, Pinget, said Henri.

—I'm glad you put it like that. I'd assumed you were dead.

—No, but at Immigration it is sometimes hard to tell! We're a couple of secret policemen who don't know the secret, old man. You know what Frémont's like, we—

—You needn't butter me up, I'm being paid to assist you. I'm the only honest man on the premises.

—Certainly, said Henri, we're looking for a needle in a haystack at any rate—

—The arrivals ledger, I said, for October 1909. The ship *Salazie*.

—Arrival of goods or of personnel?

—Personnel, I said.

—Arriving at Saigon?

—Certainly at Saigon! said Henri. At this very building!

—Patience. What sort of job would I do if I weren't exact?

—Then please be exacting, Henri said through his teeth, and bring the item requested with all swiftness.

—Customs no longer keeps those records. I realize you work in the building, so there's no way you could be aware of it, but personnel ledgers are considered Immigration's domain and are therefore kept in the basement of the Vice-Regency.

—Since when?

—Since 1924. You may be looking for a needle in a haystack, LeDallic, but it seems you don't know where the haystack is or what the needle looks like!

—Ah, I said, but we do know!

I held up the photograph and Pinget hobbled forward.

—Who is this scrumptious girl?

—Adélie Tremier, I said proudly.

I CANNOT CLAIM to be an expert on Taoism, but at the File Archives desk in the Vice-Regency's basement I recognized not one but *all three* of the Jade Emperor's legendary ministers: Nam Tao, who records births; Bac Dau, who records deaths; and Ong Tao, who records daily activities. It was as plain as if they'd worn nametags.

—What do you mean by those get-ups? Henri demanded.

They turned up their oil lamp on the counter. They may have simply been three broad-headed old men with wispy beards and scholarly black tunics—perhaps teachers thrust from their calling by governmental reorganization.

—How may we serve? one asked.

—The arrivals ledger, I said, for October 1909. The ship *Salazie.*

The three nodded and disappeared into the shadows behind them. The basement smelled powerfully of damp.

—They ought to at least wear bow ties, said Henri.

After a moment they returned and placed a thick book before us, bound with mildew-spotted cardboard. The title was illegible. I opened it to the first page.

—Smells like a cat's pissed on it, said Henri.

—It begins with September twenty-fifth '09, but this is not the *Salazie*. Can you read that, what's that say? The *Carné*?

—Skip to the middle.

I could hardly get a finger between the pages.

—For what name? asked one of the men.

—What does that matter if we can't look in the goddamn thing? asked Henri.

I opened my little notebook and showed them her details.

—Tremier, I said.

Bac Dau and Ong Tao held the ledger by its covers while Nam Tao fanned its pages over the chimney of the lamp. They each had the long yellowed nails of the venerated scholar and I fantasized that each had seen Le Loi's exploits firsthand. Henri retreated to a dark corner where he noisily opened a packet of cigarettes.

—The Cambodian frontier, he announced, has precious few nightspots.

The pages began to separate, and laying the ledger flat the three pored over the entries in each left-hand column, bending so low as to have kissed the rotten paper. I watched the arrivals of ships down the middle of the page, *Indus, Tonkin, Tourane*, while the right-hand column seemed to indicate each passenger's ultimate goal: Bangkok, Hongkong, Yokohama, Haiphong. Somewhere in those humble place names we'd find her. The old men straightened and marked a place with a ruler.

—"Tremier, Adélie," I read aloud. "Born 8 April, 1880"—

Henri seized the ledger from my hands and ran a thick finger down the page.

—Then where'd she go from here? What ... why is that space empty?

The right-hand column was *blank*—what could we do but return her portrait to Frémont and climb back up to our files and stamps? Ah, but if Captain Tremier were killed outright in a skirmish in Tonkin, perhaps no one would reclaim the portrait!

—She may have not *known* where she was going, I said feebly.

—Nonsense, we used to spend hours chatting to them as they came in, it was the least efficient system in history—they'd tell us their life stories and complain about the heat and we'd say it would only get hotter, don't take your hat off, and it dragged on thus for the whole day.

—What's *that* column mean?

—That's the entry status. But these are all French citizens, there's nothing to put.

—What's the little box? I asked.

—Clerk's initials—the syphilitic moron of a clerk's initials. I'd imagined that she'd gone to Hué. Enchanting place, they say, but hardly anybody lives there, easy to have singled her out in a crowd, then a nice cool cruise along the coast. Why shouldn't I write it in myself? "Hué." With tuberculosis, no less—come, man, what are the chances she's above ground anywhere?

—But what *are* the clerk's initials? Perhaps you know the man.

He set the ledger beside the lamp.

—"M.A.L." First name M, last name L? Could be thousands of people.

—That L might be a Q, I said. Some people write their Q tall and skinny.

—In that case it's Quinn. You know any French names that start with Q?

—Quillard.

—Son of an Englishman, little Quinn, with hair on the bridge of his nose. Been retired ten or eleven years, but he did have an eye for the girls, he might remember this one. When's the arrival?

—October tenth, I said. I've made a note. Frémont might know what became of this Quinn—we could cable him in France tonight, couldn't we, and have his answer by morning?

—Hell with Frémont! said Henri. It's half-past three, and upon the entire face of the earth I know the exact spot we'll find him. The real mystery is why he's never thought to pluck those hairs!

—Assuming that really is a Q, I said.

AN ORPHAN MAKES
HER WAY IN THE WORLD

Mlle. Adélie Lissner.

FEBRUARY 10, 1899
Dearest Henriette,
I snatch this moment before the evening service. Have I mentioned how musty this church is? The damp is like nothing we have at home. I must add that Monseigneur Childebert has hairy lobes to his ears, which I find more spiritually wholesome than anything he has said thus far, for it means he is a man of God and not of Fashion.

I am ashamed of my long silence, and yours was such a sweet letter, but Grandma passed in January and though of course I don't begrudge her it was no little job to bury the dear. I thought I would have learned after the trouble I had with Grandpa! I'd dug a hole as deep as my waist before the quarrelsome gravediggers took up their shovels. Her illness had its laughable side in the blunders she made of names and places, her past perfectly mingled with the present, leaving her every thought an embarrassment of riches. After closing her eyes I conclude I would not make a good invalid myself.

Are you familiar with the name Tremier? It does sound familiar to me. I have made the acquaintance of a man by that name and he assures me it is a name of no consequence, unlike Lissner, he is quick to say. The districts of Paris are numbered one through sixteen in a spiral, did you know? We have walked them in order and seen the most awful things. Our findings: the relationship of people to one another is like your brother's description of the Cambodian forest, where the mighty trees take all of the sunshine while beneath them innumerable bushes carry on a bare existence. The men and women in tatters do not upset me, not after seeing scores of them, but each child in such a state affects me equally. I gave bread to a gaptoothed little boy, his arms like matchwood, then bought him an omnibus ticket so his father could not snatch it away.

My thanks again for your sweet long letter. Your brother's adventures in the East sound so frightening it is a wonder he could have been bored as he claims.

Your attached,

Adél.

PS—(After service.) Monseigneur Childebert gave wonderful accounts of Sister Alphonsa the Ecstatic who sees prophecies, and he told us more stories of bleeding roses and blushing stones than I ever read in my life. N. tells me over my shoulder that I believe too easily in such things, but if the fantastic can set our hearts racing, why shouldn't we believe?

IT WAS OPENING night of the opera *Cendrillon* at the Opéra-Comique, where the Tremier family's fourth-tier box looked down on the orchestra seats as on a fiefdom. While couples sat like tombstones in the adjoining velvet-lined boxes, the hundred diverse instruments in the pit tuned like a lot of train whistles and birds and blacksmith's bellows and Adélie leaned this way and that to see it all—until Nicolas threw the curtain across, seized her by the waist and pulled her onto his lap so, if only for a moment, she'd keep still. Within the gloomy box a bar of yellow light lay across them, and she ran a fingertip over his triangular eyebrow. He gazed up at her, then kissed her quickly on the neck, his moustache soft beneath the curve of her jaw. Sparks ran down her arms and her lips went numb. She thought she heard a bell begin to ring.

"You'll enjoy this," he said.

He set her upon her chair and pulled back the curtain. As the last peal echoed the electric lights snapped off, leaving the theatre black but for the embers of distant cigars and halos upon the floor from the ushers' lanterns. Several ladies cleared their throats— timidly, yet the sound resonated as though in a canyon. Then, as the strings began a maudlin tune, the stage was bathed in a murky light, revealing a damp basement, strewn with cobwebs and ash, where a girl in lavender rags lay asleep on a great hearth.

"Cendrillon herself," whispered Nicolas.

Before the girl even raised her head Adélie's heart went out to her, and when the three stepsisters in high-collared gowns appeared to thrash her with the broom and berate her in song Adélie felt tears run hotly down the back of her throat. Of course she felt moved by poor Cendrillon, but even more so by the realization that here was Pilou's *Marie in the Ashes* come to life—a story which had once been as real to Adélie as breakfast, yet to the bejewelled Parisians around her it was just a trifle, for never in their lives had they needed magic or a prince to save them. She held tight to Nicolas' sleeve, feeling its weave beneath her nails. The sisters strutted offstage, leaving Cendrillon to sleep and dream of a ball, the most splendid Oriental ball, and a fairy took the stage now, singing that the girl was her godchild and summoning nature to her aid—starlight for a gown, a goblin to drive the coach and dragonflies to pull it. Cendrillon awoke in the midst of this splendour and joined in the chorus until every instrument achieved an unattainable note and the stage fell to black. Applause from all sides.

Adélie Lissner squeezed Nicolas Tremier's arm in both of hers, put her head on his shoulder and her forehead against his white collar. He stroked her cheek with the back of his hand. She felt her hairpins shift. The electric bulbs snapped to life throughout the theatre and with much chatter and rustling of papers the audience rose in glad anticipation of cake and a glass of chocolate. The tombstones on either side peered at Adélie and Nicolas in puzzlement, as though they'd never been in love themselves and could only shrug when they stumbled across the word in a book. Adélie bit her lip; perhaps Nicolas would *not* stir like the rest of them and perhaps this moment would not end. She heard a buzz and snap above their heads and an instant later the theatre was plunged into blackness—a woman shrieked and men laughed.

"The electric circuit has failed," someone announced plainly.

"Bring up the gas! Light the gas!" croaked an old frog.

But the gas lines had been lately removed and the ushers had tamped their lamps, leaving the hall black as the inside of a goat. Disembodied voices *always been better and if Monsieur Edison were such a genius he'd bring me a coffee can't see your hand and little pastry now play Mouche in the dark* fluttered about Adélie like moths. She could not tell up from down, and could barely discern his face in the dark though she found it was closer than she might've guessed—here was his moustache upon her neck again, here were his lips. She curled like a petal, wrapped her arms around his head and put her fingers through his hair, stiff with pomade. His neck smelled of a forest. She slid from the chair to the floor. Was that his arm? Hers? Her lips found his, her fingers found the hair curling behind his ears. She felt a silver light course through her and knew if she were only to open her eyes from kissing she would see beams shining from her fingertips like lighthouses. Her whirlwind had somehow become that and more, he'd wreaked a change in her very biology: it should not have been possible for her small hand to take his and guide it beneath her wealth of skirts to the pearl buttons of her drawers, indeed to *help* him with the buttons, even as their lips were ever upon the other's mouth. Suddenly she was inundated beneath her seven layers of crinoline but Nicolas pawed at her face to find her mouth again, and through the blackness she saw a hundred damsels abreast of her and a hundred princes arrayed like a peacock's fan around the man in her arms as the last button of his suspenders relented.

STRANGLER
QUINN

Pierre Lazarie.

HENRI REQUISITIONED a car and driver as Quinn'slocation was apparently too distant to reach by rickshaw. The dirt road was flat and straight, and we soon reached the outskirts of Saigon. Under the trees, thatch huts squatted on stilts.

—What sort of people are these? I asked. See, she has a rice-pounder under the house there! And what a lot of chickens—isn't it miraculous?

For this was suddenly agrarian Cochin-China, the seat of that mode of life which had affected my brain from the moment I first stepped into the Hall of Artifacts at the Colonial Exhibition of 1931, the typed descriptions bold and black upon the bone-white cards: wine container, clothes basket, quiver, rice baskets, sieves and hats—all of woven *bamboo,* so muddied and smoke-stained they might have been a thousand years old!—as well as the wooden shields, hoes, crossbows, gracefully curving sickles, and a mortar with a metre-long pestle. Of all the halls of the exhibition it had been the dingiest and most deserted, yet I'd stood amongst the dust motes in a beam of sunlight, felt the blood throb in my ears and leaned against a table to keep from fainting.

It had seemed to me the objects were holy, fallen to earth from the lands of the Bible yet *not* of the Bible, yet just as ancient, as sacred, and yet—and this was most seductive to a lad of seventeen whose worldliness consisted of owning a half-dozen monogrammed handkerchiefs—utterly *secret* from the realm in which I moved. What unknown hands had fashioned those blackened hats? The cards had read *Hmong* people, *Muong* people, *Moï, Dao, Xo-dang*. What calamity had led them not just to fashion crossbows, but shields? I'd just screwed up the courage to question the bearded attendant when my father appeared to fetch me, his coat-sleeves stiff with chalk though he claimed to have come from an exuberantly wet war-canoe demonstration.

—They're Annamites or whatever you call them, Henri yawned. Same as in town. There's no Khmer sculpture hiding in the grass, so quit wagging your tail. Think of something to tell that captain so it'll sound as though we did our best.

—You think Quinn won't have heard of her?

—Can you remember one name from your applications this morning? Ah, hear that? The bugle. Sound carries out here on the flats.

He glanced at his pocket watch.

—That'll be the seventh race starting.

As we passed a half-naked boy astride a water buffalo, a grandstand came into view and I was reminded of the Prince d'Orléans' observation, "In Asia we men of civilization look first for a racecourse." In the car-park lined with flowers my colleague flew out the door; I raced after him, through the gate and past a baffled-looking attendant.

—Shouldn't we pay?

—Not after the sixth! he shouted back.

A cheer went up—evidently the race was ending. I came out of a short tunnel and found the bettors' windows and a circle of laughing young women, then flew down three steps to overlook the course. A half-dozen horses danced back toward the paddock, necks slick with froth, jockeys sitting up tall. Native boys in tennis whites hurried out to meet them.

The grandstand rose to my left and I turned up the wooden stairs. A hundred-odd colonials in white and grey left off applauding to light each other's cigarettes and swirl their drinks. A fat sunburnt man, fists studded with fluttering tickets, pushed past me on his way to the cashiers, then another man equally giddy, then two stricken-looking girls in blue, and finally Henri with a bottle of wine in one hand and two glasses in the other.

—They close the bar at the start of the eighth.

The terrace afforded a lovely view of the track but we carried on up another flight of stairs until we were nearly among the rafters. Grey birds swooped past our heads as we ducked beneath their nests.

—The cheapest vantage point, said Henri. And yet pensions aren't improving! There he is, do take your hat off.

A line of café tables had been pushed against the rail to overlook the course far below, and in that whole line there was a single tenant, a hunched man in derby hat, peering into a huge pair of binoculars. He wore white shorts and extremely long black socks, while a vacuum flask, coffee cup and overflowing ashtray adorned his table.

—Where are the girls? shouted Henri. I told my friend he'd need prophylactics!

As we sat down the man lowered his binoculars. Patches of purple blood vessels sat high on his cheeks, and from the bridge of his nose bristled six coarse hairs.

—LeDallic? he asked. I'd dearly hoped to never see you again.

—Likewise. Here, I brought you a drink to stop your mouth from talking.

—Pour out, bless you. I brew my own coffee, can you believe it? Thrift. The horses are against me. But how did you manage it, wasn't that the eighth just now?

Henri filled the glasses and pushed one forward.

—The seventh.

—Seventh! Dear me, maybe I haven't done as badly as I'd thought. Hallelujah! Look at that, I had number five in the seventh all the time, "Youth's Advantage" his name. Drink to him!

They rang their glasses together. I drummed my fingers on the table.

—Young man, Quinn asked, you aren't a colleague of this cretin's? You can't have been with him long, for your eyes aren't bloodshot.

—His first day, said Henri.

—Then if I were you I'd put the gun in my mouth this instant.

—If you have a free moment, I said, we'd like to inquire whether you might—

—What's happened? he asked. Did I let someone in I shouldn't have? I turned away Germans during the war, didn't I? And I couldn't have embezzled anything, for you can see I brew my own coffee—it's unheard of!

—Don't bother the man, said Henri. Run and fetch us another.

—No such luck, said Quinn, it's nearly the eighth. Don't you keep a little something in your pocket?

Henri studied the horizon through the binoculars before answering.

—Nowadays I prefer to sit with a fresh bottle like a civilized human being.

—We've travelled from the Vice-Regency, sir, to ask whether you might recall an entry in the arrivals ledger for October 1909. A passenger on the ship *Salazie*.

—Do they require new boys to have a sense of humour now— did this cretin put you up to it? Do you realize you're talking about, what, twenty-seven years ago?

—Ah, said Henri, but only *seventeen* years before the end of your career.

—This is my career. Is the eighth likely to ever start?

—Tremier was her name, I said, Adélie Tremier. We're curious to know where she might have ended up, or to know *anything*, really, that you might recall.

—And it was supposedly me that processed your unknown creature?

—When you write down your initial does the Q look like an L? asked Henri.

—It does vaguely.

—Here's her photograph, I said.

Quinn took the portrait and held it near the end of his nose.

—*This* woman?

—They're at the post, announced Henri. I suppose you want these back?

63

A trumpet blared shrilly and the gates snapped open. Even at that distance I could see clods of dirt fly up behind their hooves. Quinn clenched the barrels of his binoculars and swayed like a metronome.

—Which is your money on? asked Henri.

—"Metropolitan," I think it is. No, he's fading. Well back now.

Quinn sagged sideways in his seat. He turned and tapped the photograph with a white-haired finger.

—This woman, he said, was she ill?

—We've been told tuberculosis.

—Yes, I remember. But there was more to it than that. We must go to my place. Did you come out by car?

—Departmental car, said Henri. Newer model than the one you used to run down poor Sainteny.

—Certainly, said Quinn, they couldn't have driven that car again. Do you have cash for a few bottles on the way?

Henri pushed his chair back and wiped his mouth with the side of his hand.

—I don't personally, he said, but it happens that Pierre here has six thousand francs.

NATIVE CHILDREN with wet noses were bouncing bald tires down the stairwell, and though one grazed my shoulder I admit it seemed a marvellous game. Quinn's place was a second-floor apartment above an out-of-business garage and a sidewalk stall that sold grimacing temple gods; I couldn't find the name of the street but we were near enough the river to smell it. Quinn patted the children's heads as we climbed past.

—*Chao ong*, he said, *chao ong*.

The pane of glass in his door was cracked. The white kitchen glistened. We followed him through to the living room, where a cluster of innocuous black chairs was menaced on all sides by stuffed fauna: a crocodile as long as the room, a thin tiger baring varnished teeth, a pair of barking deer with heads at rakish angles, a potted tree full of long-tailed monkeys. It might have been a zoo's funeral parlour or vice versa.

—Pretty, aren't they? A suicide's widow gave me all this to settle his debt.

—You ask me, said Henri, the whole lot is—

—You came to hear what *I* had to say. I have a pistol on the premises and I do think a small hole in your neck would suit you. Just here, you know, below the ear. Glasses in the kitchen, young man.

He set a card table between the chairs and poured us each a tumbler of whisky. It was no brand I'd ever heard of. He absently ran a finger across the hairs on his nose.

—Don't ask, I haven't any ice. Terribly uncomfortable chairs, aren't they? I wonder sometimes if that was what drove him to it. Show me that picture again.

Quinn lay the frame on his knee and smiled gently, cheeks crinkling like paper.

—Even when they wheeled her into the hall in that chair I thought she was lovely. Smiling just as here. All that black hair. The steward from the *Salazie* wheeled her up but then he went away.

—There was definitely no other man with her?

—Why, you young dog! shouted Henri. You want her all for yourself!

My ears tingled at that. It's likely I blushed.

—No, no, said Quinn, quite alone. I made note of that myself. She put her hat in her lap. I read her papers and asked where she was headed, and she told me she'd been sick and was going to Laos. As simple as that, as *I* might say, "My shoelace broke, so I must get a new one." She was sick, so she was going to Laos.

I wrote "Laos," then my gaze drifted into the lacquered branches. The monkeys' jaws were so badly set that their mouths appeared as ragged vacuoles.

—Of course I asked her how far *into* Laos, as we had to, and she said Luang-Prabang at the very least, maybe up toward China, so I advised her that Luang-Prabang was still its own kingdom and before setting out she'd do well to write the French resident up there, the standard line, you remember, and she smiled again, just as she's doing here, only here she's with family, it looks like, and happy, and with me I believe she might have been hysterical. She said that if she waited around for a reply she wouldn't live long enough to board the *Bassac*, and—

—What was that last? I asked. How do you spell that?

—B-A-S-S-A-C. Well-known boat then. She'd heard it would go up the river in November and I said, "Yes, but if I'm to jot your destination down shall I put Luang-Prabang?" And then the funniest bit—she told me she'd likely go up there and learn to live forever before she went back home. As *I* might say, "I'll likely get wet if it rains." It wasn't so unusual to have a lunatic stop at my table but most only screamed about microbes and trade unions until the boy led them away. This Adélie of yours wasn't like that. And, granted, outside of parroting its governmental status I'm quite ignorant of Luang-Prabang, so maybe there was something to her idea, perhaps there *is* a sort of Shangri-La up there and she lost nothing in looking for it. She looked like ashes already. I suppose I never jotted "Laos" down in the ledger, is that the problem?

My colleague looked asleep, his double chin clamped against his chest.

—Nothing at all in the right-hand column, I said.

—You were meant to tell us she'd gone to Hué, said Henri.

—Well, it was a big ship, Salazie, said Quinn. Long line of customers. I might have had a prettier girl since then, but it's this hair I remember and the photograph doesn't do it justice. That's typical of tuberculosis, I read very recently, the body wastes away but the hair, of all things, just gets lovelier. Expands like a cloud.

Henri refilled his glass and threw an arm over the back of his chair.

—Two questions, he said.

—Blasted quick, said Quinn. If my girl finds you when she brings my supper up she'll insist on feeding you supper too, and I can't afford that.

—Firstly, that film about Shangri-La only came out in the last year, yet you'd have us think it was on the tip of your tongue as early as 1909—have I, or have I not, caught you out in an anachronism?

—I did see the film down on rue Pellerin, I'll grant you, and it did occur to me I might see that girl with the wild hair wander past in the background, though I'd no inkling of her name. I've forgotten it again, in fact.

—I have a third question, I said, when you've finished.

—Second, asked Henri, what in that story was so salacious that you had to insist it couldn't be told in public, far too sensitive, barricade ourselves in at your digs, et cetera?

—Ah! said Quinn. I wanted a ride home.

—Deftly played, said Henri. I've often thought it was you who ought to have been mangled instead of poor Sainteny.

Quinn drew a cigarette from his sock and slowly lit it.

—And the third question?

—How, I asked, can you live amongst such bad specimens? The deer are innocuous enough, but these monkeys and the tiger are the stuff of nightmares! In the Hall of Natural History at the Exhibition of 1931 the tigers were—

—The past can't be recreated, dear boy, much less retrieved. It can only be. . .

He stroked the crocodile's flank with the toe of his shoe.

—Shaken by the neck? asked Henri.

—The night these arrived, Quinn said, I came in late from the course, black as a witch's tit in here, and I do think my heart stopped for a minute or two. But they've become my mascots since then.

—Just yesterday I became mascot to this young fellow, said Henri.

—We're grateful for your time, I said, and I suppose we—

—Is she really Mata Hari, this Tremier girl, is that it? asked Quinn. Why go sniffing up her trail now?

—They told us several good reasons, said Henri.

—What next, the two of you flash her photograph amongst the crones of Luang-Prabang? I must warn you, if you don't like my simians you won't like that country at all—out in the woods, the so-called human beings have tails as long as your arm!

—You mean the Moï? I said. That was disproved twenty years ago.

—They made that up to raise money for the goddamn missions, said Henri. Then some fathead called them the Lost Tribe of Israel. I knew the Moï as a youngster, old man, and you'd look as much a monkey next to them as you would beside anyone else.

—*You* were out with the Moï? I asked.

—Don't fall headlong on your way downstairs, said Quinn.

Henri rose from his chair with heavy exhalations out his nose.

—Whatever happened to that chubby girl you used to go with?

—I strangled her, said Quinn.

The sky had already gone black as we descended.

—Such a pretty turn of phrase, said Henri. With a tongue like that he could sell peonies to a German.

—Didn't the idea of hunting immortality on the Chinese frontier sound familiar?

—Yes, it's that film, I already said so! *Lost Horizon* or some—

—No, a friend of mine, a PhD candidate, was translating Wu Ch'eng-en... it's foggy now but near the start the Monkey King vanishes into the wilderness and comes out immortal somehow. Can't remember how.

—You have monkeys on the medulla oblongata. Too much sun.

At the foot of the stairs he stopped to read his watch beneath the electric light. The patch of wall facing the bulb was alive with insects who gyrated for the audience of nimble yellow lizards who'd crept out to find their supper.

—Six o'clock already, said Henri.

—What's left, I asked, report to Dubois in the morning?

—No, no, *now*. He and Frémont will be there until eight o'clock. They've had two hours for lunch, slept two more at home and gone back to work fresh as newborn babes. Only a chap with a death-wish soldiers straight through!

Our driver was asleep across the front seat but as we climbed into the back he sat up and started the engine without a word. I felt decidedly drowsy myself until we pulled into the street and I saw how the sleepy native quarter had transformed itself with nightfall—the car had to crawl through the throng! Electric bulbs hung from the branches of wizened trees and black-clad men lounged beneath them on ankle-high stools, drawing on pipes as thick as my arm and sipping from squat glasses. Their hostess leaned an elbow on a tin keg, a rag over her shoulder.

—Beer, light and crisp as an apple, said Henri.

There were five such drinking parlours down the length of the block, with the addition at the last of a sway-backed barber in possession of a straight razor, a folding chair and a mirror in the crook of the tree. Barefoot children clutching bright green biscuits rushed in front of the car, bound for the ball- or balloon- or tin-car-vendors on either side of the street who squatted beside wicker baskets of goods or sat regally behind candlelit stalls or simply stood with their fistfuls of flowers or strings of catfish. Whole families sat on stools in the street, hunched over bowls, chopsticks flying, but only when I peered through the clouds of steam to glimpse piles of organ meat on the vendor's counter, or lengths of noodle or platters of bean sprouts or decapitated, whip-thin dogs could I venture to guess what anyone might be eating. Our driver used the horn liberally. Women with shoulder-poles hurried by on either side hauling steaming kettles or pyramids of fruit, conical hats flapping against their backs to let the night air cool their brows, tendrils of black hair slipped free after the long day to curl against their cheeks.

—The cooking fat is rancid, said Henri. Who can abide that stench?

I could smell only the charcoal of the braziers. The car rolled apace with a woman around my own age, the baskets on her pole piled with dry rice, then a shrill whistle sounded, a white-clad native policeman waved his baton, and we found ourselves rolling up a wide and empty street. We'd crossed an invisible boundary.

—Is it even goddamn possible to cable Luang-Prabang? asked Henri.

In his office on the marble-tiled first floor we found Dubois writing, *scritch, scritch,* while a cigarette smoked behind his ear—a trick I hadn't seen even in college. The electric bulb swayed perpetually thanks to the vibrations of the ceiling fan so that his hat rack, the globe on his desk and the brass ashtray all appeared to sway as well, a happily familiar sensation after my weeks at sea. Dubois finished his sentence, capped his pen and retrieved the cigarette.

—I'd assumed you'd be drunk in Cho Lon as the first stage of your assignment.

—Never in Cho Lon, said Henri. I learned my lesson. Listen, we found the clerk who processed her in '09, and he confirmed the old girl had been deathly ill.

—Which clerk was that?

—And he informed us, I said, that she'd been bound for Luang-Prabang!

—That's right, too, Henri said, aboard the . . .

I lay my open notebook on the desk.

—*Bassac*, I said.

—Who was it that told you all this? asked Dubois.

—Beyond question she was headed for Luang-Prabang, said Henri.

—We'll cable the resident, I continued, and he can confirm whether or not she arrived late in the autumn of '09.

—The autumn? asked Dubois.

—The start of the dry season, said Henri.

—At any rate, said Dubois, the north-west cable has gone down at Kratié. That's a thousand kilometres short of your mark. No, the ministry shouldn't be too impressed if we only get this far. But before we wear ourselves out over the *Bassac*, the chief told me in no uncertain terms that if you track down someone named "Queen" we'd all better think twice about the information. It might have been "Quincey," I didn't write it down.

—Ah, said Henri. I know the one he meant.

—Apparently she was going north, I said, to find the secret of eternal life.

—Really? It's hilarious how starry-eyed they were in those days. But it seems to me that Luang-Prabang does have *radio*. If the Army flies a plane from here to Hanoi twice daily, let me see, and from Hanoi to Vientiane every *other* day—

70

I reached for the notebook.

—If you need arithmetic—

—If we mention Captain Tremier in our request there's a chance they'll take a circuitous route down the valley of the Upper Mekong, then as they pass over Luang-Prabang they can radio our query down to the airstrip or the resident himself, provided he's home.

—And where in that extravaganza do we hear a response? asked Henri.

—Do it all in reverse the day after! Then Hanoi back to Saigon. Have an answer in... four days, provided the weather's fine. Just write the name and dates down for Madame Louvain, and we'll see you back on the third floor in the morning.

Just off the foyer we found a teller's window marked TELEGRAPH and staffed by a middle-aged Frenchwoman with liver-spotted hands and temples. Henri wrote "Airborne Radio Communiqué" across the top of a message slip and slid the paper to me.

—You look extremely well tonight, Madame, he said.

—Thought you sailed home weeks ago, said the woman.

—That was Beyle.

—Shame.

She slid down from her stool and trudged out of view. At the rear desk a young native clerk sat pulling carbon copies apart and stuffing the resulting sheets into envelopes. He wore cellulose guards to protect his sleeves but his hands were a grubby blue, and as he'd likely not been given a four-hour lunch I guessed that he'd been at his task for eleven or twelve hours that day and would likely be kept at it another fifty years.

—Poor boy, I murmured.

—Poor boy what? asked Henri. I ought to thrash him.

—Whatever for?

—Because then he *would* be a poor boy and you'll have been right for a change! Hurry up with that chicken-scratch—we're treating ourselves to the courtyard at the Continental, and if the kitchen has closed I'll knock your brains out!

EVERY PARISIAN'S NIGHTMARE

Mlle. Adélie Lissner.

B UT DOCTORS can be wrong, can't they?" asked Nicolas, his hand on the banister. "Bonheur may not know as much as he ought to—we should wait!"

He raised his eyebrows hopefully but went on climbing.

"Wait?" said Adélie. "Look how swollen I am across the top— these lapels ought to sit flat and they're out over my shoulders. I'll have to feed the dear thing one day, but from this you'd think it was tomorrow!"

The Tremiers' echoing foyer rose three storeys, its white columns culminating in archways carved with cherubim holding the sun aloft. This was Adélie's first visit; she recalled those homes in Aix that were never visited due to a mad aunt or invalid father. As they climbed she counted the various suns out of the corner of her eye. Eighteen.

"With the heedless rubbing of a lamp," she whispered.

"You heard Marie—she has a caller already. She'll be on best behaviour."

Was Madame Tremier as fearsome as all that? Perhaps a pair of maternal claws really was necessary—her own mother had failed utterly to protect little Georges, after all, and if any mother upon the wide earth had a single job that was it.

"One day we'll laugh," said Nicolas, breathing slowly through those bottom teeth, his hand upon the gilt-and-chrome door-knob. "Proclaim this an historic afternoon."

The upstairs parlour thus revealed was an enormous onion, domed and pearly white, the chiffon curtains shifting with the breeze to give parsimonious glimpses of the gardens below. At the far end of the room a couple sat and chatted, as distant and hazy as if they'd been on the far bank of the Seine. Above the porcelain fireplace, busts of the Greek pantheon stood upon the zinc mantel, gods and muses and whatever-all-else. She knew that one had seduced a woman as a swan and another time as a bull, she'd seen the watercolour by Moreau with her own eyes, but she knew above all else that these likenesses represented wisdom and dignity. She glanced at Nicolas and was relieved to find his eyes upon her bosom; soon he'd raise his spectacles for a better look.

But they were now halfway across the fleur-de-lis carpet and so lowered and raised their chins, respectively, as they approached the figures at the white tea-table in front of the windows—though in that room every table was in front of a window. The woman had slate-grey hair, very coarse and curly, pinned simply like a pom-pom on top of her head. Her gown was elaborate, high-necked, with layers of cuffs and cummerbunds, but as every centimetre was fashioned from identically meticu-lous white lace there was no telling where the flounce ended, for example, and the bodice began, and the overall effect was that of a lizard which had failed to shed its skin and now laboured beneath a mass of detritus. But who was Adélie to pass aesthetic judgements as her distended breasts spilled from her dress to fulfill every Parisian's nightmare of the ham-fisted peasant girl clomping muddy-clogged into the parlour?

"Mother," Nicolas said from somewhere above her ear, "I am pleased to introduce Mademoiselle Adélie Lissner, of the Lissner Boutiques, you understand, and lately come north from Aix-en-Provence—like the Roumanilles, you remember, they come from there. Mademoiselle Lissner is a very *dear* friend—"

The gentleman seated next to Madame Tremier sported purple bags under his eyes, a bald, mottled pate and an upper lip so long his face seemed racked with a simian fatigue. He wore a blue double-breasted tunic with canary epaulettes, golden foliage around his collar and such a weight of coins and crosses stitched to his chest that the poor man tilted visibly to the right. Now Nicolas' mother rose and extended her hand; it had been scrubbed scarlet and felt soft as whipped turnip.

"—*wonderful* you can get away on holiday," Madame Tremier was saying. "You must call me Sabine, my dear, and this is General Subrégis. He was with Heart's Blood at Metz, as I'm sure you must have gathered."

"Ah." Adélie failed to understand but curtsied and placed her freshly shaken hand upon her belly. "Heart's Blood. Wonderful."

"And Mexico for long years before that, the two of us," the general said. "Hurried across from Saigon in Cochin-China. The battle at Chi-hoa."

"Oh, yes, all those travels." Madame Tremier touched his blue-serge sleeve, and cast her eyes toward the chandelier. "Then to a place better still."

She turned to Adélie with a smile marred by the brown discoloration that came of drinking too much tea, though any newsstand could have sold Madame Tremier a dentifrice powder to bleach her teeth even while reddening the gums.

"I must apologize," said Adélie. "I'm not familiar with Mexico."

"Nonsense!" said Madame. "As you must know, for they have the same profile, your *friend*'s grandfather was Heart's Blood Tremier himself!"

"I don't dwell on it," said Nicolas. "I've yet to even mention that Father drowned after pacifying Senegal."

Madame Tremier blanched as though she'd been pinched on the neck, then resumed her seat, seized the teapot and began to hurriedly pour out, though a young maid hovered over the service.

"I *wonder* what this house would be like today, don't you?" asked General Subrégis. "If Heart's Blood were still with us, I mean. If Bazaine had not been in command. But that's the soldier's lot, and that of his family."

Nicolas pulled Adélie down beside him onto the black-and-gold sofa.

"Are you referring to the Prussian war?" she asked softly.

"Naturally," said the general, shaking his wattles. "Your friend here has yet to go in for his national service, so it bears consideration. Oh, my dear." He turned to Madame Tremier. "There's no shame in being widowed. There's *glory*, in point of fact. And for all that, the Bazaine family have always been my dear friends, and it strikes me now that you might do them a great favour, Mademoiselle Lissner, an act of real Christian charity."

"What could I . . . ?"

"Well, just a prank," he went on, "but I see you're with child, Mademoiselle—look, you can't keep your hands away from it, can you? And what a blush, like you've stepped out of a steam bath! Sabine, have you seen anything like it? Wonderful!"

Madame Tremier put a hand to her throat. She looked with wide eyes at Adélie, then at the vast expanse of carpet. Nicolas leapt to his feet.

"Excuse me, but we're—"

"Now here's my idea I've been coming to," said the general. "The Bazaine family are still my dear, dear, friends, you understand, I see them regularly for tea, but the dear things can't show their faces in public because every six months there's a new monograph, a new analysis, a new pamphlet tearing old Bazaine to pieces!"

Cup and saucer chattered visibly upon Sabine's knee.

"Come to your idea," she murmured.

"Well, why not 'Bazaine' for the child's name? Not much of a Christian name, I realize, I see the looks upon your faces, but with that in mind it could be a male *or* female child, no one's used it before so who could tell you otherwise? Your little snip Bazaine might discover a new planet, or a race of pygmies who could produce milk for export—just hook 'em up to machines, easy as that—and even if he grows up to be an anarchist who throws himself out of a balloon, well, then, all the better, my friends can say, 'He's not a Bazaine from *our* family,' and saunter up the boulevard with heads held high."

"I've brought Mademoiselle Lissner here today to announce our engagement," said Nicolas, hands folded behind him. "We have come with nothing to hide."

"Though it is not your child," said his mother.

"It certainly *is*! And we would be announcing our engagement even if there were *not* a child. As it is I am more inclined. Doubly so."

Madame Tremier drained her cup. There was an audible click as she swallowed.

"And what, Mademoiselle Lissner, do you bring to these proceedings?" she finally asked. "Have you a tongue or only a voracious womb?"

"No harm done, you two," said Subrégis. "Difficult to think straight when the blood vacates the brain for the nethers."

"I am no different than you, Madame." Adélie's saliva felt sticky against her teeth. "I want only what is best for your son, which is to honour the family name—"

"Of which you claim to know nothing!"

"Mother," said Nicolas, "I hereby give you vast warning that under no circumstance shall this child enter the military, he shall—"

"Nonsense, but even so. Mademoiselle, I trust you aren't the sort of child who believes youth makes her invulnerable to folly, that years will dim the impact of—"

"The military doesn't work like that," said the general. "After one mistake you'd be dead!"

"I suddenly feel as though someone *had* died." Madame Tremier sunk her fingers into the cloud of lace upon her chest. "I have this weight here. Subrégis, tell me, were you there to see off Colonel Bertrand? They said a great parade of gentlemen went in carriages."

Nicolas collapsed onto the sofa.

"Bertrand?" asked the general.

"Bertrand had that bit of flesh cut out of his nose which impeded his breathing, I told you, then he went out in the cold before it was healed. Erysipelas set in."

"Better to have died at Querétaro," said General Subrégis.

He managed to lean near enough to the table to lift his cup and saucer, and Adélie saw that the fingers of his right hand had somehow been fused, the bottom three together and the index finger to the thumb, so as to resemble the soft pink claw of an enormous crab.

"*That* would have been a far better death," nodded Madame Tremier. "I pity a man who dies poorly. Why live at all, without a good death? Berenice, would you? It's gone as cold as ice."

She and the maid fussed with the teapot. Adélie and Nicolas stayed just as they were, hand in hand upon the sofa. The coming generation would know nothing of war or suffering, they had decided. The wedding would be a small one, just down the road at Saint-Gervais, where a lovely Infant Jesus watched from the glass above the organ.

"And then grow old together," Adélie said.

THE COURTYARD
AT THE CONTINENTAL

Pierre Lazarie.

U P RUE Catinat I followed Henri through successive squares of light cast by milliners' shops, antique dealers, jewellers, bookshops, barbers, chemists and resplendent perfumeries. We passed gaunt couples in silks and counterintuitive furs, stretching their legs between acts at the Théâtre Municipal; bell-bottomed sailors of every maritime nation; and cloth-capped men under each mango tree and lamppost, too drunk to stand—hence the lampposts—and roaring at the tops of their lungs until I concluded that on average these countrymen of mine were 86 per cent louder and drunker than any Frenchman then living in France. Dodging spark-showering streetcars and automobiles ancient and modern, Henri and I crossed this august boulevard and passed into the lobby of the Continental Palace Hotel.

And there, in the relative quiet, we passed girls.

Girls humming Strauss waltzes with folded parasols on their shoulders; girls wearing pearls and cardigans and mules, wandering in twos and threes before display cases of monogrammed hand towels available for purchase; barefoot, willowy girls of nineteen and twenty in sleeveless blouses, ruined by the heat and so curled up on divans with their heads in their mothers' laps; girls, five of them, crowded between a mirrored pillar and an enormous fern so as to share a single cigarette, perhaps hoping that no one would see, though *I* saw them, even the one with the tennis racket behind her back, hair in pigtails and a finger-length of brassiere strap visible on her freckled shoulder. What exactly did she gain, I wondered, in revealing so much? What man was ever more blessed than Adélie Tremier's husband, who in 1905 spent a half-hour undressing her, beginning with her white gloves? Then unpinning that black hair.

And what part of Marguerite, I wondered, was Aldo kissing at that moment?

—Promptly at eight-thirty every night, said Henri. They set the clocks by me.

We stepped from a carpeted corridor onto red tile and were in the open air again, in a courtyard. The rooms of the hotel looked down upon its glass-topped tables and wicker chairs and twisted black trees so full of chattering birds that had we been courting they'd have drowned out our whispers. Henri strode past the bowing maître d' and selected a table himself.

—Such incredible trees! I said. Fronds coming out of the trunk!

—What do your studies indicate it signifies—the Annamese messiah will be born in the morning?

—These are the largest napkins I've ever seen.

—Ah, Nguyen's sent his man over. Let him pour, let him pour. Paternina Gran Reserva, 1928, I swear by it. Get your hand out of the way.

—Spanish import? You're none too patriotic.

—All countries can go hang themselves, I bear France no allegiance. Oh, onion soup to start—no, we'll have everything to start—mussels with fried potatoes, *salade Niçoise*, a little bread on the side and duck however he's making it, if it's confit so much the better.

—And I'll have—

—The same. Quit wiping your face, didn't I tell you that sweat sustains you?

The courtyard was not crowded; I assumed at that time of the evening the fashionable crowd had finished their meals and gone dancing, but months later I'd learn that the fashionable crowd did not even put their shoes on until midnight.

79

—I cherish the outdoors, said Henri, but except for the race-course this is the only spot where you may commune with nature and still enjoy yourself. Racing, however, relies on day-light. See him there.

—Who?

He gestured magnanimously toward a slender Vietnamese in a tight-fitting white tunic, standing behind the bar. He wore spectacles halfway down his nose and from the incline of his head I wondered if he might be asleep.

—Nguyen! Looks as though he's doing nothing whatsoever when in fact he has committed his mind to solving all of the world's problems with a single thrust: Trotskyites, protectionist tariffs, the complaint I lodged against you regarding the mul-tiple-party ordinary residence application—thanks to Nguyen all of these will slide noiselessly into the ether. Memories! In fact he has solved them already, if not last night then early this morning.

—He told you as much?

—I can sense it about him. Each problem is resolved and now he strives merely to present his solution in as elegant a package as possible. No doubt he will set it to waltz time and have Nijin-sky perform it before the League of Nations.

I swirled the wine in my glass, peering through its purple lens at the frangipani branches. The waiter reappeared with a fresh bottle of Paternina Gran Reserva and crept away with the spent one. Henri's glass, refilled the moment before, sat empty again. He was staring at something over my shoulder, and I turned and saw blue sparks spray from a second-floor balcony. Welders repaired a railing.

—I can't abide these disturbances at my Shangri-La, said Henri. To hear a single nail hammered overwhelms me with the notion that all things must crumble to dust.

I cannot speak for my colleague, but at that instant my own thoughts were not piloted by the seeming-lucidity of drink so much as by hunger, exhaustion and the exhilarating cool of a Saigon evening after the day's injurious heat.

—But if a nail can be hammered occasionally, I said, there's no reason why anything should crumble.

—Ah, I'd prefer it to be made to last forever from the start. I'm an idealist in entirely impractical ways.

—I'd heard that most idealists are.

—Is that what you'd *heard*? I think you ought to ask the other patrons about the conquest of the city by the Tay Son brothers in 1789—go ahead, I'll be in the Men's!

Even with an entire bottle inside him he walked straight enough to have demonstrated plumb to a party of surveyors. He crossed the courtyard, ascended a single tile step and disappeared through swinging doors. The step looked extremely slippery.

—Isn't it just a matter of time? I asked, upon his return.

—Are you being metaphysical? Beyle, too, was like that at this time of the evening.

—It's a matter of time before you brain yourself on the step into the Gentlemen's.

—And the river will rise, empire will fall and all laws of thermodynamics will come to fruition. I was reminded as I relieved myself that last night as I relieved myself I'd thought I'd better tell you about this old bite rather than have you believe that complaining of tiger maulings is some tired affectation amongst us inmates, like tying the spare onto one's car with liana vines. Though this nectar *does* dull the pain of the thing.

—I'd had some real anxieties regarding tigers, I said. But I was enlightened aboard ship by Coderre of the opium works.

—Coderre! He's impotent, did he tell you that? Gets a girl and just fiddles around with her breasts.

The waiter hovered beside us with a fresh bottle.

—I'd been in the country two years, Henri continued, on a three-day leave to Dalat, playing *boules* with a lemonade in my hand, financiers' daughters winking from the porch, you understand, when an old gentleman ambled through the gate, clamped his mouth over my shoulder and proceeded to drag me outside.

He drained his glass and the waiter saw an opening.

—The local *gendarme* had followed him up the road at the languid pace expected of a resort town, and as we emerged into the street this officer appeared at my side to empty his magazine into the back of the old fellow's neck. He collapsed with teeth still in me, and of the two of us I have a fair idea which one suffered the greater—if he'd had a bullet left I would've asked the *gendarme* for one through my skull. Ah, the food!

A small army of waiters set bowls and plates around us, repositioned cutlery, then retreated silently to the fringes of the courtyard.

—Fried potatoes ought to be cut longer, said Henri. I've always thought these much too short.

—Agh! I said. The ketchup comes out too quickly.

—And it's too sweet. You could pour it over ice as an aperitif. Now I have some thoughts on the tiger's place in natural history, shall I share them?

I licked my finger and nodded heartily; the mussels were in an excellent broth.

—First of all, considering his relationship with man, his colouring is altogether wrong. The garish palettes of the peacock, the parrot, the flamingo reflect the frivolity with which we regard them, while the shark—or the timber wolf, say—is grey, muddy black, and that's only revealed if you can glimpse him lurking about the periphery of our existence. And a tiger *lurks* even more. He is an insubstantial black cloud with yellow eyes and a spring-loaded jaw who has as much right to be a lively white and orange with delicate brushstrokes of black as the bubonic plague does, or the depths of the Mariana Trench.

The mussel upon my fork paused in mid-air.

—And second of all?

—Second nothing. I've made my position clear.

I swirled the wine in the bottom of my glass before swallowing the last of it.

—When you were with the Moï? I asked.

—In a Cambodian forest. Our troops sat on hilltops for eighteen months, waiting for a Siamese incursion. I was there as the esteemed representative of the Ministry of Colonies, great with anger as it was, and as I was a downy little duckling and it was a posting no one wanted it had trickled down to me, just as this Tremier affair has come to our attention like a bedpan emptied out a window. I was given a tent and a Moï family to look after me, and I watched bugs smother my lantern and cried myself to sleep over Saigon, over Hanoi, over any shack with a deck of dirty playing cards, I didn't care where because I hadn't yet realized Indo-China is a kingdom of pickpockets, that's all I can say for them. But the Moï are children, really, as unspoiled, as meddlesome. Look!

He pushed back his sleeve to reveal those copper bangles.

—Welcome bracelets, I said.

—My Moï knew when anything was afoot in their village though it was thirty kilometres away, maybe the birds told them, but the old girl would hobble in and the other two would jump to their feet, and at first the one who mumbled French would ask if I'd mind coming with them—I'd been herded out of the army camp, I ought to have said, thanks to my irreplaceable position with the ministry—so I went along whenever there was a ceremonial tooth-pulling, and how many kids were there? Eleven. And what a life to be born into: falling out of trees, chasing after deer with a dog at your ankle and a knife between your teeth, and once you came of age screwing whoever you liked provided both parties were amenable. When I was a kid I couldn't read about such things! For my dad it was the slate, the belt and the ink-pot, the Bible on Sunday, and on my birthday I'd go to the bakery to smell the hot bread. Climbing a tree was an unnecessary risk, so he'd batter you until you'd think the ground really *had* come up to meet you.

—That's love in most cases, I said quietly. Didn't want to lose you.

—He had *nine* of us—let's not mention him again. To earn a bangle I'd have to drink whisky from the Moï's jar until my head hit the floor. Oh, under my father's roof I'd never had a drop, but the Moï taught me—damn it, I *did* mention him again!

He rose and retraced his steps toward the Men's, and as he slowed to ascend that tile step I flinched as though I'd closed my teeth on a live wire. Why should I be filled with mortal dread on behalf of a man who'd battered a half-starved coolie with an oar? I ought to have soaped the tiles myself! Instead I gazed about the tables for a woman in a large hat of an age between twenty-five and fifty-six, her black head perfectly poised, and instead saw only the insipid denizens of my own generation.

Henri strode back looking so self-satisfied that the outer tables might've guessed he had Frémont's job rather than his own, despite his dishevelled hair. I shifted in the chair and felt the somewhat-less-than-six-thousand francs nudge my hip.

—Did you ever go back to your Moï? I asked.

—I was sent directly to Dalat for my holiday—I'd been a great success, of course, in that the Siamese never appeared. And after I was dragged into the street by the old gentleman I spent three days in a backfiring car, raving with fever and shitting my pants before I was deposited at our fair city's Pasteur Institute, and I've not left our fair city since. My band of Moï have probably been killed and eaten. Come to that, the amount of morphine the Pasteur Institute pumped into me would've finished them off to a man.

—Did you at least visit Angkor?

—Well, a fellow goes into the world with his mind open, you see, his very spirit salivating to accomplish, oh, all manner of good works—

—"To care for others first and enjoy happiness after."

—I would've got a prostitute if I'd wished to be interrupted. Now one morning when a fellow is twenty-five or thirty-seven he wakes up and thinks, "Damn it, at this rate I won't have anything to leave the wife and kids," even if he doesn't have wives or kids, and his generous disposition narrows like a closing umbrella.

I might have argued that thanks to faithful Marguerite I'd regained my open-mindedness, but hadn't our dark-eyed quarry altered my perspective already?

—Well, I said, I'll entertain the fantasy that it may not happen to me.

—The universal ambition is to die with an army of grandkids at one's bedside, the wind roaring through a vineyard fat with grapes. Incidentally, I've decided we shouldn't fight over the bill.

—Shouldn't we? That's very kind of you.

—Not at all. You won so much lucre playing cards you can afford to buy me a piece of bread now and then.

By the time we trudged back through the lobby the flocks of girls had dispersed. A Vietnamese boy in black oxfords dusted the display case.

—Won't be a single rickshaw to carry us home, Henri predicted. Too many ships in port. Sailors scurry from one bar to another like the town was a damned roulette wheel, can't hunker down to the hard work of drinking. Most of them, anyhow.

Sure enough, on rue Catinat there wasn't a rickshaw to be found—had all of my gateway-nappers really found employment? Another thesis to amend. Two French girls on a bicycle, one straddling the book-carrier to swing her bare legs, bellowed in unison:

They give him soft looks
but it's me
he likes the best!

They whirred by. Car horns shrieked as they passed the Théâtre Municipal.

—You know that one, *"La Petite Tonkinoise"*? asked Henri. About some Prince Charming up Hanoi way. If Dubois gets his way those'll be the last girls we ever see. Step lively! No, casual, more casual than that! Someone's left their engine running. I'll drive—you can barely stand, child, much less sit up.

I climbed in and collapsed into a leather seat as soft as a kangaroo's pouch; I considered that a comparison of great lucidity. While Henri heaved himself behind the wheel—the car had excellent suspension but I was jostled like a joey regardless—I gazed through the Continental's picture window at a monocled gentleman pacing the lobby between the foot of the stairs and the concierge stand while consulting his pocket-watch with every third step. Waiting for a girl, I concluded with my keen detective's brain.

—The owner of this car is bent on romance, I whispered.

—He's given his driver the night off, said Henri, so romance would be the least of it. Depravity to make a seaman weak in the knees.

Eventually we turned into a dark boulevard of trees. As our headlights flickered across each tamarind I felt sure, slumped as I was against the door, that faces etched in the bark peered back at me. I descried clear-cut cheekbones and regal brows, but with each successive tree the faces became more primordial, grotesque, and as a barrage of moths struck my face through the open window I fell horror-struck against the seat.

—Anywhere in the car is fine, Henri said. But by God don't be sick on me.

—We may be the pinnacle of civilization, yet the Khmer kings of Angkor thought the same, didn't they? And what became of them? *You* claim to know Cambodia.

—What's this I'm supposed to know?

—The bloodthirstier ones might have come back us as *smer*—really, werewolves!—and their ministers are the emaciated *beisac* who scrounge the—

—You ought to film chillers instead of coughing up those generals of yours!

—Ah, that's because force of arms makes an impression! I *want* to study blackened old baskets of the Hmong and Xodang, then wend my way home, but it will make for a far better career to demonstrate that if the Mongols conquered the world, the Annamese defeated the Mongols in 1288, and the French conquered the Annamese, then *we* are therefore the dominant species on earth. Lecture tours up and down the country!

I was drunk on Paternina Gran Reserva, yes, but to a greater extent I'd been upended by the chance that we'd soon be striding though the very jungles of the vanished Khmer. An astronomer studying charts of Saturn is told to pack a bag, he's going.

—Witches, some say, are now *srei ao*, crawling heads searching for excrement to devour while their intestines trail behind
them, and as a favour to the department I'd like to prove it! But
the kings who commanded slaves in their tens of *millions* wait
until the end of days as emasculate trees, and if that's what
became of such a glorious people I can little wonder what will
become of *us*!

We lurched to a stop in a street I didn't recognize—Henri
gripped the wheel as though to strangle the thing.

—Which is why, he said, I've no urge to gambol through the
forest!

ON FRIDAY MORNING I visited the Bank of Indo-China and
wired 5,800 francs home to my mother, enough to rehire the
housekeeper—was Aldo Masson ever such a paragon of fil-
ial duty? I knew real love existed and was merely waiting to be
found while poor Aldo had already sewn himself to Marguerite
Gély, as constant as a weathervane.

It only remained for Luang-Prabang to summon us. I used the
"To Be Filed" stamp unerringly for hours, trading folders with
Henri and ringing for the clerk without uttering a word to either.
In the three days previous I'd learned all that was necessary to
perform my duties, and if not for watching the door for Dubois
it would have been an extremely tedious morning, but thankfully, yes, there was Dubois to watch for. Yet he did not come,
so I opened my journal to record what I could of these events.

Henri kicked his chair back and pounded the bell.

—There! he shouted. All work done in a single hour, and if he
tells us never mind, the trail's gone cold, then we'll spend the
day with Nguyen. My brain's gone soft.

—You've spent the week with Nguyen.

—Simply contemplating him. You ought to have been there,
it's very calming to contemplate Nguyen. Oh, and I've had him
arrange supplies should we have need of them. Drop that pen—
how many times have you written "Adélie Tremier" by accident?

—Twice.

—Ten or eleven for me. The boys at the docks will think we've tightened our restrictions down to a single name, that wouldn't surprise them. On your feet, now, don't make me pull you by the ear.

Dubois' office was hot as a baker's oven as sunlight poured through the window behind him—even I knew when to draw the rattan blinds, and I'd only been in the country five days! He sat scrutinizing a newspaper, following each line with his finger, and my first thought was that perhaps news of the discovery of Madame Tremier had already been leaked to the press, and if so how quickly could Captain Tremier and I be rushed to her side? Dubois looked up with a grin.

—Have you read this one? "Blum's Hat Crushed In Royalist Riot," when the fact is the Socialist bastard nearly had his ear lopped off and the Royalists took his hat home for a trophy! It's like something out of Puccini, it's so ridiculous!

—That was last year, that hat business, said Henri. Haven't you got a new paper in all that time?

—Now they say he's next in line for prime minister, I added.

—Well, yes, the steamers have brought a stack, said Dubois. I'm current as of six weeks ago. I like *this* one, though, there's a good recipe here at the back, especially if a chap can get his hands on a good-sized salmon. Oh, good morning, Madame Louvain!

Our friend from the telegraph window stood framed in the white doorway. She dangled a slip of paper between thumb and forefinger as though it were rancid.

—Set it down here, Madame, said Dubois. That's awfully good of you.

Only after Henri and I stepped back into the very corners did she deign enter and drop the message into Dubois' fat fingers, and whether she left the room after that I can't say. I thrust my hand into my pocket and gripped the little portrait as tightly as I dared.

—Ah, yes, said Dubois. "Army dispatch." It's come down from Hanoi.

Henri massaged his left shoulder.

—Kindly tell us what it says, sir.

—It reads, "Yes." Not a word more.

I couldn't help grinning.

—Confirming Madame Tremier's arrival?

—Have to assume so, won't we? You understand that Frémont will want you to travel into Laos yourselves? Remember there are no roads into the country, there is only the Mekong—weeks or months on the Mekong.

—You're not funny, Dubois, said Henri, so there's no sense in your trying to be.

—I'd send you by air, but the Army is notoriously jealous of cargo space. They'd rather fly a pig north than a civilian.

—A *private* plane could take us! said Henri.

—Frémont has done so, yes, said Dubois. But in this instance cost is prohibitive.

—The cost? shouted Henri. You'll pay our salaries while we vegetate on a paddleboat but won't pay to get us there and back so we can carry on our proper work?

—*Modern* steamships, keep in mind. May not take an entire month. And in the meantime, should the Ministry of Colonies inquire whether this office was able to help Captain Tremier of the Third Army with his problem, Frémont wishes to say that at this moment two of our best men are en route to Luang-Prabang to pursue our investigation.

—But why not fly us up and back so we can report to the captain that we've *found* his mother? I asked.

—Twenty-seven years later? You won't find her. When the ministry performs its audit you will be en route, and after the audit I won't care if she's been skinned and sewn into a book—*after* the audit you can tiptoe home whenever you like!

—If you don't want us in evidence, asked Henri, why don't we float over to Hué?

Dubois pushed his chair back. He passed between us on his way to a print on the wall, tucked behind the door, showing Josephine Bonaparte astride a lion. Swinging this aside, he opened a wall safe and took out three bundles of white-and-orange five-piastre bills; he threw a bundle to me and two to Henri.

—For passage to Luang-Prabang. Messageries Fluviales will at least get you to Cambodia, and it's Friday, yes? They sail on this evening's tide and you'll reach Phnom Penh on Sunday, and after that be sure to detour up the Mekong, rather than sailing to Angkor in the company of every man in the world lucky enough to own a camera.

The ends of my fingers suddenly tingled.

—How *near* to Angkor will we pass?

—Put the innovations of the vanished Khmer behind you. Once into Laos I believe you'll have to switch boats due to the cataracts, but that's not my worry. Go home for your topees and revolvers, and Mailliard will have your safe-conducts ready when you stop in on your way to the dock.

Dubois hurried behind his desk and shut the blind with a clatter.

—You must've heard my wife has just arrived from France and she gets *agitated,* shall we say, if we're apart too long. Go ahead, gentlemen, I must lock this door. You'll be in my thoughts day and night, I assure you.

THE ONE
HUNDRED WOUNDS

Mme. Adélie Tremier.

EMANUEL WAS born at dawn on New Year's Day, after a long night of rain drumming against the window and the doctor standing at the end of the bed with his fingertips pressed together, the lamp's light illuminating the underside of his nose and—visible only when she lifted her head just so—shimmering across the steel instruments laid out on a square of muslin, as though the doctor were selling them piecemeal from a park bench on a Saturday. He did not observe her progress himself but was informed of it intermittently by Suzanne the hired nurse, who'd been watching Adélie minutely for all of the previous month and who now squatted, mannish hands between her knees, on the ottoman. He was a wicked old magician of the damned, hired by Madame Sabine to ensure Adélie's death should the childbirth not kill her, and as the agony rose up her back into her shoulders she saw the nurse for what she was, too, a hag who only waited for the child to be born before changing a poor girl into a grasshopper and mashing her into the ground. Lord, no, not a grasshopper—but then she could only throw her head back and abandon herself to fate.

When Manu appeared pink and steaming the doctor spoke a few words of congratulations and Suzanne spirited the infant away to a windowless chamber down the corridor until

Adélie insisted, shouting through her haze, that his bassinet be wheeled beside her—she might have been from Toumbadou but she knew how germs worked—and spent the rest of that day gazing across at his perfect walnut of a face and dozing, even while the ever-more-grim Suzanne changed the gauze between his legs followed by the gauze between her legs. Adélie studied the white lace collar of the nurse's black dress, heard the clatter of her heels as she stepped off the rug onto the floor, and realized her agony had seared the old notions from her brain. The world according to Pilou, crowds of goats—that had all become vapour. She saw only the child opposite.

"Mother said I mustn't pick him up," said Nicolas.

She watched him circle the bassinet, a thick finger tracing its crocheted edge, his face so drawn the very brows hung in pouches. Would he lift his spectacles to better know his child, or simply pat the mother's hand and stride from the room as a Society Father must? Yes, her Nicolas, he was doing it, lifting the glasses to his forehead!

"He has your colouring, certainly, though he's a little purple. And my—oh, that is strange. To see my own forehead there asleep."

For the first week and into the next she and Manu stayed in that room, daylight and moonlight both so slate-grey that sleeping and waking became indistinguishable. She would suckle her son, and when he cried the nurse would change him, then Adélie would carry him, her white gown and his trailing across the floor to the window, where they'd watch the wind lift sheets of newspaper over the wall. And her child who had wisps of hair growing from the tops of his ears would gaze out at the grey city and blink his black eyes, and she would wet her finger and wipe the crust from his lashes. He smelled like a roll fresh from the oven. She would love January forever afterward because of those colourless days. January the golden month.

SEPTEMBER, 1907.

"Aha!" said Madame Sabine, straightening in her chair and clapping her hands. "Here is my little morning apple!"

Manu strode into the breakfast room, bowed briefly to his grandmother, then lifted his hands, palms down, to the level of her face. The autumn was still warm so he was dressed in spotless white, with a great looping black tie. She scrutinized the state of his nails while he surveyed the expanse of table behind her. Here, had anyone wished to explain it to the boy, was a practical lesson in the geography and economy of France's empire: bananas from the Ivory Coast, Algerian sardines, Indo-Chinese tea, cocoa from Guadeloupe, coffee from Madagascar, a soufflé flavoured with Tahitian vanilla, croissants from the kitchen below them, all served in crockery rimmed with Guianan gold upon a sheet of cotton from Chad. The maid Marie poured him a cup of cocoa.

"But what's happened to your sleeve?" asked his grandmother, flaring the nostrils of her slender nose. "Crawling in the grate at your age?"

"Charcoal! I was up early so I made a sketch of the garden."

Sabine frowned deeply, right into her neck, then bent to re-examine his fingers.

"And nails clean enough for the barracks at St-Lucien!" she said, and noisily kissed the back of each hand. "What's become of your parents? The poor soufflé can't wait another minute."

"Papa said I was too old for Guignol so Maman hit him with a slipper."

"Did you tell Pasdeloup about the carriage?" asked Nicolas. He dropped a briefcase onto the settee then kissed his mother. "The investors must sign the contracts by noon and my quarrelsome wife has a League meeting. No bread? Only soufflé?"

"I do like the fish." Adélie slipped into her chair. "Is this pot the coffee?"

"Marie, are there any more croissants?" asked Nicolas.

The maid's face was as leathery as a sea captain's, Adélie thought, except for a nose which looked as though it had been moulded from yellow putty, nor was her aspect improved by the loop of brown hair she'd pinned to her grey head as though the fashions of 1875 could never be outdone. Marie curtsied and vanished from the room.

"The mail has come," Sabine announced.

"And?" Nicolas lifted an overloaded fork. "An invitation for cocktails with Major-General La Mestrie?"

She held out a creamy typewritten page already free of its envelope.

"The Minister of the Interior. For you."

"And you've read the thing?"

"It *does* say 'Tremier,'" Sabine muttered into her cup.

Adélie shook her head with theatrical disgust. Her son blinked comically.

"But this is quite serious," said Nicolas, eyes flying down the page. "'In keeping with your family's close ties with this government...'—no, here it is, '...more than accommodating in deferring your two years' service but as your thirtieth birthday has recently passed we feel we *can no longer...*' Damn it!"

Marie, hurrying in with pastries, flinched as though a blow would fall.

"About time, too," said Sabine, stretching her neck like a bird. "Years now."

"'Though you have stated, in writing, your disinterest in the military...'"

"No!" Adélie said. "More than 'disinterest'!"

"'However, it has been resolved that due to an extreme want of talented...'—here, now, listen—'...that your present field of *engineering* could be an acceptable substitute.'"

"But that's tremendous!" said Adélie. "Nico!"

"'...which you may undertake at an *extremely junior* position'—that *does* sound tempting—'at any number of government job-sites in France, or as a *supervising engineer* in Laos, constructing a twenty-kilometre road alongside the Mekong opposite the Island of Khône.'"

"'Khône,'" echoed Manu.

"'The Minister of Marine and Colonies assures me that this challenging project would place you amongst the top men of your profession in the whole of the Indo-Chinese Union. We except to hear your definite answer within the week.'" He lowered the page so that a corner dipped into his coffee. "Sincerely, sincerely, sincerely."

"Too long in coming," said Sabine.

Nicolas wiped his neck with his handkerchief then meditatively chewed his lip.

"Considering the amount of detail they lavish on the jobs here at home, it would seem my mind's been made up for me!"

"But dredging this harbour in Brittany," said Adélie, "is that somehow not worthy of them?"

Nicolas shrugged. "It's a private contract—"

"A *private* contract, my dear," said Sabine. "Not government."

"A tiger pulled a boy out of his school," said Manu, sitting up with a sardine on his fork. "In Annam it happened, that's Indo-China—ate him up, one, two, three!"

"Hush your boots," Adélie said softly.

"Where did you read that?" asked Sabine. "In your little newspaper?"

"Master told us for Geography!" said Manu, neck straining from its collar.

"At St-Lucien they'll never prattle on like that! Why, in a whole *day* there—"

"Enough, Maman," said Nicolas, slipping the letter into his pocket, stain and all. "He'll stay with his academics."

"St-Lucien has academics," she said, beaming at her grandson. "They'll take you the instant you're nine years old, that's not so far away! And think of the fun, to wear a proper tunic and polish your brass alongside all the other boys!"

"We have four days yet to decide." Adélie raised her chin from her breast. "If you write for details regarding the junior positions we might hear back by this evening."

"I'm still digesting all this," said Nicolas. "But that Mekong River project did sound interesting, don't you think? And only two years, in any case."

"Or a junior position for two years. Here at home time would hurry by."

"Manu would miss early enrolment at St-Lucien if you went for two years," said Sabine. "But think how many have sacrificed themselves for the empire, and will—"

"Hang that, I love the people at *this table*!" Spittle flew onto Adélie's lip; she daubed it with the napkin. "For yesterday's sermon Monseigneur Childebert described the well-meaning gentlemen who went to do God's work in Indo-China, and not so many years ago, either, only to be put to death in the most obscene ways by the grateful natives. Decapitated and dismembered, martyred with red-hot tongs—cut in two and cast in the river! After a quarter-hour I realized I'd stopped up my ears. One I remember, a Father Marchand from down in Passavant, they took *him* and they—"

"Darling, would you *please*—"

"Better to hear it now than have to go there! Think of it, arriving, full to bursting with good intentions, just as *you* would, my love, only to look down and see your lower half no longer attached. And this Marchand was sentenced to something the mandarins called 'The One Hundred Wounds,' as if every man on the street would know what that meant! Why stir a finger to help such people? 'Just forget everything he's saying,' I told myself yesterday. 'That world can never intersect with ours.'"

"Marchand was in the *Martyrs Newsletter*," remarked Sabine.

"I want all the world to love God." Adélie gritted her teeth. "But the life God has given me is too valuable to throw away. When I was eighteen I was the only one left in my family, did you know that?"

"Of course, yes, I—"

"Better to live a peaceful life, a *boring* life, perhaps, but for the sake of our boy I suspect God would rather I live a *long* life. And forgive me, Sabine, for it may not be a sufficiently patriotic sentiment, but God did not put a family together to break it apart. Husbands with wives, fathers with children."

"I see comically congested parade grounds," said Sabine.

"I can't see the harm in *asking* after their junior positions." Nicolas polished his glasses on his shirt front, which he'd never done before in front of his mother.

"Marie," said Adélie. "I have that tonic if your head's no better. Forgive me, I'd forgotten."

VÉTHEUIL-SUR-SEINE, FRANCE. NOVEMBER, 1907.

"Here's Tremier," said Simoneau, gazing down the span toward the southern bank. "He'll say whether we carry on."

At the working edge of construction the span swayed terribly. The eleven foremen, gathered in a haphazard crescent around Simoneau, dipped their midday bread into their midday coffee and stared out from beneath the brims of their derby hats.

"When I'm up to my neck in work I don't notice the Jesus wind," one muttered.

"See what *this* one makes of it," said his neighbour. "Then we'll go down. I want to buy apples."

He leaned against the little thirty-two-tonne traveller crane, already laden with enough girders to see the fitters through the afternoon, and flexed his hand as though it pained him.

"They ought to have cleared us off first thing."

"What's Yvan say the other side is like?"

Four diamond-shaped steel spans had been erected from either bank of the Seine, and in two weeks' time—according to the foremen's well-thumbed timetables—the anchor span which joined them would be lifted into place by hydraulic winches. Then, according to the Ministry of Public Works, the mill towns beyond Vétheuil would no longer have to sail their cotton upstream but for generations to come would enjoy rail transit to the markets of Paris. In the meantime the outward-most spans jutted out into thin air forty metres above the river while each foreman ferried his bread through the gap between the bottom of his moustache and the top of his woollen muffler.

"I bought apples from that barrow by the church."

"Nice ones?"

"Mealy. Just about made me sick."

"What a happy bunch you look," said Tremier, shielding the smouldering end of his cigar with a gloved hand. "And the wind isn't all that bad out here!"

The two engineers seemed cut from the same cloth, with their check suits and sandy moustaches, though Simoneau had grown whiskers clear to his ears, neatly bisecting his face.

"Bidou noticed something," he said. "Go ahead and tell him."

Bidou stepped forward, coat unbuttoned, hands crammed into the pockets of a waistcoat which welding sparks had burnt in a hundred places.

"Half an hour ago, sir, one of my boys climbed up to tell me he'd noticed a bend in one of the plates. Not one of the *big* plates, I asked him that first, it was a small one. So I climbed down and had a look for myself. And? Well, a buckle has developed in number twenty-six on the left."

"Developed since when?"

"They all agreed, sir." Bidou fidgeted in his pockets as though feeling for a watch spring. "It wasn't like that day before yesterday."

"Can you show me now?"

"*I'll* take you down," said Simoneau. "I'll show you."

"You come as well, Bidou," Tremier said, pulling quickly on his cigar. "Does anyone have anything to add? Anything unusual?"

The other foremen curled their lips at such a question.

"It was one of the smaller plates," Bidou repeated.

The foremen filed past, shaking out the dregs from their coffee cups. Tremier pressed his thumb against the bridge of his nose.

"I imagined you'd clear the bridge!" said Simoneau. "Shall we go straight down?"

"I wonder if we shouldn't get Fouquet on the telephone first."

They started back toward the third span, and Bidou pulled a corner of his moustache into the side of his mouth. Suddenly Tremier tugged his hat down and took three short leaps, the iron grillwork ringing beneath his heels.

"Solid enough," he grinned. "Why should we worry?"

"You're not fooling me," Simoneau said. "Get the old man on the telephone, and what then? What's he likely to suggest?"

"Remove the stricken plate and hammer out the buckle, that's what," said Tremier. "The immediate result being, less one plate, that the buckle extends through every plate on the section."

"They transferred me," Bidou said. "On the other side, they've a girl who brings around little cakes."

Tremier pocketed a stray bolt lying on the crane tracks.

"I'll tell the old man to wait. Wait until the anchor span's in place. We'll have structural support from either side then, and this plate can come off without a whisper."

Before them the little town spread across the bank. Black branches swayed over the stone houses.

"I can point it out on the drawings if you'd rather telephone from the office."

"No, no," said Tremier. "From the box. If we hop into town they'll think we're running for our lives, and what happens to a battalion's morale if the officers clear out at the first trouble?"

"Why should *you* talk about battalions?" Simoneau frowned.

They'd reached the third span, littered with metal slivers that habitually sliced through shoe leather. The midday meal had been scheduled in shifts, and the two engineers nodded to the first of the workmen returning to their sections.

"I feel an increasing nausea," muttered Tremier.

"Measure and calculate then measure again," said Simoneau.

"Excuse me, sirs," said Bidou. "This is the spot. If you'll just . . ."

A half-dozen ropes hung from the railing, and Bidou automatically pulled one around his waist.

"You wait for us here." Simoneau tugged his own knot tight. "You said number twenty-six on the left?"

"On the left," Bidou repeated.

"Here, finish this off."

Tremier handed his cigar to a workman with a deep scar across his chin. Bidou kept his rope in his hands and the corner of his moustache in his mouth. The two engineers tested their knots then hoisted themselves over the rail before feeling with their boots for the girder below.

"Was I the one who said it wasn't windy?" asked Tremier.

"Lower your right foot. There."

They clambered like apes from one girder down to the next. The steel was achingly cold beneath their fingers and Tremier wondered what the maid Berenice would think of his blackened cuffs.

"They get word to you already?" someone called. "Thought it'd take all day!"

The engineers looked between their legs at a blond boy of seventeen, who peered up from a wooden platform nestled amongst the steel. He had a rivet gun in his hand and a kerchief round his neck.

"That the buckled plate?" shouted Simoneau.

"That's down the bottom, sir," replied the boy. "Monsieur Bidou said I ought to be across the way by now, but you see how it is—they keep popping! Come see how it is so you'll vouch for me."

The two men dropped onto the platform as the boy waved his cap at a plate of three-centimetre steel; ten rivets ought to have held it against the girder but Tremier lifted his spectacles to his forehead and saw only seven alongside three empty holes.

"You say they *popped*?" he asked.

"Watch those a minute, then tell Mr. Bidou if I'm shy of work!"

"What about the other end of the plate?" asked Simoneau.

"Just these here," said the boy. "Listen now. Hear that?"

Tremier heard only the cross-breeze whistling through the girders, but then his ears picked up a rising groan like a fog horn. Suddenly the seventh rivet shot like a champagne cork from its place and rang against the plate behind them.

"There!" said the boy. "What did I—"

"Get off the bridge!" Tremier was already climbing, the rope looped over his arm. "Bidou!" he shouted over the wind. "Sound the horn!"

IN HER DOWNSTAIRS parlour Sabine sat with a novel by Huysmans in her lap, for though austere in many habits she did not shy from purple prose. The evening edition of *Le Figaro* suddenly dropped across the volume, cutting off its narrative in mid-sentence.

"Berenice!"

She glared up at the most junior of the maids, who for several years had been presenting *Le Figaro* with far more subtlety. But neither had Berenice ever had such an ashen pallor, for that matter, or such a tremble in her chin. It was imperative that a servant maintain control of her emotions at all times, Sabine reasoned, but wasn't it just as imperative that she not display the *struggle* to maintain that control? No doubt the afternoon sermon at Saint-Gervais had effected her physically.

"Are you ill, child? Have you smoked a cigarette?"

"No, Madame!"

"Was that a telegram at the door?" asked Sabine. "Not for me?"

But as Berenice would only stare wide-eyed at *Le Figaro*, Madame Tremier glanced down at the front page herself. What was this, some new disaster?

"What have—?"

She drew a breath up her nose before carefully reading the headline.

<STOP PRESS EDITION>
VÉTHEUIL BRIDGE FALLS
Carrying Over Three Score of Persons to Death in
The Crash and Causing a Loss of About
60,000,000 F
Calamity Caused by Collapse of the Total
Steel Superstructure of the South Shore
Engineer Son of Late Gen'l Tremier Among Dead
Channel Blocked—Piers Still Remain Intact

The story carried on in large type, then into many columns of small type, yet each word swam away from her eyes. She wondered—if it *were* true—how a sheet of white paper could be granted the power to strike a man down. Not a cannon, or even the sea.

"They mean my boy," she said.

Sabine heard the electric lamps buzz, then falter, then buzz again. She felt the contents of her lap slide to the floor. Then she too was sliding until Berenice's strong arms enveloped her.

FARMERS

Pierre Lazarie.

As we sailed down the Saigon River the city's lights vanished one by one until only the blue beacon on the cathedral spire remained, then it too vanished behind the curvature of the earth. Electric bulbs flared up across the deck of the *Ton-Le-Sap*, revealing clusters of passengers blinking like moles, women in long white travelling skirts, each white-suited man ruffling his hair after its long afternoon beneath the topee. I inhaled the riverborne perfume of a Cochin-China evening, hummed snatches from *Rigoletto* and recognized, over the engine's din, the hemisphere of tongues ready to sing ancient Angkor's praises—Parisian and Provençal French, dawdling American, lisping Spanish, bilious German. By unspoken agreement their cosmopolitan grey and olive suits had been abandoned; in the wilderness of Cambodia we'd recognize each other in white.

In our cabin I found the Paternina Gran Reserva crates stowed neatly beneath LeDallic's bed, his suit on a hanger, his bed turned down, his shaving equipment arrayed around the sink and the man himself barefoot in one of the wicker chairs, that evening's edition of *Le Courrier Saigonnais* upon his lap. Unfortunately he still wore his grey undershirt with the appendicitis stain.

—Listen, he said. This is a thing of beauty!

He flipped back through the paper, those incongruous copper bangles jangling merrily. As I unlooped my tie I couldn't help but stare at his perfectly hairless white feet.

—"The Cleaner in the Tiger Cage," the item's called. "Vinh Anh, a Cochin-Chinese employed by the Saigon Zoo since 1927 as a full-time cleaner of mammal pens, met his end this afternoon when the Bengal tiger unexpectedly entered the front portion of its cage where Anh was mopping out drains. At the time of the incident Zoo Director Monsieur Douvillé was demonstrating to a group of dignitaries the ingenious system of gates designed to keep the great feline separated from staff at all times. Monsieur Douvillé assures the public that an internal investigation will not be necessary. Monsieur Douvillé also reminds parents that on Saturday the 17th balloons will be given free of charge to all primary-school-age children accompanied by a paying adult." Stupendous, isn't it? A cleaner in a tiger cage is the ideal metaphor for the civil servant of Indo-China! Think of it, microbes and spores to the left and right, insurrectionists on all sides, and we're expected to mild-manneredly sweep up after everyone. This Tremier today, and who-knows-what-else tomorrow! Here, are you gawking at my feet?

—No, I'm—

—Like bedroom slippers, aren't they? They betray the delicacy of my soul.

I unrolled my pyjamas.

—Going to bed already? I'll do the same, yawned Henri. I've already made my inspection of the services offered. It's a different sort of life out here in the wilds.

—We're only a couple of dozen kilometres from Saigon!

—"Only," you say.

I opened a fresh notebook, uncapped my pen and began the day's entry—one which would ultimately be lost, I confess, to the Mekong, but which I'd recreate to the best of my ability in a tumbledown restaurant in Ban Din. Henri extricated himself, with a generous supply of grunts, from that undershirt, and which detail of his upper half caused my eyes to widen? Not the

bony chest or prominent stomach—no, it was the divots of puck-
ered white skin, two in the front of his left shoulder and two in
back, each deep enough to have hidden the joint of a finger. He
twisted his head to admire them.

—My souvenirs of Dalat. The surgeon did remark they'd
healed rather badly.

—I, uh—you're full of surprises, truly.

—Had you thought them some glamorous invention? Since I
was a boy, I tell you, people have underestimated me!

I TOOK TO the deck again at dawn, surveying ever-present palm
trees in the ever-present hazy distance. The water was brown,
the passing sampans were no different than those of the Chinese
Canal, and that vast plane of water kept the floating hulks and
grey villages too distant to properly study, though this was not
even the Mekong proper but one of the nine streams that made
up its fabled delta! I confess I'd expected more of the place.

—Here's my sidekick! said Henri. We're making up a governmental party to chase those tourists from the buffet!

An entourage of whiskered men followed him, balancing coffee cups on saucers. One with a monocle jostled my elbow.

—What do these Germans know of eating croissants, anyway?
Open a dozen tins of cabbage and they'll be happy!

An elder brother to my Marseilles cutthroats sucked at his
pipe.

—We ought to quit the rice business, Lassay—get the farmers
growing cabbages. Think of the inroads into the Slavic market!

—Rice fields are too wet for cabbage, I said.

—So *drain* the fields—never know until you try!

—Keep up the wheat-field lobby! blurted another. Those cabbage countries are poorer than dirt.

Lassay of the monocle wiped the dregs from his cup and
sucked his finger.

—Those cabbage countries ought to build more colonies. Look
at the land concessions here, every decade they lower the limit
but even so any Frenchman with the wit to sign his name can

have three hundred hectares if he wants them! Needs approval by the regional agent, mind you, and *he* needs to keep himself in bread and butter—

—Your brother in Sadec, suggested the gaunt one.

—Who will step out of his *fifth* Packard next time you see him.

—Don't these concessions displace a high proportion of natives? I asked.

—Breakfast-time, said Henri.

—"Displace"? Ah, you're the lad from the Sorbonne—yes, you *do* look pale. As for the natives, well, for every starry-eyed Frenchman who didn't like farming as much as he'd imagined, there's a mandarin ready to buy fifty hectares from him, and *these* notables are always generous toward any landless, yet industrious, families in leasing acreage in exchange for 70 per cent of the harvest. And provided they've enough to pay their taxes these farmers are quite content—the greatest single boon of their primitive culture is that the paying of taxes is absolutely endemic. At the very start, our men at the Sorbonne informed us of the fact so we quintupled the old head tax, initially, which met with miraculously little resistance. Picture the farmers of France being treated like that!

—Guillotines! laughed the others.

—How, I asked, do they survive on 30 per cent of a crop? It's my understanding that merely to have enough seed for the next season they—

—I don't mean to upset you, lad, but it *is* the best system in the world, wherein the cream rises to the top, financially speaking. Speaking of which, LeDallic, I forgot to ask how long *you* had been striding around these parts!

They surrounded Henri, younger than he but with silver cigarette cases, gold fillings, and shoes so glossy I might have shaved in them. He shrugged his bad shoulder.

—Not long, he said.

—In any case, young man, to have done with the agrarian topic, these "displaced" families possess no formal record of ownership, therefore—

—No *record*? I blurted. Forgive me, sir, but the Imperial Court at Hué has kept *exact* records since the rise of the *quan dien* system in 14—

—Chase the tourists from the buffet! shouted Henri.

After breakfast the *Ton-Le-Sap* tied up at My Tho, a rust-coloured town spread across a treeless bank. A row of slate-roofed houses with wrought-iron rails looked demurely out on the river as though its builders believed it to be the Seine, despite oxcarts and unchartered rickshaws shambling past its porticoes. A party of white-clad arrivals climbed our gangplank followed by a queue of coolies with hatboxes and trunks.

—Unruly stragglers, said Henri. And there's Robequain! Lucky for him to have caught us here, the debaucher!

—On the contrary, Sir, said the steward, these ladies and gentlemen caught this morning's half-past-six train from Saigon.

Henri threw up his hands.

—You might've spent the evening contemplating Nguyen, I said.

—Dubois really must open a travel bureau. He's wasted in government.

A row of cone-hatted locals gazed up at us from the wharf.

—Loiterers, said Henri. You see how the vestiges of civilization are stripped away? In Saigon they would have been ushered off in a twinkling.

—How long until we resume? I asked.

The steward took a carpet-bag from a sallow-faced matron.

—Ten minutes.

—Care to savour the local colour? I asked.

—The local colour is yellow, said Henri. Just look at them. I'm going to see how many horrid young entrepreneurs will stand me a little refreshment.

At the bottom of the gangplank a native family squatted amongst the broken crates, staring at a lower gangplank as oil drums were rolled into the hold.

—*Chao ong!* I grinned.

The father glanced at me before resuming his study of oil drums. Making a great show of stretching my back and arms—as though such activity were impossible aboard ship—I studied the picturesque little group: the parents and three children were a matched set with their threadbare indigo jackets, grime-streaked faces, and bamboo hats so battered they'd have been cast off and burnt by the discriminating residents of Saigon. Only the father did not stare with open mouth, lower lip slack as a dead thing; he grimaced instead, interrupting his vigil every fifteen seconds to glance over his shoulder at the train platform. Odder still, he had a burlap sack tied around his arm. I couldn't imagine more deserving recipients of a dozen five-piastre notes.

—Friend, I asked in Vietnamese, what is your name?

He took a step back and touched the shoulder of the lank-haired eldest child—male or female I couldn't guess.

—Tat, he murmured.

—Where are you going?

To you or me this might sound vaguely accusatory but I'd been taught it was an expected step in casual Vietnamese conversation.

—We make our home in My Tho.

—Are the children hungry? I asked. I want to help.

My stomach turned at this lack of nuance. The mother looked up from between the younger two and murmured something. She had a long cut down the side of her foot.

—I don't understand, I stammered.

—We need to get away, she repeated.

—Where are you going? I asked again.

The father glared at the last drum disappearing up the gangplank.

—We did not pay what they asked, he said. We did not pay.

—Perhaps *I* can help, I offered. How much—

—No. The body tax was collected two days ago.

—Two days they have looked for us, she said.

—Perhaps if I speak to the . . .

Administrator? Representative? I couldn't have translated such a term had I known the appropriate title.

—Thang died, stated the eldest child.

—Who is that? I asked.

—Our boy, the mother said.

—I went to them, said the father, to ask for more time. Without Thang in the field I cannot. After the rent, there was nothing. They chained me up ...

He lifted his burlap-wrapped arm. I felt the hair rise on the back of my neck.

—The French did this?

—What French?

—Thang was alive at the start of the year, said the mother. So we must pay his tax now. Then they said the tax is three piastres, not two piastres and four dimes.

The father stared at the deserted gangplank.

—We sold our eldest girl to Mr. Pha, he finally said. For two piastres and four dimes. In his kitchen. We will not see her again.

—Then they told us the tax was not two piastres and four dimes.

—We ran, said the father. No one has done that before.

—We will not sell any others, said the mother.

—I have enough, I stammered, to pay the body tax for everyone! I can write to—

—It is too late, said the father. If they see us again ...

I didn't understand what he said next, but the mother dropped her gaze to the paving stones. Who did he expect to see on the train platform? The youngest children stared only at each other.

The *Ton-Le-Sap* was a Tourist Special, so natives couldn't buy tickets. The lower gangplank was still down, though, and none of the crew in evidence; it would take only four strides to cross. I looked up at the rail and saw the back of the steward's coat.

—Follow me, I said.

I started across the gangplank, its slats creaking horribly. I could hear voices in the dark hold ahead, the oil drums thudding against each other. I stepped over the lip into the boat and as I turned around the father's forehead struck my shoulder. He carried the two youngest and the mother carried the eldest. They carried nothing else.

—Where do we go? he asked.

Due to the late hour of our reservation Henri and I had been given the least desirable cabin: below decks and off an ill-lit corridor. I'd seen crewmen pass our room to disappear behind a stout door—perhaps it led to the hold? I groped my way in the vague direction of the stern, the family at my elbow, silent as wraiths.

A few minutes later I found the dining room empty except for a few young women smoking cigarettes, white elbows dangling over the backs of their chairs.

—I'm still really very hungry, I said to the mess-boy. Couldn't you wrap a few potatoes in a napkin? And what about that ham? I don't mind how dry it is.

In our cabin I found the family much as I had on the wharf, sheltered under their decrepit hats with emaciated arms hugging their matchstick legs, Tat standing ever-vigilant in the centre of the room. I silently shut the door and handed him my plunder. I couldn't be sure whether smoked pork was a traditional component of their cuisine but, regardless, the five of them tore the ham-steak apart as though it was their worst enemy. In the case of the potatoes they took the time to pass each around the circle, savouring the smell before devouring it. I leaned against the door, feigning composure, but when the knob rattled beside my hip I felt my stomach leap into my throat. The family rose to their feet, frantically chewing.

—I'm here, I stammered. Just a moment!

I scanned the cabin to be sure nothing near at hand might be used as a weapon.

—I've come down for that newspaper, Henri said, I want to—

He stopped, lower lip pinched absently between finger and thumb. I ushered him forward a step and closed the door. The family sat down and began to dissect the stale rolls, evidently believing there was nothing to be feared from a random Frenchman. We'd imposed the murderous taxes, after all, but had never deigned to collect them.

—Please keep calm, I said. They'll get off a little farther up the river.

—*Calm*, did you say? "A little farther" is Phnom Penh!

—Please, if you could—

—If it weren't for the little ones I'd kick their teeth out! Why'd you sneak little ones in here? Tell them if they raise their eyes I'll knock them down. Tell them!

—It is very safe, I said in Vietnamese. Do not be afraid.

His gaze never leaving the wretched group, Henri crossed to the table and seized his vaunted copy of *Le Courrier Saigonnais*. Tat shook out the napkin to see what other treasure it might contain.

—Lose *our* berths if they're found out, Henri muttered. What could possess you?

I confess I hadn't considered that. The family couldn't help us in our mission, but was I to suspend all functions of my heart until we decamped at Luang-Prabang?

—I wished to demonstrate that we are not universally oppressive.

—"Demonstrate"? If you're phenomenally lucky no one will ever know about it!

The eldest child drank from our washbasin.

—If *these* people know, I said, I'll be satisfied.

—I'll put this down to hallucination provided you lock yourself in and keep them from pissing on my clothes. And give it a good airing at Phnom Penh! Eighteen hours. You'll excuse me if I pass the time in the salon with affluent crustaceans who've so far refused to let me buy a round.

—Eighteen hours? I asked.

He shut the door behind him and it seemed as if a dozen people had gone out. The younger children were asleep, back to back, at the foot of my bed, and Tat reclined against the wall, arms around his bony knees. The burlap sack was sodden with blood.

—My name is *not* Tat. I wish you to know.

—Do you know people in Phnom Penh? I asked.

—I do not know the place.

—Ah, I said.

He asked something.

—I don't understand, I said.

He mimed smoking a cigarette. I shook my head.

—*Không có chi*, he murmured.

His wife crawled to him, clutching my hand towel, and as she began to unwrap the burlap I turned to the porthole—through its oil-smeared glass the sky was the colour of smoke. I took a Messageries Fluviales leaflet from my trouser pocket and fanned myself. Now and then she cooed sympathetically but her husband made no sound.

From the forward deck I might have witnessed our arrival at Phnom Penh the next morning and seen, as the leaflet described, "that huge and magnificent sheet of water formed by the Anterior Mekong, Posterior Mekong and the Great Lakes of Angkor, and overlooked by the pagoda of the Phnom." Instead I would have the porthole, and the leaflet. I felt too exhausted by the family's very presence to quiz them on any improbable knowledge they may have possessed of Ly Thuong Kiet or even Adélie Tremier, too exhausted to hear the story of Indo-China from the mouths of its people—I felt thus though I was not leaking blood nor had I missed a single meal in my lifetime.

The mother had curled into a ball at her husband's feet so I stalked to the far end of the cabin and sank into the armchair.

—Will she sleep there, in that kitchen? the mother asked. Will they even give her a blanket?

After a long time the father sighed.

—Maybe, he said.

AN INTERLUDE IN
THE SULTANA'S PALACE

Mme. Adélie Tremier.

NOVEMBER, 1908.
"*Caw!*" Manu shouted. "See? It recognizes me. *Caw!*"

A thin crow sat hunched on the garden wall, its chest feathers wet and askew as though to demonstrate how its species *en masse* might benefit from mulled wine and a glowing fire. Manu set his easel down in the gravel path and took a case of pencils from his coat pocket.

"You were right not to bring pastels," said Adélie, stopping behind him. "Everything's black and grey out here." She felt a flush in her cheeks as sweat trickled from her hair onto her temples. "What do you imagine, the trees as well?"

But Manu had already twisted up his face like a nautilus, indicating that he was busy about his work. Two deft strokes on the paper—unmistakably a crow's beak.

"A work of art," said his mother. "But I must leave you in ten minutes. There's an office I've yet to visit."

The boy tilted his head to again study the crow and without glancing at the paper quickly began to sketch the feathers down its chest. Sabine had dressed him in his "garden attire" of brown boots, tan riding breeches and a black woollen jersey, topped with a beribboned straw boater which he'd tugged down to his brow in order to increase the fierceness of his aspect. With a softer pencil he began to sketch black swaths across the bird's body. Other crows raised a din in the neighbour's yard—would his model fly off? No, it only stamped a wiry foot. A chill breeze rattled brown stems in the beds.

"Do you really think I'll get into the Académie d'Italie?"

"Nothing definite yet."

"He's the most boring bird in the world! I'll see if he can even fly."

The gardener had not been lively in his work, for a dozen pears lay mouldering in the grass. Manu picked one up as nimbly as possible so as not to soil his cuff.

"The Krupp breech-loading cannon!" he cried.

The crow gazed nonchalantly at a passing cloud just as a three-kilogram Prussian shell struck it squarely between the wings. The bird dropped behind the wall without a stray feather to mark its passage.

Manu looked to this mother for applause but instead found her massaging the bridge of her nose, her hand beneath her veil.

"My boy," she sighed, "you haven't any notion what a cannonball like that would really do, have you?"

"Now I'll see if there are frogs!"

Easel beneath his arm, Manu ran for the rain barrel. The crow on its flapping page looked far more dignified than it had in life. Adélie rose to start after him but the blood rushed from her head. She thrust her arms out as though balancing in a rowboat before dropping solidly onto her behind.

Through her veil she watched Manu run back to her. In his open mouth his teeth looked exceptionally white.

"Up," she said, "up."

He helped his mother to her feet then let her lean against him while she brushed gravel from the back of her skirt.

"Not a word to your grandma, you remember?"

"A man with crutches is standing at the gate," said the boy.

Gripping Manu's shoulder, she stepped carefully along the gravel toward the narrow side entrance. A hawk-faced man with a brown beard peered in at them.

"Good morning," Adélie called.

"Yes, Madame. I was with the 2nd Foreign Legion Regiment in Algiers."

"Well, do come in."

Manu slid the bar across and the veteran hobbled in. A checked trouser cuff flapped where his right foot ought to have been.

"Couldn't you get a wooden one?" asked the boy.

"Hush," said Adélie. "This way to the kitchen, sir."

"They strapped one on, son, but it chafed like whipcord."

With that he hopped ahead of them toward the house; obviously he'd been before, though she couldn't claim to recognize the soldier. The Battalion of Forgotten Men, she called her veterans, and now it seemed she was forgetting them herself. For years now Isabelle had kept a pot of soup simmering at the back of the stove.

"If it happens that I'm not here," she said to Manu, "you can let them in yourself."

"Not *here*?" He squinted up at her.

NOT UNTIL SHE'D first clad herself in black and peered through a veil did Adélie notice how many women dressed likewise were walking through the streets of Paris. Even now, racing up rue St-Honoré so as not to miss her carriage home, here were a half-dozen climbing up from the Métro. She swam through the mass of shoppers as sweat streamed down her cheeks, stinging the corners of her eyes and ultimately pooling beneath her stiff collar. She'd burnt her tongue gulping coffee at Le Petit Fumoir—she ought not to have stopped in at all, but it had been months since she'd been so far abroad.

"Ah! Here's our patroness of the arts," Sabine told Mauriac. "Find us at the Rivoli exit in fifteen minutes. Don't stand gaping!"

"Aren't you going home now?" asked Adélie.

"Nonsense!" smiled Sabine. "Let us enjoy a moment together!"

With a pneumatic hiss the two pushed the revolving door until an overeager shopper trod on the hem of Adélie's gown, and she seized her mother-in-law's arm to keep from falling. At least the door was wide enough for their hats.

"Can't you *see* through the veil?"

They were disgorged into the store. A pewter-haired concierge with braided epaulettes smiled wryly at them—obviously retired military. Hundreds of shoppers shouted and whistled, the tearing of wrapping paper and ringing of signal bells sounded from all directions, youngsters gazed sparrow-like from the walkways three and four storeys up and escalators rumbled like waterfalls down from Millinery or Silks while their counterparts rose toward Flatware or Furs or Mezzanine Café.

"I require a sideboard for an upstairs corridor," Sabine told the concierge, who beckoned to the page, a thin lad who'd gnawed his bottom lip bloody. Even working *here* would be preferable to St-Lucien Military College, thought Adélie. Braving the crowd's sharp elbows, the boy led them onto an escalator.

"As you have nothing to report," said Sabine, "I assume they were unresponsive."

With her great lace ruff Sabine resembled an aroused hen. Adélie gripped her clutch-purse and the clattering rail.

"I left a portfolio in case they changed their minds," she said.

"Though they'll accept no students younger than twelve."

"So they continue to maintain."

"I marvel at your efforts, don't misunderstand me. I suppose it doesn't matter to these painters that you've worked so tirelessly for the downtrodden with the, what is it, the Anti-Penury League?"

"I haven't time to dwell on that." Adélie pinched the bridge of her nose. "I must adopt an entirely different tack."

Alighting at the next storey, the page led the women to an over-rouged girl with a tremendously tall head of copper hair who in turn led them into the jungle of furniture.

"They certainly know their business at St-Lucien, taking them as young as they do! Honestly, I don't think either of you will mind so much as you make out—they don't arm them with bayonets in the *first* year, you know!"

Adélie smoothed the black veil against her cheek, an old habit by now.

"If there really is no alternative," she said, "I will take him away and disappear."

Sabine's mouth dropped open to reveal her tawny bottom teeth.

"Madame?" asked the copper-headed girl.

Sabine pirouetted and ran gloved fingertips across polished beech and deep mahoganies as though her mind had never been on anything else. She banged drawers and jangled latches as the girl intoned a litany of economical prices.

Adélie dropped gratefully onto the first of a row of piano benches. Three narrow-trousered young men passed without so much as a glance at her boot-clad ankle—there really was only a hair's breadth between widowhood and actual death, wasn't there? No, she ought not to even joke about it. Dr. Bonheur had told her to remain positive.

"I'll have to ask the department manager," the salesgirl said.

Sabine turned back to her daughter-in-law, lips pursed so tightly as to produce unnatural dimples. Her voice was soothing as a pot of cream.

"I know the modern widow need only wear her veil six months, yet you acquiesced to twelve, as well as a good deal of seclusion. I do appreciate the gesture. After the year is up I won't begrudge you a party, what do you say to that?"

Adélie rose from the bench as grandly as she was able, steadying herself on a pole-lamp topped with a turbaned Negro in porcelain—Nicolas would have laughed at such a thing. She placidly folded her veil onto the brim of her hat so that, unobstructed, she might meet Sabine's gaze with one equally candid.

"I will accept your generous offer."

"Splendid!"

"Provided that our agreement still stands that I have until his birthday to find another college. Need I remind you, yet again, that St-Lucien's entire graduating class of 1869 was killed in a single Prussian advance?"

"Oh, I would *never* renege," said Sabine, "though I don't see how you'll do it in, what, five weeks—you've stained your hands blue writing all of those letters, and the bruise hasn't gone where that door hit you! Don't you have another appointment with that Bonheur? See what *he* thinks of your bruise!"

The copper-haired girl returned with a most accommodating offer but Sabine replied that none of the pieces were really suitable after all. The grand lady led Adélie to the escalators but they stepped onto the wrong one and found themselves amongst women in drooping hats pawing through bins of discounted yarn.

"I admire good painting," sighed Sabine, "but I can't name one instance when a painter saved a village from cannon fire, can you?"

"No," agreed Adélie, "artists seldom do anything so grand. But they'll *respond* to what is grand, I have no doubt of it. They demand spectacle."

"My dear, is that a new-found determination I hear?"

"It isn't new," said Adélie.

Over the gleaming back of a clockwork elephant they finally glimpsed the exit to rue de Rivoli.

"Mauriac is going to be peevish," said Sabine. "Time was not with us."

And never will be, thought Adélie.

ONE MONTH LATER

"Thank you for coming up early, Marie." Adélie balanced her black hat atop a porcelain head on the vanity. "I can't imagine how long this might take—trading these weeds for Oriental vestments."

"I was just trying to sponge the coffee stain from your magazine," said the putty-faced maid, "and I noticed something about these Musical Society grand balls given at the Académie du Palais Royal by, oh, what was the name—"

"Greffuhle is head there."

"Yes, Count Greffuhle—and not to presume too much, but I wondered did you think to invite him?"

Since Berenice's decline Marie had become Adélie's absolute confidant; Sabine would've choked on her tongue to hear how the two carried on.

"He has yet to respond. The name Tremier is too synonymous with military offensives."

"Sponging your edition did little good anyway."

Adélie lowered herself to the pink ottoman. Marie pulled the pins from her hair.

"You're wonderfully pale! All women should be made to wear veils, Madame, you ought to write your magazines to say so— you won't need powder. Berenice could have had the day off if she'd been here! I asked after her this morning and Madame said the poor creature is a good deal better, if doctors can be trusted!"

"You're all aflutter!" laughed Adélie. "One would think a ball had never been held in this house!"

She lifted her black cloud of hair and the maid set to work unfastening the buttons at the back of her collar. As the blouse fell open Marie gave a start—there was only a white shift upon Adélie's back.

"Madame! Did Isabelle not fit your corset?"

"Why should she? I've gone thin as a breeze through a keyhole."

Marie frowned at the back of the mistress's head then cracked her knuckles mechanically and crossed to the wardrobe, lifting out three muslin-wrapped garments and laying them with a sweeping motion across the chaise longue.

"The sandals too," said Adélie.

Something crashed in the adjoining room.

"Who's that?" Marie drew herself up. "Sylvie?"

The designer Lepape appeared in the doorway. He tucked his bowler hat beneath his elbow, unfolded his handkerchief and placed it atop his bald head.

"Only a little vase I ran into," he panted.

Marie seized his wrist and dragged him from the room.

"We are *dressing*, sir!"

"And who do you suppose fit her for it, my minx, Franz Lehár? When I create a thing I do it top and bottom!"

"Ask him what his business is!" called Adélie.

"But a *dressing* room! And now you're in her bedroom, it's no better!"

"Here behind the armoire, will that be acceptable, my vixen, just here? Tell Madame that according to the caterer the sherbets will be spoiled utterly if the incense is lit any time prior to eight o'clock, while I maintain the incense ought to be there from the beginning or not at all. If one or the other is to go she must decide."

"What if we separate the two at either end?" Adélie held the dress to her chest despite the wall between them. "Would the sherbets be all right then?"

"Incense as they enter and sherbet the destination? Genius, Madame! The panther won't be disturbed either way. Incidentally, those birds flew straight—"

"Out, sir!" Marie shouted. "I'll shatter your *skull* if—"

ADÉLIE PUSHED the tall door open and found a battlefield. The governess Sylvie was curled on the couch, sorting pastels on a tray, while every other surface of the bedroom—floor, counterpane, windowsills, desk, shelves, toy boxes, the tops of the wainscotting—was crowded with tin soldiers as well as a single company of intricately folded playing cards. Manu crouched on the seat of his desk chair, patiently positioning canvas tents upon his pillow. With the exception of the crucifix over the bed, every centimetre of wall space was crowded with his artwork, despite dozens of pieces having been moved to the downstairs gallery. Sylvie straightened up but did not venture to put her feet down.

"Oh! Good evening, Madame!"

The girl's high bun suited her slender neck, Adélie decided, but failed to compliment her enormous ears. Manu affixed a regimental banner to one of his tents.

"I could pretend it was Saarbrücken if I had more artillery to put on the hill. Oh! Maman . . . what are you dressed as?"

"As a sultana. Do you not think I look terribly artistic?" She passed between battalions, took up a clothes brush and attacked his black wool coat hanging on the wardrobe—but wouldn't it better serve its purpose daubed with paint?

"You never said it was a costume ball!" said Manu. "Will there be pirates?"

"Well, I believe the nature of pirates lies in their unexpected arrivals."

Manu's mouth hung open with his tongue upon his bottom lip—his most common expression, she recalled, from when he was four years old.

"I mean to say I don't know whether there'll be pirates," said Adélie.

"That coat cuts into my armpits!"

"I see the cavalry is making good use of your *Mon Journal* collection. Have you read the one that arrived yesterday?"

"I like the story about the orphan boy, but the dancing bear isn't in it anymore."

"Anything's preferable to Saarbrücken, I should think."

"Is the ballroom really full of birds?"

"Five dozen larks, Lepape says."

"Can they sing 'The Heavenly Fire'?"

"They cannot sing 'The Heavenly Fire' and I wouldn't want them to if they could—larks are meant to add to the sense of natural splendour. The trilling birdsong of the East."

"Did they come from the East on a Messageries Maritimes boat?"

"They were most likely caught in a Métro station."

"See what I found out!" He wrenched a rider from its saddle— the poor man was dreadfully bowlegged. "He looks like he's wet his trousers!"

"Hush with such things," muttered Sylvie.

"He does," agreed Adélie. "Remember, I'll bring you down when it's time to meet all those people I mentioned. Can you remember what you're meant to talk about?"

"Um, yes," said Manu, an artillery piece between his teeth. "Marc Chagall."

"Chagall, yes, but what are you meant to say about him?"

"Emotive colour. *Rich* emotive colour?"

"Certainly, but what *movement* is he in, what do they say about him?"

"Um. Oh, avant-garde!"

"Finally, yes, avant-garde. You *must* remember it."

"But," asked Manu, "do I paint avant-garde?"

"No, dear, but they wouldn't want you to. Ninety minutes, Sylvie? We'll ride up in the cage together but I don't want dancers stepping on him beforehand."

"I'll step on *them*!" said Manu, scattering a company of infantry across the rug.

"I have your colours ready, Emanuel." With her tray Sylvie tiptoed between rows of medical tents. "Which part of the battle did you mean to draw?"

The boy looked up attentively. Three nights before he'd awoken with fever and when she'd appeared in her nightdress he'd glimpsed a beguiling stripe of hairy calf.

SEVEN BUTLERS had been engaged to collect hats and overcoats and to usher guests the ten metres from the front door to the ballroom. After the first two hundred people arrived there was a brief lull and the butlers sat in a row at the bottom of the grand staircase, though a conscientious few leaned their elbows on the banister so as to not wrinkle the tails of their hired coats.

"Show me where I can vomit."

"Is that what incense is?"

"I thought a load of dung was burning in the lady's furnace."

"We ought to keep towels over our mouths."

"You'd look like a brigand."

"A good sultan needs brigands."

"Why's that?"

"To violate the harem."

"Just keep your head between your knees. That any better?"

"Why shouldn't he want to violate the harem himself?"

"Takes years to become sultan. The average sultan is a withered old man."

"Keep a look out for vacancies all the same."

"Show me where to vomit."

"On your feet, here comes the lady."

Adélie had seen an illustration in *Fémina* of the very scene: a girl in a daring ensemble descending a wide staircase toward a crowd of broad-shouldered admirers, a girl whose only concern, according to the caption, had been to find a husband.

"Have Greffuhle and Fouquet arrived?" she called. "Or de Vaux?"

"We were told not to inspect invitations, Madame," answered the butler with the faint blond moustache.

"Don't stand staring," she said. "Attend the door."

Their fourteen heels clattered across the marble as she passed into the gloom behind the peacock screen that acted as gateway to the Tremier ballroom. Another screen, painted with minarets, stood ahead of her, and in the facing mirrors on either side of the vestibule she seemed to walk abreast an infinite number of Adélies dressed in billowing pantaloons of ochre chiffon below gold-fringed, wire-hemmed white chiffon tunics held in place by gold lamé cummerbunds, the heads of those infinite Adélies crowned with gold lamé turbans surmounted by sapphires shaped liked eggs. The turbans' line across these limitless sultanas' foreheads accentuated their Provençal brows while kohl made their black eyes seem enormous. No sultana painted by Faléro was ever more beautiful.

She rounded the screen through a pink cloud of incense so pungent she couldn't draw breath—the trouble reasserting itself—but she was gladly distracted as her eyes took in the torchlit scene. First of all there were the acrobats: olive-skinned, hairy-chested men dressed only in sequined vests and pantaloons. On trapezes strung from the vaulted ceiling they dipped and flew, executing somersaults ten metres above the floor, one man after the other like a whirligig caught in a wind. Cymbals, dulled by the din of voices, crashed in accompaniment. The long room was lined with white-pyjama'd boys who circulated the air with palm leaves far larger than themselves, while above all dangled a gilded cage three metres square and festooned with peacock feathers. Flushed male guests sat on aquamarine cushions around bubbling houka pipes as bare-midriffed girls with raven tresses fed them oranges and calves' sweetbreads from silver trays.

Adélie had had the door removed from the corner cloakroom and a bead-curtain installed, as though the little room were a cave of irresistible allure. The electric lights within threw a triangular corona across the ballroom floor. This was the Emanuel Tremier Gallery which every guest would enter, God willing, inhale sharply at the sight of its diverse framed marvels—pencil sketches of neighbourhood houses; watercolours of irises; a charcoal portrait of poor Berenice at the hearth; Marie with her hair down, glaring at the viewer; a scene in oil of a son and greying mother clinging to floating wreckage; a watercolour study of the Seine's dappled surface—then let their breath out before gratefully signing the register and reaching for Manu's visiting card. For the present, however, her guests skirted the entry as though they feared its bright lights would dissolve them. She felt some caustic substance creep up her throat.

A shirtless Negro handed Adélie a goblet of shaved ice infused with mint, and she held it close to her chest. For weeks she'd been clipping the most noteworthy "Gentleman of the Orchestra" columns from *Le Figaro*—the multitude of cabinet ministers attending the Ballets Russes' *Boris Godunov,* for example, had made that performance "a politico-artistic manifestation of the highest importance"—and sending each list verbatim to the printer, though she wouldn't have known any of those notables to see them. This golden-haired boy at her elbow, however, did look familiar.

"Do you know, is there coffee? I came in a bit tipsy to begin with."

"There's a service at the far end of the room. Shall I see if a girl is available?"

"Oh!" he said. "Are you not . . . ?"

"I am Madame Tremier, your hostess." She tipped her head. "Your sultana."

"I don't need coffee then. I don't! I can fetch it myself."

"Nonsense, there must be a girl—but I'm afraid I don't know *your* name."

"Fouquet. François Fouquet."

"Fouquet of the Académie d'Italie?"

"Have you seen my sculpture at the Colarossi? Did you like it?"

"But you aren't the new head of that school? Overseeing admissions?"

"Ah, yes, that's true as well, and somewhere there waits a mountain of unsigned papers as proof—ah, I see that look in your eye, you believe I'm too young! The committee wanted new blood, that's all, so I said blood was what I'd give them."

The sultana gripped his arm and he did not resist.

"How new?" she asked. "We have a gallery through that beaded curtain, you see, where a ten-year-old boy of enormous talent—"

"When you said 'Tremier' did you mean Nicolas Tremier? You're the widow?"

"I—I, well, yes."

"This is remarkable! My father was Fouquet the engineer."

"The man who . . . designed the bridge?"

"Ah, the commission of inquiry's still ongoing! Though he's passed away now—say, will there be dancing? I'd love to spin you around the floor with that getup on."

"But the admissions at the Académie d'Italie—surely there's no need to go onto these lists, if I could show you his artwork you'll see the genius is there already, he—"

"A genius, yes! Hello, I believe that's Caroline Uzanne, do you know *her*?"

With the shaved-ice Negro two new arrivals stood chatting: frog-physiqued Louis de Vaux, portrait painter and vice-chancellor of the École des Beaux-Arts, alongside Caroline Uzanne, much-photographed editor of *Fémina*, rumoured not to have blinked since childhood. As the Negro moved on with his tray, Adélie was upon them.

"You *owe* it to yourself, and she'll never know," Uzanne was saying, pulling back her coat—a green velvet design embroidered with palms—to indicate her thigh. "Be honest, when was the last time Cecile took a really good look at the top of your leg?"

"With her I shouldn't think any bit of me was safe," said de Vaux, and with his fingertips smoothed his thin hair down his forehead.

"Practice on the maid, then, until you never leave a bruise."

"Mademoiselle," said Adélie, squaring her shoulders, "Monsieur. Pray allow me to introduce myself: your hostess, Madame Tremier."

She brought her sapphire down to the marble floor with a flawless curtsy.

"The *Sultana* Tremier, I should say!" barked de Vaux. "Mavellous affair!"

"It *is* Adélie Tremier, is it not?" asked Uzanne. "They told me at the office you had a grown boy, yet here you're a slip of a thing! And not lacking for *style*, eh?"

"It runs in our blood perhaps, perhaps it does—my father founded the Lissner shops. And this boy of mine, well, he's nine, but without saying too much I must admit I have a better eye for painting than for—what would you call this? *Spectacle*."

They both nodded, deeply engrossed.

"With a pencil or brush, the name Emanuel Tremier will loom large in this city, and in a very few years. A guest of ours just lately, and a military man, I must admit, so he has no investment in such things, mistook one of his drawings for a photograph!"

"Of what subject?" drawled de Vaux.

"A woman on a café terrace. He is nine, but his eye is that of a man."

"That *would* be worth seeing. I represent the École des Beaux-Arts, Madame, which you may not know—"

"You say you must have protégés, Louis." Uzanne bumped him with her hip. "This fellow sounds the find of the century! Like little Korngold, that composer in Vienna—only eleven!"

The cymbals were louder now and somewhere a zither played.

"Yes, but where are these drawings?" de Vaux asked, hair fluttering up from his head. "Upstairs? I tell you, before I step into my carriage you will lead me upstairs!"

"You need only put your head through that bead-curtain!" cried Adélie.

A cloud of larks swooped overhead—multiplied tenfold as shadows across the ceiling—and a towering Negro hurried past with a bullwhip in his sash. Caroline Uzanne seized her companions' hands.

"I should like to see where *he* goes," she announced beneath unblinking eyes.

"But the gallery's just there!"

Adélie followed the pair as they shouldered their way between mauve gowns and dark jackets smelling of wet wool and sweat, between women clad in menswear or in tasselled, uncorseted kimonos. The room smelled of hissing pitch and the acrid pong from the black panther which lay upon the tiled dais, separated from the chattering crowd by a ring of torches. Its urine ran down the side of the dais and across the floor.

"I'm quite overwhelmed!" cried Caroline, her face betraying no such emotion.

"In three hours," de Vaux called to Adélie, "you may lead me upstairs!"

She passed a hand across her sapphire, in a calculatedly coy response, and noticed men's heads turning from every direction. If women had abandoned girdles the husbands clearly had not— each waistline resembled the thin end of a chop—while each moustache had been waxed to such ruthless points they might have been instruments of assassination. She lifted her arms and turned so her diaphanous sleeves rose about her in the manner of Salome's famous veils, and tongues paused mid-word, as she'd hoped, but she found the flow of air against her naked ribs disconcerting. Now to lead them like the Pied Piper toward that bead curtain, and all because St-Lucien's entire graduating class of 1869 had been killed in a single Prussian advance.

"Madame, er … Adélie?"

126

A curly-haired man in a brown suit gesticulated with an empty wine glass. She felt suddenly ridiculous in her Oriental garb.

"Doctor Bonheur! I *am* glad you came!" She lowered her voice. "I thought I would need a *friend* in the midst of all this."

"But it's ridiculous!" he hissed. "You know very well how contagious you are!"

"Sultana Tremier!" someone called.

Adélie turned but saw only a trio of Sabine's cronies: Major-General La Mestrie, Brigadier Moreau and General Subrégis in their double-breasted tunics with canary epaulettes, each man with a glass of brandy in one hand and the other upon the hilt of his sword. But who were these women who'd set them chuckling? As a tray passed Adélie traded her goblet of ice for a tumbler of gin, which she gulped in a single mouthful.

"Sultana Tremier!" one of the women called. "What a success!"

"What a rattling success!" called the other, raising her glass.

Impossible—Julia Cahen Astruc and Monique d'Anvers, who *Le Figaro* had labelled "the Great Jewesses of Art," mingling with the French military under her own blessed roof! A politico-artistic manifestation of the highest importance, true, but what role did either play in academic admissions?

Brigadier Moreau took Adélie's hand. "I like your hat," he said.

"Only just now," exclaimed Julia, smoothing down her great ropes of pearls, "we said that if she'd climb onto that panther it would rival Mata Hari once and for all!"

Two new arrivals joined their little circle as the ostrich plume in Monique's headband swayed precariously: Count de Choiseul, with crimson earlobes and a nonexistent chin, and Countess Renée, half his age, in a floor-length, skunk-trimmed mustard coat. If Caroline Uzanne set eyes on her she might grace the cover of *Fémina*.

"We wondered if you expect Madame Sabine to come down," said the count.

"But it occurs to me," said Julia, "that for a *real* Oriental ball you ought to have chosen a man for the sultan!"

If I smile gaily, thought Adélie, perhaps they'll say no more about it.

Countess Renée ran her tongue over her teeth. "Without a *husband*, you mean?"

"Quite right," Brigadier Moreau smiled, brandy upon his lip, "and the sultan ought to have cracked his whip and chased her all about that cage!"

"Oh, my *dear*." General Subrégis shook his wattles at Adélie. "There's no shame in being a widow, there's glory! I saw that child of yours take tea—what a future for the country, with boys like that! And look here." He pulled back the corner of his tunic to reveal a pistol tucked into his belt. "I've brought him a little gift."

Major-General La Mestrie clipped the end of a cigar. "A Chamelot Delvigne?"

"Blew some Bantus' teeth out with this, I should say," grinned Subrégis.

"You never think of anyone like *us* being killed like that," said Countess Renée. "Imagine, a falling bridge! *Far* worse than coughing to death in one's garret."

"Block up your ears, Sultana, this is hardly a learned society!" Julia took up a length of Adélie's sleeve. "But did Lepape make all this for you?"

"He designed every aspect to my specifications."

An acrobat yelped not far above their heads.

"As we came in," Monique said, "Count Greffuhle told me your spectacle may yet turn his gaze from Berthier."

"Greffuhle of the Académie du Palais Royal? You know, I was told they admitted a boy of *twelve*—"

"But Adélie!" a woman screamed over Julia's shoulder. "How could I have known that a *count* is the son of a *marquis*? How could *we* have ever known that?"

Adélie turned and stared the woman full in the face. Here was that light-headed feeling again. Here stood her Henriette, to whom she had not written in a year, still dressed in the high-collared black gown that even in 1899 had been a decade out of fashion. She threw her arms about Adélie's neck and knocked the breath from her.

"If I'd known Arabia could be like *this*, I certainly wouldn't have come to Paris!"

"Henriette? How did you—"

"So it *is* a surprise! Your wonderful mother-in-law intercepted my letter, you know, and invited me at a moment's notice—such a giving soul!"

The Jewesses of Art vanished like shadows.

"But you must understand," gasped Adélie. "It's for Manu—"

At the clatter of chains she looked to see the glittering cage begin to drop from the ceiling. Had the dancers begun? Where were her boy and Sylvie? She had better—

"Strawberries soaked in *laudanum*!" Henriette looped an arm around her waist. "I expected I'd feel sleepy! Ah, Arabia! But you ought to have chosen Indo-China!" She straightened up, fingering her pearl choker. "Did you not see my monograph on temple architecture? Oh, but look how your sleeves blow around!" Henriette grasped the chiffon between two fingers. "If this is tulle you must be a Rothschild!"

"Excuse me," said a waistcoated gentlemen, "but are *you* from Tulle?"

"Certainly not!" Henriette set her fists against her hips. "I'm from Aix!"

The man grinned—the line of moustaches behind him looked more poisonous than ever—and Adélie realized with a start that this was the legendary Poulenc himself, *Le Figaro*'s "Gentleman of the Orchestra."

"And is that *near* Tulle?" he asked.

Adélie scanned the crowd for big-eared maids but none were in evidence.

"Surely you know where Aix is!" cried Henriette. "Why it's—"

"They don't," stammered Adélie. "Trust me, dear, they *don't* know."

Here was her mountain of sophistication reduced to a provincial molehill!

"Goodness, my love, you're fainting!" said Henriette. "Where's a chair?"

"I must see the panther's not agitated," murmured Adélie.

"Is *this* the girl?" A copper-bearded, barrel-chested man seized Adélie by the wrist. "Let me kiss your hand, Sultana, and wish you every success! There!"

"Count Greffuhle!" said Adélie. "Welcome to—"

"Sultana!" Sabine, resembling a pigeon behind her lace bodice, appeared with Subrégis on her arm. "Is it possible you've forgotten to give Manu his introductions?"

"But what the devil's become of Sylvie? Ah, my mother-in-law, sir, Madame Sabine Tremier—we discuss my son, who is a protégé in the visual arts. If I could beseech you to look over his work, a gallery's been assembled a few steps away. Just—do you see the bead curtain? I understand there's school protocol to be observed," she shouted above the crowd, "but in this matter, I beg you, time is of the essence!"

"I will visit your gallery," said the count, "if only to see you into a chair."

"This mob has worn her out," said Henriette. "And I am pleased to make your acquaintance, Madame, for down in Aix your daughter-in-law was my dearest friend."

"Do you mean to say she really *is* from Aix?" Sabine asked.

"For God's sake, Maman, go find him!"

"Thank you, Monsieur, Mesdames, a thousand times!" Lepape, in aquamarine caftan and sable hat, bowed with courtly grace. "Sultana, your hand? It is time."

"You'll deprive us of her company?" asked the count.

"Not yet!" said Adélie. "He—"

"We have brought down the gilded cage, you see!" Lepape seized her wrist. "The labour of weeks comes now to fruition. She ascends to the heavens!"

Acrobats stood motionless on their trapezes as he led Adélie through the crowd; he ignored her attempts to pull away. The cage stood upon the marble floor within its ring of torches, their light illuminating a hundred expectant faces. But Manu's face?

She recognized no one. Perhaps blond Fouquet, at least, was admiring the gallery. Perhaps de Vaux had meant those things he'd said but would be too drunk to remember—if only he could awake with "Emanuel Tremier" ringing in his brain!

"Manu?" she called.

She would kick Sylvie to death! A Negro led her into the cage and seated her on a pyramid of cushions. The door closed and she found herself swaying a metre in the air, then two. Snatched from the earth, despite all her machinations, and Manu left behind!

"Our grand spectacle!" Lepape proclaimed from below.

She watched the ring of torches widen beneath her, and the raven-tressed serving girls, each with a red scarf in hand, circle within it. The panther's silver chain reflected the flames; the beast licked its paw and the Negro cracked his whip heroically. A cluster of dark women in shimmering headdresses assembled before Lepape, the witch-master from Pilou's stories, transforming spiders into women.

With a clang the cage ran against the pulleys as her ascent reached its zenith. In the shadows against the wall she discerned the pyjama'd boys gripping the chains, leaning back, shuffling . . . the cage was too heavy, the poor lambs! The smoke was suffocating there against the ceiling and she wiped her eyes with a chiffon sleeve. He ought to have been swaying there with her.

Now the cage heaved—the descent! Below her the girls spun one way then the other, their whirling scarves companions to the torches. She watched Lepape spread his arms and the women began their ululation, the staccato *ayayayayay* that was the very sound of a desert wind cresting the dunes. The crowd swirled beneath her, white faces twisting to take in the whole of the spectacle, wineglasses flashing like rubies on a cave floor. She coughed into the back of her hand. That smoke! A pair of dancers sprang into the ring below her and began to leap all about the poor panther, which flicked its tail. Adélie felt near vomiting; she sought out Lepape's eye. The dancers spun like dervishes in peacock feathers and silver pantaloons, and the female dancer was lovely even as she flew backward while the man's simian features made him her ideal ornament, and indeed they were Nijinsky and Karsavina of the fabled Ballets Russes, hired by Lepape to portray a pair of genies. Every guest clapped, whistled, shouted like a schoolchild.

Adélie gazed down at Poulenc, his arm around Henriette, his poisonous visage transformed—his portrait of the evening would shine off *Le Figaro*'s page!—and Caroline Uzanne and Louis de Vaux, grinning like cats, and that bumpkin Bonheur scowling up at her, and François Fouquet clutching Countess Renée's breasts through her chemise while they madly kissed. Then furiously waving hands—her Manu! Beaming in his black suit, he bobbed above the throng on the shoulders of General Subrégis while La Mestrie and Moreau each gripped a leg. They laughed together like great chums.

The whip cracked again, the red scarves flashed across the blackness and the panther turned an agitated circle. Adélie could not remain upright on the cushions. She knew she ought to acknowledge her admirers with a wave, but that *ayayayayay* carried more force than gravity. The cage bumped against the floor. She had to climb to her feet but even without a corset she felt as though her chest were pressed between two bricks. The crowd swarmed around her cage, dragging back its shimmering feathers.

"The Sultana Tremier!" shouted Count Greffuhle.

Her guests roared as if a long war had been won. She stretched forward until her hands could grip the bars, then dragged herself up, clinging to the side of the cage as though it were timber after a shipwreck. The peacock feathers smelled rank as a tanner's yard. Lepape unlatched the door, beckoning, and beyond him stood a Negro holding aloft the fabled lamp— yes, bought just the week before from J. Quille Et Fils. She finally relinquished the bars and set a foot outside the cage.

She would wish. She would wish that Manu grow to have children of his own.

But then the sea of faces became a sea of *sideways* faces passing before her eyes. She had an idea she might be falling, and felt a dozen hands seize her in mid-air. Now she was set down on her back while firelight danced just beyond her eyelids.

"A faint, perfectly fitting! This, the night of her life, and the family—"

"Oh, but! Do you see?"

"Move away, yes, just—"

"Back away, you see—"

"She's not injured." This was Bonheur. "Look her over, there's no wound."

"But that *blood*—" Sabine stammered into her ear.

"All from the mouth," said Bonheur. "Haemoptysis. She's hemorrhaged."

"She injured herself!"

"Tuberculosis, Madame."

"But just like *that* she couldn't have—"

"Doesn't start with the haemoptysis, not hardly. Now don't make a face like that, lad, she's breathing in and out! She's not dead, you'll have your Maman yet. There, good! Cover her up and take her out of here."

Strong hands lifted her to move Adélie through the heat of the crowd. It was a great comfort to feel so warm.

"Gruesome," someone hissed.

THE LEDGER
AT LEIT TUHK

Pierre Lazarie.

IN PHNOM PENH only Henri and I transferred from the *Ton-Le-Sap* to the *General Subré-gis* for passage into Laos, and though I steeled myself for more shipmates of Lassay's ilk we met with only one other white passenger, little Charton, and as he did not immediately blow tobacco smoke in my face I felt a weight lift from my shoulders.

Upriver the Mekong was still the colour of café crème, and even in the worst heat of the day I couldn't keep myself from the strip of deck in front of the rattling wheelhouse. The wind whistled through the air-holes in my topee, tattered villages appeared around each long bend, copper-coloured basalt crags came into view only to disappear in the silver haze, and for three days I kept a mental list of the waterborne detritus sweeping past: fish traps, gold-mining sluices, straw hats, stripped and numbered logs roaring past like locomotives, two dogs swimming to save their lives, pulverized canoes, entire living trees, drowned buffalo, a teak balcony railing and one drowned monkey. This last I could never have identified if not for Duc, the *General Subrégis'* navigator, who slumped beneath the wheelhouse window day and night in red-striped pyjamas and a black fedora. He tugged my trouser leg and raised a black-nailed finger.

—Monkey, he intoned.

I squinted at the matted black ball shooting past in the tawny foam. As our location was too blustery to ignite a match, Duc kept an unlit Turkish cigarette between his lips and sounded like a character from Pourrat speaking the French of the Middle Ages.

—Flowers! he croaked.

This next wasn't a bunch of Marguerite's daisies, either, but raft after raft of vivid pink water lilies, the lotuses of myth, somehow cast adrift from the tranquil ponds of their child-hoods. The wooded riverbanks looked dustier still as these tender islands swept past and I couldn't help ruminating on the Buddha, their venerated sponsor. What was it de Carné had written? "One must have *been* to the East to realize the inde-finable sensations which make the Nirvana of the Buddhists comprehensible." I'd once taken umbrage with that passage, believing I understood Nirvana as well as anyone. In Cambo-dia the flame-shaped roofs of the Buddhist temples had first appeared on the bare banks and then amongst the trees, some with freshly painted gold *stupas*, some with collapsed walls, but all capable of setting my pulse thumping behind my ears. It is one thing to wander through Saigon to the clangour of auto-mobile horns and say to oneself, "This is the East"; it is quite another to whisper it as a thousand-year-old temple juts out from a hillside to vanish the next moment behind the jungle canopy. "The East"' is an ever-fleeting thing.

Yet even as I congratulated myself on the exotica of my locale—our carbon paper now a week behind us—it struck me that the exotic is never an absolute but merely *otherness* taken to its extreme, and that the coffee-coloured Mekong, its surface coruscating with skimming white birds, must have been mun-dane to that boy paddling a log along the shallows, just as the mildewed spires of Notre-Dame Cathedral, which to me spoke only of wet shoes and stalled buses, were doubtless the stuff of fairy tales to a Mexican farmer or a mechanic from Soviet Rus-sia. I decided that an essay entitled "On the Nature of the Exotic" might prove instructive if only it could be contemplated under less thrilling conditions.

—Ah, Duc said behind me. *Monsieur le directeur*—

—Jesus, these Malays exasperate me! shouted Henri. The minute we leave home it's as though they only know three words, *"Monsieur le directeur," "Monsieur le directeur."* Do I look as though I could direct anything on the face of the earth?

Indeed he did not. A bona fide *Monsieur le directeur* would have looked anxious, while I'm certain Henri LeDallic had never looked more relaxed in his life. His gait along the narrow deck was straight and erect, and his hair was not twisted into rat-tails but blew about his head like the mane of a modestly arrayed lion.

—What've you been quizzing him on? he asked. "In what year did the Le Long brothers win the Battle of Jericho?"

—Charton must've been after you, I said, for you to have climbed up here.

—He holds his drink too well. Last night he started me talking.

—Then found you again this morning.

Henri unfolded his tartan handkerchief to wipe his streaming eyes. That stinging wind, sultry though it may have been, had rushed all the way from Tibet.

—I believe I was extremely erudite in explaining this Tremier situation.

—Explaining *what* exactly?

—It seems perfectly clear to me, said Henri, that the woman chose between this pipe dream of life eternal and certain death at the hands of tubercles in her lungs—pipe dream or no, would any of us have done differently in her dainty shoes? Yet Charton is *angry* at us for going after her, can you imagine? Apparently if she was dying of consumption in Paris with a nine-year-old boy dependent upon her, she ought to have gone to Lourdes for a miracle rather than abandoning him to drag herself off to where the word of God falls on deaf ears. Now what sort of medical opinion is that?

—He's a missionary.

—Don't try me—is he really? Honestly?

—He gave us Saint Pancras medals when we came aboard! Didn't you look?

—I thought it was a fishing lure. He's not a salesman either?

—Certainly he's a salesman!

—Ha! That's true, I'll tell him that. At the very least he ought to tell your chum here not to eat his own filth. Say, these hills take me back to the Siamese incursion!

A pair of thick knuckles rapped the inside of the wheelhouse window, and we peered in at Captain Malraux. He looked very much the skipper with his blue cap, red kerchief about his neck and thick black moustache, the only anomaly being that at thirty-five he was nearly toothless because he sucked all day on sugarcane as the deck passengers did. He pointed at a village unfolding along the next bend. Duc leapt to the rail, eyes fixed on a crooked wharf, one hand clamped over his fedora while the other hand flashed urgent signals to the steersman, and the sudden quietening of the engines told us that we might go below if we desired to explore the place.

At the bottom of the ladder we met Charton, dressed as we were in white suit and topee. Saint Christopher graced the ring upon his finger and his freshly shaven cheeks were badly pockmarked. He spoke with the sort of drawl I associated with Normandy fishermen who've been swept once too often into the Atlantic.

—This is Leit Tuhk, he said. Stretch our legs? I do apologize for monopolizing your time. I feel I must speak French as often as I can before excusing myself at Pak Sane, though it will be fine to see my Moï friends again, certainly.

The *General Subrégis* shuddered against the current and on the bow Duc threw ropes to men upon the wharf. The loincloth-clad locals gazed at us coolly, hands folded behind their backs like altar-boys listening to the radio. Our deck passengers rolled up their sleeping mats and over their shoulders slung bags laden with rice, dried fish, bananas, peppers dried and fresh, limes, cabbages, suckling pigs, bolts of embroidered cloth, brass lanterns and commodities I couldn't name. I wanted to slip the *General Subrégis*, its passengers, its crew and the river itself into a bottle and preserve them, for therein lay the minute insights of every essay I could hope to write. The sticky infant who blinked at me over his mother's shoulder might easily have been my life's work.

—Tell us about this village, Monseigneur, said Henri. We're tourists in these parts.

He gripped a black bottle wrapped—rather prudently, I thought—in a banana leaf.

—When it is not your first language you can hardly communicate what is in your heart, said Charton. I have taught French to my friends on my mountainside, but—

—What's that to do with anything? Keep your wits about you, man!

—Give me time, said Charton. I believe there is still a countryman here at Leit Tuhk, a learned man. We'll give him a drink and he may divine something from your apocrypha of the woman who sought immortality in these parts. This invalid of yours.

Dozens of natives tramped down from the village and onto the wharf, old women with white topknots, young women in square blouses that left their shoulders bare, old men with red betel dripping from their lips, all staring at the *General Subrégis* as though it were Leviathan risen from the depths. The engines had been tamped down to a hiccuping purr; I could hear the young men calling to acquaintances aboard ship as the several dozen children flung themselves, with backflips and howls, from the muddy bank into the river. An impossibly tall white man in ash-coloured trousers, singlet and hat appeared at the top of the hill, knotting a grey tie around his neck; no jacket or shirt, yet from the angle of his elbows I could see he was taking great pains with the tie. The deck began to smell overpoweringly of *nuòc-mâm*—viscous fish sauce.

—After all, said Charton, it's written, "The people who sat in darkness saw a great light." The deeper the darkness in which you find yourself, be it literal, spiritual, or geographical, the more brilliant the light when it appears. That's from Isaiah. I end all of my letters that way and my friends tell me it's very annoying.

—Do you know that man coming down the hill? I asked.

—That's our countryman, said Charton.

—The dweller in darkness, said Henri.

—Don't single *him* out.

—I'll show Madame Tremier to him, I said. Perhaps he'll know her.

From over the upper rail Duc tipped his hat to us and exhaled a stream of blue smoke. I couldn't help but agree with Frémont's insistence that Bolshevism only took root among the young and privileged, for if the navigator could be taken as representative of an older, less-affluent population then they seemed entirely satisfied with their lot. Captain Malraux appeared beside him.

—Three-quarters of an hour, he called. Have to be in place to run the Kemmarat at first light.

I stared at my boots as I crossed the gangplank, paying the swirling water no heed, and was most grateful to the loincloth-clad men who took my arm upon the wharf.

—*Aw kohn*, I said.

They flashed brown-toothed smiles but said nothing in response, leading me to realize that we were no longer in Cambodia—we had sailed clear into Laos! I marshalled my brainpower to recall the musty basement room of our language seminars.

—*Khàwp jai*, I gasped.

—*Baw pen nyang!* they replied.

On shore the entrepreneurial passengers set their bags down beneath a cluster of red-and-yellow parasols; with great ebullition, children slick with mud hurried to join the throng inspecting the wares. I hurried up the hill to where Henri and Charton shook hands with our tall countryman of the impeccable tie.

—Do *you* have the parcel? he asked me.

—Gironière, you still misunderstand! said Charton. We are merely passengers aboard the boat and have come to wish you well. You and I have met before!

In the shadow of his wide hat Gironière's close-set eyes crouched beneath blond brows while his shoulders were absolutely bronze, their sinews tensing and slackening.

—Which is the man from the Messageries Fluviales?

—Not one of us, said Charton. Shall we sit and have a drink?

—Has the parcel broken apart? Because I must say, even if Quiroga de San Antonio is lost I'd be grateful for the Lefèvre!

Malraux now ascended the hill, stepping as brightly as if he were about to address a graduating class though he carried a parcel that rose to his chin.

—Gironière! he called. I saw you mooning around the wharf last month but we'd left your lot behind. Asked my mate to collect for you but he's thick as a mule, so who had to write F. H. Schneider? That the whole amount, you're not shirking? There!

The captain took a thin envelope from Gironière then heaved the brown parcel from his hip into the poor man's waiting arms. In the shadow of his hat Gironière's eyes had grown big as saucers.

—The full order? he gasped.

—The receipt said eleven volumes! Malraux called over his shoulder. If there's any left behind you'll see us at the end of February. But I can't stop here to chat anymore, not since they took the commissioner to Kong!

Gironière lifted the parcel atop his head as though the eleven volumes were feathers, and turned toward the village proper with great strides of his five-metre legs. At a leisurely pace Charton started after him. The sky burned blue overhead and muddy boys chasing a bicycle wheel raced past a mouldering yellow bungalow—presumably some European had once lived in it, but what had become of him? Two women compared recent purchases: a large cabbage versus a battered number of *Hollywood Cinema* magazine. Goats slept beneath the towering mango tree around which the houses were gathered, and had the villagers been Moï or Mau I would've ventured that the tree housed their tutelary spirit, but, no, these were lowland Lao, Buddhists, whose boys would be sent to wear saffron robes. Teetering on two-metre pilings, the only variation among the huts arose in the number of quibbling chickens and hairless napping dogs beneath;

Charton started up the ladder of that with the most chickens and least dogs.

—Will you have that drink now? he called.

Gironière's gloomy front room was lined with clay jars. Scraps of laundry hung from the rafters. The house, made as it was of rice thatch and woven bamboo, swayed perilously under our weight, and the chickens' cackling became all-encompassing. The parcel rested on a low table and Gironière sat cross-legged before it, slowly unknotting his tie. From the tilt of his chin I could see he was no longer the man we'd first met.

—Drinks? Praise God, yes! he said. Though I haven't glasses nor an opener.

From beneath his tunic Henri produced a corkscrew on a string.

—I have the one, he muttered, and won't need the other. Let's please hurry.

—If you've not read Lefèvre you'll find him worth waiting for, I said. I commend your self-control.

—You've read *The Fate of the Sip Song Pana*? asked Gironière. For leisure?

—There must be soup plates, said Charton. Pour into those.

Henri, foraging in the corner, produced an assortment of clay bowls.

—Come, you don't know Lazarie by reputation? he asked. I serve as government-sanctioned mascot to the author of "Sculptural Innovations of the Vanished Khmer," who now travels merely for his health!

Gironière slowly removed his hat and placed it on the floor.

—Young man, he said, my heart is racing. If I owned a chair I'd show you to it.

—Good French conversation sets any heart racing, said Charton.

A Lao woman, small as a child, appeared from the rear of the hut and smiled broadly at us.

—*Monsieur le directeur,* she murmured.

Gironière said a few quick words and she backed out again.

—There isn't much to eat, said Gironière. Just fish. You don't have time for chicken, do you? No, the Messageries Fluviales must keep to their schedule, and in my opinion she takes far too long in plucking. You know the fable of the beggar? Not one of you does?

I knew several, in fact, but seeing him smile as he passed his spinning hat from hand to hand I saw no reason to curtail his hilarity. Henri distributed the bowls of wine.

—Tell! said Charton.

—A beggar comes before a rich man. He asks for the table scraps but the rich man shouts, "Go to Hell!" "Ah, forgive me," says the beggar, "I went, but they had no room. Hell is too crowded nowadays." "Crowded?" asks the incredulous mandarin. "Ah, yes!" says the beggar. "Hell is full of rich men."

Henri laughed as though he had a trumpet lodged in his throat then drained his bowl in one gulp. Charton took a loud sip through his teeth.

—In summation, announced Gironière, I'd rather be a poor man and live here. I explain that to her every evening before I sleep. Lazarie, tell me again about your work.

—Yes, carry on talking, said Charton. I'm like a sponge.

—What we must ask you, I said, is in regards to government business.

—What the hell should they want of me?

—On behalf of her son, my colleague and I are attempting to trace a Frenchwoman believed to have passed this way in 1909. You see—

—I am sorry to interrupt, said Charton. It is a problem of mine, and my Moï friends at Pak Sane will agree it's very annoying. Now, Gironière, have you ever heard the theory that a person might live forever if they marched north of here? Not properly forever, with the Light of the World—I mean that they'd live on as they are now, as clay.

—I don't see why not, said Gironière. I've been here since I was thirty-three and don't look a day older. But you say 1910? I'm not so old as that! No, none of our people have been in these parts that long, they'll have gone mush-mouthed or dropped dead. Ah, here's the food! Not hot, of course. She stepped over to the neighbours' for it.

—This bottle didn't last long, said Henri. What's the neighbour got in that line?

The woman set down chipped bowls full of rice, smoked fish and thick noodles with mushrooms, carefully keeping clear of that long-awaited parcel. I saw wrinkles around her mouth and strands of grey in her hair, but while she busied herself her gaze never left Gironière, and her eyes were large and shining. Tossing morsels of the fish into his mouth like peanuts, he looked at me meaningfully.

—Go on talking about your academic study.

—Khmer sculpture *was* my previous interest, I explained. Now I'm preparing a treatise on Indo-Chinese generals prior to French involvement, specifically the Tay Son brothers' capture of Saigon.

The Lao woman straightened up, her eyes wider still.

—But, cried Gironière, not—surely not Ly Thuong Kiet!

—Repelling the Song Court? Oh, sir, imagine the drubbing I'd take if I forgot Ly Thuong Kiet!

—And your epigraph? Gironière murmured.

—It may be entirely irrelevant, but lately I've had Le Quy Don on my mind. "Verdant spring passes quickly, man ages rapidly like a bamboo shoot, and one should marry in good time." Yours?

—"If only I could make the Heavens descend," he said, "and ask them if I have committed such terrible wrongs in a former life as to merit this." Also Le Quy Don.

—But surely our work will be complementary! I insisted. If you're reading San Antonio's account of Cambodia you can't be concerned with Ly Thuong Kiet over in Hanoi, can you? Sir?

Gironière gazed at me over his forearm.

—I intend to read everything written on Indo-China, he said, and to digest it perfectly. *My* Ly Thuong Kiet will be the canonical text, comprehensive, exhaustive, it will not be a rhyming poem for nursery children!

Then he was on his feet, stooping low beneath the thatch roof and dangling laundry. He swept up the parcel and raced after the woman into the back of the house. We heard a crash, then the woman speaking in soothing tones. We listened a full minute, food still clasped between our fingers, and heard not a syllable from Gironière. Charton finally swallowed his rice and carefully wiped his hands with a handkerchief.

—That is annoying, he said. The language can really be delicious when spoken in anger by an educated man. I've a medal of Saint Antony of Padua for him—shall I leave it?

—Hide it in that vomitous fish, said Henri. He can choke on it.

Charton descended the ladder in less time than it takes to tell, backing down with his bottom in the air, but Henri, too dignified for that, slid down on the seat of his pants and ripped them seriously just above the rear pocket.

—Never mind, he said. Tell me, did our hermit do some sort of work before he retired, or is he a Bourbon in exile?

—He was a scholar of some repute, said Charton. Came out to work for the Indian & Australian Chartered Bank.

I noted that in the mango's trunk an ingenious shrine had been fashioned, stuffed with flower chains, incense, ribbons, oranges and nuts, and in the centre an exquisite little standing Buddha of dull gold, hands clasped in the *wai* greeting. I confess that my first scholarly instinct was to nail the whole tableau in a crate. I heard a distinct *hsst* and turned to see Gironière's diminutive housemate bent in her doorway, patting her sarong just below the knee as though summoning a dog.

—*Monsieur le directeur!* she whispered.

Scurrying down the ladder, she raced past with a demure look over her shoulder.

—Perhaps she has a sister to sell, said Henri.

—No, no, said Charton. I shout myself hoarse to discourage that!

She waited for us before the yellow bungalow, then hurried up the steps, across the veranda and through the black, doorless entrance.

—This a devil of a place for entertaining girls.

—*Monsieur le directeur!* the woman whispered.

Cobwebs dangled from our topees. We followed the sound to a back room, blinking back the gloom to the drone of unseen flies. She stood in a corner, pointing gravely at a stack of books.

—Ah! said Charton. If this was the commissioner's house these must be his ledgers.

My heart gave its accustomed leap—could I even entertain the hope that *her* name would appear?

—He is at Kong now, Charton went on, but for thirty or forty years a poor devil holed up here, waiting for the boats to stop and register.

—And he left the things behind? asked Henri. I must say our Vice-Regency would take better care with *its* records!

I lifted the half-dozen books; they smelled fusty as a tomb. The woman hurried out of the house then away up the hill.

—Yes! I called. Thank you so much!

I set the ledgers on a bench on the leaf-strewn veranda.

—Only a trickle of people through here, said Charton. Not exactly the Gare du Nord on Maundy Thursday!

—Don't let that boat get away ahead of us, said Henri.

—Here, this is '08 to '14.

I opened it in the middle and flipped back ten pages to the entries for 1909, and there under the heading for November 2 amongst the pressed flies of yesteryear, I read the words *Adélie Tremier* written in the most spidery hand imaginable.

—Here she is, I whispered. Here she is!

—Ha! said Charton. "The people who sat in darkness saw a great light." That's Isaiah. Say, her scrawl looks like *my* writing when the fever's on me.

—She wasn't well.

—If I had my guess, they carried her up from the boat!

—Agh, verminous curs! said Henri. Don't sniff me there. Back away!

—The day is cooling, said Charton. Wakes the dogs up.

—Here, hoist that book. Don't let Malraux abandon us.

Vendors' parasols had been taken down and we could see passengers filing back across the gangplank. The disc of the sun had dropped close to the treetops on the opposite bank, the river had turned shades of cocoa and gold, and Leit Tuhk, accordingly, was coming alive. Smiling men ambled down the hill carrying paddy rice and bananas, men came up the hill with dripping harvests of catfish, old women clubbed chickens over the head, young men hacked branches apart for cooking fires and a battalion of children raced madly after that beleaguered bicycle wheel. The *General Subrégis'* engines throbbed on the air. On either side of the river families balanced in long pirogues, silently hauling in nets, each shadow as long as a banner across the rippling water. Could Eden have been much different? Before Leit Tuhk our path had been demarcated with hearsay and shrugs. Now it was as though Adélie had taken my hand, and I did not shrink from the sensation.

—Don't sniff me there! Filthy hairless things. If my father were here he'd brain them with his clog, said Henri. Look at these ones coming, green with pus!

—Buddhists are adverse to taking life, I explained.

—Well, they may *all* live forever at this rate, he replied. But it's disgusting!

At the foot of the wharf we hurried through a cloud of white butterflies and a moment later were walking the *nuòc mâm*-scented deck of the steamer. We climbed to the perch before the wheelhouse, Captain Malraux gave a great blast of the whistle and we backed out into the current. Duc looped ropes in the bow below us. On shore the bicycle wheel had evidently lost its appeal, for the children shrieked and waved farewell and flung themselves in the river. I held the 1908–14 ledger to my chest.

—When I look at the Mekong at this time of evening, said Charton, I must always think of Camoens. You know him?

—He threw that Russian queer through a plate-glass window, said Henri.

—Sixteenth-century poet, I said. Portuguese.

—That was he. He was once shipwrecked, you know, in the Mekong Delta, and swam ashore holding his poems over his head, and after that he wrote a paraphrase of the 137th Psalm in reference to the Mekong. Can't remember it now. Supposed to be very beautiful. What I do remember is his swimming—with only one arm, can you imagine?

—Ah, said Henri. Action rather than words.

—I believe his woman might have been Moï, said Charton.

—Your rotten Portuguese had a Moï?

—Gironière's woman.

—She may have been, said Henri. I had a native wife of my own for a while.

—Really? I asked. But you had your differences?

Henri shielded his eyes. We were well out in the river by then, and the day's final radiance painted the landscape gold and black and nothing else.

—I was not kind to her, he finally said.

The huts had melded into the trees. I could discern the children only from their mighty splashes.

—Easy to see why Gironière stays on, I said. Easy to imagine Madame Tremier staying on, for that matter.

—The place can have him! said Henri. Too nervous to do any proper work. What's he contribute to the world at large, eh, living out here off the fat of the land?

I studied my colleague, his ruddy cheeks, the mucus in the corners of his eyes, the scant patches of beard he was cultivating, and pressed my tongue against my teeth to keep from shouting, "But in God's name, man, what are *you* contributing?" Nevertheless he could read my face—doubtless in his forty-four years he'd seen the same expression a hundred times for each kind word he'd heard—for he sniffed hard up his nose and stared at the back of his hand on the rail. My disgust died away.

Then a sudden noise from the forest caused us to start—Charton straightened like a pointer. The sound rose from our left, upstream of the village, and even over the engines was perfectly audible: a deep ripping, like the trunk of some dry-rotted tree giving way, then turning by slow degrees into a piercing shriek. It was such an extraordinary noise that it seemed in the meantime that all other sounds, the engines, the river, the ubiquitous clattering of rivets and bolts, died away completely, and we dwelt in perfect silence with this one exception until its echo faded over the water and the old din reasserted itself. The fluttering leaves of the jungle betrayed nothing, not a bird had flown up, but fishermen in their pirogues called to each other and pointed. Charton crossed himself and immediately Henri did as well.

—*Ong kop,* Charton said quietly. *Ong kop.*

As I looked astern the wharf at Leit Tuhk disappeared behind a bend. Its blithe denizens would have to fend for themselves.

"Lord Tiger," he had said.

SHIT MIXED
WITH ORANGES

Emanuel Tremier.

THE COACH smelled like roast goose and the sky above them looked grey like a cannon muzzle. The painted kind. The unpainted ones always turned orange after they'd been out in the rain and then Manu would give them to the Spanish battalions, he wasn't sure why exactly. He set his upper lip against the window frame so he'd feel every jolt as the coach flew over the rutted road like it was a locomotive flying down to Lyon, but after he counted three breaths in and out the woodwork jumped and knocked him in the teeth. He rubbed his lip and looked at Maman and Aunt Henriette as though nothing had happened.

"Is this Ivry now?" Aunt Henriette yelled out the window.

"Not so far out as that, Madame," Mauriac yelled from up above their heads. "But this is the street we were given."

"Not so cheery as I'd imagined," said Aunt Henriette.

They drove beneath a big dead tree that could have been drawn eight different ways but she hadn't even let him bring a pencil so Manu went back to looking at his mother's reflection in the brass-work, where her skin looked even whiter. Whiter than carp! They would only stay long enough to see Berenice walk about on two feet, Maman had said, and congratulate her on her recovery. That morning Isabelle had run into one of Berenice's brothers at the market and he'd insisted that she was better, oh, so much better!

"Gives us all hope," Maman said. In the reflection her lips looked long as mussel shells. "It's no wonder the dear stayed at our house on her afternoons off—she couldn't have *walked* here in her four hours!"

"This is the number," yelled Mauriac. "Two more carts here. Hope it's not a doctor and priest, or you'll have come out for nothing!"

Then they had to wait for Mauriac to climb down, so Manu looked at the house. It looked mouldy like it had been dragged up from the ocean and the people who lived in it would have gills like codfish! If he'd at least brought a pencil he could've shown Eugène afterward what they'd looked like.

"*This* bit of news will make Bonheur think twice," said Maman. "I'll start to chair the League meetings again, and you won't fret either, Manu, will you?"

"Will I what?"

"Will you quit following me everywhere like a puppy?"

He slid across to look out the other window but there was only a field of broken window frames. Crows hopped around on scraps of crockery and blowing curtain. A dog barked in a yard somewhere, then three or four more barked somewhere else, making a noise like his bicycle chain in those days when he'd been allowed to chase ducks through the park but the chain had needed oiling. The coach door opened and Mauriac reached in to take Maman's arm.

"If it *is* a priest, he's here to congratulate her," said Maman.

Aunt Henriette climbed down and Manu jumped from the top step and half-landed on a rock so he thought his ankle might turn and throw him down on the ground like a Prussian grenade had been lobbed at him, but his ankle didn't turn.

Then quick as a wink the sun came out and everybody had to squint. The puddles were too bright! Two men spied on them from behind two other carriages. They looked like Prussians and after what had just happened with the grenade Manu felt the spit well up in his mouth. Mauriac and Aunt Henriette took Maman's arms to walk her to the house but she shook them off the same as always. Grandma's chestnut horse scraped its iron shoe across a stone and right then the dogs in the yards stopped barking. Queer. He'd tell Eugène about that.

"Didn't we come to see Berenice?"

"Of course," said Maman.

"Why doesn't she come out?"

Aunt Henriette banged on the door with the handle of her umbrella.

"Wait!" he yelled.

He'd thought the house might topple over. Mauriac took out his tin of cigarettes and said to the Prussians by the puddle that they could help themselves.

The door opened halfway before thudding against something, maybe a crate of lead animals. A red-haired boy in a shirt with no collar leaned his head around.

"Yes?"

He didn't have gills or even catfish whiskers.

"Does Madame Berenice live here?"

"Of course, *Mesdames*! Come straight in."

He pulled his head back in. Maman and Aunt Henriette walked through sideways and the bones in their skirts creaked against the door. Manu kept right behind them so Maman wouldn't get too far ahead because he was looking after her now, everyone knew that. The corridor was black as the inside of a molehill but far away he saw a glow that was the same colour as a mortuum-red pastel.

"Not good for your lungs in *here*," he heard Henriette say.

Then her silhouette and Maman's appeared against the mortuum-red. Grownups were talking. He followed Maman and Aunt Henriette into a gloomy room where a lot of old people sat in chairs and a lot of young people leaned against the walls. Everybody was watching a bed beside the fireplace. The room smelled like somebody had shit themselves and Manu thought that those horses on the muddy street were already having more fun than he was. He'd asked Mauriac what horses would do if they could do anything they wanted and Mauriac had said,

"Rut." He'd also told him Berenice had spread plague by spitting on Maman's boots.

Manu grabbed Maman's hand before she could stumble into anything.

The red-haired boy sank to the floor between two buck-toothed girls. Men smoking cigarettes made red lights in the corners. Like a Vermeer. Everyone kept talking quietly like in church before the priest came in.

"Your groom is a prognosticator," Aunt Henriette whispered to Maman.

A prognosticator told the future at carnivals but he couldn't see what that had to do with Mauriac. Why didn't anyone give Maman their chair?

"Berenice?" Maman asked.

Nobody answered, not to say "Here I am!'" or even "She went to buy soap." Rude. He'd tell Eugène. And who'd shit themselves? There weren't any babies. A priest as big as a strongman crouched at the head of the bed, talking to the old lady lying there, while a skinny man with a beard shoved a lot of metal things like knives and forks into a bag like Doctor Bonheur's, so he was another doctor.

"From a benevolent society?" he asked.

"We've come to call on Madame Berenice," Maman said. "She worked at our house, and we learned she was much better. Has she gone out?"

The doctor shut his bag with a snap.

"She is *no* better. Though before you wag your finger at the dread consumption, go back in the kitchen and cast your eyes on the quarts of Garden of Eden Cure-All these people have put into her. I'll write 'tuberculosis' on the certificate, I'll have to, but tonics killed her as neatly as a knife between the ribs!"

"Sir!" a bald man yelled. "If you're quite—"

"Yes, yes, I'll find my way out," said the doctor.

"I'll pay your bill," Maman said. "My driver can write down the address."

"I would appreciate that more than you know."

"Did she say 'pay the bill'?" a woman yelled.

Manu held the back of Maman's dress. He didn't want her to fall down in front of so many people.

"Madame *Tremier*?"

The lady in the bed was talking. She sounded like Berenice the time she'd imitated the man who sold clockwork monkeys under the Pont Neuf.

"Yes, dear, I—"

Maman walked forward with her skirts dragging across the old people's knees and Manu kept hold of her hem like he was a girl at the neighbour's wedding.

"Forgive our intrusion! You've been on my mind, of course, and I thought if I could . . . I had heard your illness was quite a bit *better*."

"Ah, I'm to blame for that," the bald man said. "Just being polite."

Two girls a little bigger than Manu helped Berenice to sit up. Her eyes looked the same, and her ears, and the hair trailing from underneath her cap, but otherwise she *looked* like the man who sold the clockwork monkeys.

"Hi, Berenice." Manu waved with his free hand.

"What, have I done something wrong, Madame?"

Then red stuff like blood spurted from Berenice's mouth onto the sheets, and right away the two girls tried to wipe it up with towels. Berenice started to cough, but not regular coughing. More like gypsies grinding knives. He watched Maman. Her mouth was hanging open and her front teeth were lit up by the mortuum-red.

When Berenice finished the girls laid her down again.

"It's all right, love," said a man with a grey beard.

"You ought to change the pan," said the priest.

The sheets were pulled back, and Berenice's legs looked as puffed-up as an elephant's. The girls took out the bedpan and the smell made Manu sneeze, and he wished he hadn't in front of so many people. A hunchbacked woman smiled at him. Maman squeezed his shoulder as he wiped his nose. The smell wasn't just shit but shit mixed with oranges. He wouldn't tell Eugène about that.

"I *had* hoped you might be better," Maman said.

The man with the grey beard kissed Berenice's forehead then fell back in his chair. It creaked like a coal grate. The strongman priest kissed his crucifix and put it in her hand even though Berenice's eyes were already shut.

"Submit," the strongman said, "and be content. I speak now of the comfort of that holy and blessed revelation of the divine which with power and goodness opens its arms to the afflicted. Be still now. Be content."

Maman turned so her face was in the dark. She found his hand and squeezed it. He squeezed back hard. Berenice was sick in a different way than Maman was, he knew that, but how many different ways *were* there?

The red-haired boy led them through the molehill. Aunt Henriette was blubbering. Then in the sunshine Manu had to shade his eyes just to make out the horses. Maman wiped her neck with her handkerchief.

"I brought a roast goose," she said, "though I suppose it can't be of much use to her…"

"I'll take it off your hands," the red-haired boy said quickly.

Mauriac's *Salome Without Her Veils* postcard peeped from his trouser pocket. He took Maman's arm and helped her up the step.

Nobody said anything in the coach for a long time, not until they were back on proper cobbled streets. That made the horses feel less gloomy.

"Will she die?" he asked.

"Yes, my love." Maman leaned against the curtain. "She may be dead by now."

"My dear!" said Aunt Henriette. "You shouldn't—"

"It's the truth. No harm in it."

"But what's the matter with her?" Manu asked.

He remembered what Mauriac had told him, but did Mauriac know everything?

"Tuberculosis," said Maman. "They call it consumption some-times."

"But that's not what's the matter with you!" Manu smiled at them. He snapped his fingers. "*You* have influenza!"

Maman leaned across and took his hand. She rubbed his knuckles and kept blinking like there was smoke blowing in her face.

"I'm sorry you thought that, my love. I have tuberculosis."

"But a different kind. You'll get better."

"It *will* be different." She kept her eyes open wide. "I will get better."

"We can pray, child," said Aunt Henriette.

"Sylvie prayed for rabbit for dinner." His voice shook, like a baby's! "And we *never* ate rabbit for dinner!"

"I swear to you I will do anything and everything possible," said Maman.

When Papa had been crushed flat it hadn't been like those people watching Berenice dying, sitting there quiet, not doing anything, because Manu and Maman had run to the station to take a train toward the place but there were no more that night and Grandma wouldn't let Mauriac drive them in the sleet so Maman had taken the heads from the upstairs mantel and dropped them three storeys, and the way they'd smashed on the hall floor did seem funny now. But as he'd watched he'd screamed into his hands.

Now he wanted to punch someone in the mouth until their tooth dropped out. He didn't want his mother to ever shit the bed the way Berenice had.

"You swear?" he asked.

At home he followed Maman upstairs and stood outside the closed door while she coughed and coughed and coughed, and after a while he could hear her spitting.

ADDRESSING THE EASTERN IMMORTALITY FABLE

Mme. Adélie Tremier.

THE NEXT day Mauriac drove the two women up boulevard St-Germain. When the horses balked at climbing a sidestreet, however, Adélie insisted they walk the final block lest they be late for the lecture. Henriette wanted to hear it so badly.

The cobbled hill rose, Adélie guessed, toward the Panthéon, though its great dome stayed hidden behind the tilt of neighbouring roofs. She regretted not having brought an umbrella, as Henriette had, to have leaned on as she climbed.

"I'm not so depleted as I look," she called after her friend.

They came to an arched doorway with a slate propped against the step, and Adélie assumed it was the *plat du jour* menu for yet another bistro until Henriette produced her notebook and nub of pencil.

"I'll jot this down for my brother before we step in," she said, adjusting her pince-nez. "He's fascinated to know how his part of the world is received."

The Left Bank Orientalist League
presents a lecture & debate
"Addressing The Eastern Immortality Fable"

"Surely there'll be a program," Adélie said slowly—she did not wish to betray her lack of breath. "You might send him that."

"Oh, you're quite right!" Henriette clicked her tongue and slid the pencil back into her sleeve. "Though keep your gloves on. Their leaflets tend to smudge."

"Is there time for coffee before we go in?" asked Adélie. "There's a wonderful place in the Place de la Contrescarpe, but if that's too far we—"

But Henriette had already lifted skirts and jogged merrily beneath the archway, rushing across the foyer toward the upward-spiralling flagstone stairs so as to report with all-the-greater efficacy to Marco, the lieutenant in Cambodia.

That morning Adélie had believed this would be one of those good days Bonheur had promised, but now the pain so racked her knees and hips she imagined she was climbing in a suit of armour. Even her blameless *elbows* ached—perhaps it wasn't tuberculosis at all, but a vindictive rheumatism! But, no, now her cough struggled to assert itself and in her mind Berenice, withered as a centenarian, reared up yet again from her pillows.

Three boys in cloth caps hurried past on the narrowest turn of the steps.

"... and harem girls who won't ..."

"Adélie?" came Henriette's echoing voice. "Shall I wait for you?"

There were enough empty seats that the two women could set their immense hats on either side of them.

"Are you still chair at the Anti-Penury League?" asked Henriette.

"I was asked to step down after Poulenc's column."

"Ladies and gentleman!" called the Orientalist League secretary. "A change this afternoon from our usual program of caliphs and camels, odalisques and Ottomans—"

"And none too soon!" called a woman muffled to the eyes.

"Female guests may have privileges revoked if we cannot keep order in the place, thank you. Yes, the Anarchist Society is one floor down!"

The hall was a theatrical studio with pink cherubs carved into its proscenium arch and a half-dozen rows of creaking, tobacco-imbued seats. A section of battlement stood at stage left behind Lacheroy, the secretary, as he stomped his boot at the podium. He wore liberal amounts of hair oil along with a Van Dyke beard.

"The impresario," whispered Henriette.

"Yes, yes, this afternoon we move our sphere of inquiry from Asia Minor"—one hand waving low—"to Asia *Major*, as it were"—the other waving high, as though he stood astride a globe—"for the reason, yes, that our treasurer, Roux the Mystic, has only yesterday returned from his tour of China, Japan and our own delicate East Asian possessions, consulting dusty books and learned men as well as dusty men and learned books, while dallying, no doubt, amongst the local delicacies, yes? Roux, you peered *beneath the veil*, one might say?"

"Uh, why… *no*." The respondent sat in the front row—Adélie could see only his bald head and a slender neck protruding from a high collar. "They do not generally wear veils in those parts."

"Yes, *yes,* but you know I was speaking metaphorically, that to peer beneath a veil is to… be made privy, shall we say, to a woman's secret places, and then—"

"Give Roux the stage!" shouted the muffled woman, though she'd pulled her scarf down the better to shout, revealing a face mottled with age-spots and heavily rouged. "We've a scholarly talk this time, not your dancing girls!"

"My wife, Louise, yes, ladies and gentlemen." Lacheroy grinned like a cat. "She anchors me to this reality, bless her."

"Is it true every sultan keeps a hundred girls?" chirped one of the cloth-capped boys.

This drew deep chuckles from several bearded gentleman, and a fat man with a torn lapel clapped enthusiastically. Henriette clicked her tongue.

"I'm afraid it's true what she said, boys." Lacheroy leaned heavily on the podium. "No dancing girls today."

He unfolded a chair at the rear of the stage while the afternoon's speaker rose and carried his carpet bag up four steps to the podium. Roux wore heavy glasses and a black-and-white tie, and something about his soft-cornered mouth hinted that it shied from strong cheeses. Henriette gripped her nub of pencil.

"Li Baozhen!" he shouted. "Sought immortality!"

With sheepish creaks of their vacated seats the boys crept from the hall.

"Eleven hundred years ago Li Baozhen was a Tang general who, like great men before and after him, sought to achieve life eternal. He engaged the alchemist Sun Jichang to mould pills of gold—now, can anyone suppose what supposition lay behind this belief that swallowing *gold* would lead to immortality? Yes?"

"Because of the exorbitant markup," called the fat man with the torn lapel.

"From a practical perspective that's quite likely, yet the purported theory was simply that gold does not tarnish. And so Li Baozhen ingested twenty *thousand* of these pills until he became exceedingly uncomfortable, yet one night he dreamt of flying on a crane to the court of Shangdi, which inspired him to practice balancing each day upon a wooden crane of his own design. A Taoist monk cured his stomach ills with a combination of laxatives and lard, at which point the alchemist upbraided the general, asking, 'Why abandon the immortality you have so nearly achieved?' So Li Baozhen swallowed three thousand more pills, at which point, understandably, he died."

Gentlemen shifted in their seats, perhaps out of sympathy for Li Baozhen, as light applause rippled through the auditorium.

"Would it be safe to assume," asked Lacheroy from his upstage seat, "that the general had serving girls at his disposal?"

Why abandon the immortality you have so nearly achieved? wrote Henriette.

"Do not consider what follows to be a scientific survey," proclaimed Roux. "Nothing was preserved in formaldehyde and at no point did I so much as take my own temperature. Rather it is a survey of the rude art of the people, and if I tell you that certain things are done in a certain place, it is solely in the *literature* of that place. These things are real only to those who dwell in unreality."

"I wonder whether the young woman with the masses of black hair might have a question," called Lacheroy.

"To achieve life eternal," Roux went on, "the three primary causes of death must be overcome, these being disease and old age as well as physical trauma. A man might live for centuries with his belly full of gold, for example, but if he is crushed beneath a millstone he will have no advantage over a man who is succumbing calmly enough to stroke..."

Adélie found her head increasingly heavy after the exertions of the day; she could only listen with half an ear.

"... in India there is an insistence that *spiritual* immortality can be achieved through metempsychosis—that is, jumping from one physical body to another, and in 1874 the yogi Vallalar disappeared *entirely* from a locked room, never to..."

Why had they turned up the radiators? She stared at the oiled mane of a gentleman in front of them while Roux's voice flickered past like so many fish.

"In our Asian capital at Hanoi I chanced to meet a missionary recently returned from the great and royal city of Luang-Prabang, within our protectorate state of Laos."

Hanoi! wrote Henriette, and circled the word.

"Equally versed in fables of lowland farmers and half-savage hill people, she enlightened me with the following tale over a supper of succulent noodles and dog."

Lacheroy licked his chops with aplomb.

"To wit: atop a mountain shrouded in cloud there lies a spring, a holy lake, that anyone who set out to find it has never found. The spring has only been visited by hunters who've *chanced* upon it, and on its shores they have encountered fowl and deer which no arrow could harm, grandiose fruit which the vines refused to surrender, and the largest and most vigourous stalks of rice in the world, for the spirits tend them. These fortunate men were at the extreme of thirst and starvation, yet one sip from the spring so sustained them that they could descend and return home, and it is even said—and this is what drew Mademoiselle Fleeson and I together—that these men have gone on living thus forever. They have nothing to prove their stories but the evidence of their own bodies returning home, but, as

I jotted down, 'the little ones, who have hearts free from guile, believe.'"

Adélie realized she was sitting bolt upright.

"I attempted to achieve synthesis with my existing research." Smiling, Roux produced a sheaf of papers which he dropped with a thud. "It is difficult, of course, to ascertain the *exact* whereabouts of Mademoiselle Fleeson's delicious Lao spring. Mansarovar, the holy lake at the foot of Mount Kailash, leaps to mind, but as Kailash is in Tibet it seems unlikely that Lao hunters might chance upon it even in legend. In China the cult of Ma Gu, protector of females, is said to have centred on Ma Gu Shan in Nancheng and a *second* Ma Gu Shan in Jianchang, near Nanfeng."

"Where are these places?" Adélie asked.

"Around about Laos," whispered Henriette.

"There is one fable of a Maid Ma—doubtless an incarnation of Ma Gu—who could walk across water. She was murdered by her husband, of course, but at the close of each lunar month her ghost may yet be glimpsed walking through the mist across the water. Out of reverence to her, hunting on those shores has been forbidden, which in *practice* makes it rather like our Lao spring, though—"

"And where is Maid Ma's lake?" asked the man with the mane of hair.

"Ah," said Roux, mouth pursing again, "with such specifics, it does sound like an actual place, doesn't it? I might also mention Yaochi Jinmu, Queen Mother of the West, who dwells beside a lake—perhaps the same one—where she tends a tree which produces *p'an-t'ao*, peaches which confer life eternal. And you will recognize this Yaochi Jinmu, should you chance upon her, by the Peaches of Immortality dangling from her headdress."

"Wearing the headdress and nothing else?" asked Lacheroy.

"What's more, there is the fable of the Monkey King, who tells his subjects—let me find it, here—'Someday I will grow old and weak but I shall go down the mountain and wander to the ends of the earth 'til I learn how to be young forever and escape the doom of death.' And he does just that! The first sage ..."

Adélie gazed down the row to the seats vacated by the cloth-capped boys. They'd been well-groomed—were *their* mothers still alive? And would their lives be markedly different if they were not? After *she* died, would the unspooling yarn of Manu's days take an untoward turn? It would, yes, straight to St-Lucien.

". . . yet for all that, the Cham of Indochina were amongst the most barbaric peoples in history, slaughtering six thousand subjects at a time that their emperors might bathe in the collected gall. Why? An attempt, yet again, to win life eternal."

"Boo!" called Louise.

"My point exactly," said Roux.

As the fabled Manu would be sacrificed.

". . . and they reasoned, quite magnificently, that to venerate an infant was to call it to the attention of evil spirits, so that Dog, Rat and Weevil became common sobriquets, and a long line of Cham kings were named Excrement."

The bearded gentlemen smiled and Adélie breathed a laugh out her nose—she might easily travel east, then, and leave Manu under the protection of a new name: *Shit*. But, no, she couldn't go without him!

Called Excrement, wrote Henriette.

"Throughout my time in Phnom Penh, I reflected, as anyone might, on Chou Ta-kuan's observations of the thirteenth century, that—"

"I understand, sir, one does not fall ill *once* an immortal," Adélie called, climbing haltingly to her feet, "but if the monkey had been ill at the moment he *became* immortal, would he have become healthy, or would he have kept that affliction forever?"

Over his spectacles Roux regarded her balefully.

"Well, Madame, in *theory*—"

"Certainly, 'in theory'—I don't pretend any of this is real!"

"My dear, really!" whispered Henriette.

"In theory, the Monkey King would have simultaneously transcended death *and* illness, assuming he had not been so incapacitated by his theoretical illness as to fail the various tests offered by the sages."

"So it's possible one might . . . *already* be too ill to achieve it?"

There was a pathetic catch in her voice. No one cast her a scornful look now, and even Lacheroy sat wide-eyed. She gripped the seat in front of her.

"My understanding," said Roux, "is that a human being who achieves immortality has had his body *propped up* by the ascension of his spirit—I base that conclusion on my studies. But to draw upon my personal experience, I've seen a man's spirit defeated by illness long before the body had deigned to succumb."

"The hour grows near!" Lacheroy waved a pocket watch.

Adélie sank into the seat. Mucus churned in her lungs.

"If I may broach a question of a more practical nature," Louise called. "Might it not be possible to arrange a tour of this Laos place and glimpse this hinterland for ourselves, but with comfortable beds and proper food? Any *number* of us could profit by a dip in a magic lake, I dare say!"

"Ignoring the fact that my spring exists only as a metaphor," breathed Roux, "it gives me great pleasure to inform this assembly that Laos remains one of the most inaccessible countries upon the face of the earth. With enough time and money you might sail to the Orient via the Messageries Maritimes, true, but whether you then travelled overland east from Siam, south from Yunan or up the great Mekong during the rainy season, you would require weeks, if not months, to reach your destination, and only if you could secure translators and were willing to eat native slop and to sleep on the bare ground. Have your learned husband locate the place on a map, Madame, and you will observe that Laos may well be those very ends of the earth the Monkey King sought."

"Yet *you* went there."

"No, Madame. I travelled only for a year so I hadn't the time."

"Would the obstacles be insurmountable," asked Adélie, "if travelling with a nine-year-old boy?"

"On the contrary," said Roux. "I believe nine-year-old boys to be just as adaptable as thirteen-year-old girls."

"What do you make of our position in the East?" asked the oily-maned man.

"Ah!" Roux removed his glasses to wipe his eyes with his handkerchief. "I believe there are diverse biomes of men just are there of plants and animals, but from what I know of France and of Indo-China, gentlemen, I will state *unequivocally* that we have as much business there as a tiger in a field of ptarmigan."

"How dare you—?" cried one gentleman.

"And should Indo-China ever rouse itself in conflict, I hesitate to guess whether we should be the ptarmigan or the tiger."

"Yes, yes, yes, my friends, yes!" Lacheroy very nearly pirouetted to the podium. "For his insights Roux the Mystic will doubtless achieve that immortality of our greatest thinkers, namely undying fame! And now to pass the cuspidor for the Eastern missions that those who sit in darkness will see the light! Fascination with pagan culture, my friends, is no excuse for allowing souls to fall to the wayside—so says our patron the bishop. A few centimes, gentlemen and ladies, to plant crosses upon their graves instead of buffalo skulls. And yes, to Guérande's question, it *is* the very cuspidor Debré brought back from Turkmenistan."

"I understood from the advertisement," said one of the bearded gentlemen, rubbing his cropped head, "that there was meant to be a debate on the topic."

"I had noticed that myself," said Roux, adjusting a cufflink.

"THREE TIMES I've submitted my monograph on temple-building," hissed Henriette, eyeing the men descending below them, "and still not a word!"

They passed beneath a great brass clock in the foyer.

"Quarter past three?" whispered Adélie. "Come, get a cab! I want to be there when Manu comes home from school."

"But, my dear," said Henriette, "on Mondays he's home at *noon*. Surely he's in dependable hands with his grandmother and a staff of six!"

"The poor lamb. My mind is going."

Her hips ached from that torturous chair; she thought longingly of her bed. She hurried down the hill and somehow kept upright, skipping over the uneven pavement though exhaustion clung to her like a shell. At St-Germain she heard a cry and turned to see Henriette on her knees.

"Just my idiotic notebook." Henriette propped herself up with her umbrella. "Dropped the thing. Ought to make a fine letter for Marco."

"I embarrassed you terribly up there," said Adélie.

"I will recover," her friend nodded.

Arm in arm they wandered toward the cab stand, forcing a knife-sharpener to steer his grindstone around them, then a hurdy-gurdy man and his seven children, bleak-eyed between songs. Without a backward glance Adélie slipped a franc coin into the sunburnt hand of the youngest.

"Café Gimlette," she suggested. "Or would you rather go on walking?"

"I *must* stop. You may not realize it, love, but I'm carrying you."

Adélie had not been in the place in years, yet the waiter set a demitasse before her even as he took Henriette's order. A flower-seller came through and Adélie bought a carnation for Manu.

"There was no program after all!" laughed Henriette. "The Left Bank Orientalist League has fallen on lean times."

Adélie swabbed herself with her handkerchief.

"I wonder what a Provençal Enthusiast League might discuss."

"I beg your pardon, love? Your voice is going."

Adélie repeated herself.

"I shudder to think!" said Henriette. "Those stories in the newspaper, when—"

"The wife who bit her husband to death," rasped Adélie.

"Or those women killing each other with frying pans!"

"Then set each other *on fire*. Because of a chicken that got loose, wasn't it?"

Henriette wiped her pince-nez on her apron.

"And each time they used an umbrella—"

"Or a pitchfork!" croaked Adélie.

"Or a pitchfork, it would be broken to pieces 'from *the force of the blows*.'"

"And what shall the Provençal Enthusiast League conclude?"

"We conclude—"

"Friends—"

"Ladies and gentlemen, friends, we conclude that the nature of the Provençal is to keep beating at something until the matter is well and truly *concluded*."

As Adélie laughed the afternoon light caught the delicate pink of her upturned nostrils and Henriette decided her friend was as lovely as a painting, until Adélie fell, inevitably, into a fit of coughing—eyes distended, handkerchief over her mouth—and Henriette lifted her mulled wine from the table to keep it from spilling.

"Get me a croissant to dip," Adélie gasped, eyes streaming.

When they went out she insisted on walking unassisted.

"But you aren't *much* better, dear, are you?" asked Henriette. "Heated gas in one's behind is one remedy, I believe, though I shudder to mention it."

"Well, I may yet travel to Laos, dear, in order to bathe in that magic lake."

"Oh, don't make fun of Monsieur Roux!"

"I will write to the Messageries Maritimes," Adélie said plainly, "and if Bonheur can offer no cure Manu and I may simply steal away."

"And wear the Peaches of Immortality at your next ball! You might have a thousand pairs made up—but don't look at me like that, you weren't serious!"

Adélie strove to keep pace with the draught-horses plodding up the street.

"Those things are real only if one dwells in unreality," Henriette went on. "He said so very clearly, and I can't see how anyone could justify journeying to an unchristian country just to end with her dead eyes closed by unchristian hands!"

Adélie leaned a shoulder against the rain-blackened wall.

"You've been too good to me today," she stammered. "You mustn't miss your omnibus." She wiped sweat from her throat. "I've left that flower behind."

A tradesman with a ladder stepped lithely around her.

"But my dear!" said Henriette. "Don't cry!"

Adélie's face was damp and creased. Mucus caught in the roof of her mouth but she refused to spit.

"I was only *musing*, wasn't I?" soothed Henriette. "Just take my arm. This is the modern world, you must realize, and medicine can—"

"No one ever died of tuberculosis in *our* experience," rasped Adélie.

Then ignoring her friend's hand she stepped from the curb, so erect she might have been held aloft by diamond-shaped steel spans. A teamster twisted reins against his chest to keep his horses from running her down, their shod hooves sparking against the cobbles, while automobiles braked frantically. Every klaxon in Paris seemed to sound rancorously in her ear. Boys jeered from the sidewalk. In prim deference to them all Adélie pinched the brim of her vast hat and walked ever-forward; she would walk ever-forward until the matter was well and truly concluded.

THE KEMMARAT
RAPIDS

Pierre Lazarie.

W E'D BARELY been served our coffee the next morning, monkeys in the canopy still shrieking their sunrise hymn, when crewmen swarmed over the ship, lashing barrels down, clamping portholes shut and nailing tarpaulins over the hatches. I felt a clap on my shoulder and there was Malraux, unshaven and hollow-eyed yet on tiptoe with excitement. We pressed against the rail as the deck passengers were herded beneath a canopy in the stern.

—If they're sitting on the roof and we tilt even a little, *whoop*, that's the last of them, said Malraux. Please go to your cabins.

—Are the cataracts that dangerous? I asked.

He sucked voraciously on his sugarcane.

—For an hour today, you'll feel alive. Every moment is a trial.

—No margin for error, said Henri. Our work is like that.

—We've been up the rapids at Preatapang, I said. Is this so much worse?

He wiped his moustache with the back of his hand before climbing a ladder.

—Keep an eye peeled for her bleached bones, Henri said. This may be as far as she came.

My stomach clenched at the thought, though my father could already have calculated, to the hundredth decimal, the unlikelihood that she was still living.

—I once made the mistake of describing these rapids to my Moï, said Charton, and they made me promise to lock myself in and crawl under the bed.

Inside our cabin it was difficult to relax—the frenzied stoking of the engines had started every piece of the ship shuddering like a franc coin on a tramline. From beneath his bed Henri pulled the wooden crate, reinforced with copper screws by Nguyen himself. In an entire week my colleague had consumed only a sixteen-bottle case, though our evening at the Continental had seen the end of five.

—Your economy has been remarkable.

—Yes, put that in your report, you wretch.

He pulled a pry-bar from his valise. Through our porthole I could glimpse only dark trees passing, yet one sound was ever-increasing and I thought of putting my head out to see if an aeroplane was flying over. Henri looked up from the crate.

—Are those the rapids now?

Suddenly the cabin tilted, our trunks slid out from the wall and foaming brown water burst in from under the door, soaking Henri to mid-thigh where he knelt. I lifted my feet above the inundation. A chorus of alarm sounded from the stern. A moment later we tilted just as sharply in the opposite direction, the water rushed out, the trunks resumed their original positions and Henri, extricating a single bottle, climbed to his feet.

—In the name of the Vice-Regency we shall see what this is about!

We opened our door onto a whirlpool as large as a house yawning just below the rail, a teak log thrashing in its jaws like a matchstick in a drain. Spray lashed us and our ears roared. I seized the rail—for I had no wish to await the inevitable in that rat-trap of a cabin!—and Henri looped his arm through mine while he struggled with the opener around his neck. I shook him off, abetted by reprehensible language which neither of us could hear.

The stairs to the wheelhouse stood adjacent and we crept up like delinquent schoolboys. With Henri gripping my elbow I slid the door open, staggered backwards a step then pitched headlong into the cabin as the *General Subrégis* heaved sideways. We found a chart table which was bolted to the floor and clung to it gratefully. Captain Malraux grinned over his shoulder.

—The pleasure's all mine!

He wore only trousers and the kerchief around his neck, and every cord in his back stood out as he gripped the creaking wheel. At his barked command a crewcutted Cambodian pushed the brass handle forward for more steam. I pitied those stokers, whose boiler room must have been bucking like a colt.

—Current holds the screws back and the rudder can't respond! yelled Malraux.

I nodded sagely in response. Through the window we watched Duc leap and contort like Nijinsky himself as he rushed from one side of his deck to the other. Beyond him lay a panorama of cataracts so alarming that my gums suddenly tingled—these rapids were a mill for breaking ships into splinters. Malraux barked at the Cambodian and I guessed that the requested pressure had not been forthcoming. Duc pressed his face to the window, a baleful cigarette crushed against his chin. Henri proffered his half-empty bottle of Paternina Gran Reserva.

—No to worry! shouted Malraux. The starboard screw's lost pressure so the port . . . screw's . . . having its way with us!

The boat rattled like a car in a mine shaft as we sailed on a perfect diagonal toward a thrashing whirlpool. I saw the achingly calm water just beyond it as the Cambodian turned a crank above his head.

—Hold on! shouted Malraux.

I wrapped my arms around the table leg. We tilted to the right and the empty wine bottle rolled past to thud against the wall. The bolts securing the leg groaned like invalids. How far could we lean before capsizing?

The Cambodian shouted again but, remarkably, with less alarm.

—Pressure's back! called Malraux.

Despite our wretched angle I climbed to my feet. The river broke heavily over the bow but that lovely stretch of water lay immediately before us, and an instant later the *General Sub-régis* surged mightily onto the calm eddy. The boat righted itself—the worst was past us! I looked to see what gripped my wrist and saw it was Henri's hand.

But then I saw that we were still under maximum steam, flying over that glassy water like a torpedo—Malraux shrieked an order and the Cambodian threw the handle into reverse. Boulders the size of churches rushed toward us. Malraux fell back as the wheel spun like a windmill. I dropped to one knee.

When the impact came I was thrown against the back wall.

Then the cold-sweated relief of opening one's eyes, to be *able* to open them, if only to look through a row of broken windows at a tangle of greenish-black trees.

—Lazarie, whispered Henri. Are you cognizant?

Though our engines were silent, the roar of the rapids was as loud as ever. I heard distant shouting. I sat up and the side of my head throbbed. Henri crouched before me, wild eyes scrutinizing mine, his face still ashen. His lip was cut.

—Hm, he said.

Then he vomited over my boot, and his purple sick felt so hot against my leg I thought I'd been burnt and was instantly on my feet. I looked down at him, wiping his mouth with that handkerchief, and wanted to smash his mottled head. Mist drifted in through the smashed windows. The abandoned wheel creaked pitifully.

—Where's Malraux? I demanded.

—Someone coming, said Henri.

The wheelhouse door shuddered, the knob rattled, then frame and door both fell inward with a crash. Duc peered in at us.

—*Monsieur le directeur?* he said. Everything is broken.

I helped Henri to his feet, collected our topees from the corner then followed Duc down the stairs, of which only three remained. The morning sun was hotter than should have been possible, and a cadre of flies swarmed over my defiled boot and up to my face and ears, serving to distract me, if only vaguely, from the view: the topmost half of the *General Subrégis* lay nearly recognizable upon a shelf of rock stretching between river and forest, but the lower half had been pulverized against the boulders below.

Duc led us to the riverbank. Wreckage lay piled on the rocks as though some careless giant had dropped a deck of cards and a box of toothpicks. The mate, feet bloodied as he scaled the rocks, overturned one heap of boards after another.

—Captain? he shouted.

Planks swirled in the whirlpool and at first I failed to associate them with the *General Subrégis*. Deck passengers wrung out their garments and coughed, having been thrown into the eddy—Malraux had been right, the stern was the safest place.

—Only some drowned, they told us.

It was with something near ecstasy that I lay my eyes on the sticky-eyed infant and its mother as she sat nursing the child in the shade. Had I been a little more confident I would've obeyed my impulse to wrap them in my arms. Instead I stood fast beside Henri LeDallic.

—Where's that little Charton? he asked.

The natives laid the injured on the grass. They ripped clothes for bandages. One fellow sat at our feet with his hand pressed to his face and blood coursing down his arm. Those in better repair helped the mate bring down the new-found dead. After a quarter-hour we deduced that the crewmen in the holds, the stokers in the boiler room and the passengers in their cabins, including our Charton, had all been crushed to death or drowned. At any rate they would not be found without heavy equipment. Duc limped by, carrying the body of a loincloth'd old stoker whose head lolled like a rag doll's. They lay him out on the bank.

—The starboard screw had lost pressure, said the mate. That's an engineering error, that wasn't the captain's fault.

I have seen additional tragedies in Indo-China since the wreck of the *General Subrégis*, some bloodier, some more infuriating; none so infused with that dreamlike quality of normal existence being turned on its side by the fact that I was still alive. Not to say that the world was brighter, or smelled more sweetly— the sun beat down malevolently, for one thing—but it was as *different* as walking out of a dark matinee into the sunlight of two o'clock.

—How far to the nearest village? I asked.

—There is Kemmarat. Not far. Through these trees, then I think to the left.

—What should we bring back?

—Bearers, said Duc. Wagons. Water and food.

—How far a walk? asked Henri.

—I know the headman likes the French very much, you will not have any problems. A little whisky for the sick people.

He resumed climbing the rocks—an unlikely place to find the captain, I thought, but as Malraux was nowhere else I had nothing to suggest. The brush above us was wet with spray and I relished the idea of wiping the sick from my boot.

—Do you have your credentials, asked Henri, or were they locked in the trunk with mine?

With a start I thrust a hand into my pocket—yes, yes, the little oval frame was there, along with the odd scrap of paper. The '08–'14 ledger was lost, of course.

—Yes, here, I said. Crumpled.

I started uphill, picking my way over the slick branches but making headway over the rock, thinking again how little trouble it would have been to have dragged Charton up to the wheelhouse, though I reassured myself that for the sake of his Moï he'd have refused. I did not give the riverbank a parting glance—I wished the young mother to know we'd be gone only a moment.

—A corkscrew, said Henri. That's what I have.

We met a great tangle of black thicket and I bent double to hurry through, spiderwebs breaking across my face, then we strode between stands of creaking bamboo, brown lizards scattering before us among the leaves. I felt sure that whisky would be the very thing for our wounded, or, better still, the headman might offer soothing opium. With my newly minted functionary's mind I calculated the number of pipes we'd need to requisition.

—He told us go left, said Henri.

—Stay perpendicular to the river for now. The path will run parallel to it.

—You assume a logic within the Malay brain which may not be warranted.

—Good God, if you *must* call them—

—When my grandparents saw a photograph from the colonies they'd point and say 'Malays,' and I always felt that had great style.

Marks of bare toes lay in the dirt before us, and looking left and right I noted the undergrowth to be generally passable in either direction. French paths are more conspicuous as French pedestrians tend to wear shoes. I started to the left, grateful for the lack of scrub for the speed it allowed us, obviously, and because of an anecdote which had long lingered in the back of my mind and now flared like fireworks at the front. In Henri Baudesson's book a tiger makes his lair behind a fallen tree blocking a path, and after making the necessary detour one unsuspecting Moï after another has his skull polished clean by the cat's coarse tongue.

Next I realized that we hadn't a grain of quinine between us though rural Indo-China is malarial in its entirety. Just then we came to a tree across the path and my heart came up into my throat.

—Duck around it! said Henri. What's so mysterious?

The surrounding brush was not impassable or even thorny—indeed, the beginnings of a new path were already visible—yet I hesitated. Didn't the air possess a distinctive funk?

—We'll be *another* twenty-seven years and how old will your lady be then?

He darted past me, arms parting the branches with a sort of breaststroke. The white of his tunic disappeared, leaving me the noise of cracking boughs and his curses. But weren't those more branches breaking on the other side of the log?

I dove after Henri. The roots of the fallen tree rose well above my head and I found him meandering through this labyrinth of snaking wood and cobwebs, the ideal hideout for every reptile imaginable.

—Will these people be the sort who insist we have a drink? he asked.

—Hi! Who's that? a man's voice called.

—Heavens, a countryman of ours! said Henri. We'll have a heart-to-heart!

We rounded the great whorl of roots to find, breaststroking forward, my mirror image: a long-faced youngster in white. He put out his hand. He wore binoculars and had a cigarette in the corner of his mouth.

—Besançon, he said, of the Telegraphic Service! And here you are without a scrap of luggage—you must have porters stretched to the horizon!

We introduced ourselves somewhat shakily.

—Our steamer has crashed with great loss of life, I said. We're going for help.

—Good God, you're joking! Which boat?

—Now we're looking for goddamn Kemmarat-town, said Henri. But Kemmarat's gone up in smoke.

—But you're headed for Amnach! Not to worry, though, I carry a little of everything—blankets and beds, and carts to haul them. Where can I find these people?

—Straight back this way, said Henri, and—

Just then a bullock cart burst from the brush, the creature's hooves flattening the foliage while a black-turbaned driver flailed its hips. Besançon clicked his tongue and patted the beast's great hump of a shoulder; the wagon was loaded with tent poles, rolls of canvas and spools of copper wire.

—Our line's gone down somewhere in here, he said. Nothing's getting through between Vientiane and Saigon, so our regional director got me out of bed!

Another cart crashed by, loaded with pots, pans and tin cans that rolled with every bounce of the wheels.

—Got wine or brandy? asked Henri.

—I'm a teetotaller, said Besançon. Where did you come onto this path, will I spot it?

—You'll see, said Henri. We walk like a couple of club-footed elephants.

—Nonsense, I said, we'll lead you to the boat!

—No, you carry on to Amnach, said Besançon. You both look like death!

—Is that a Gitanes Maïs? asked Henri. Got any more?

—Take the packet, said Besançon. Amnach's not far, then you might carry on to Ban Din—that's your nearest telegraph. Hope I get the thing mended!

We passed one cart full of ladders and cables, then five others. I gave up inspecting their contents. After a minute we trudged out of the trees into open country where cicadas buzzed with determination and a hawk circled far overhead.

—First find a drink, said Henri. *Then* Adélie Tremier.

IF THE FANTASTIC CAN
SET OUR HEARTS RACING

Mme. Adélie Tremier.

ON HIS NEXT visit Bonheur resumed his lecture.

"... and some days you will feel much more yourself. Some *months* you may feel more yourself!"

Adélie regarded the great bed all around her. Its lace counter-pane. The carved bee surmounting each post.

"... you'll hear of a hundred remedies but I'm not going to dabble in any of those. When Nicolas first brought you to my rooms with Emanuel on the way, I said to myself, 'Here is a girl of uncommon will.' I've seen a farmer lose his arm in a block and tackle, couldn't provide for his children, so what did he do that winter? Grew it back again. Think of that! Have you been out of bed?"

"Not for a few days." Her hair had been tied into a smooth braid which lay like a dead thing on the pillow. "I thought I'd go down to the garden, but I can see the new leaves from here. See them?"

"Haven't they been changing the sheets every day?"

"They move me to the settee!" she said cheerily.

He took her temperature—and it must have been high, for he shook the thermometer in exasperation and replaced it under her tongue—then set the cold and ominous disc of the stethoscope upon her chest. By now her rattles and wheezes were audible to anyone who stepped inside the room, so through his miraculous instrument the gratings of her inflamed pleural layers must have sounded like milk cans falling down stairs. He leaned over her as he listened so that his forelock brushed her face.

She twisted her head away and studied the faithful objects of her bedside table: the carafe of mineral water, the coffee cups, the enamel cuspidor, sprigs of lavender in a jar, the hardbound copy of Thérèse of Lisieux, the untouched tin of ginger lozenges, the half-empty bottle of Vin coca Mariani, the charcoal sketch of a plane tree on a square of cardboard, the well-thumbed copy of de Maupassant, the watercolour sketch of her hands on the back of an envelope, the unopened pint of Garden of Eden Cure-All, the women on magazines looking down from their balloons and whispering *the world is vast, my friends, the world is vast.*

"It's progressing much too quickly." The doctor grimaced at himself in the high mirror. "You aren't used to lying around like a bale of hay. You need to concern yourself with something!"

"My benevolent societies?"

"No, I've told you, nothing so riotous. If you had a telephone up here you could decide what you wanted to hear on the *théâtrophone.* Last night my landlady and I listened to *The Merry Widow.*"

"Was it about me?"

"Are these paintings by Emanuel? They're quite good."

She sat up on her elbows.

"He's been told to apply at the École des Beaux-Arts and the Académie d'Italie when he turns twelve, and what's more his grandmother has agreed to wait! Shall I construct any other Byzantine plans? He'll be home in a minute, will you wait for him?"

"Well, don't plan a trip to the moon just to upset yourself when it doesn't come off—no, hang that, if you feel well enough I won't discourage you. There's a thing they call *spes phthisica,* 'the hope of the tubercular,' that means, which may have just commenced, considering the gleam in your eye. What are you smiling at?"

178

"FORGIVE MY tardiness," he said the next time. "A great many calls."

He took the chair beside the bed and felt her pulse.

"Your practice is improving?" she finally whispered.

"In leaps and bounds." He glanced at his wristwatch and adjusted his hold on her wrist. "The floodgates have opened now that Greffuhle can cope with his rheumatism. Every imaginable sort of friend, that man has, with every imaginable complaint."

Her arm set free, she dutifully undid the top three buttons of her nightgown then settled in to stare at the right-hand bee. She flexed the calf muscle in her left leg. And then the right. Whenever Bonheur set the stethoscope to her chest she was sure that he'd already done so three times that day, even if in reality three weeks had passed. It was not his listening that pained her so much as the ramifications of his listening. The stethoscope was her veteran waiting to heave her from the bridge.

As he took out the earpieces Bonheur swallowed hard. He tilted her head and peered into each eye. His lashes flickered as he gave a tight-lipped smile.

"Was that the sort of practice you imagined?" she rasped.

"What, Count Greffuhle? No. Never." He bent his head to write in his notebook. "You know, I bicycled down from Montrenard to come to college. Met your Nicolas. I only wanted to learn enough to be able to patch fishermen and potato farmers back together." He closed the notebook and opened his bag. "I've told you this at some time or other."

Adélie shook her head.

"No? I pedalled between the smokestacks to see these chalk-faced little souls dying for a gasp of oxygen without ever conceiving of such a thing, then I sat through a five-hour lecture where they took a litre of blood out of a corpse's neck but didn't give us the least indication of how to stitch together a hand that's gone through a thresher. There have been peaks and valleys, let me assure you."

"How did you pay the tuition?"

"Money my parents left me."

"An orphan who made his way in the world!" she rasped.

"Yes," he said flatly.

She missed the Bonheur who'd stumbled into her ball in his church-deacon's suit.

"I am too," she said. "But my boy won't be. I'll outlive him yet."

"Yes, perhaps you'll see a hundred." He filled a syringe and held it to the light. "But if you can take anything from my tale it's that even the simplest plans go wildly awry." He made the injection in the crook of her arm. "Wildly."

"Now tell me straight off, without your niceties. Are you optimistic?"

He looked down at her and gave his tight-lipped smile.

THREE MONTHS LATER Manu sat on the side of her bed, marching two lead soldiers—lately painted purple—across the back cover of *Mon Journal*'s most recent number.

"It is a lovely picture there, isn't it?" his mother rasped. "Who are they?"

"It's who I've been telling you about!" Manu drummed his heels against the side of the bed, jangling the spoons on her tray. "It's Carlino and his godmother—reunited!"

"But they'd never met before, you told me, and that was—"

"But with her arms out, I think, 'Oh, they've been reunited!'"

Her black eyes were very large as she studied the boy.

"How does the dancing bear figure in?"

"*He* hasn't been in it for months and months!" Manu dug a bayonet into the godmother's forehead, the better for that particular soldier to stand on his head. "Carlino lives in the mountains but his father has weak lungs and dies, so the grandmother says to Carlino that the greatest thing in life is to know one's godparents, provided *they* haven't died, so Carlino says goodbye to the gypsies and goes into the world to hunt for them."

He glanced at her, expecting to be asked to continue, but her eyes had closed.

"That seems like a hare-brained errand," she finally said.

"I thought so too, but not Carlino!"

"I wonder how you'd like to travel the world," his mother murmured.

Sabine hurried in, the hem of her gown dr[...]
fully across the carpet, while Henriette tiptoed[...]
hearty outdoor scent emanating from her cotton b[...]

"She's asleep, child," Sabine said softly. "Go lo[...]
until Isabelle calls."

Manu looked stricken. "*Are* you asleep?" he asked.

"No more than usual," Adélie murmured.

Collecting his things, Manu slid to the floor then tur[...]
kissed the air a half-metre from her florid cheek.

"Enjoy your supper," she whispered.

He marched out the door like an admiral of the navy.

"It's been *weeks*!" said Henriette. "You look rosy as a bus[...]
of apples!"

The women smiled, though they all knew that the spots on[...]
her cheeks, stoked by fiery bacilli and vivid as badly applied
rouge, bore no relation to blustery good health.

"My boy?" quavered Adélie.

"Yes?" he called from the corridor.

"*Wash your hands.*"

Henriette set a copy of *Le Matin* on the bed, folded open to an
interior page.

"If the house went up in flames I couldn't yell fire," rasped
Adélie.

"I've brought camphor cigarettes," said Henriette. "Lacheroy
announced today that Proust smokes them."

"Does Proust have tuberculosis?" asked Sabine.

"Oh, *no*," said Henriette. "Asthma."

"Do you wish to doze?" Sabine asked. "Don't lie there fretting. He told us he'd communicate the results of his conference
as soon as humanly possible."

Adélie lifted her head to allow her mother-in-law to savage
the pillow.

"Manu can come with me to Switzerland," whispered Adélie.

"What's this?" asked Henriette, forcing a smile as though they
were discussing seaside villas. "You have a line on a sanatorium?"

"The very best one, in Davos." Sabine stroked her daughter-
in-law's smouldering forehead—the fever hour had come on—

ickly crossed to the basin
...irector. He is speaking at
...he's achieved an unprece-
...use he refuses to take on any
...ng."

...ou, my dear," said Henriette.
...nodded.

...rom way over at the Sorbonne?"
...a culture of my sputum," rasped

...Switzerland. But how was Lourdes?"
...ed over your postcard but—"
...ays' travel in either direction." Sabine set
...ow. "She had a hemorrhage on the train
...he queue, and went into such decline that we
...days longer than planned. And to find a doctor in
...veryone in Lourdes needs a doctor."

...u go with an open mind," murmured Adélie. "Yet there
...e so many thousands, I asked, 'Holy Mary, how can I ask for
...nything when so many here suffer?'"

"But the Virgin reads every heart simultaneously!" insisted
Sabine.

"Did your Thérèse find serenity in a crowd?" Adélie asked.
"No. In solitude."

"You'd had such hopes," said Henriette.

"In that grotto where the crutches are left behind," said
Sabine, "I realized it's cripples who profit from the trip. So long
as they stay off their feet it does a cripple no harm to travel, but
for someone like Adélie, who is really *ill*? Suffice to say there are
no cuspidors left there. Doctor Bonheur has pinned his hopes
on Switzerland, but it seems to me that further travel would be
disastrous. Disastrous."

Adélie lifted her hand and scrutinized its green veins.

"Manu was very good about pushing my chair at Lourdes."

"That one will remain cheerful," said Sabine, "come what may."

They stared at the lamp. Through the open door a fly could be
heard circling Adélie's dressing room. She suddenly smiled.

"What did the Orientalist League discuss?"

Henriette rolled her eyes. "British influence in Palestine! Guérande talked so long his cigarette burned down to his fingers."

"Did you keep the notes? From when I was there?"

"Yes, *yes*! Marco has been very sorry to hear about your difficulties."

"I should like to look over that notebook."

"Oh," said Henriette, "would you? Ah—"

"I won't spit on it, dear. Not one infinitesimal drop."

"Why, the very *furthest* thing from my mind—my only thought was that it might not be *legible*! I shall make you a copy."

The maid Marie appeared in the doorway. Sabine strode across and received a small parcel in brown paper. Marie curtsied.

"From Bonheur!" Sabine lifted a vial from its wrappings and held the label to the light. "This is odd. 'Sixteen grains of opium, to be administered as required.'"

"Why should he send that?" Adélie shifted her head in order to squint up at Sabine. "I don't have diarrhea."

"What does his note say about Davos?" asked Henriette.

"There is no note," said Sabine.

When Adélie opened her eyes the lamp had been turned down. On the settee Henriette and Sabine sat silhouetted in a rectangle of light from the corridor—Sabine with her grey head in her hands, Henriette very erect with the vial cradled in her palm. A demitasse of coffee waited on Adélie's nightstand, and smelling its aroma she felt as content as when her mother had awoken her by wetly kissing her ears. Yet the other women looked as dour as statues at Père Lachaise.

"I know what it means," Sabine said. "It means he can do nothing else for her."

"I beg your pardon," Adélie whispered.

Henriette started at the voice from the dark. The vial dropped from her hands onto a cushion embroidered with doves.

"Do you know what he told me?" Adélie said blearily. "I have good news, I'd forgotten! Bonheur said I have amenorrhea."

"And—and what is that?" Henriette asked.

"It means the monthly visitor will not visit."

"Oh!"

"I suppose that's good," said Sabine.

"One less job for Marie," rasped the patient.

After they'd gone Adélie turned up the lamp and reached for Henriette's *Le Matin*, while a moth beat itself senseless between the window-shade and glass.

· "Nothing could be more salubrious to the lungs," ran the article atop the page, "than the pure air enjoyed in the course of sea-voyaging and foreign travel." The author then claimed that the life of a consumptive might be prolonged *indefinitely* by some years' residence in warm climes. Adélie guessed the piece might be a cunning advertisement for the Messageries Maritimes until it grew suddenly pessimistic: "The female patient's happiness is more intimately blended with tender associations of home, however, and the sacrifice of these when her body is infirm cast a shadow over her health." Ah, yes, but what if those tender associations were to stride at her side, sketching palm trees by the thousand?

After dinner Adélie read the article a half-dozen more times before nonchalantly dropping the paper for Marie to spirit away alongside the shell of a soft-boiled egg, then her mind's eye roved once again over that vast painting she and Nicolas had seen at the Universal Exhibition, showing children sleeping in a spring amongst swans. She became drowsy herself just as the unfortunate moth succeeded in beating itself to death.

In the morning Marie carried the cuspidor and bedpan away without meeting Adélie's eyes. The mistress called her back, though, to make a quiet request, and a few minutes later goose-faced Isabelle appeared with her fountain pen and bottle of ink to jot down Adélie's message to the lawyer: would he stop at the house at his earliest convenience in order to undertake certain financial arrangements?

"My father *recovered* from consumption," said Isabelle as she blotted the page.

"Did he?" Adélie whispered.

"I never said so before? By breathing over a pan of maggoty

beef! I'll set a piece aside, Madame, and fetch it up for you when it's rank."

"FATHER CHILDEBERT asked after you," Sabine purred. "He wishes to come up soon."

"Have him come," rasped Adélie. "Provided he's not bent on discussing last rites or funerals."

"But that's precisely what he wants."

"I've no use for those things. Set him ladling in our soup kitchen."

"Which reminds me." Sabine picked dead fronds from the fern and dropped them in the grate. "I opened a letter from the Anti-Penury League by mistake. They say that despite your years of good works and leadership you've been stricken from the membership roll as you haven't paid the 1909 dues. Ridiculous, considering. Shall I send a cheque on your behalf?"

"I'd prefer," whispered Adélie, "that you hand the money to the first hungry child you pass in the street."

"Of course. I'll write Isabelle a cheque to cash. You've also had a letter from the Messageries Maritimes. I'll set it here. No doubt they're also soliciting memberships."

Adélie raised herself feebly on her elbows, then dropped again.

"But let me draw the curtains," said Sabine. "Your fever will come on soon."

She stayed in the corner with her back to her daughter-in-law.

"What can I do for him in the time left?" Adélie whispered, throat full of ashes.

Sabine dropped to her knees beside the bed, and Adélie guessed that her mother-in-law would end another conversation with yet another rambling prayer, but instead Sabine fastened wet eyes upon her and grasped her white hands.

"Be still now. Forget about St-Lucien. I don't want that anymore."

"My boy's life can't be like those others'!" rasped Adélie.

"I only want to see him grow to be a man. Have children of his own."

"*Only* that?"

Adélie dropped her head onto the pillow. Tears slipped toward her ears.

"If I go away," she said, "I will come back."

"Be still now," Sabine murmured from the counterpane.

Then the grand lady raised her regal head, eyes still wet, nose dripping, yet did not produce her handkerchief, which struck the younger widow as signally heroic.

"If I can *prop up* my body," Adélie said as she rolled over, "I might—"

But then a quantity of yellow-streaked mucus seized its opportunity.

THE LAST
OF PARIS

Mme. Adélie Tremier.

OR DAYS beforehand her legs had felt swollen with a thousand Lissner dyes so that she could have been drained, had any enterprising soul had the will, to colour the resplendent frocks of Julia Cahen Astruc and Monique d'Anvers. Yet on the perfect end-of-August morning that she swallowed back whatever had risen from her chest and suggested an expedition in the chair, the swelling had actually subsided enough for her to fold her legs beneath her. She felt nimble as a dancer!

"It may relieve the pressure," she whispered. "Where shall we go?"

"Théâtre Guignol!" said Manu, hopping from one foot to the other.

"But which one?"

"Luxembourg Gardens!"

"I'm sure you're too old for *that*."

Yet he ran to his own room to change from his pyjamas into the expedition clothes. With a comparable spring in her step Marie threw open Adélie's wardrobe and lifted out the riding coat the mistress wore during trips around the garden.

"More substantial," rasped Adélie. "Where's the travelling cloak from Lourdes?"

"So much, Madame? It's to be a fine warm day."

"And a scarf and gloves."

"Of course, we'll pile you with rugs."

"Only one. The clothes must be substantial."

And so, after being washed, Adélie was dressed in pearl-buttoned blouse, woollen skirt, waistcoat, cardigan and riding coat as well as her various underthings. With a timid rap at the door Mauriac entered, tie stuffed in his morning-coat pocket, and waited for the young mistress's nod before lifting her from the bed and carrying her along the corridor, down the grand staircase, across the echoing foyer and so out to the street and the carriage, horses, nine-year-old boy and iron wheelchair with bamboo ornaments that together waited there. Adélie now weighed forty kilograms and in truth Mauriac could have carried her twice over. Marie, under a severe black hat, piled her with rugs then perched attentively on the backward-facing seat should the mistress signal for another.

"You've no sketchbook," whispered Adélie.

"I'll watch Guignol with all my might," Manu announced. "He always makes me feel I've missed something. He tells us what he's doing, but all the time he has a plan."

"Those wooden eyes never blink."

It might be said that Marie watched her like a hawk if only hawks were more single-minded and intense. The carriage rocked forward, gently, gently at first.

"There's a cuspidor behind Madame's cushion," murmured Marie.

Months had passed since Adélie had been abroad in the city, yet the posters on the boulevard kiosks hadn't changed: a moustached and cockaded officer recruiting for the army; the boastings of various newspapers; a thick-necked soprano appearing at the Opera; brand names of soaps and cigarettes. But now there were more automobiles, perhaps one for every thirty carriages, their drivers in goggles and scarves, merrily beeping at each other and waving to passersby, the cars' elegant frameworks sputtering through life just as she did. A vegetable market spilled out from the sidestreet, a card advertising black bananas at fifteen centimes a kilogram. In Laos they'd fall yellow and perfect from the tree.

"Everything is a parade," said Manu.

The previous autumn this might have been a gay remark from the child in the straw boater, but beneath his cloth cap he spoke with new-found solemnity. It had been months since Eugène or anyone else had come to the house—well, and wouldn't she have forbidden it if she was Eugène's mother?

"Do sit back, Madame," said Marie. "There'll be drafts off the river."

Though the windows were shut she gave each pane a fastidious shove. Mauriac clicked his tongue and flicked the whip to guide his horses between the pedestrians and onto the Pont Neuf. Beneath them excursion boats steamed up the grey Seine, their coloured lamps sparkling in the sunshine, and Adélie smiled despite herself to think that when the boats' flat roofs would be piled with snow she and Manu would be far away.

The Luxembourg Gardens swarmed with families bent on enjoying themselves while the season allowed, and Manu bumped his mother's chair up the gravel paths with a zeal he hadn't demonstrated at Lourdes.

"Mind this grey pony," rasped Adélie.

"Mind the droppings!" called Marie.

They rounded a copse of trees and came upon the Théâtre Guignol, its red-satin roof already flapping from its pulleys, its benches nearly at capacity, the occupants of the front three rows cuffing the backs of each other's heads—and so sending straw boaters flying—in anticipation of Borgne Baigne's comeuppance. The back rows were filled with anxious little ones on the laps of mothers and governesses.

"Why don't you sit up beside me, Maman?"

"I can lean back," Adélie whispered. "It's better for me."

She dared not raise her voice lest she reveal herself to the maternal audience as not just a feckless cripple but a dire consumptive, to be rolled into exile by the sword-wielding bathroom attendants. But her cheeks felt so hot, surely they—ah, Manu chewed his nails with excitement like the rest!

Suddenly the red curtains of the little theatre flew open and there stood Guignol himself, his burgundy coat flecked with brass buttons, black hair tied back in a ribbon, his long head square as a brick. The front three rows sat absolutely still.

"I'm so happy to see you all!" called the puppet.

Manu studied his mother for a moment, his mouth in a tight knot, then returned his gaze to Guignol as he flitted about the stage like a squirrel.

"So much to do today—do *you* remember what needs to be done? Pick up the cows' eggs, shear the hens—"

"No, no!" shouted the first three rows.

Manu smiled and Adélie saw his molars had gone yellow—they could buy tooth powder on the way home, certainly, but he'd have to make it last until they returned from Laos. Though who could say what the spring might do for one's teeth?

Mother Bigoudis appeared—looking like a wooden Sabine with her hair in a bun, her grey dress surmounted with lace—and squabbled amicably with Guignol. Then each raced from the stage in pursuit of their own agenda. Out of sight a harpist produced a trill of lighthearted notes, then a dark, trembling melody. The little ones threw arms around their mothers' necks. Borgne Baigne stalked onstage in a patched coat, his bald head bruised and battered, and glared out at the children from beneath his black brow.

"I escaped from prison," he gloated, "now I'm looking for a place to stay. Maybe you have room at your house? Show me your hands!"

A flurry from the front rows.

"Drop those hands!" snarled the convict. "Let me see your feet."

He stalked off just as brass-buttoned Guignol rushed onstage carrying a cudgel larger than himself.

"And children," the hero warned, "if you see the thief you must scream loudly for Guignol, understand?"

Borgne Baigne crept up behind him, bent on mayhem, but the gallant members of the audience leapt to their feet *en masse*, pointing and screaming—with the exception of Manu, who leapt to his feet only to study the unfolding drama with his chin between his fingers—until Guignol finally understood and turned to beat the villain insensible. He threw his weapon down and applauded the audience's vigilance. Mother Bigoudis appeared to embrace the hero, all pettiness suddenly behind them.

Though he was an old man of nine Manu stood cheering with the rest. The status quo had been restored, after all, thieves and cudgels had been laid to rest and everyone would sleep in their own beds. The first three rows cleared out immediately so as to throw one another into the pond. Mothers and governesses gripped the little ones' hands and helped them step precariously from bench to bench.

Mauriac steered them home via the Pont Royal. On the left bank bowler-hatted men buzzed around the booksellers' stalls, scanning a few lines of each book, moving on to the headline of *Le Figaro* or *Mois Parisien* or even *Culotte Rouge*—what was the sense in such fluttering, when life was so short?

"I should like these clothes left out overnight," rasped Adélie. "To recall the day we've spent. Leave Manu's over his chair."

The boy bit his white lip.

"I still think Guignol wasn't telling something."

ADÉLIE LIT ONE candle, then, much abetted by strong and silent furniture, made her way across to shut her door so that the pale light should not flicker in the corridor. As she gripped the knob she found her chest heaving and mucus rattling in her throat, though only because she was sobbing. She did not have the strength to carry herself to Laos, much less Manu too, yet she would not make an orphan as her own mother had!

To her relief she found her fingers as capable with buttons and clasps as they'd ever been, though the arrogant blouse had pearl buttons up the *back*—some kind soul in a Gare de Lyon powder room might fasten her up, she hoped, and in the meantime three other layers would cover her spine. Manu might have helped but she wanted him to sleep until the final moment, lest he cry for his grandmother when Adélie explained their plans. Only when the waistcoat was buttoned did she realize the blouse might have been worn backwards—what did she care whether it was, if she was already throwing her life away? But perhaps a backwards blouse would call greater attention to her fugitive status than burning cheeks or even haemoptysis—first-class travellers were not expected to recognize *tuberculosis,* after all, they were expected to read the fashion magazines!

There was nothing technically difficult about putting her arms into the coat, but the manoeuvres entailed were utterly debilitating. By the time she'd heaved the tailored shoulders over herself she had to scramble for the cuspidor, and an instant after the blood swirled in the bottom she was sprawled across the bed, face-down while dressed for travel like a fortunate train-wreck survivor, *thrown clear onto a goose-down mattress!*

She awoke in the dark. The candle had burnt down. She lit another and saw by the clock that it was nearly five. The train went at eight. She slipped her feet into the boots without lacing them, then tied hand towels around them to dull their clatter on marble stairs she'd once descended as Sultana Tremier. But first she lay down to await a cough; after so many months such cacophony from her room wouldn't cause an eyelid to flicker, but echoing from the foyer it would bring the household on the run. She suddenly saw herself returning north to Paris, her coffin locked in a baggage car.

She awoke coughing, her hairline dripping sweat. She saw by the guttering candle that it was past six. She saw that she had hand towels tied around her feet.

She crept down the corridor without so much as a valise in her hand. She stopped to rest against the new sideboard before taking the additional step and grasping Manu's doorknob. Without a sound she swung open his door.

A sliver of wan daylight lay across her boy's cheek. He breathed silently through his nose, though his head was twisted backward on the pillow as though he'd sat up only to collapse again. Over the bed he'd tacked a watercolour of a rosebush that could not have been improved if he'd studied in Vienna for ten years. His fingers trembled on the blanket as he dreamed.

And as she watched those restless fingers Adélie changed her mind.

She hardly knew where she was going or how she'd survive from one hour to the next once she arrived. If she did not expire on the way and leave him alone mid-ocean, she would likely die in Indo-China to leave the boy ten thousand kilometres from home. For Manu she needed to go on living, but she had no right to take him.

His clothes waited expectantly across the chair.

She did not walk any nearer. She was too contagious to kiss him goodbye.

She sat on the first step to begin her long descent to the foyer. Tears ran down either side of her nose. Her behind dropped silently from one marble step to the next; the high arched windows reflected across each.

On the hall table she found stationery and a pencil, scrawled a note, then folded the page and wrote *Emanuel* on the back.

At bedtime Manu had been absorbed in festooning trains with flags, but he'd marched in distractedly to kiss the air, as tradition dictated, a half-metre from her cheek.

"Good night, Maman," he'd said. "Don't cough too much."

And she'd long remember these phrases while he, poor boy, would be left wondering what he'd last said to his mother. If she recovered she would write to tell him, and if she did not then let that note be the end.

My darling, I must go away. You must believe that I can do or think nothing but what springs from my love for you.
Maman.

Through the gate she looked back at the house's high windows, its balconies, its chimney smoke dispersing into the dawn sky. His was the fourth window from the left on the second storey. Perhaps at that moment he was waking from the dream, calling for her, and she truly felt well enough to climb back up those stairs and slip beneath the sheet with him, her cold cheek upon his warm one. But perhaps it was her mind only telling her she was well—her spirit, even, to draw Monsieur Roux's distinction. The chimney smoke meant that at any moment Isabelle might slip from the kitchen door on some errand. Was that a light in the dining room?

She lifted her fingers from the gate and began to walk with great deliberation toward the boulevard and its cabs bound for the Gare de Lyon. Balancing the contents of her lungs in a champagne flute, she drew infinitesimal breaths.

She carried her money and papers in her coat pocket; in Marseilles she would buy anything else the journey required. She *had* to travel austerely, she would tell anyone who inquired, because she was hurrying to the side of her ailing father who was in the clutch of paroxysm. She paused beneath the gaslight to catch her breath and reminded herself that ordering a cab would have been pure folly. Yet the boulevard, five houses distant, was unattainable. A rag wagon heaped with rotten blankets creaked past.

When she boarded the *Salazie* in Marseilles she would declare, perhaps even describing in detail a road under construction on the Island of Khône, that she was joining her husband at last.

THE MESSAGERIES MARITIMES office in Marseilles loomed as vast and solid as a bank. She was still in France, of course, but outside the doors palm trees swayed and the air that settled in her nostrils was rich with spices and sea foam. She sat in a borrowed wheelchair and wrote her name in the register. The attendant across the table was so leathery he might have been raised on a date farm.

"Do you wish to book . . . a return voyage?" he asked.

She felt the heat in her cheeks as plainly as if candles were being held to them, and despite the long-rehearsed shallow breaths up her nose she didn't doubt that the clatter in her lungs could be heard in the manager's office. Perhaps on his farm the attendant had actually *seen* tuberculosis.

"Not just now," she whispered.

He folded her tickets but did not immediately hand them back.

"Leukemia is not contagious," she blurted.

His face fell. Adélie knew only that leukemia was a disease of the blood—*could* it be contagious?

"Of course not, Madame! But once you're aboard I'll have the doctor introduce himself."

Sure enough, a white-tunic'd doctor, lean as a whippet, hurried into her cabin just as the steward wheeled her to a stop between bed and vanity. A stethoscope protruded from his hip pocket—aboard ship they evidently took their roles seriously.

"I'm Turgot," he intoned. "I'll only be a moment, Claude."

The steward set a mahogany stool beside her chair then sprang into the corridor.

"Leukemia, eh, Madame? Unfortunate." The doctor must have attended a college where diagnoses were obtained by scrutinizing one's toecaps. "Who attended you prior to this, might I ask?"

She rolled her glove down from her elbow while gazing covetously at the bed.

"Doctor Bonheur of Paris," she whispered.

In the corridor, trunks scraped against metalwork and men laughed heartily, but she knew all that would sound quiet as snowfall if Doctor Turgot were to press his stethoscope to her chest.

"Bonheur? Ah," he said, not raising his head. "In any case we'll endeavour to make you most comfortable. You see the bell-pull?"

He helped her onto the bed then went out and shut the door, reducing the noise of the corridor to an intermittent grating. Her eyelids slammed shut like furnace doors. She still wore her boots and one black glove, but the power of *spes phthisica* had deserted her so entirely that even now she couldn't remember which hand wore the glove. Yet something roused her, forced her eyes to open—Lord, there was no cuspidor!

Ah, but the lilies could come out of that vase.

THAT NIGHT she was woken by the baby bawling from its room. Why didn't Suzanne go to the poor child? Adélie threw the blankets back, sprang to the floor and, astonishingly, felt it tilt beneath her. She'd never heard him so angry—could he be as hungry as all that? Her breasts did not feel ready. Not at all. A dull roar echoed through the house. She staggered forward until her fingertips touched the metal doorframe, then all at once she knew where she was and that the child crying so near at hand was not Manu. Would never be Manu—not for a long time.

THE
RUINED TEMPLE

Pierre Lazarie.

WE DID not come immediately to Amnach. Instead there were fields, punctuated by an occasional stricken-looking tree with the inevitable buffalo beneath it, its tail shooing flies like a pendulum ticking off our days—such was the timbre of my thoughts.

—We must go back to the boat, I said. We've been away too long.

The sun rapped upon our helmets and though my legs believed the path grew steeper it was inexorably flat. Sweat sat so thickly upon my face I might have been peering out from inside an aquarium.

—Never, Henri grunted. The hero Besançon has that in hand. And what's more I've seen them buzzing around this country like flies, and gruesome as it may have been to see those Malays gouged up I can't help but wonder how ten or fifteen could possibly be missed. Across Indo-China at this moment there are boys in their thousands falling off buffaloes to drown in paddy-fields, and though it grieves me deeply I can't rush a life-preserver to each one, can I?

—What would be the point in doing what she did? I asked.

—Why would Madame Tremier sit and talk to Quinn for fifteen minutes? I thought about that and realized she was physically incapable of running away.

—But what do we know with certainty? Quinn said she intended to go up into Laos and live *forever*, if we—

—Before I run out of breath I ought to point out that your academic mind is making a nine-course meal of that story of Quinn's even though you've only Quinn's word that it's true. If that's the vanguard of French thinking I'll weep tears of blood!

—How is it you haven't run out of breath already?

—You haven't heard of Ban Din whisky? This won't be the first time good whisky has made me forget Paternina Gran Reserva, once in Cho Lon—

—But what did the dear woman imagine would *become* of her? It's only people's intentions we can second-guess—what happens in the end is beyond their control. The fact that we're walking to Amnach without a sip of water is proof positive of that.

—It'd be worth living forever, said Henri, to have more conversations like this.

—Well, the *other* thing that occurred to—

—I'll slash your throat straight across, you wait and see.

The path took us up a rise of crumbling rock, and if there hadn't been saplings to grasp, Henri would have capsized. Yet the stubborn ox never begged a rest. The branches over our heads appeared as a lacework of shadows at our feet.

—These trails were made for smaller men, he said. Every species develops to perfection in its own place, yes? I may be the apex of Darwinian creation but this was not the place in which I developed.

I needn't go into detail describing how thirsty I was at that point; suffice to say I coveted the sweat at the corners of my mouth.

Finally we ran up against a gate of horizontal rails. Henri slid the top three from their holes in the post and stepped nimbly over the lower two.

—I expected a hinge, I said.

At our feet fresh cow droppings, perfectly liquid, lazed in the sun. The forest disappeared, replaced on either side by overgrown vegetable patches, the fences thick with creepers.

A farmer in a black loincloth sat in the shade, machete in one hand and half of a pink-fleshed melon in the other. As I tried to guess the dialect in which to best frame a greeting he murmured a few words then held up the melon, its syrup coursing between his fingers. Lust must have been apparent in our eyes, for he bisected it with one neat stroke and we clamped the quarter-sections over our faces, swallowing pulp and seeds without discretion. The farmer's smile revealed large square teeth.

—Ask him if he's got onions, said Henri.

—*Hua phák bua?* I asked in Lao.

The farmer huffed a reply, then disappeared over the fence with a bound.

—Just wait, said Henri. We'll teach these people sophistication.

A breeze rippled the creepers; the sun was finally dipping toward the horizon. Three hawks circled high overhead and farther down the path dogs set to yapping. Considering the events of the day I felt calmer and more refreshed than ought to have been possible. A triangular shrine on a fencepost offered rice-balls to Lord Gautama.

The farmer reappeared with a handful of tear-shaped golden onions. Henri pulled three half-cent coins from his trouser pocket and jangled them in his palm.

—I won't haggle! That's what I have.

He dropped the coins in the dirt, seized the onions from the farmer's hand and strode off down the path. Rather than associate for another minute with a walking signboard that read BOORISHNESS, my instinct was to lay beside the fence and consume an infinite number of melons. Yet if this *was* Ban Din there would be telegrams to send, clothes to wash, our damsel to retrieve. The farmer bent to collect his coins and I pointed meaningfully at the ground.

—Ban Din? I asked.

—Kong Lom.

He placed a coin in the shrine. The dogs barked with renewed fervour and I hurried after Henri, suddenly afraid lest he come to some harm.

After a paddock of cattle hung with clanging wooden bells, huts appeared, efficacious matrons sweeping their porches with twig brooms, and the whining dogs who'd escorted me into the village receded into the shadows. I realized what a glorious place this Kong Lom was, with its naked children herding ducks and a pink-flowered frangipani tree framing each roof. And here was Henri, walking unsteadily up the street behind a tall monk in a flame-coloured robe.

—Hurry! he called. I've found their representative of the Chamber of Commerce!

The sound of energetic chopping drifted from the kitchens, children with infants tied to their backs raced in every direction and the smell of cooking rice wafted over all. It struck me as preposterous that only the evening before we'd visited Leit Tuhk, the last twilit village Charton would ever know.

The further I sauntered, the more villagers stopped cold, in the local fashion, after only just resuming what they'd been engaged in before Henri had walked by. Most men affected nonchalance but the careworn women were less subtle, frantically herding black goats out of sight or freezing, mid-stroke, in the act of chopping wood—perfectly posed, it seemed to me, for the Colonial Exhibition of 1931's artful dioramas.

Sweeping each wide step as he ascended, the monk led us into a building which caused my poor pulse to beat even harder: a weather-beaten Buddhist *sim*. Either side of the red-tiled roof swept nearly to the ground in the Luang-Prabang style and I recognized the deathless characters of the *Ramayana* in the latticework of each window. But why were there no other monks, no freshly shorn novices, no bent elders who ought to have been chanting the twilight in at that very moment? Stepping onto the tile I saw that much of the roof and far wall had been destroyed by fire, including the platform where the Buddha's image must have rested. The air was sour with creosote.

—Tell him he can bring whisky now, said Henri.

The monk beckoned us toward a side door. Henri sat down heavily.

—Tell him to hurry, man! I'm not long for this world.

Outside, the monk led me down a path, barely discernible among the vines, to a bamboo outbuilding where he showed me a bucket of water. He mimed scrubbing his face, and though I must have known the Lao for "wash" at one time I was too exhausted to recall it. He pointed to a yellow robe on a peg, and without any sense of nostalgia for that particular linen suit I stripped naked. Collecting my foul clothes, the monk left me to my ablutions. I dropped the portrait into my boot.

In a temperate clime the wash-water might've been considered tepid, but to my roasted skin it felt absolutely glacial and therefore sublime. Dousing my every corner, I allowed my ears to fill with the murmur of a stream somewhere down the hill, calling night-birds, and myriad insects' thrum.

Then with the yellow robe about me like a cumbersome apron, I convinced myself that I'd lost the path in the gloom until I looked up to see a whitish glow and recognized the ruined roofline. I hurried in to find Henri dancing a sort of polka around an oil lamp.

—You look dressed for a birthday party! he said. Have you brought the whisky?

—What? No, of course not, I don't intend to—

—Look, the Chamber of Commerce brought blankets so we can sleep right on the ground like in an imperial palace! And my Malay must be improving because I'm sure he told me he'd bring food—in fact I felt sure that by the time I got back we'd have it.

—Why, where did you go?

—To find the headman! Back up the boulevard and up the hill. He's got a tumbledown porch twice as big as his neighbour's. And a wonderful little boy there, he kept showing me a chicken head he had under his bowl, *peep, peep,* a little devil he was, a little beggar! And they aren't Moï here, no, I know that because he brought a lot of bottles out instead of a jar, and I wouldn't mind a little rice now to settle my stomach. That's the only reason I ran back.

He finally stood still. Moths of every colour and size hovered over the lamp, and several dozen, singed, dragged themselves across the tile. With a hop he crushed them.

—And whisky's called *lao Lao*, he said. You might have told me!

—I didn't know it. In our seminar we—

—And he brought pots! I can make my soup now!

—Most likely they're to wash in.

He drew the onions from his pocket and sat in the circle of light. I set my wet boots before the lamp, where they were instantly festooned with moths. Henri flicked open a clasp-knife.

—Left to me by the late, lamented Beyle.

—You never said he was dead.

—Gone from *this* world. Abandoning his opportunity to bed down in that rarest of things, a shack too rotten even for a Malay.

With a ponderous *clack, clack* he sliced his onions. I squinted to examine the wall's spirited depictions of the Buddhist Hell, with demons slicing tongues from bound victims, tugging off noses, tying offenders to trees to be impaled by elephants or throwing them to grinning tigers or into vats of boiling oil. The painting may have been centuries old but the demons still relished their work, especially the big-eared devil proffering the lottery bag out of which punishments were allotted, and I couldn't help but wonder how I'd select to be dispatched were I honoured with the choice.

—There! said Henri. Into the pot. And now for a little water.

—What are you trying to make?

—Why, onion soup *à la* Continental Palace Hotel! By the heat of the lamp!

—But we've no butter!

He had just risen, and froze, pot in hand, on the balls of his feet.

—Couldn't we find some?

—We'd find our Adélie sooner!

He brought his arm back and flung the pot out into the night, flecks of onion trailing after it like the tail of a comet. He collapsed onto his blanket.

—How can a fellow survive without butter? We ought to have colonized Denmark—the Danes wouldn't have made a fuss!

Suddenly the monk set down a pot of rice and plate of fried fish, pressed his hands into the *wái* and withdrew without a word. Henri and I ate quickly and methodically, forever waving away insects, until all that remained were thin bones and rice burnt to the pot. This Henri attacked with his clasp-knife, and it took me a moment to recall why the act should seem so alarming.

—The M'nong insist that scraping a pot with a knife invites disaster.

—Our riverboat smashed to kindling, for example?

He scraped merrily, extricating a brown crust now and then to crunch between his molars. I heard soft footfalls on the steps and expected our monk to reappear in the halo, but with a start I saw it was a young woman, carrying my suit over her arm. She wore a neat patterned skirt and, draped over her shoulders, a simple scarf which stayed in place for no reason I could ascertain. Yet though I stole countless glances as she darted over the tiles, I was unable to glimpse a bare breast. She lay the garments over a drooping length of rafter, and, catching my eye, wrung the jacket-sleeve to show it was damp. Then she hurried down the steps. Henri leaned back on the heel of his hand.

—So tomorrow I'll wallow in rags while you go about like the Emperor at Hué.

He sat smoking while I studied a mural of Gautama's reincarnations, and quite despite myself my imaginings took a sordid turn as I mounted the girl amongst chicken droppings and circling dogs, staring down rapturously at her silken forehead, and out of sheer embarrassment my academic brain constructed a metaphor. She was Indo-China and I France, and though as colonizer I could rest assured of my own pleasure I had to *assume* she was enjoying herself despite all evidence to the contrary—which had been the ministry's policy, after all, since 1868.

I rolled over on my blanket. What would my Adélie think of such depravity? Outside, murmuring villagers drifted past in the dark and a gong repeated two slow beats, *dong, dong,* followed by four—these more rapid—*ding-ding-ding-ding.* The odour of creosote and Gitaines Maïs was disrupted by a waft of the evening's perfume.

—My father smoked these, said Henri. The smell of the corn husk is distinctive, don't you think? My first ten years here they weren't available, then I smelled one in the street and vomited. Look here.

He climbed stiffly to his feet and bent so the lamp lit one side of his face. He tapped the side of his neck—a neat round scar.

—That was a Gitaines Maïs. He said he'd show me once and for all, though I can't remember what exactly. I don't believe I'm going to vomit so that proves I'm now a healthy, forward-thinking man—not the child anymore, am I?

With a flick of his wrist he extinguished the lamp, and in that sudden darkness the bewildered moths cascaded over me. I pulled the blanket to my ear. Then I couldn't help but consider the deck passengers of the *General Subrégis* and wonder if Besançon had managed to transport them to Kemmarat-town as promised, and if so, what each of them might be thinking themselves as they lay in the dark. Then, through a haze of near-sleep, I heard the rustle of blankets.

—I'm going to see the headman, whispered Henri.

THE PALACE AT
LUANG-PRABANG

Mme. Adélie Tremier.

FROM THE last boat—of how many, five?—
swaying up the Mekong to the cadence of
its oarsmen, water throbbing beneath like
some hydraulic contrivance invented solely to keep her alive,
Adélie was lifted by many hands to a litter, gingerly set beneath
its canopy and onto its cushions as though upon a funeral bier,
and so carried beneath the palms and uphill as effortlessly as a
twig in a stream, past thatch huts all a-tremble on bamboo stilts.

"This is the lower gate," a man informed her in French, "of the
Royal Palace."

"Of what country?" she asked. Could he even hear her?

"Of Laos, my dear. This is the Royal Palace at Luang-Prabang."

Her head rolled onto its side, and through the gauze curtains
she discerned thick walls of whitewashed mortar which made
her think of Holland though she'd never been to Holland.

"Soon you will have your audience," the voice told her.

TINY LIZARDS trafficked the white mouldings. With her neck
over a triangular pillow that allowed her to gaze at nothing but
that space where the wall met the ceiling, Adélie was unable
to ascertain how many women had been assigned to her head-
lifting detail; it may have been one, with dry hands strong as
pliers, or it may have been a dozen. Rolling her eyes to the top of

her head Adélie could glimpse teak floors on which distant windows reflected as white, wavering rectangles. But she did not *like* to lie with her eyes rolled back in her head—she imagined the horror with which Manu, for instance, might regard her.

Yet it was a relief to be off the Mekong. Through her veil and lowered lashes she had been aware of the tops of great trees sailing past, and staring at her canary-yellow gloves over the course of days she'd watched black spots of mildew form on the fingertips and spread onto her palms. And while she'd been able to sit up she had written her son. *We have tied up for the night; the sound of the jungle is of an untuned orchestra.* And each time she'd ended, *Not long now, my love,* though her hand had become increasingly spidery. They had carried her ashore to sign some mule-headed document and grimace at a riverside official who couldn't raise his eyes to her, stealing minutes from her evaporating life, and the worst of seeing the cavorting denizens of dry land was trying to fix Manu in her mind's eye, for within her weary brain he was still every age he'd ever been. Two brothers on a dock playing with a tin bucket, a tiny girl hurried by her granny out of oxcart traffic, an infant in a sling. Just as Lepape's mirrors had multiplied her in pantaloons and turban, so her son stalked every corner of the world simultaneously. And when she'd become too weak to sit up she had merely stared at the pitch smeared between the planks of her cabin's ceiling. Her only demand then had been for her evening bath, and in this she was aided by a party of novice nursing sisters bound for Xieng Khoung. "You'll be washing corpses," she'd said each time, "so practice on me." Two of the nuns had even laughed. Starved for levity.

Now in the palace a teacup would be placed in her hand and, if she could signal her intent by folding fingers around the porcelain, then her head would be lifted, even her hand and the cup would be lifted, and she would drink. The tea tasted of dark earth, subtly different from the iron tang of blood which loitered around her back teeth. But each time she drank she fell asleep to awaken with an ache through her body for the simple reason that she had *stopped*, because the sustenance of voyaging was no longer hers. And before she could return to Manu she would have to move farther from him, farther still, while that perilously shaped pillow smelled too much of wash mornings and candle smoke.

In the palace the only voices she heard were from outside, chanting not discernible syllables but a sound hand-drills might produce as they bored through an oak. If anyone were to so much as whisper in Adélie's ear she would be sure to ask them what it meant. People came and went from her side but their steps were inaudible; the room, in short, was populated with spirits and genies. They circulated through the tea-kettle-humid air of the Royal Palace specifically to take her measure so they might know what to expect when she came across to their dominion.

The instant someone whispered in her ear she'd have them post the letters she'd written Manu while she'd been able to sit up, *Not long*, in her spidery hand, then she would dictate another to this unmet benefactor, and so feel that she was moving again. *Their chanting is increasingly mysterious; were you here I'd set you to investigate.*

Now her scrutiny of the moulding was interrupted by a dark-brown form—from its thin and pendulous breasts Adélie guessed it was a woman stripped to the waist. Her hair was short as a soldier's and so thin that patches of black skin were visible on her scalp. She danced on the balls of her feet, clearly enthralled by the spectacle that Adélie Tremier presented with her chin pointed at the ceiling. She'd have profited by a gingham apron over her elaborate sarong, for her nipples were as long as thumbs.

"*Sabai di*," the woman said, and pressed her palms together.

The upside-down face broke into a black-toothed grin.

"*Sabai di ba?*" it asked.

Then there was soft chatter all around them and fine-boned young women appeared on Adélie's left and right, hair fixed atop their heads with golden clasps, their tawny shoulders bare above chemises of turquoise, gold, vermilion—they might have modelled in a Lissner shop.

"Mán yu sai?" the old woman asked the mannequins, but none seemed to know the answer. The old woman waved her arm to dismiss them and one of her lolling breasts struck Adélie on the side of the head.

"Owp!" the woman laughed. She patted Adélie's hand, still curved around its teacup, and skipped from her perspective.

Imagine Sabine being struck by a madwoman's dug—she'd have demanded a duel! *Satisfaction!* With her head back Adélie began to chuckle. She felt her cheeks fold into a smile. Why had she gone so long without laughing? Because the chuckle rolled into a cough, then she felt the old steam-press upon her chest and a moment later the multicoloured girls had lifted her by the shoulders and thrust a gold cuspidor beneath her dripping chin. Through the hemorrhage she caught glimpses of the white wall, thick foliage outside a window, the perfect curl of one of the girl's ears, the cuspidor inlaid with ivory parasols and elephants and at the bottom a large-eyed frog awaiting the rains.

"I'M THE DOCTOR," a man was saying.

She'd been asleep on her side. In that position the pillow was put to better use. The doctor wore a brown beard, a long black tunic with black trousers and splendid white shoes. He carried his leather bag and a white helmet in the crook of his arm.

"The queen mother fetched me herself," he went on. "I see it's tuberculosis. When were you diagnosed?"

"Last November," she whispered.

She could not see the cuspidor from where she lay and she felt it vital to learn whether or not it had been emptied.

"You've had an *annus horribilis*, then, from the look of you. I'd say you weigh thirty-seven or thirty-eight kilos. Where is your husband stationed? If it's as far away as Muang Sing you'll never make it."

"He died two years ago," she rasped.

The doctor lifted a stethoscope slowly from his bag, as though reluctant to use it.

"I am sorry to hear that. Whereabouts in Laos?"

"At home in France."

"Just a moment—you bewilder me! Whatever are you still doing here?"

The rectangles on the floor shimmered ecstatically.

"I'd prefer to tell the king himself," she finally said.

Then she slept.

"—no mustard plasters here since '04," the doctor was saying. "So blistering is out. And you can scream and shout for laudanum, you wouldn't be the first, but if I ever get any it's gone in three days—they take it like it's candy. If you could only travel I'd send you into the mountains for the air. Diverse benefits of ozone. How many hemorrhages have you had since your arrival?"

"Only the one."

He asked the question again but in a snarling voice, and a girl's voice murmured a response from somewhere in the room.

"Lungs are worse than anything we had at the training hospital. Are you awake? Never mind, you *have* earned a rest—nothing but willpower keeps you alive now. If we could but bottle *that*!" He crammed the stethoscope into his bag—where was the olive to set between her teeth? "The commissioner had asked me to design the festivities marking your arrival. You don't by any chance feel like attending a formal tea party tomorrow afternoon? After all, you're the seventh white woman to ever visit Luang-Prabang." The doctor pressed his white heels together. "We know the next-of-kin from your passport, but what's your denomination?"

"Catholic," she whispered.

"As expected." He brushed his helmet with his sleeve. "It's best to know for certain, that they might bury you with confidence."

SHE FOUND the weight of one leg upon the other oppressive, and though she concentrated dully on the range of movement her hip once enjoyed, that heavy leg did not stir. Her foot at the end of it, though, seemed light as eggshells, and as she turned it

merrily on its ankle the foot must have resembled a rabbit foraging for seeds. She felt certain the young ladies in the room would
read the movement as a signal to lift her leg.

Yet she received no assistance. Adélie opened her eyes to see
whether any young ladies were in the room at all; three stood
beside a wide doorway in their splendid blouses, hands folded
before them. She glanced down at her whirling foot. Her boot
had been unbuttoned and removed, leaving it quite bare. Her
old clothes were gone. She wore a white chemise and a single
petticoat.

"A gift of the king," one of the young ladies said in French.
She had glided out from the wall, and now glided back.

"Here *is* the king," said another, and all three dropped in genuflection, foreheads against the teak.

The man in the doorway had black hair short as eyelashes and
the thick neck of a cheese-maker. He presented Adélie a long,
pitying look, in contrast to the deep laugh-lines around his eyes,
and it was this expression that suddenly made her realize what
a sorry figure she must be. The doctor hadn't looked at her that
way because his beard had leached away all compassion. The
king came forward.

"Madame Tremier? I am Sisavang," he said in French.

In acknowledgement she raised a hand in front of her face.
The mildewed glove was gone and the bare hand looked young
and slim.

"I had planned to wait for your official reception," he said.
"But my mother insisted I come at once."

With heads bent low the young ladies pushed an ottoman
forward and the king sat astride it. Adélie's eyes began to sting.
Sweat trickled into them—submerged in fever as she lay before
the king!

"You come from Paris?" he asked.

"Yes," she gasped, "near Saint-Gervais."

"I do not know it."

A cool cloth wiped her face clean.

"I should like to dictate a letter to my son," she said.

"Certainly. I have a competent staff. Do you know Poulenc of *Le Figaro*?"

"Yes."

"I attended school in Paris. I count him as my great friend."

"After I gave a ball, he wrote revolting things about me," she whispered slowly. "My mother-in-law struck the mantel, she was so angry. Cracked a bone in her finger."

"Yes, he has opinions. But a fine singer."

He tilted his head as if envisioning gentle Poulenc. She stared at the chain of scarab-shaped medals stretched tautly across his stomach, each inscribed with an enigmatic Chinese character and encircled by a dragon. Such items brimmed with magic so the king's stomach would live forever.

"Do they still read Huysmans?" he suddenly asked. "You might carry a volume with you . . .?"

Her eyelids were too heavy for her to form an answer.

"You have children?" she finally asked. "A son?"

"Yes, yes." His wide knuckles brushed the ottoman's upholstery. "Savang Vatthana is crown prince."

"My only wish is to return to my son."

"That is why you've come? No one would explain. The boy is here in Laos?"

The dainty women wiped her face again.

"In France," she said.

The king gripped the knees of his trousers. He glanced at her bare foot.

"But then why are you in *our* country? Why were you brought to me, Madame, rather than to your own people?"

An iron taste rose in Adélie's mouth.

"I've come to find my cure. In the hills. But the bureaucrats I met in Saigon, the Frenchmen, they couldn't . . ."

"It's all right. Take your time."

"I will be frank, King Sisavang. There is a blessed place in your country where I can find relief, where—"

"Ah, you mean Wat Xiang Thiong! Something of course can be—"

"What place is that?" she rasped. "Away in the hills?"

"Only down the road! The most famous Buddhist temple in Laos. I myself—"

"No!" choked Adélie. "Oh, forgive me, your honour. Be patient. There is a place in the hills, perhaps near China, yet I don't know how to reach it and all the way up the river I thought, 'If only King Sisavang Vong will help me in Luang-Prabang, I might be all right!' It has never been my habit to go begging, but—"

"Please," said the king. "I do not think it is good to become excited."

She slept. When she awoke the young ladies were kneeling in a semi-circle by the door, singing a quiet song that involved clapping their hands lightly every few bars. The king stood by the window, smoking a cigarette. From beyond the window the mechanical chanting went on unabated.

"Begging your pardon, your honour."

He turned on his heel. She recognized a medal on his chest as one of the many worn by Heart's Blood in his portrait on the first-floor landing, though it didn't seemed likely that Sisavang Vong had fought at Querétaro or pacified Senegal.

"I'd like to ask two favours in addition to all you have done already."

"My mother encouraged me to fulfill any request, Madame."

"Before I go away I would like a glimpse of your son."

"Which son is that?" he asked.

"Why... the crown prince. You mentioned he—"

"Savang Vatthana! I only ask because I have five sons already, you know. The crown prince is the *oldest*, of course. He is two years old."

"Only... two? But how did—"

"There are *four* mothers, you see. In Paris no one believed that my father had thirty children, but when you next have a drink with Monsieur Poulenc you can assure him I was not joking."

"I also wish to know the meaning of the chanting we hear."

She was sliding back into sleep.

"For the Boonmahasart Festival?"

"Any medicine you like."

"No, you misunderstand. This evening there will be a great feast, Madame. You will hear them with gongs in the street, and in the monasteries they chant the tale of the Buddha's life as Prince Wetsantara—from what I can hear they're only halfway through! But, to give a sketch. The prince is forced to leave his home and go away into the forest to live as a hermit on a particular mountain, and one by one his servants and possessions are stripped from him, and before the end even his children."

"Because he is ill?"

"Ill? No. Because he gives a beggar his sacred white elephant."

"Does he find his children again?"

"At the end, yes. A black-skinned beggar comes to the mountain and asks for the children, and Wetsantara calls the boy and girl over and tells the beggar, 'Take them.'"

"With no mother to defend them."

"But she was there! She'd dreamt that a black bird chewed off her nipples, then awoke with a burning within her breast and told the prince it was a grim omen!"

"Within her breast."

"The story is complicated, of course, but in the end the prince is welcomed back to the city and reunited with his children, and there is a parade. But there is my sketch of Wetsantara—the lesson is that because of his virtue everything which he'd lost was restored to him."

"No," rasped Adélie. "He had to go to the mountain before he could find his children. That's the lesson."

Tobacco ash fluttered onto the king's white trousers.

INTO THE
UNPACIFIED REGIONS

Mme. Adélie Tremier.

BENEATH THE morning sun they waited upon the grassy quadrangle formed by two walls of the palace and the long L-shaped shed which contained the king's automobile and gilt carriages. Attendants held an enormous white parasol over the king and over Adélie in her litter, but from beneath that shade the whitewashed palace was altogether blinding. She once again wore her skirt, trailing to her feet, and that faithful companion her blouse, its back studded with pearl buttons.

"Do you feel great anxiety?" asked the king. "But I must beg your pardon, perhaps it is not appropriate to..."

"The most welcome symptom," said Adélie, "is an unreasoning calm."

A flock of blue-green pigeons flapped overhead, hurrying back to nest and young before the heat began in earnest. From latticed windows the second, third and fourth kings and their myriad attendants peered down in their finery, each face appearing to Adélie as if carved from mud. She was relieved to see the king perspiring just as freely as she—perhaps the renewed sustenance of travel had driven her fever out!

The four posts of her litter were carved with intertwining elephants and crowned with cobras; the king crouched to tap one with his nail.

"When you are well we will cook a feast—*foie gras, pla buek* caviar and timbale *à la Sisavang*. You must tell Poulenc about the timbale *à la Sisavang*."

He shifted his gaze. Ten men, hair cut short and square, hurried across the grass in single file. They wore baggy patterned breeches and white tunics with buttoned necks.

"From my personal retinue," the king said gently.

"As in all things," she whispered, "you are too generous."

Upon reaching them the retinue fell into a mass genuflection, the seats of their breeches catching the sunlight like a range of dawn-lit mountains. Perhaps the Pyrenees. The king threw his leg over a carved wooden saddle upon a grey pony, clicked his tongue and cantered away, at which the retinue leapt to their feet, grasped the teak stays on either side of the litter then straightened in unison, lifting Adélie a metre off the ground. Where shall I spit, she wondered, when the time comes? These curtains are too lovely.

In the wake of the harried parasol-carriers, the litter circumnavigated the palace. Adélie gripped her bed-sheets, for there was no bar to keep her from tumbling to the ground. She perspired terribly beneath the white bed linen embroidered with rampant elephants, yet knew she could not throw it off before she spoke her last *Until we meet again* to the king. But with whom would she talk then? And what was this new procession falling into line from behind the garages?

"Aha, bullock carts!" The smiling doctor had sprung up from the lawn like a beanstalk. "Their king *has* looked after you, and no mistake. All these fellows went around town last night complaining they wouldn't be able to sleep late—and no doubt he's cleared the shops of tinned consommé, to the detriment of all! Forgive me, Madame, here is Monsieur Grand, commissioner of Luang-Prabang and personification of civilization west of the Annamite range. Grand, here is Madame Tremier."

A bespectacled man with thick black moustaches and a bowler hat strode on the opposite side of the litter, thumbs jauntily in his waistcoat pockets.

"You may not remember, Madame, that I met your boat, and yesterday I meant to raise a glass of champagne to you!"

"But you did, Grand. Several," said the doctor.

"But *in person*, surely," said the commissioner. "Though in my extemporaneous amateur's opinion, dear lady, we could have toasted your health a hundred times with little hope of improvement."

"So, you *do* agree with me!" the doctor cried.

"I can give no reasonable argument to hold her back. I did see a number of tubercular cases in Algeria who might have been a little more wan, a little more wasted, but I confess they lay all in the morgue."

Beyond the bobbing parasols Adélie saw for the first time the front of the palace: colonnaded porches meeting at an entryway surmounted by golden elephants beneath yet more parasols— the royal coat of arms telling its subjects *Remain in the shade*. At the foot of a driveway lined with coconut palms Sisavang's pony blinked up at a steep wooded hill, itself crowned with a gleaming temple. Her knight ready to take to the lists.

"You'll want plenty of tobacco," said Grand. "The heart of malaria country up there, and nothing else can keep 'em away."

"Hills are *not* malaria country," said the doctor. "Not much standing water on the side of a hill!"

"You'll want plenty of tobacco. Keep off any ailment."

"Even tuberculosis?" asked Adélie.

"Ah! Madame, your wit is undiminished. Look here, I'd wondered at Sisavang riding at the head like that! Now he's remembered himself, you see, and we'll have to file behind the buffalo and their mess, in this heat. Where'd the boy leave our car?"

The king spoke a few words as they approached, and indeed the litter did pause to allow the carts to precede them up the driveway, bare-chested men in white turbans half-heartedly waving flies from the bullocks' eyes. Sisavang spoke sharp words to Adélie's bearers, who murmured between themselves until their apparent leader, at the front left, spoke a syllable at which the ten men lifted litter and occupant, with a jolt, onto their shoulders. Adélie flew up from her cushions and landed painfully on her elbows.

"I had wondered at that too," said the doctor. "Hadn't looked efficient."

"Yesterday at your party we told everyone your plans," said Grand. "And one of our army gents proclaimed that he'd go with you to write an article for *Tour le Monde* titled 'Into the Unpacified Regions.'"

"Will he *really* come?" whispered Adélie. "He knows the country well?"

"Just left town for a gambol on his elephant," said Grand.

Then she must have slept, for she looked up to see they were nearly at a gate opening onto a dirt road which led the good people of Luang-Prabang alongside their wooded hill. But at that moment the good people simply stood upon it in their thousands and stared. Their ornament and costume were too varied to describe, though a member in good standing of the Left Bank Orientalist League might have paused to make a photograph for the quarterly journal. Ebony chickens flapped their wings importantly. Tall palms stood at diverse angles. A golden temple stood to their left, and from its tiled courtyard a dozen children spilled forth, dashing between the plodding bullocks to hide themselves, with piercing laughs, behind the ornamental shrubbery. A tall girl, laughing and smoothing her skirt down, seemed to be searching them out.

"There, Madame." The king rode up beside the commissioner. "There is the crown prince."

Adélie followed his dignified nod, which indicated a small boy emerging from a bush. The lad jogged haphazardly into the temple courtyard where he lifted a coconut husk above his head—arms barely long enough for the job—and yowled victoriously. But for a string tied around his middle the little fellow was quite naked.

"He's darling," rasped Adélie.

The bullocks moved onto the road and the chattering crowd gave way.

"We'll take our leave of you, then," said the commissioner. "Glad to have seen you off. Be sure to stop past, you know, on your return."

"Yes, I shall need the details," said the doctor.

"Here are a few more of our folk in the crowd—see them wave to you?"

When she next opened her eyes she saw five white elbows on either side of her and beyond them the brown backs of dozens of Laotians, their faces pressed in the dirt. In black shadows formed by roadside foliage and stalls selling wizened limes, Adélie saw grey heads, heads of shining black hair, heads in ragged turbans. A cart jounced ahead of them, its rails bulging with goods—meant for her, she realized, and the king must still be riding behind the litter, hence the faces to the ground. The king of Laos, her benefactor. Manu would think it fiction when he read her letter.

Then stillness. Shadows lay across long grass, and the shadow of a lithe column carved with cobras lay across her legs. Hours had passed. She heard men's low voices and a crackling fire, and insects duplicated the unceasing hiss of the radiators in her grandparents' apartment. Brass-coloured shoes with pointed toes stepped through the grass, then the wearer's slim white trousers, then his legs bent at the knee and the king's solemn face appeared just below her roof.

"Ah! Madame. The eyes *do* open. I've come to tell you I must excuse myself. The party is waiting for elephants to take you further into the jungle. There is still a road, you see, but soon only a path."

"Elephants?" she said hoarsely. "But I do not need so many supplies, your honour. The bullock carts—"

"Even if the litter returns empty to Luang-Prabang, to my eye your spirit will recline there. Tell them *ahan* when you want food, and *nam hawn* when you want water."

"I do want water."

"*Nam hawn!*" the king called.

A boy, his hair wispy and reddish, offered her a dripping brass dipper. But she could not sit up; she seemed to lack muscles. The king nibbled a blade of grass and said something in Lao. The boy crawled into the litter and tipped the tepid water into her mouth. A good deal ran down her blouse. When the boy crawled out she noticed there was also blood down her front—she had hemorrhaged and no one had thought to tidy her up! She would have to ask King Sisavang for a nurse.

He was still looking in at her, lips moving as though speaking. He pressed her hand between his, then rose. The crease in his trousers was lovely.

AS THEY TRAVERSED the overgrown forests she safeguarded her strength so that she might speak if they were to enter a village. She would ask the bearers to inquire when a villager had last passed away and so determine unequivocally, upon receiving the answer "Never," that the party had marched into a village of immortals.

Each time she murmured *"Nam hawn"* the swaying would stop immediately, though she would fall back to sleep before so much as tasting water from that eight-cornered brass dipper. Did they pour it between her lips? Now the evening sun dipped over the hills, silhouetting the patterns of leaves against a red sky whirling with insects, yet none of the retinue came forward to offer a bath.

The bearers' hair and beards grew ragged, and each time they dropped her she awoke: once when crossing the side of a hill on a path of loose rocks—from the light it must have been early morning—and once upon the bank of a clear stream where the air smelled acrid and small birds skimmed the water. Each time she would see, fleetingly, their entire faces, rather than a snatch of profile, as they peered between the curtains. *"Kaw thot,"* the bearers' leader would say—his chin was very square, with a scar down one side—and she guessed that it meant "Forgive me." She would memorize it and say the words back to the men, *kaw thot, kaw thot, kaw thot.* They deserved to hear it every day. Had the famous Thérèse of Lisieux, with her galloping tuberculosis, her perpetual bleeding from the mouth, ever been such a burden? She'd shivered in her monastery's hospital and before dying announced *I have reached the point of not being able to suffer*—Sabine had done the passage in needle-point one winter, so Adélie knew it well—*because all suffering is sweet to me*. But Thérèse of Lisieux had had no loved ones dependent upon her survival, for a nun forswears such things, and in any case five of her siblings had died of tuberculosis already.

SHE SMELLED a pig on a spit, and the swaying ceased. She waited to be set down. Instead the litter shuddered as the bearers expressed guttural arguments. Her bed dipped and jolted but still she was not set down. Would it be worth the effort to open her eyes? Perhaps they had arrived at the place they'd set out for, though the cicadas here sounded distinctly predatory. Dogs barked and birds bickered hoarsely.

"*Sai,*" said the bearers' leader. "*Sai, sai.*"

She looked out through the nets of her veil and the curtains to see the copper path had turned dull grey. Her fragment of sky was slate-coloured and full of circling birds. She saw four bearers in profile to her right and three to her left.

"*Pai su su!*" they said. The leader kept saying "*Sai, sai,*" and because he was outnumbered she took his side.

Before them the grey path forked in a field of scrub, and amongst those pewter-coloured leaves Adélie glimpsed the brown shoulder of a crouching Chinaman clad in a black sort of jacket, his face straining—the poor soul was relieving himself! At his shoulder a stout pig waited for him to finish. Up the right-hand path a crow pecked at the eyes of a dead woman, her torso attended by vultures, their wings sweeping up dust as they hopped through ropes of innards. On a rise of hill a column of black smoke rose amidst a handful of huts; human forms slumped in and out of view and dogs looked down on the litter and barked.

The man who relieved himself called to them and stood, only to collapse forward into the scrub. The pig wagged its shoelace of tail.

"Pai su su!" someone hissed with finality.

Adélie realized the bearers had succeeded only in finding a village rotten with cholera. She read a thousand times in newspapers how it killed within hours using nothing more elaborate than diarrhea—Poulenc himself had described the unstylish travesties of the Berlin epidemic! Forever a question of water supply. Dogs on skeletal haunches sat waiting around the dead woman. More vultures arrived and in their enthusiasm the corpse was lifted and dropped.

The bearers took the left-hand path. On foul cushions suffused with infinitesimal insects and her rusty blood Adélie's head lolled so she caught glimpses of a mountain shaped like a dog's molar and a crimson sun showering it with sparks. As her bearers whispered she peered beyond the outline of her feet at teetering branches knotted together in imitation of a dangling man, its willowy arms beating the air—it wouldn't have seemed a sign of welcome even in happier times. The trail dropped into a hollow where thickets of bamboo stood in dank water, and though the sweat poured off them the king's own retinue did not lower her and drink. Adélie blessed the wisdom of their respective mothers. The path continued away from the village then, but no, it began to climb and the lead man had to sing an encouraging bar. Thatch roofs came into view. The gusting bonfire lay directly ahead of them, and she saw it was fuelled not just with wood but corpses. No vultures circled overhead because they were already feasting in their dozens amongst the huts as the village dogs stood yowling.

People lay in doorways or curled against posts beneath the houses, and the living and dead were indistinguishable. Old women tottered past with bundles of wood on their backs, or carrying between them corpses wrapped in brown cloth. They stopped to raise clenched fists and shriek at Adélie, reading some relevance in her arrival. Her poor lungs inhaled the miasma of burning hair.

Swinging a hoe, an old man in a rag knocked a vulture onto its back before toppling to his knees himself. With a flutter the vulture resumed its meal. The old man attempted to wrap the little body in a cloth and this dissuaded the bird, who hopped away to join its fellows beneath the nearest house. A party of crows, though, immediately helped themselves to the leavings, and the old man's sob drowned out every other sound.

Rotund pigs snorted at their passing until the bearers found a path out of the village across a grassy ridge. A young man appeared in front of them, filthy with soot, clad in ragged black trousers and holding a spear. With a yelp he threw the weapon, and to Adélie's left the front bearer dropped from sight. Then the path stood empty.

The remaining bearers began to run with the litter, and Adélie flew up from her cushions to crash down again and again.

SHE DREAMT of a wood-panelled kitchen, a forehead-warming glow emanating from its open hearth and the pans of steaming milk balanced on every countertop and table, until the wall to the right of the fire gave way and she was looking out onto a busy street, indeed it was the Pont Neuf and she was passing from the First District to the Sixth, walking rapidly in a pair of high-heeled boots that were uncommonly comfortable, the pavements crowded with tall-hatted men. A group of them turned and spoke inaudible syllables. How freely I'm breathing, she thought. Yet the bridge's gilded salamanders gradually evaporated and her lungs filled with pus and rising seawater.

Opening her eyes she saw silhouettes of four long-horned beetles as they wandered nonchalantly across her veil. The smallest of the four ascended to the top and balanced there a moment before she heard the scrape of its armoured legs skittering down the brim of her hat.

She lay upon a platform of branches, her clothes wet through. Below her the litter rested on its side, curtains in shreds, sheets and pillows as black as if they'd been hauled up a chimney. From a branch dangled an open white parasol, blotched with mildew. Ahead of her she saw a clearing strewn with dead leaves and white mushrooms the size of franc coins. A millipede as long as her arm rustled past on life-or-death business. She did not hear the men's quiet talk or a morning's crackling fire—they'd gone as a party to hunt firewood, she decided—and instead of smoke she smelled only the jungle's odour of wet horse tack and mouldy bread baked slowly together.

I will wait one minute more before I sit up and look behind me, she thought, then she batted the beetles from her veil and slid her feet to the ground. Were leeches tumbling down her back? She steadied herself against a tree, head spinning—how did the world appear to people whose heads did not spin?

She knelt in a thick humus of ruddy leaves when only a moment before she'd been standing. Her lungs were not distinct organs inside her but a great slough of brackish water that surged inside her chest, its only intention to burst out of her mouth. She pulled the veil from her face, ripped the ribbon from beneath her chin and threw the whole mess away. Now her hands were in the dirt and the blood poured out of her mouth, peppering her sleeves afresh with rusty pin-pricks. She felt as though sand were being forced against the roof of her mouth, her throat and esophagus seared with embers, yet there was such a *rightness* about the blood coming up and out of her. It was not *coughing up* the blood that was killing her, of course, but its transformation within her—it was diseased, putrefied, it would do more good spilled amongst the ants and mushrooms and worms.

She coughed until she'd been drained from the soles of her feet. A ghastly illustration from *Mon Journal* entitled "A Hemorrhage On The Jungle Floor." She spat one last string of mucus into the pool between her hands.

Snatched from the earth, despite all her machinations, and Manu left behind.

BETWEEN THREE and four o'clock in the morning she had let him nurse from one breast until it was empty and then from the other, so that with a full belly he might sleep until first light, though Suzanne in her iron cot had sat fingering her long braid and glaring at Adélie all the while, muttering that it was *her* job and a lady ought to sleep. And Manu, loudly sucking, had blinked up at his mother by the light of the lone candle.

Now he would never be more substantial than that memory. She opened one eye and saw that she lay on her side on black soil teeming with grubs. Rivulets of sweat trickled from behind her ear and down across the back of her neck. Her every pore gaped for oxygen, absorbing the jungle's fetid breath as though she were a sponge upon the ocean floor, yet the heat was so delicious that she could not recall how the chill of fever had even felt, though her bones ached from it.

The puddle of her blood and mucus, only a hand's-breadth from her face, coursed with the wings of insects wading and leaping like children at the seaside. Surely her face was coated with them—yes, as she exhaled she saw them flutter from her nostrils. Her hat lay opposite the puddle; the beetles had worried great holes in the veil with their crooked legs. A species with great ambition, she thought—wasn't her brain delightfully nimble? She wished she could have worn the veil for these final moments. Like the Cloth of Saint Veronica, it might have retained her image. She lay frozen there.

The grubs must have moved against her face but she was not aware of them. Had she possessed pen and paper she might have written a few words to Manu, written *Kaw thot*. Now she was returned to a tadpole's existence, confined within her mind, as in that split-second when she first kissed Nicolas and lightning had flashed behind her eyes and spread like quicksilver to her extremities. Perhaps approaching ecstasy and approaching death were not so different.

Her eyes fixed on the triangles of yellow light breaking through the branches.

LORD TIGER

Pierre Lazarie.

I N SAIGON, I have learned since, it is possible to awaken in a strange bed and, judging from the quality of light upon the wall and relative cacophony of street traffic, be unable to discern whether it is early morning or late afternoon—though I should add the caveat that if the sweat on the back of your neck has had a chance to congeal it is probably morning. Upcountry, however, the morning is unmistakably colder and the villagers' din consists only of spare halting calls between mother and child, but above all it is the hour of choice for poultry to voice their many and varied opinions. In some linen-sheeted hotel I would gladly have bunched up my pillows, rung for coffee and enjoyed the musical program, but a bone-bruising floor is no place for such things.

Retying the yellow robe, I carried my damp suit outside. As I picked my way down the steps, our host, wherever he was, rang his morning gong. In the frangipani trees before the temple fluttered hundreds of house sparrows, so mundanely brown that they immediately transported me back to Paris and the Place Denfert-Rochereau, where Mama had taken me to watch the birds while sensible old women threw them breadcrumbs and addled old men merely pretended to—in my youth that had been nature at its most virile. I hung the components of my suit over a dead branch as a clutch of thin-legged lads hurried past, sticks balanced on their bare shoulders, tin buckets dangling from either end. Beyond the monastery wall they turned down a path into the forest.

—I do miss that rat of a porter, said Henri. Never failed to have my bath drawn.

He stood at the top of the stairs, barefoot, in trousers and undershirt.

—Follow the boys, I said. There must be a stream down below.

—And on our return he'll have brought our rice.

—He'll go collecting alms about the village first.

—I've never second-guessed where my breakfast came from. I won't start now.

He managed to break a thick branch from the dead tree and strode after the bucket brigade. I lifted my robe to trot after him.

—You're moving at lightning speed this morning, I said.

—To convince myself I'm not about to collapse from the effects of their liquor. Tastes as though I snored, did I? I believe Ban Din's only another hour or two.

—Though if we've learned anything it's that the telegraph between Saigon and Vientiane is inoperative a good deal of the time.

We heard splashing far below and the boys' sonorous voices chanting a round. The light became gloomier as we descended, though on the stream sunbeams danced in parallelograms.

—I've become quite perturbed thinking of Madame Tremier, I said.

—Yes, I've seen you caressing that picture like it was a new-born kitten, and it doesn't bear thinking what must go on under cover of darkness.

—What upsets me is that she'd undertake this quest *by herself*. I mean, why go to such lengths to achieve what would at best be an eternity of loneliness? I can imagine someone of *your* type choosing to live as an everlasting hermit in order to spite the human race and growing exponentially more miserable—I see what forty-four years have done to you and it's mind-boggling!

—Damn it, I just remembered our money from Dubois. And Sainteny himself gave me that valise! When that whirlpool spits our piastres out in a thousand years the Malays will find them and say, "What the devil's the Indo-Chinese Union?"

And he spun his stick jauntily, stepping high over the snaking roots. I looked down the hill at a row of shining brown backs. The boys had evidently enjoyed a swim and were only now filling their buckets.

—There's a dipper in the wash-house up above, I said.

—Never mind that. I plan to throw myself in whole-heartedly.

The ground at the base of the path was flecked with tiny grey mosses. The boys looked up and curtailed their chatter—one lifted his buckets to his shoulder and hurried past us. The youngest lad, perhaps eight years old, trotted across the ankle-deep stream. Still intoning their chant, he climbed a flat rock on the far bank.

—This looks a likely spot, I said.

An older boy crouched, the pole poised across his thin shoulder; I watched with fascination, for the two buckets must have weighed as much as he did. He called a few syllables in the direction of the child on the far bank, but mid-sentence he shouted and dropped onto his behind.

A tiger approached from our left toward the youngest boy, who looked up, bemused, in the direction of his squealing compatriot. Of the cat's massive bulk three features remain clearest in my memory: the vividness of the orange stripes across his immense flank, all its blackness having merged with the undergrowth; the white front paws, as broad as shovels, each stealing unhurriedly in front of the other; and the impassive features of his surprisingly long face. The child turned and saw the tiger, then with a half-swallowed cry fell onto his behind as well. At this the tiger paused to lower his head, a dozen fern fronds caressing his back.

He lunged. The boy raised a spindly arm which the tiger seized in his mouth before pulling his muzzle back sharply. The arm gave a distinct snap.

Henri was no longer at my side but moving across the stream, stick above his head, silver water leaping high with every footfall.

—Get off! he was shouting.

The older boys and I yelled ourselves hoarse. Shaking the child by the arm the tiger backed into the undergrowth. The little chap could only beat its broad head with his fist, yet an instant before the foliage closed over its great face Henri ascended the bank and rained blows between the tiger's ears, at which, quite amazingly, the cat opened his mouth to release the little arm and receded without a whisper into the undergrowth.

LeDallic had scared *a tiger* away! He dropped the stick, clutched the boy's good arm and lifted him to his feet. I shouted ecstatically alongside the others while every insect in the countryside suddenly whirred up a song of congratulations. Our triumphant pair peered down the bank for the easiest descent. A smile played about Henri's lips.

Then with a rush of black leaves the tiger sunk his teeth into LeDallic's shoulder. The boy toppled into the stream. My colleague lifted his hands to somehow defend himself but in the same breath the tiger gave his white-whiskered head a vigorous shake, like a dog dispatching a duck, and my friend's hands flopped to the ground. His neck must have broken. The tiger retreated once more into the oily-grey underbrush, and the last glimpse I had of Henri LeDallic was of his delicately tapered feet bumping over a root before the forest closed over him.

The injured boy splashed toward us, galvanizing the older lads—and me—into action. He'd sustained a compound fracture just below the shoulder and was bleeding badly in a dozen places, but all I could think to do was straighten the arm despite his sobs, and knot my robe around it as tightly as possible. Then, quite naked, I lifted him in my arms and started up the hill. Half the boys had run on ahead but those with me crashed through the brush on either side, cupping their comrade's head, massaging his feet, doing anything that might soothe him. The boy's snot smeared my chest and shoulder. At the top, the village women spirited him from my arms as a cadre of bare-chested men tore past us on their way downhill, .22 rifles held high. The older boys breathlessly told the story, one vividly re-enacting Henri's performance with the stick, and despite my nakedness I was treated to a score of deferential bows and murmurs.

—*Khàwp jai,* they said. *Khàwp jai!*

No one mourned the boy's ruined arm, it seemed; rather, they celebrated his escape, and with a carnival air they carried him home.

—*Baw pen nyang,* I murmured.

Thus I stood once more beside the monastery wall; perhaps ten minutes had elapsed since I'd listened to Henri pine for warm baths. But for the snot upon my chest and shouts ringing from the gully I might have dreamt the incident.

I found myself on hands and knees in the dust; evidently I'd been vomiting. Struggling to my feet, my mind fixed on the one person who might take my hand to lead me clear of my disorientation, to give me wise counsel. Adélie Tremier.

My suit upon the tree was still damp, though the underthings, thankfully, were dry. After dressing I retrieved our belongings from the temple. I hung Henri's topee and boots from the dead tree—where house sparrows immediately undertook an investigation—then slung his corkscrew around my neck, pocketed his clasp-knife and Gitaines Maïs and started along a wide path under clusters of palms. A gunshot echoed up from the gully, then another, but too intermittently to bespeak success.

A NATIVE IN a Postal Service truck drove me into Ban Din. He let me down at the government rest-house and a Frenchwoman affiliated with the Agricultural Bureau sauntered across the road. I shook her hand and realized I was still in a cold sweat.

—I'm afraid I've lost my papers, I said.

She poured me a tumbler of water.

—What a strange thing to say. Why should anyone want to see those?

—I must send an urgent telegram.

—There's a band playing at Savannakhet tomorrow night. Do you tango?

I was muddled. In fact I did have my papers, though sodden from washing, and showed them to the elderly clerk inside the clapboard telegraph office.

—I haven't any money.

—According to your papers, sir, at no cost you may send a cable of not more than twenty words to any government address.

—Oh, God, what day is it?

—Friday, sir.

I'd been terrified it might be Sunday. I carried a telegram blank and pencil to the table, where the white rectangle of paper grimaced up at me—Dubois would certainly be in the office, I could reach him within minutes, but where to begin?

—Twenty words?

—Yes, sir.

DIFFICULTIES, I began. But that was a word wasted, for surely whatever else I wrote would convey the same. I crossed it out.

KEMMARAT SHIPWRECK, I began. Two extremely potent words. SUPPLIES LOST, I added. LEDALLIC TAKEN BY TIGER. HEROIC ACT SAVED CHILD. MYSELF STRANDED BAN DIN. ADVISE. LAZARIE.

But what of our mission? I needn't sign it as my name would appear on the form—that left three more words. SOME SIGNS TREMIER, I added. ADVISE.

At the desk the clerk's eyes widened.

—A tiger *killed* a friend of yours? When was this?

—This morning.

—Not in the daytime!

—Yes, I said. In the daytime.

I loitered on the Telegraph Service veranda; until Dubois replied I was absolved of all responsibility. A yellow dog with every vertebra visible skulked up the steps to collapse beneath a bench. I retrieved Henri's Gitanes from my breast pocket. I finally lit a cigarette, my first in Indo-China, and inhaled deeply as it crackled.

But a moment later I threw the thing away, for while savouring its rough sweetness upon my tongue and contemplating a dragonfly hovering over the rail I'd quite forgotten that my friend had died, and what is the point in any of us living if we're to be dismissed from the consciousness of those nearest us as readily as that?

Judging from what I knew of his life prior to that morning I wouldn't have been optimistic in guessing the destination of Henri LeDallic's soul, but, on the other hand, I'd recently been informed that Hell was already full to capacity. I contemplated the smouldering cigarette until the dog padded over and ate it.

The clerk called me inside.

ENTIRE STAFF SHOCKED OVER LEDALLIC, the telegram read. AUDIT POSTPONED INDEFINITELY FOLLOWING FRANC DEVALUATION. RETURN SAIGON IMMEDIATELY. IRREPLACE-ABLE HERE. NECESSARY FUNDS FOR AIR TRAVEL WIRED SAVANNAKHET.

—Another cable? asked the clerk.

THE BUS WAS a bald-tired relic of Chinese design, I ventured to guess, for the total distance between the back of one's bench and the one ahead was a hand's-breadth shorter than the length of my thigh. My fellow passengers, meanwhile, might have stepped nonchalantly from the still-intact deck of the *General Subrégis*, for they wore straw hats and threadbare blouses, carried the same chicken baskets, bulging vegetable sacks and unconscious children, and were able without exception to lower their feet to the trembling floorboards, liberally decorated with flattened roaches, and drop off to sleep with their heads upon their neighbours' shoulders. Henri had speculated that Laotian forests were made for smaller men, but their buses were manufactured for a more diminutive race and no mistake. Happily the natives left me alone that I might sit diagonally, my legs in the aisle, while they crowded three to a bench.

Dusty cattle flashed past like phantoms as our anemic headlights guided us through the night. As we limped off the bus to relieve ourselves in the foliage it began to rain, and I saw Adélie's long skirts trailing over the wet grass. At times I believed that LeDallic had simply hurried ahead to find her, and that at Savannakhet I'd find them drunkenly playing dominoes and firing guns in the air.

Through the rest of the yawning hours I composed a mental introduction to *A Cursory Guide for the Indo-China Visitor*. "The patient Lao," it began, "goes through life with three maxims nestled to his heart: that even the most contemptible object, carried far enough, will find a buyer; that a machine of any size must produce an ear-splitting shriek; and that any human being, though in particular French nationals, might disappear from the face of the Earth without a moment's notice."

As we shuddered up those wet roads Adélie Tremier stretched over the scene as an umbrella against trouble, smiling beatifically down on us with lips that were meant for kissing. I offered the monks across the aisle a Gitanes Maïs but they declined, as in the clucking-chicken darkness they couldn't possibly have known what I was offering.

But Adélie Tremier accepted. She puffed languidly, a dimple in her cheek.

BECAUSE ITS STRIP lay on an expanse of scrubland a hundred metres from the Mekong, the airport at Savannakhet must not have operated at all during the rainy season, but at seven o'clock on a February morning its red dirt was hot as a frying pan. Dust devils jogged ahead of the rickshaw. The periphery of the strip was scattered with tin-roofed shacks and a shirtless, grey-bearded Frenchman uncurled himself from a folding chair as I stepped down. With his deeply tanned hide and brass-studded belt he might easily have been made into three dozen wallets.

—Thought you'd be older! he said. You really from the Vice-Regency of Cochin-China?

—Lazarie's the name. If you have a plane ready I must get to Luang-Prabang.

—No, no, my name's Delaporte, he said. But they all call me Knuckles. Heard the big news? Charlie Chaplin's at Angkor! Came over the telegraph. You believe that?

—Certainly. If you have a plane ready I really must get to Luang-Prabang.

His head only reached my shoulder. He wrapped a bare arm around my back.

—Hey, what do you want to go north for? Don't you tango?

I couldn't decide if he and LeDallic would have got on famously or knocked each other down. He led me into a shed, where lumps of machinery sat in pans of noxious-smelling gasoline, then out across the field. To our right a pair of water buffaloes copulated lethargically, still chewing cud, while to our left a black plane shifted in the wind while two native boys with oil cans peered under the hood and three more lay in the dirt and watched. Its wheels were ensconced, beautifully, in tear-shaped boots.

—Get your luggage and we'll be on our way, said Delaporte.

I did laugh at that. Three minutes later the ground lurched out from under us, the ever-diminishing riverbank scrub permitted to comfortably hug the earth while I scrambled for something to hold on to. A pair of bronzed baby boots swung from a hook in the ceiling. Delaporte, still shirtless, sat at my left elbow.

—Do not touch the wheel! he shouted.

Instead I put my hands to the glass and gazed out at Savannakhet's fields of tin roofs and the rising dust clouds that likely indicated roads. I saw that the Mekong lay below us but I did not relish looking straight down.

—Should we not be flying *toward* the mountains?

—Ah! Delaporte shouted. Yes, but the cloud's low today! For now we'll stay over the flat! Conserve fuel!

Tongues of vapour flashed across the windscreen and an instant later we were engulfed in whiteness. After the disasters of LeDallic and the *General Subrégis*, I saw for myself that one could leap headlong into the atmosphere and alight in Luang-Prabang. When I saw Dubois I'd punch his face—he couldn't have put us on a plane at the start? The air in the cabin was suddenly cold as an icebox. Delaporte was all goose pimples.

—Makes for a change from the heat! he said through chattering teeth.

How high had we climbed? I couldn't guess which of the eight dials to study. Through rips in the cloud below, dark-green forest flickered past. Forests Adélie had walked. For a time

I observed how the air around the propeller shimmered like a mirage, then I shut my eyes and slept. I had sufficient room for my legs.

The instant I awoke I saw a dial circled with N, E, S and O — obviously a compass. But why did it say we were headed south and slightly west? Green squares of rice field spread below us. I tapped the disloyal compass.

—How, I shouted, are we possibly headed for Luang-Prabang?

—Ah! grinned Delaporte. Had a wire from your bosses! Said to bring you to Saigon no matter what you said!

I sat back. I confess I felt perfectly calm.

—And you'd better not smash me in the mouth, he shouted, unless you know how to land the thing yourself!

I picked grit from my ear, then found my matchbook and lit a Gitanes Maïs. Evidently if gasoline could combust at such altitudes there was ample oxygen for lighting cigarettes, and before long Delaporte and I finished the pack.

ENJOYING HAPPINESS
AFTER OTHERS

Pierre Lazarie.

IF NOTHING else, my trip up the Mekong had taught me not to let chickens disturb my slumber, so on my first morning back in Saigon I slept until ten past six, when the porter carried in my washwater. I wiped the sweat from my chest with the pillowcase.

—And a note, sir. Came late last night.

In my half-dreaming mind it contained news of Adélie Tremier, but the note was only from Frémont: he wished to welcome me back with coffee and a pastry. The porter brushed talc from the bureau into the palm of his hand.

—And Monsieur Henri? he asked. Comes back another day?

—Ah, no, I said. He won't. He... passed away. Uh, *chet*, you understand?

He stood in his neat white shirt, eyes big as headlights.

—Dead? Monsieur Henri?

—I'm afraid so. I realize you must have—

—Do you want his room? he asked. It's bigger.

I told him I'd consider it, gratefully stepped into freshly ironed clothes and hurried out. It was my first day in Saigon without Marguerite to dream of or Adélie to pursue, and I felt at loose ends. At the top of the stairs a red-headed figure stood immobile, his hand upon the banister; at my approach he shuffled backward and I saw it was my once-garrulous housemate of the acne scars. He smelled like a kennel. He'd lost considerable weight since advising me on the economics of soliciting prostitutes, and his skin looked as though the dye had been wrung from it. I had heard that the rare opium-smoker actually thrived on the stuff.

—She gives me too many, he muttered. I can't stop her. Do you know? She'll be the death of me. My ruin already.

—Ah, I said.

—Yet . . . doesn't everything look so sweet?

As I descended I might have taken this exchange as a warning, a harbinger of the day's trials, but instead I climbed into a rickshaw and asked for boulevard Norodom.

Frémont sat outside a café opposite the dome of the Governor General's Palace. In the morning light the tabletops glittered like new coins as each patron threw one creased leg over the other and refolded his newspaper. Frémont rose and we shook hands, then I lifted a four-sheet paper from the seat opposite him—*The Struggle,* it was called, with the banner headline, "Form a Representative Indo-Chinese Congress!" I saw that a copy lay on every untenanted chair.

—Trotskyites, muttered Frémont. They paint those notices about electing Workers' Candidates to Municipal Council, but why should they complain? Now that you've seen a bit of the country you know what I mean!

With alarm he raised his eyebrows, then slowly brought them down.

—Ah, here are the éclairs! Let us toast Henri!

After which I could say nothing for a quarter-hour as every white-skinned passerby, to a man, had to exchange pleasantries with Frémont—he was an extremely competent tennis player, among other things.

—Now then, he said, smoothing his napkin across his knee. How shall we report your lack of progress to Captain Tremier?

I would've wagered the topic to be the furthest thing from his mind.

—Oh! I said. Dubois indicated we were no longer obliged—

—Dubois thinks one crisis means the end of everything. No, no. Our country, this country, it all goes around in cycles. Even if the issue were foreign hordes invading rather than, what, franc devaluation, do you believe it would dissuade the fellow from looking for his mother? Dubois ought to take the long view—study Le Loi and the Tay Son brothers, don't you think? This part of the world requires perspective.

Perspective? I thought of Gironière, exiled at Leit Tuhk to study Le Loi and the Tay Son brothers while a woman who loved him waited at his side!

—We might, said Frémont, make mention that Henri met his end, and what else? Your riverboat troubles. "Yes, but what now?" the captain will ask.

—We could write to the outstations, I suggested. Lai Chau and—

—Yes, good. If there were only some way to get a man to Luang-Prabang besides these dinky little boats, you might nose around with a good deal more efficiency!

I took the notebook from my inside pocket and dutifully jotted down the point raised. I did not mention that I'd been sitting in a contrivance called an aeroplane only sixteen hours before, because I'd already learned that great deeds can only be accomplished within the parameters of ego.

—We might cable them again up in L-P, he said. A few more enquiries, or—what did I read yesterday? They've advertised for a supervising bookkeeper up there, you've certainly the experience, but then what would be the sense in your going if Captain Tremier's mother was no longer your responsibility?

—I might be *posted* to Luang-Prabang? I asked. As simply as that?

—But she can't really be dead. I have given this some thought. There have been any number of times that a tribal has walked into a police station with a watch chain or half a boot and said, "We found this man or that man dead in the woods," but a woman's things have *never* been brought forward in such cases. You know, she might wander back into town at any moment—even after all these years, it wouldn't be unheard of!

—It wouldn't?

—Even me—in my early days I got away from my detachment out on the Cambodian frontier, damn foolish, and only lived to tell about it by getting captured by Siamese slavers and winning their favour by giving dance lessons every night! So if you ever see a tango in that part of the world that doesn't look quite right, well, you'll know why. Then I had to skipper a steamer across the gulf to get back here, with just a lot of Burmans for crew!

—And you were gone for years and years?

—Eighteen months, but that was only because things went my way. A misstep here, snake bite there—or if they'd actually sold me!—then I'd be lucky to walk back into town today or tomorrow, and that's forty years later! I wouldn't be married then, would I, wouldn't have kids—it beggars the imagination what I'd do with myself! Now, if you ask any of these gentlemen they'll tell you my instincts are keen, especially returning serves, and my instincts say that the captain's mother will return!

—But even thirty years ago, sir, she had tuberculosis.

He waved a large hand dismissively then called out to a gentleman adjusting the wing nuts of a racket case while standing on the running board of a parked car.

We eventually shared a rickshaw to the office, and while Frémont nattered on about the recent paucity of typewriter ribbon I stared at the rickshaw man's abnormally wide fingers. I imagined stepping off the aeroplane in Luang-Prabang to accept the bookkeeper's position, then using every syllable of my Lao language to cast an ever-widening net over the countryside—this was my line of thought as I climbed flights of Vice-Regency stairs—even if it took me, bearded and sweaty, across China and Outer Mongolia to the islands of Japan, to find Adélie breathless in a white skirt, ropes of pearls draped down her chest. Waiting for me all that time. Just as I reached our office door Dubois came charging out—I'd forgotten how diminutive he was!

—Ah, Lazarie! Wasn't sure you'd make it back. I've just had the boy pack up LeDallic's things, you can do what you like with them, I suppose, and Madame Louvain brought up a cable. Must have slipped from the envelope because I believe I saw the Sorbonne's address across the top. Must be the alumni association!

I felt my hair stand on end, yet I refrained from knocking him down so as to get to my desk.

—You've lipstick on your face, Dubois.

He rubbed either cheek vigorously with the heel of his hand.

—Not surprised! Tonight we're making a foray into Cho Lon, and Georgette says you must sit beside her cousin. Bring the car at half-past eleven?

—Georgette?

—My wife—surely you know *Georgette*!

He hurried off, wiping his palms on his trousers, and I stepped into our office. The ceiling fans hung idle, and in that grey room smelling of mothballs and feet only the rectangles of window stared back at me. My scalp went on tingling. A cable from the Sorbonne could not be bad news—they couldn't take my baccalaureate *away*—so I savoured the anticipation just as my parents had puttered about drying dishes on Christmas Eve while we'd thrown fits jostling gifts beneath the tree.

I took off my jacket and hung it on the hook. Three towers of files stood on each of our desks. On the corner of mine sat Madame Louvain's envelope. A wooden fig box, balanced on the edge of Henri's desk, contained a rusty jackknife, three wadded handkerchiefs, five dice, a mummified orange, a great many pen nibs and a long, battered box of J.W. Spears-brand dominoes. I went to the window and looked out but in my distraction my eyes took in nothing. At the coat hook, I pulled my notebook from the jacket pocket, took the Tremier family photograph from the inside cover and stood the portrait against my inkwell. Adélie was somewhere in the world yet. She watched closely as I slid the cable from its envelope.

DUE TO KOSSUTH'S ILLNESS LECTURER POSITION NOW AVAILABLE IN RUDIMENTARY HISTORY AND LANGUAGES. TWO COURSES THIS SEMESTER, THREE NEXT. HEARTY HANDSHAKE ON YOUR RETURN.

C. LAMBERT, ORIENTAL STUDIES.

Then I was standing at Madame Louvain's window in the foyer. Without returning her baleful gaze I took up two telegram blanks and wrote carefully with a stub of pencil before addressing the slips and sliding them across the counter. Madame glanced at the first, her lips languidly mouthing the words.

REGRET THAT RESPONSIBILITIES KEEP ME IN INDO-CHINA, it read. KINDLY FILL POSITION WITH ALTERNATE.

She passed it to her visored assistant, who carried it with great deliberation to the Morse key at the rear of the room. I had every opportunity to call him back. Madame registered the telegrams in her ledger.

URGED BY FREMONT, the second read, TO APPLY BOOK-KEEPING SUPERVISOR POSITION. CAN COME LUANG-PRA-BANG IMMEDIATELY.

Because if I'd learned anything from Le Loi—not to mention from the great Le Quy Don—it was that, while the caprices of the mind might win a battle, the heart spurs one to fight in the first place. And the heart moves quickly. It does not deliberate.

—Anyone *I* know in Luang-Prabang, Madame Louvain said, has gone to pot.

AS I HAD those six towers of applications to review I told Dubois that the car might pick me up at the office rather than at home if he'd be good enough to lend me a dinner jacket. All day and evening I waited for word from Luang-Prabang. At twenty past eleven the watchman telephoned to inform me, a bare two-and-a-half piles into my task, that I was wanted on the street.

I hurried out, yawning, to find a black Renault idling at the curb. Beside it a tall, thin woman stood cracking her knuckles, a cigarette between her lips. The cut of her gown left her long back quite bare.

—Ah, you're right! she said. That jacket is aggressively wrong!

—Madame Dubois? I asked.

She stepped on the cigarette and we kissed each other on each cheek, though my kisses were far gentler than hers. Her eyes were bright beneath the streetlight, and her smile extremely wide.

—The one and only! shouted Dubois through the window. That's Georgette!

The cousin had apparently gone ahead into Cho Lon, leaving me alone in the back seat while from the front Madame Dubois described the parties people in France were throwing despite their rainy spring and how a certain girl had found a new gown designer and the very same night had started stepping out with a ravishing young man who had quite rightly climbed the Alps. She inevitably described each desirable young man as "tall." Behind the wheel little Dubois remained intent on the traffic, which was light.

But, crossing into the Chinese district of Cho Lon, the streets filled suddenly with keening hawkers, fortune tellers' tables, honking rattletrap cars and jostling rickshaws, and again and again Dubois asked Georgette to remind him whether there'd be a valet to park the car. Had Cho Lon been so riotous when Adélie had last seen it, a gloved hand pressed to her cheek? Georgette wanted to buy a bottle to smuggle into the club but Dubois was disinclined.

—Well, the fact is, I said, that the Chinese only built Cho Lon after the Tay Son brothers burnt down their village at Thanh Ha.

—And when was that? asked Georgette, her lean arm across the seat back. Nine thousand BC?

His spare jacket was too short for me, particularly through the arms, but by fussing incessantly with either cuff I hoped to not betray too much wrist. It was undeniably for the best, though, that I had left my serge jacket in the Renault, for besides the club girls in high-slit *ao dai* gowns swaying alongside black-tuxedoed Chinese gentlemen, the Triple Lucky Room was rife with vociferous, bowtied Europeans in white suits—for once I could've made use of those misbegotten things! Even the Oriental musicians, nodding onstage with their banjos and brass, would have looked equally at home boating on the Seine—which flows only blocks to the north of the Sorbonne, I thought despite myself.

As we manoeuvred the smoke-filled room en route to our table I couldn't help but notice a slim blonde girl in a tight-fitting tunic dress, a cigarette in either hand, chatting affably with a clutch of stout moustached men at the bar. She spun on her stool as I passed, blocking my way with a firm white calf.

—Hold on! she said. Stay awhile!

I bowed my head, turned red as an apple, I confess, and hurried around the end of her foot after Dubois. In my wake the stout men laughed as though I'd emitted nitrous oxide. I looked after her as I took my chair but saw only the back of her tightly coifed head, so I attempted to shake hands with Dubois' many large-toothed friends as they threw peanuts into the bell of the saxophonist's horn.

—Come, come! said Georgette, seizing my hand. There's space on the dance floor!

There was only space enough for Georgette and I to press tightly together. Over her shoulder I watched Dubois buy a cigar from the passing girl, then puff with determination, glaring at us all the while. Georgette was perfumed with jasmine.

—You met Mariette? she asked in my ear.

—Who is Mariette?

—My lovely cousin!

With a long finger she indicated the blonde at the bar, nearly jabbing a smiling club girl in the eye.

—She *is* lovely, I said.

—Every planter from here to Yunan wants to marry her, but those planters are terribly unreliable, aren't they? Ah ha, see the face she made? She likes you! And she's a city girl, wants to settle in town, not on some muddy plantation!

I tried to glimpse the cousin again but we'd made too many turns into the throng. And what was the sense? Georgette backed away and seemed to stare at my feet, her arms still looped around my neck.

—She likes kissing, that's what, and some chaps don't know what to make of it!

—You must forgive me, I shouted. I like kissing too, but—

—You'll dance the next with her, won't you?

—The fact is, I won't be in town long—I'm on my way up to Laos!

She gave a pained look before we stepped away from each other to applaud the band as the high-hat neatly ended the number.

—And what's more, I said, my heart belongs to another.

Perhaps I ought to have given the blonde more consideration. Perhaps I half-believed I was still travelling north with Henri with that one goal before us.

—Ah, Georgette sighed. Another with a girl a world away!

Despite my admissions I was led to Mariette and told to kiss her cheeks. She really was lovely, with a smile just as wide as her cousin's, but the place was too loud, too modern, and I longed for my bed. Georgette frowned at my glazed expression.

—My Dubois will kill me for saying so, so you must keep this between us, but a love affair conducted across vast distance is no affair at all. It was nearly the end of us.

—That's good advice, I nodded. I'll give this business a few more weeks.

—You might let *the girl* have some say in it! Is she from Paris?

—Naturally.

—They're all the same, winked Mariette.

The cousins drank a good deal after that, and they snored together in the back of the Renault as we sped back into Saigon.

—What's this about a transfer to Laos? asked Dubois. You can see very damn well how much work we have!

I put my elbow out the open window and amiably told him of my morning's chat with Frémont. But the moment I mentioned bookkeeping he began to giggle.

—Oh, there's no way you could have known! he sputtered. It's just that every year the resident up there advertises for this bookkeeping supervisor, to keep up appearances, you know, as though gold were dropping out of the trees and he didn't know how to count it. In twenty years of posting the job they haven't hired anyone!

He chortled. I watched black buildings whirr past.

I'd already been in Saigon far too long.

Though it was three o'clock in the morning the porter sat barefoot on the steps of the villa, smoking a long pipe beneath the lamp. As the car purred away he stood up and said good evening, and I nodded hello. I no longer attempted Vietnamese.

—Do you want Monsieur Henri's room? he asked again. It is bigger.

—It seems I may be here some time, I said. How much will the rent increase?

He led me into the slumbering house and up the stairs.

—The same price for you, sir, he yawned. But for the room it goes up. Monsieur Henri paid the same rent since 1918, and if we sent an increase he called the police! Yes, go in.

He left me in the corridor, turning Henri's key.

If I'd expected any sort of museum I'd have been disappointed, for its four walls enclosed no busts of LeDallic, no selected letters, for what exactly does the uncelebrated man leave the world? In the glow of the hallway lamp I saw the bed was freshly made and the wardrobe, its doors hanging open, stood empty. I straddled the cane chair to admire the many yellowing portraits, evidently clipped from newspapers, of '20s film actresses beaming coquettishly from behind palm fronds and parasols. One blonde in particular, Huguette Duflos, had been tacked up a dozen times above the chiffonier.

I undressed and threw my clothes across the bedspread, where they lay as though their occupant had dissolved. Like burning incense. I sat on the cane chair, and as the moths flitted down my bare back I listened through the window to the night that stretched too far in all directions to even be called night. Night was when one was meant to sleep.

After an hour I rose and circled the room, ripping the ladies' pictures from the walls. Then I methodically tore each one to shreds. Their mouths in two. Their ears.

—Forgive me, I murmured to Huguette Duflos. My heart belongs to another.

YOUR SPIRIT
WILL RECLINE THERE

Mme. Adélie Tremier.

A CHICKEN BELOW her. Clucking resentfully, like a maid muttering into her chest while counting silverware. Then a younger chicken with a question in her voice, distinctly ignored by the first. Then two more, flapping and reproving, until the quartet's clamour nullified their voices as individuals. Evidently some excitement was afoot—in Toumbadou certain green-backed beetles were often the cause—but suddenly it all subsided, leaving the first chicken to her embittered soliloquy. Then Adélie heard two women pass by quite close, old women or genii, speaking handfuls of words. As predicted she was in her shroud, then, ready to begin anew as a spirit. Yet she knew from their inexplicable language that the genii had not been so generous as to transport her to France so that she might have glimpsed her son's progress, even if only fleetingly and through her shroud and even then only on All Souls' or some other prescribed date. She remained in this other country. Evidently the genii had bureaucratic niceties to observe here just as anywhere, to which she too would have to conform. And it was difficult to reconcile this notion of ephemeral genii with the undeniable fetor of chicken droppings.

She suddenly heard a man's guttural drawl near her elbow. *"Boi, dindah."* Then a sigh, a catch in his throat. *"Boi, boi, boi."*

"Dindah poo-ay," said a woman's voice from just above Adé-lie's chest—she evidently floated there. *"Poo-ay."* There was a great tenderness in the word.

Then Adélie was made aware of her physical body as cold water poured over her middle. A wonder she didn't jolt! This could only mean that she was not in the sphere of the genii at all, or that genii were nothing like she'd imagined.

She opened her eyes onto a dark room; yellow light filtered in through numerous slits in the walls. She saw a rivulet of water poured haltingly over her chest, a teaspoon at a time, from the lip of King Sisavang Vong's eight-cornered dipper. Her head was propped on what felt like a block of wood, and she gazed at her own body as though it were on a slab: her white torso, nipples red as boils, the two halves of her ribcage protruding upward like housetops, then a greyish petticoat clinging to her thighs. She gazed up the dipper's handle to a lean brown arm, then a shoulder, and finally a weathered female face round as a nut. The woman's eyes slanted slightly, smiling in their work. She in turn was watched by a man somewhat younger, with a nose which looked to have been broken numerous times, and large brown eyes that stood out so prominently that at first she feared he wore some macabre mask. But, no, he leaned forward on the heel of his hand and blinked his lashes just as anyone would. His waving hair sat back like laurels on a bust of Caesar.

"Alla," he murmured. *"Tangan-tangan."*

At this the woman poured the last of the water over Adélie's hands, crossed elegantly below her navel; with the final drops Adélie unconsciously drew a deep breath—and found the action effortless. Her lungs were cleared of tubercles. In the same instant the pair gaped down at her and seized each other's hands.

"Dindah boos!" whispered the man. *"Sisil!"*

"Baw poo-ay!" The woman lifted Adélie's hand and pressed her forehead to it.

"But who are you people?" Adélie asked, and the resounding volume at which she spoke alarmed her.

They wrapped her shoulders in a mat of woven grass and helped her to sit up in a corner where the bamboo floor was not

246

so wet. The woman sat up very straight in front of her, and in that reeking shed the sway of her wrinkled breasts reminded Adélie of a she-goat.

"*Kaba kama,*" the old woman said slowly, "*Pak.*" She patted her own bare chest and said it again. "*Pak.*"

It had to be her name.

"*Kamili,*" said the man, with similar reverence.

The woman patted his hand. "*Kown brah kama,*" she told Adélie.

What could it mean? Ah, as Pak glanced again at the man Adélie knew without question that she was his mother. Wherever Adélie had landed, it seemed a place where mothers took great pride in their sons—and perhaps before long she would be telling Manu that he was her *Kown brah* and that no *Kown brah* would stay an orphan for long. She inhaled deeply again, her lungs unfettered. This was not *spes phthisica*, she was not fooling herself—the tubercles were simply not there.

She brought her hands to her chest. "Adélie."

"Adli," they both intoned.

Kamili turned to refill the dipper from a wooden bowl and Adélie drew her sharpest inhalation yet, for the arrangement of lines as the man twisted his body—trapezius muscle flowing up into the back of his tawny neck, sturdy hand pivoting on his nimble wrist—was indistinguishable from Nijinsky in his role of genie. This inspired her to rise to her feet and visit the bowl herself. But though she drew up her legs and pushed from her shoulders until the grass mat fell away, she succeeded only in raising her behind an inch from the floor; the muscles in her legs were as dough.

Kamili rushed to Adélie and with his free arm around her back eased her down to the shuddering bamboo floor.

"*Yeut, yeut,*" he said reassuringly, and brought the dipper to her lips. "*Boi.*"

It was tepid yet clear, and tasted vaguely of lemon. She managed to take a deep drink, then another, at which time Pak spoke a few sharp words and Kamili withdrew his arm. By the third swallow the hairs on her arms stood on end.

"Boi," she whispered.

He blinked lavishly from either side of his ill-used nose and pressed the dipper on her until she had swallowed it all.

"Alla!" said the mother approvingly.

Beneath the floor the chickens awoke from their naps. Pak slid forward and began to massage Adélie's enervated leg, up the calf into the back of the thigh until it became altogether too ticklish and Adélie waved her away. Pak chortled happily while she dished rice and tiny peppers onto woven plates. Already the light in the room had changed as though hours had passed. Adélie wondered if she might yet be feverish and not realize it. An unseen child called from outside the hut and Kamili murmured a response, then a woman called more questions and Pak answered laughingly, saying *Adli,* among other things. Kamili shook his head.

"Sisil," he murmured, and touched his chest before gesturing toward Adélie. *"Sisil kaba shin!"* he said lightly.

There was *him*, he was saying, and there was *her*...was this his name for her? Sisil? Pak set the plates down and began to emit a high-pitched whine. With her thumb and forefinger barely apart she seemed to indicate the flight of a wayward insect around the room—then, suddenly, she slapped herself on the forearm and ceased whining. *"Sisil!"* she cried.

It meant "mosquito."

Kamili held his hands a centimetre apart in front of Adélie's emaciated frame. *"Sisil,"* he said yet again. He could not call her "Adli," apparently, as he had already named her "Mosquito"—because she was *small* like a mosquito?

Pak resumed her chortling—she plucked an ant from the rice and held it out on the end of her finger. *"Kamili!"* she cried.

And Kamili, the man, sat up proudly.

After the first mouthful of rice Adélie felt tremendously thirsty. She climbed to her feet and crossed to where the dipper floated in the bowl. As simple as that.

SHE COVERED herself with the grass mat before stepping outdoors, though Pak, gnawing one pea pod after another,

248

obviously had no such scruples—the Queen Mother of Laos had had no such scruples. But the giggling children, the itinerant pigs and whip-tailed dogs, the chattering women carrying their weaving down the path that ran in front of the house—it was unlikely that any of them would have to wait long before Adélie revealed more. The mat was as itchy as any hair shirt. Yet it surely was cause for celebration that she was so sufficiently recovered, after months of numbness and horror, as to resume dwelling on trifles. What were these, for example, on the backs of her hands—flea bites?

Those red crags stood in the west, she calculated, if the sun dipped above them, and if she could assume her mind not to be addled. Far to her left she discerned a jagged mountain in the shape of a dog's molar—the reverse of the hill she'd spied from that choleric village. Was this geography she was practicing now?

Dark-browed men congregated at the periphery of the crowd, arms folded in front or behind. Each wore a sheathed knife hanging unobtrusively from the small of his back. One carried a large rodent, its throat slashed.

The first of the crowd to hurry over was a toothless old woman, "Ama," who chattered conspiratorially with Pak before reaching up to brush her hand across Adélie's bare ankle, her leathery fingers nearly black against skin which hadn't seen the sun in eighteen years.

Adélie had expected a chief or even a party of dignitaries to come forward. The house to the left was larger and boasted something resembling a porch, and though no residents were in evidence Adélie imagined the chief living there. The small house opposite, however, its front wall in a state of near-collapse, was well-tenanted with chickens and grim-faced men. Six more houses could be seen from Pak's ladder, though to reckon by the villagers still ambling up the path there were more scattered elsewhere. Sixty-odd people now lounged before her and the figure of each, though slight and none too clean, was perfect enough to have stood in a museum; the old people sagged where old people will, yet backs and legs were never less than athletic. The children looked at Adélie and laughed while miming that they carried a great load on their head, firewood, or hay, no, it was hair, *her* hair, which, unencumbered by hats or pins, was expansive as a treetop. All of the villagers wore theirs in a lop-sided bun or in a plait down their back.

They wear it in a lopsided bun or plait down their back, she'd write Manu.

Men vanished down the paths, hands full of arrows. The sun dropped, this first day suddenly over, and the air filled with dragonflies. A trio of young women waded through the throng to set down sloshing buckets of water, and, ducking beneath the haphazard wings, the villagers lined up to each drink from a weathered gourd.

THE WORDS were not difficult to learn if she took them one at a time. *Boi*, after all, was not so different from *bois*, French for "woods," so if Adélie kept a picture in her head of a forest in the rain she could remember that *boi* meant water.

Beneath the crags further up the valley, the surface of the spring lay dappled grey and yellow by the morning light, its banks hidden by a profusion of overhanging branches full of lustily singing unseen birds. Pak set her shoulder-pole and buckets down, knelt on the damp ground and motioned for Adélie to do the same. They pressed their foreheads to the moss as though Sisavang himself dwelt in the water. Then Pak drew a burnt chicken wing from the hem of her rough skirt and placed it within a square of stones already crowded with ant-ravaged fruit, adding the sprig of purple flowers she'd picked on the way.

They'd walked a quarter-hour to reach the place, and Adélie wondered at the distance since its surroundings seemed just as inviting as around the village—why not live beside the spring? Now Pak lowered her head again, whispering into her bosom. The place seemed a sort of cathedral, albeit one filled with the raucous cries of emerald birds wheeling dizzyingly over the water. Adélie's people had revered their spring in Toumbadou, true, but they'd built their church in town.

"*Boi uah,*" Pak finally said, and sprang to her feet—though her face resembled a walnut, she was remarkably spry.

Adélie guessed that *uah* meant "bucket" since the old woman dipped hers in, again whispering a sort of incantation. Suddenly Pak whirled in the direction of the village.

"*Sek! Sek!*" she shrieked.

A black hen with a party of chicks ambled up the path. Pak lobbed twigs at them until they scuttled away.

"*Sek,*" she chuckled, "*te boi.*" She waved her arms dismissively—chicken, no water. "*Sek boi, te laha.*" If a chicken has water, no—?

"*Laha?*" asked Adélie.

Drawing a knobbly thumb across her throat, Pak thrust her purple tongue out the side of her mouth. "*Laha! Te laha!*"

Laha was "kill"? A chicken that drank water had to be killed? Or couldn't be killed? Neither made sense. The surface lay perfectly calm and the two reflected women towered like deities. Pak whispered confidences to the spring and dipped the next bucket.

Halfway back to the village, Pak motioned that Adélie set her load down and rest in the shade of a spreading fig tree, the earth trampled smooth beneath it. Pak stared up at a house nearly invisible amongst the scrub.

"*Oruma,*" Adélie said with confidence—house!

"*Baat,*" said Pak. Yes. "*Oruma sadet.*"

"*Sadet?*"

Pak raised her lean arm and pointed. A tall, pot-bellied old man meandered before the place, gazing into the air. Smirking, Pak raised her hands like a pouncing cat.

In the village, a boy Adélie had seen disappearing into the woods with Kamili now stood on Pak's ladder; his eyes sat far apart and black locks twisted past his shoulders. Pak tousled his hair. With a long string he dragged a corn cob across the ground, collecting a dozen brown ants with every pass.

"*Kown brah,*" she solemnly told Adélie. "*Kown brah* Kamili."

"Kamili?"

"*Kaba* Gani."

Apparently this was Kamili's son, called Gani—but who was Gani's mother? Adélie followed Pak up her ladder with an armload of firewood, and inside they found Kamili in a dark corner. He gnawed a cucumber.

"Sisil," he said, and held out his hand.

Before Adélie could fashion a greeting his mother unleashed a torrent of sharp words; he shielded himself with the cucumber. He hurried to his feet and down the ladder, just as Pak turned an aggrieved paragraph on Adélie.

"*Te lako*," she concluded. "Kamili *te lako!*"

Apparently there was something that her son was not, or did not have. Adélie stacked the wood beside the hearthstone and tried to appear both submissive and appreciative. She was still not strong enough to start for Luang-Prabang.

A FULL MOON had risen on her first night, and it rose again now. In the space of one month Adélie had memorized the overlapping patterns of woven bamboo, the fact that black corn was for people and yellow for pigs, and the words for sun, night, dog, monkey, mat, deer, fire, child, smoke, flower, slowly, knife, louse, moon, house, bird, tree, blood, and a few dozen more. She did tangle them on a regular basis, though, as when she'd believed *kapéna* was an entire housefly before Gani demonstrated that *langow* was the housefly and *kapéna* merely its wing. She certainly knew enough words to understand that the *noi ban*, the headman, did indeed live beside Pak but had gone away to hunt elephant, *s'in*, and had taken away enough water in pig-stomach bags to last a long time. Gani had been particularly ingenious in teaching her *s'in*, she thought, waving his hands at the sides of his head and swaying dolefully around the flickering hearth before dropping to his knees to give his freshly whittled top a spin.

Kamili no longer visited his mother's house. Whenever Adélie padded across to visit Ama her sons would leap up and excuse themselves, making it abundantly clear that unmarried men and women could not intermingle and that an unprecedented exception must have been made during her illness. Crouched beneath her ladder to sharpen knives on the wet stone, Pak scowled toward the *noi ban*'s house as they discussed this, from which Adélie intimated that the exception could never have been made had the headman been at home.

One morning beside the spring she found Kamili asleep on his side beneath a tree, knees drawn to his chest. In sleep his face was that of an exiled child, the infant Moses, a rough bow and quiver of arrows in his hands, ferns swaying over him as on the bank of the Nile. She saw a knife or a bow or spear as equivalents to a pocketbook full of money in France—they were how one acquired what one needed on a minute-to-minute basis.

She'd learned that *lako* meant "wife" and that Kamili no longer had one. She'd asked Ama and Pak what had become of the woman and each time been told, "She fell," but whether fallen from a cliff or fallen like Eve she'd had no opportunity to ascertain.

A *langow* buzzed up Kamili's nostril and he sat up licking his lips. Adélie filled her buckets as though she hadn't noticed him.

"Sisil," he said.

"Can you hunt here?" She felt as though she had to chew each word. "Deer and birds drink at the spring. You could not hunt here."

"No hunting, no." He explained that he had only come this way for the *sadet* to talk over his arrows. To... bless them? "The water here is good for animals." Kamili rubbed his taut belly appreciatively. "Good for people."

So, with this agreed upon, she tried to explain her plan as he scratched the back of his neck: that a party might carry spring water around the dog's-tooth mountain all the way to the choleric village where the water's healing properties might save them—and serve as a precursor for her return to Luang-Prabang, though she did not articulate this. He seemed to understand what she meant in describing a dog's tooth and a mountain, since he looked over his shoulder in that direction, but beyond that she may have merely been explaining that the water in her buckets had to be carried back to the village where people sleep.

"I can walk beside you," he said, and picked an ant from his ear.

PUT TO DEATH IN THE MOST OBSCENE WAYS BY THE GRATEFUL NATIVES

Mme. Adélie Tremier.

THE FULL moon had gone away and come back and gone away—that night there would be no moon at all. It was late in the afternoon, and as a reward for their labours Adélie instructed the children to gather on the path and join hands, but not in a straight line, no, no, she moved each of them by the shoulders until they formed a circle, then she had Gani and Uroh, the snub-nosed girl, step forward to be the example pair even as Gani pulled a bamboo splinter from his palm. Old Ama's house had been beautifully rebuilt with a new crossbeam, dark teak carved with intertwining elephants and cobras, and now the old woman herself sped down her ladder, winking at them as they stood holding hands, boy-girl-boy-girl, before waving her skirt at chickens picking over the sesame seeds drying on a mat. Adélie continued her instruction coolly so as to not make the young people aware of her shock—Ama wore Adélie's Parisian hat! With its veil folded back, the better to wink at passersby! Behind another matron Ama climbed into the headman's house, as boldly as if *La Samaritaine* had put silk stockings on special, and during the next quarter-hour swept his floor with leafy twigs, shook out his mats and even patched the holes in the *noi ban*'s walls. Adélie wondered at that.

When she explained that the line they'd formed would move like an *ular*, a snake, the boys wound lithely into the undergrowth—with far more subtlety than French children could ever have managed—and the girls, accordingly, struck at them with sticks. Then Adélie cut branches with her knife and, reforming the line, demonstrated with a hop for every two skips how their long serpent was meant to coil and uncoil while they held the twigs between them, even going so far as to wind the line back through itself before she renewed her attempts to have them break into pairs and touch the toes of their right feet to their left knees. A steady beat was kept by the *shush-shush* of women beneath the huts tossing rice in woven pans, stopping only to pick out the husks, and as Adélie's bare breasts danced more than the rest of her she realized that corsets and stays might have some redeeming value after all. And when she saw Pak saunter back from the corn fields beyond the ridge Adélie gladly told the young people *moleh oruma*, go home, and followed her friend up the ladder.

"I did good work today!" she announced.

But Pak told her to get the pot on the fire before it was time to line up for the water, though she needn't have said it at all as this was their ritual every night—indeed, was the ritual in every house, though Adélie reasoned that the telling was just as important as setting a pinch of rice aside for the Spirit of the House. So while she rubbed the fire-stick in the shavings Adélie described breathlessly how she and the children had spent the entire day—except for one nap under the trees during the worst of the heat, with a child and a stick on guard for centipedes—cutting bamboo from the hillside to carry to the spring—the groves below the spring being impossible to cut—and assembling the first sections of a pipe to bring water down to the village. It was a hundred paces long already! And to fill the pipe she'd placed a wheel of bamboo cups right in the spring. Think how much trouble it would save!

Pak sat pulling apart the broad leaves that looked so much like spinach.

"You make a good story," she said. "The spirit flies out of the water that way. And to leave anything in the water will poison it. You make a good story!"

"I dropped the wheel into the spring," said Adélie. "I did! Should I take it out?"

Pak sat up, wide-eyed.

"The *noi ban* comes back tonight—Kamili saw his smoke on the hill this morning! He will be there now to make thanks! The law is bad for you, Sisil! The spirit flies out of the water that way!"

Adélie's arms trembled as she descended the ladder for the evening water, and the mosquitoes in her ears alarmed her more than ever before. She stood in the line swatting herself. Kamili waited to one side with his arms folded.

"What?" asked Pak.

He stared at Adélie, his mouth grim, yet she thought his slow-blinking eyes looked as large and bright as ever, even as the Light of the Day climbed into its cave in the crags and its sibling the Darkness struggled yawning to its feet.

"I had water," he finally said. "I have been to the spring."

"The *noi ban* has come back," someone was telling Ama. "He took no elephant."

"None?" Ama still wore the Parisian hat. "That has never happened!"

"That has never happened," repeated the other woman.

And they stared past the whirling bats at Adélie, who cupped her ill-used breasts.

After swallowing their fill each hunter lined up beside Kamili. The cooking fires were unable to alleviate the gloom; each figure seemed dipped in charcoal. Uroh ran up to greet Adélie, her teeth shining, but the girl's mother called her back.

"We must go see the *sadet*," Pak said flatly.

"Take the rice off the fire," Adélie said, but her friend was walking up the path, and though her legs felt incapable of carrying her, she followed. The rest of the village tramped silently behind. The shrieks and whirrs of insects in the undergrowth seemed to enunciate, "We are hungry," but nonetheless the evening's sudden cool felt delicious as she willed her feet to climb the rocks. The sky had turned the indigo of her father's thumb, and between the black leaves she made out Orion, each star glaring like an incandescent bulb. Orion had been Georges' favourite constellation and revealing him tonight was surely his summons to her from the *actual* Dominion of Genii where he'd been dwelling so long. Whether or not she was ready to join him.

Beneath the fig tree, two men sat within a circle of torches. Moths and huge, dim-witted mosquitoes hovered over the flames, where the canny bats made quick work of them. The pot-bellied *sadet* stood up.

"Only Sisil inside," he called.

Her feeble legs propelled her between the torches. She had seen these villagers kill all manner of animals with a twist of a knife, a prod of a spear, with less remorse than if they had blotted a letter. The two men sat behind a mat bedecked with a dead chicken, a bowl of speckled eggs, a small bucket of water and one of the big knives used for cutting down trees. The man beside the *sadet* looked no bigger than a child, his grey hair sticking straight out over his ears, and one shoulder distinctly higher than the other.

"Speak a greeting," he croaked.

"*Noi ban,*" Adélie murmured. "*Sadet . . .*"

"What?" asked the *noi ban.* "What?"

She knelt and pressed her forehead to the black dirt.

"*Alla,*" intoned the *sadet.* Then he spoke too quickly for her to follow, delivering a well-rehearsed speech, that was clear, with the crowd outside the ring calling a response at pertinent moments.

"*Mondo-mondo,*" they groaned, which meant "monkeys." Head still pressed to the ground, Adélie realized that the lilting sermon might have nothing to do with her, might instead be a formality like the singing of the *Marseillaise.* The *sadet*'s voice grew strident, angry.

"The boy's mouth," echoed the crowd.

She raised her eyes, and they fell upon the long knife. The earth beneath her knees felt supernaturally cold while the torches slowly roasted her back and shoulders. She was in the cage hovering above the crowd again, dancers whirling beneath her, smoke pervading her lungs.

"Sisil," the *noi ban* croaked.

She looked up at the two men. The *sadet* held an egg length-wise between his thumb and forefinger. The *noi ban* produced a length of bamboo and dropped it in front of her, and Adélie's stomach fluttered like a bat as she recognized the notches she'd cut into either end of the tube so that it might be joined to its neighbours and so form that mighty pipeline from spring to the village, whose residents were to have shouted songs of her innovative spirit forever after. Had not a single child known what would happen?

The *sadet* climbed to his feet, egg still in hand, and swayed as though the words he was about to speak were inscribed on leaves above his head.

"I was the one!" he announced.

Adélie's heart leapt like a frog—the *sadet* shouldering blame for her blasphemy?

"I came upon this thing!" he cried, and went on to explain that *he was the one* who had first discovered the trouble at their great and sacred spring, the bad work of man, the insult to the Spirit of the Water. As he'd climbed to the spring to pray he had even passed Sisil and the children returning to the village, and they had looked so happy!

Beyond the torches she saw boys hang their heads.

"Not to punish the children!" shouted the *noi ban*.

"*Te*," agreed the *sadet*. "Now the children say what else was done."

What *else*? She looked over her shoulder at the boys and girls filing into the circle behind her. Bless their hearts, they each held a twig between them! The torches flickering against their shoulders, eyes gazing wide at the two men, the children began to wind a serpentine around her, hopping twice for every skip, and though they had that part backwards she had to smile.

"Stop," grunted the *noi ban*.

The children hung their heads and filed out again.

"Now Uroh will say what else was done," said the *sadet*.

The snub-nosed girl hurried into the circle and cleared a place in the dirt to set her top. The girl's father had carved it from a block of teak. She wrapped the bark strap around it then set the top spinning with an expert tug. It skipped over a pebble but stayed upright, and Adélie realized with a start that the *noi ban* was scurrying past her—he stood over the toy, gnarled hands gripping his knees, until it collapsed in the dirt.

"Again," he said.

His fascination might save her! But when he straightened she saw a grimace so deep it might have been wrought in clay, and he resumed his seat beside the *sadet* while poor Uroh reached for her still-spinning top. Her father grunted a syllable, though, so that she silently walked out to him and abandoned the toy within the ring.

"We have *this*," croaked the *noi ban*, pointing at the top, "and I kill no elephant. Before this, there is no number for the elephants I kill. Count the leaves in the forest to make the number."

"Who has done these things?" shouted the *sadet*.

Adélie watched for some signal from the men—was she meant to stand up? No, the *sadet* merely held the speckled egg aloft. Had blame for her crimes somehow, wonderfully, been transferred to the egg?

"Did Ama do these things?" called the *noi ban*.

Adélie glimpsed the old woman standing quite close to the fig tree—no longer sporting the veiled hat, of course—but Ama said nothing in her own defence. In fact no one, inside the ring or out, spoke a word in response to the question. Everyone stared at the egg gripped between the *sadet*'s fingertip and the point of his thumb.

"Did Pak do these things?" called the *noi ban*.

The ground beneath Adélie's hands felt colder than ever—yes, by nursing her to health Pak had certainly abetted in her crimes! But still no one said anything.

"Did Kamili do these things?" called the *noi ban*. "Did Tangan do these things?"

And so it continued, as the torches spat and hissed and the *noi ban*'s eyelids looked to grow heavier. Salaka, Me'ek, Masu and Bunga were each accused without effect. Then the *sadet* licked his lips.

"Did Sisil do these things?" called the *noi ban*.

The *sadet*'s thumb penetrated the egg's shell with a dramatic *crack* and its yellow innards gushed down his wrist. The wizened *noi ban* sat up very straight, though this only brought him as high as the *sadet*'s shoulder.

"The Spirit says it is Sisil," he announced. "Tomorrow when the sun sets we will take her to—"

"I must speak!" called Pak. She looked ancient in the flickering light, her voice unnaturally high.

"*Alla*," said the chief.

"My love to the Spirit of the Water, the *sadet*, the *noi ban*," she went on. "I say that it is not a person that did these things." She stretched out her lean arm to indicate Adélie. "Did she find the spring with the rest of us? No. Sisil is not a person."

Adélie watched the *sadet* set a new egg in the palm of his hand.

"Gani found Sisil in the forest," said Pak. "She is our animal. If a pig or a dog had done these things, would we kill it right away? No. We would say, 'Keep it tied up. No more trouble.' We would not kill it right away."

"Kamili is head of that family," croaked the *noi ban*.

The *sadet* set the egg on the mat. "He must decide!"

"Kill her or tie her up," said the *noi ban*, "or let her walk free or put her in the cave where Darkness sleeps."

Pak stepped back and Kamili reappeared in her place. He already wore his quiver and bow.

"I will decide," he said quietly.

"What?" asked the *noi ban*. "What?"

"I will decide what to do with her."

"And make gifts to the Spirit of the Water," said the *sadet*. "Then there can be no more trouble!"

"Sisil," said the *noi ban*, sitting straight as a rooster. "Follow this man."

The children clustered around Adélie as she slipped out of the ring, their eyes shining, but not one stayed beside her as she started after Kamili. They entered the yawning forest, orange and red from the torchlight. But whose feet scrambled after her?

"Gani!" Pak's voice called from beneath the fig tree. "Not now!"

Adélie couldn't say whether Gani went away then or not; she was staring too intently at the bending branches that hinted at Kamili's place in the blackness. It would be better to be beside him than all alone, whatever his intentions. Since she'd first awoken inside Pak's house the memory of dying in the woods had never been far away.

She followed him through the village—deserted but for animals shifting in their sleep, embers winking dully from the doorways—and down the path that led south. When she stopped to pluck a thorn from her heel she saw Kamili's silhouette stop as well, without a backward glance, until her feet shambled after him again.

The forest air grew damper and colder, and she knew that insects were curling up in their cellars and blowing out the candle. She let her mind wander after Manu. She wondered if he had yet walked the slick streets of Paris at such an hour, as news vendors unfastened padlocks and lit braziers to boil their coffee. No, she surely had not been away more than a year, could only have missed one birthday, his tenth, therefore he wasn't old enough to walk pre-dawn streets. And surely Sabine had not sent him to St-Lucien at all, but tucked him in with a tumbler of water next to his bed.

The Darkness had gone into its cave and the Light of Day yawned as Adélie picked her way over fallen trunks—no doubt teeming with invisible centipedes—and found Kamili waiting in the trees twenty paces ahead, in the gloom of an impenetrable canopy. The ground was peppered with white mushrooms the size of franc coins.

"Here," he announced. "Gani found you here yesterday."

She'd learned after numerous misunderstandings that "yesterday" might mean one day or a hundred years before.

"Walking here, and he found you."

Like the shepherd boy who stumbled upon the Virgin and so founded Toumbadou. She stopped in front of Kamili. He drew an arrow from his quiver.

"Do not," she whispered. "I must go back to my son."

He kicked away the dry leaves beneath his feet.

She heard a sudden downpour of rain then realized it was only breezes rattling the bamboo. He ground the balls of his feet into the dirt and lowered his gaze to set the shaft against his callused finger. As a girl Adélie had lain awake imagining the nausea Isaac must have experienced as Abraham raised his knife, but now she guessed that Isaac had felt nothing at all, for here again was her unreasoning calm. An orange fungus upon a tree looked like flame frozen in place. Now Kamili murmured to his arrow.

Her eye caught a white movement behind his shoulder.

"Gani," she said.

Bow drawn, Kamili retreated a step—the boy, running from between the trees, carried an open white parasol.

"*Shin*, Sisil!" called Gani. All smiles.

He dropped it upside down between the adults and, rotating the handle like a fire-stick between his palms, set the mildew-blotched parasol spinning. It turned a half-dozen times before tumbling into the leaves.

"*Toupie*," said Kamili, still holding the arrow to the bowstring.

"*Baat!*" Gani agreed, setting the point on a rock.

This time the top stayed upright for several seconds, long enough for Gani to grin up at his father and for Kamili to blink. Then the boy carried the parasol to Adélie, who demonstrated how it could be collapsed, to Gani's open-mouthed delight, then opened again with a single motion. Kamili allowed the bowstring to go slack. She lifted the parasol aloft and strode out of the grove into the quavering morning sun.

The boy hurried after her to hold the very big top over her head as she picked her way over the fallen trees. In the shade of this fashionable artifact she felt her lack of a *hat* even more keenly than her lack of clothes.

"*Toupie tom-tom* Sisil!" Gani called again to his father.

"*Baat*," said Kamili, carefully returning the arrow to its quiver.

WHEN SHE RETURNED there were no chickens beneath Pak's house, for they had all gone to the *sadet* and the Spirit of the Water.

Pak led her over the ridge for papayas because in the spring's vicinity they refused to come away from the branch, then they spent the afternoon beneath the house, languidly shaking hot ashes from a bamboo tube onto a burgeoning anthill that sought to undermine one of the stilts. The two women killed and plucked and butchered one of the scabby-faced black-and-white ducks, but they looked at each other with some alarm before placing the pieces over the fire, for Gani had not taken his place in the corner. Would the food even cook without him in the corner? Kamili, of course, took his dinner at home by himself, and they never discussed what, if anything, he might be eating.

"What can have happened?" whispered Pak.

Adélie leaned outside and realized that Gani already stood before the hut. A sleeping mat was draped across his shoulder, and he carried his bow and a basket holding his top and pipe and knife and arrows and a half-dozen little animal skulls.

"You sleep at his house now," Gani announced.

"Ah, good," said Pak from behind the thin wall.

Gani climbed the ladder and spread his mat beside his grandmother's. The duck was over the fire now and flames leapt as the grease dripped onto the coals. Adélie sat with her arms around her knees. The interplay of orange-brown light and orange-brown dark across bamboo crossbeams and layers of roof thatch conspired to convince her that there had never been a Manu or a Nicolas in her life. She was not convinced, of course, yet what was the tangible evidence before her? That the world consisted of one village.

In deference to Pak she left Sisavang's eight-cornered dipper hanging from the rafter, but picked up a single papaya so as to not arrive empty-handed. Then she descended the ladder.

Women threw wash-water out their doors and hens fluttered from their roosts to pick it over. Adélie started along the path that ran beside Ama's hut. As an unmarried woman she had never before approached his house, and the vague trail carried her beneath dark trees as high as canyon walls, the evening air given texture by insect orchestras. She emerged in a small clearing, a tangle of green-and-black scrub. The glow of a fire hovered a metre above the ground. That was the house. During the cycle of seasons about to unspool the hours and days would continually bury each other, but Adélie would always remember the leaves brushing her head and the red glow beckoning.

"Sisil," his voice called. "This way."

He took her hand to help her up the ladder. He was naked. He set the papaya in a basket. In the quivering light of the flames Adélie saw that he was ready for her, and as she lay down next to him she realized that she was ready too.

The house smelled of smoke, of course, but Kamili moving on top of her smelled of horse tack. She pressed her nostrils beneath his ear and decided that, no, he smelled of horse. Sour and welcoming.

No lights shone from her fingertips. No phantoms arrayed themselves about her. There was only his face disappearing into the shadow, re-emerging, disappearing, and ants scrambling across her hairline to drink her sweat.

He collapsed in sleep. The forest was overrun with shrieking animals. There was still an Emanuel Tremier somewhere in the world, she told herself again and again, and she was in the same world.

When the chilly morning came he quartered a cucumber for her, then, just as on that first day, wrapped an arm around the small of her back. Looking down at herself—naked, scarlet, streaked with grime—she wondered if she was a she-goat now.

"Sisil," he said softly. "*Lako kama.*"

My wife.

"You decided?" she asked.

"When I did not kill you," he whispered, "it was better."

At this he crushed a small brown worm that had crawled across her knee and she heard, as ever, the distant thud of firewood being chopped.

BEFORE THE rainy season they would require a house that did not leak, so while Pak and Gani hoisted palm thatch atop fresh

264

posts across the clearing, Kamili built a fire beneath their old house, cut a new set of arrows and carefully, carefully brought a basket down from the rafters.

"To make the poison."

"Why? You can knock a bird out of the sky!"

"If a wound is small, the deer escapes. With poison it does not."

The basket held nine ingredients: shavings of *wourali* vine and of a nameless bitter root; stalks from two varieties of bulbous plant, each containing a glutinous green sap; tiny scalding peppers from the bushes around the hut; pounded fangs of the deadly *labari* and *kouna* snakes which he'd cautiously stockpiled over some months; and two gourds with tight stoppers containing species of ant collected that very morning—one large and black with a bite that induced fever, one small and red with a sting like a nettle.

"I have not even shown Gani how it is done."

"When will you?" she asked.

"When he is older."

Using water from the streams beyond the ridge, he rinsed the shavings in a colander of leaves; a liquid resembling coffee drained into the pot. He squeezed the sap from the stalks, unflinchingly added the ants, broken fangs and peppers, then placed the pot over the fire, which had burned down to coals. As the mixture thickened he added more *wourali*. Sweat dripped down his crooked nose and he was careful to wipe it away with his clean wrist rather than the flat of his hand. When scum collected on the surface he removed it with a leaf, which he then burnt, and when the mixture had become thick brown syrup he lifted it from the coals and dipped in the tip of a single arrow before pouring the poison into a gourd which he sealed with several layers of hide tied with a cord. He picked up his bow.

"I will see if it is strong."

He returned ten minutes later, swinging a small red deer by the feet as though it were a fashionable handbag. Its only wound was a neat hole in the back of one leg.

"*Alla,*" he said. "Take the baskets to the new house."

The new house did not yet have walls.

"Can we stay here tonight?" asked Adélie.

"No, no." He lowered his brow like an actor in a farce. "We made poison. The spirits have abandoned this place."

She and Pak butchered the deer beneath the new hut while Gani finished lashing the roof down and Kamili carried his mixture away to the *sadet*. Besides a bluish tinge to the meat immediately around the wound—and that was easily cut away—the wondrous poison did nothing to pollute the flesh. Adélie ripped the flank away from the hip and then, while flies circled in a frenzy, she licked the sweet blood from her thumb.

"Is the *wourali* vine bad?" she asked him that night. "It could kill an animal?"

"Oh, yes!" With his front teeth he freed a strip of meat trapped beneath the tendon. "*Wourali* is very bad."

"Then why do you also put in the *labari* and the *kouna* and the peppers?"

"Ah, with them my poison is perfect." Kamili threw the long bone in the air then caught it. "It is all bad things put together!"

"Then what is all *good* things put together?" she asked.

"Come here."

Not to contradict his extremely incisive theory, but as he slept with his arms about her neck she decided that the distillation of all good things instead had to be the spring itself. Rather than being *possessed* of any good spirit, though, it simply *was* the good spirit in and of itself, self-perpetuating, like the human race.

ONE OF THE pigs beyond the ridge became pregnant, mottled sides stretched tight with unborn hooves and vertebrae, shuffling about the enclosure as though gravity sought to crush her beneath its thumb.

"*Goh bibo!*" the children sang happily, waddling sideways while lobbing shrivelled limes at each other, and it was only then that Adélie learned *bibo*, "pregnant."

"Why are none of the women pregnant?" she asked Kamili.

"A person cannot be pregnant." He lay face-down on their mat in the midday heat. "It is not possible."

"But there are babies!"

"Them? They were born before we came here. They were always babies."

"When did you come here?"

He feigned sleep. Or perhaps he did sleep.

"How many times has the moon come and gone?" she prodded.

"There is no number for that. Go outside and count the leaves!" He swatted something from his face. "More rainy seasons than hairs on my head!"

It was a village where the ancient walked upright, after all, and bacilli vanished like vapour. But from then on she sat on Pak's ladder and watched Gani and his friends string their tops and lob their spears and play farmer-and-pig, and found their habits less endearing than she had. Because if Kamili was not misleading her—and why should he?—then each moment of sing-song posturing was no longer the fleeting treasure of a single season. She realized with a chill up her spine how the simple introduction of tops had transformed the village, and she sympathized suddenly with the *noi ban*.

IN THE *leh* she was going to learn to *stu'ung*: plant rice shoots in a flooded field. Smoke from the breakfast fires still hanging from the trees, she hurried over the ridge behind Pak until they came to the wet ground. To the chirrup of frogs she found her row between Ama and Me'ek, whose infant son clung to her back in a sling. His mouth lazily drooling, the child blinked sagely at Adélie as he pitched up and down with the motion of his mother's toil. He looked away, then back at Adélie. He appeared to be six months old, but was he a wise ancient trapped in the skin of a baby? Did Gani and the rest *think* as children, or was it simply their sacred occupation to endlessly play games and run races, just as it was the women's to plant fields? Soon the women would stop to eat their bananas that tasted of potato, then, as the sun began to dip, they would fill their baskets in the corn-field and walk home with hands on the smalls of their backs and thumbs over their hips, and after dark Kamili would bring bleeding meat home over his shoulder to eat with Pak and Gani, then in their own house she and her man with the ill-used face would drink their water in the firelight while she washed her-self from the bucket of spring water and he taught her to speak. She could hardly remember what he looked like in sunlight.

Suddenly she heard a bleating from the woods, and thought *ular ahan beh*. She did not think, in French, "a snake eats a frog," and then translate each word in her mind. She simply thought *ular ahan beh,* and in the same instant the bleating ceased.

For each sprawling *leh* planted, another waited further down the hill; woven between their perpetual tasks of preparing meals and collecting firewood, the *stu'ung* was a mammoth undertaking for the village's twenty-five women. Considering that they had cured her of tuberculosis, Adélie couldn't imagine how she might with any dignity begin her walk back to Manu until the job was well and truly finished.

"TODAY I GO," she called to Kamili.

"Go?"

Jungle cocks crowed to each other across the distance. Pak filled a net bag with onions and wizened oranges and hung this over one of Adélie's freckled shoulders and a brimming skin of water over the other. They went to the headman's house, where the other women were still stretched on the floor, and she bowed and said her thanks and her goodbyes. The women fur-rowed their brows.

"Go?" they asked.

Kamili sat on the floor of the hut they shared, gripping his big toes.

"It is too late to travel today," he said.

The Light of the Day was only now stretching its arms across the sky.

"It will take all day to reach the starting place," he continued.

He and Gani cut the path before her all the way to the parasol grove, only to stand hunch-shouldered at her side.

"It must be that way," Kamili said, nodding vaguely in the direction of the dog's-tooth mountain, unseen now beyond the canopy. "Take this."

He untied the cord from around his waist and handed her the machete in its scabbard. Father and son gazed at her until a red-eyed fly landed on Gani's neck, rubbed its legs and flew off. Then they trotted away in the direction from which they'd come.

Adélie walked south through the grove. If I always travel downhill, she thought, I will eventually meet with a stream, and every stream in this country must run into the Mekong, and by following the Mekong I will come to Luang-Prabang. She had no theories as to how long this might take.

She scrambled down a satisfyingly steep slope, the water-skin thudding against her ribs. When the ground levelled she brought out the machete, for all around her towered thickets sporting thorns as long as her finger, and as she began to hack energetically at their depths she imagined Marie collecting, from the postman's liver-spotted hands, the latest number of *Mon Journal*, with Adélie herself pictured on the cover under the title "A Hard-Fought Reunion."

By the time she'd penetrated a metre she guessed an hour had already been wasted—but perhaps the thorns were not so fearsome as they looked? She sucked an orange, shut her eyes and leaned against them. A minute later she counted the twenty-two places where she'd been cut, and fifteen thorns had to be pulled from her flesh yet she refused to climb up the slope and find another way. If torrents and deadfall and thorns could deter her so quickly she might as well turn back!

She resumed her more-laborious method, but as she was streaked with blood the flies harassed her more than ever. The spring water would stave off infection.

She finally broke through to a game trail gouged by what looked like the hooves of cattle; greyish hair hung from the thorns. As the path descended she imagined the dugout canoe she would ride into Luang-Prabang, but after ten minutes she found herself in a swamp where cadres of insects flashed across black water. She slipped across half-submerged logs, following a line she'd drawn in her head. If there were loitering snakes she refused to see them. Her breasts were caked with mud, and insects came and went from her nose and eyes as though these were long-established neighbourhoods, but even so she could not complain because she was not lying dead of consumption. One day she and Manu would cross the Place de la Concorde on the way to his school and she would think, "Remember when I was in that swamp?" She listened for the stream the black water had to empty into. She thought of the waterborne animalcules swarming into the twenty-two places where her skin had been broken, then sat on a knuckle of root to drink her spring water. But she found the skin held only a mouthful. It was as full of holes as she was.

When she climbed onto solid ground the hoof-marks did as well, but now orange hair hung from the thorns too.

She came upon a tangle of fallen trees; cracked shoulder blades and skulls and leg-bones were strewn around carelessly. The air was thick with flies and smelled of acrid piss. She consoled herself that she'd already penetrated this far without this tiger eating her, and that if it slept during the day, as she was sure she'd once read, it must possess some alternate abattoir where it was curled up already. She walked silently forward but just as she stepped over a metre-wide pair of horns the thicket suddenly darkened and a wall of rain washed her clean of mud and blood and insects. The drops fell so hard she could hardly stand upright, and the path, the trees, the thorns all suddenly became invisible behind their grey curtain. She struggled forward, hands extended like a sleepwalker, and though the thorns cut her in a dozen places she still did not find a trail. Rain thudded on her scalp like hammers. She struggled back the way she'd come only to crash headlong through a worm-eaten ribcage. She crawled forward, taking care not to set her knees on a row of teeth.

When she reached the swamp she decided, as wild-eyed rats swam to higher ground, that it was not a sensible place to wait either.

The next morning Kamili had great difficulty in starting his cooking fire with such damp wood—he'd never seen such a downpour in a dry season! He blew a dozen times on the tinder, then looked up to see Sisil climbing their ladder. She'd come back?

"I will leave another time," she said cheerfully.

A FAMILY'S WEALTH
IS NOT ITS JARS

Mme. Adélie Tremier.

IT WAS laughable that she'd ever thought of *boi* and *bois* as distinct notions, for now the words were interchangeable—in every direction Adélie saw forest and rain together, for now it was the wet season. Kamili held an ember to the bowl and drew on his pipe again and again, but the tobacco refused to ignite.

"*Kai fliang,*" he said with a smirk. The wet season.

Was it possible that the *kai fliang* coincided with a tilting of the earth's axis and that gravity increased its duration? Because during those downpour mornings she could do no more but lie animal-flat against the floor, only climbing to her knees to raise her switch and slaughter a dozen or two of the hundreds of flies the weather drove indoors.

In a home without furniture muddy feet beget a muddy floor, which beget muddy bottoms and backs and hands, begetting grit between teeth at mealtimes. While the meat cooked she would pluck the swollen leeches out of Kamili's armpits and from between his toes, and without even moving he somehow spread mud over the floor and walls. The leeches would burst on the embers.

From Pak's door she watched Ama take a single step outside and fill her wash-water bucket from the torrent off her roof. Corn cobs and lime peels, thrown down for the animals, tumbled along the creek that had once been the path. Adélie watched the children creep beneath the eaves of the houses in an attempt to keep their tops dry, otherwise they did not spin evenly, and she concluded—and wondered how many times she had concluded—that the greatest achievement of an advanced society was the manufacture of objects to keep youngsters occupied during wet weather.

The adults spent many mornings around the *noi ban*'s whisky jar, and through the accompanying haze Adélie studied the eight water-skins on his wall and tried to imagine how many mouthfuls she would need when she next returned to Manu. It was unanimously agreed that no path was passable during the *kai fliang*. Old Pak ran leathery fingers over the frogs and tigers cavorting across the great clay jar.

In the wet air, smoke could not rise properly through the holes in the house-tops but seeped sluggishly through the roofs and the walls so that after dawn the whole village looked to be smouldering disastrously. She'd had such difficulty finding tinder for her own fire, though, that Adélie took great comfort in the sight.

Intertwined upon their mat, Kamili squinted down at her through his lashes.

"Warm and slippery," he grinned.

The same words he used to describe the mud at the foot of their ladder.

ONE MORNING, to her great confusion, it did not rain, and everyone she met told her that the *kai fliang* had ended as quickly as it had begun and now the *kai brung* was with them again. Just like that, they clapped, it was with them again!

That night the villagers trooped once more to the fig tree so that the *sadet* could bless the upcoming burning of the fields. He stood within the ring of torches and repeated his droning speech, and to keep her memories of the previous ring of torches at bay Adélie concentrated with all her might upon his words, for now she understood every one and could respond along with the giddy children whenever the *sadet* bowed his head. Often they simply said *Spirit of the Water Spirit of the Water Spirit of the Water.*

But just as the story ended the *noi ban* led the children away with a scowl and wagging finger, which made Adélie so anxious that she left the women and wrapped herself unashamedly around Kamili's arm. There was not a speckled egg in sight. The *sadet* exited the ring and, from the back, little Uroh stepped in. She wore the broad Parisian hat and veil and walked on tiptoes. Another girl followed in Adélie's pearl-button blouse, then a girl carrying the shreds of petticoat, then another with Adélie's bloomers over her arms, then two boys stumbling, each wearing one boot, and finally Gani wearing her moth-eaten skirt as though it were a cape, and the parasol over his shoulder. The adults, unsuccessfully hiding their smirks, watched Adélie more closely than they did the children.

The hissing torches and insect-hum now sounded extraordinarily merry; Gani and the others formed a circle and twirled in a spectacle of high fashion that Lepape himself couldn't have envisioned, and she applauded rapturously. The *noi ban* had such a smile on his face that, after killing the pigs over the stalks of seed rice, the *sadet* had to lead him to the moonlit spring and ladle water over him.

Following Kamili down the path, she repeated the *sadet*'s fable to herself, without the *sadet*'s repetitions or flowery asides, as she might write it in a letter to Manu:

> *Once a rich man was so miserly that he chose to live in the forest apart from other families. Leaving on a hunt, he told his son, "Watch over my jar while I am away, for it is our family's wealth." But the son fell ill with fever so that monkeys were able to enter the house and take great sport in rolling the precious jar out the door.*
>
> *Because he was blustering and loud the rich man was a poor hunter and caught nothing, and so returned home in a rage, and was so angry when he discovered the jar stolen*

that he dragged his poor son into the forest and raised his knife. Because he was pure of heart the boy's last words were not "I do not wish to die" but "I wish that no one would die." Then his father left the little body unburned and unburied so that wild beasts would devour it. But instead the Spirit of the Water caused a spring to gush from the boy's mouth.

That night the rich man's relations, hurrying to invite him to a feast, took their rest beside the spring. They were surprised, for in all their years of travel they had never seen one in that place. They were no less surprised when they stumbled across the murdered boy as they made camp. They could no longer recognize him as their nephew, so they agreed that they would make no funeral but simply burn the little body in the morning.

They boiled water from the spring. They threw in their dried fish, and then the most surprising event of all occurred: live fishes leaped from the kettle! The water of the spring, the relatives suspected, was rife with spirits. They splashed water on the murdered boy and he sat up and through his mutilated lips described what his father had done.

The enraged travellers raced through the night to find the rich man. Hearing their cries he ran out of his house—but because he was blustering and loud he blundered into a tiger's jaws, and afterward this tiger suffered incurable diarrhea.

Meanwhile the son discovered the jar where the monkeys had abandoned it, and with this recovered wealth he founded a village below the spring. Of course the rich man should have known that a family's wealth is not its jars but its children.

It was a wonderful tale. Evil was punished, innocence triumphed, magic carried as much significance as biology or the Napoleonic Code, and children, it was stated unequivocally, were not to be sacrificed on any parent's whim. Only the epilogue was not entirely to her liking, for to make his fortune this particular orphan did *not* have to go out into the world, and she couldn't help but wonder at the young protagonist's fate, resurrected by benevolent forces yet bearing such scars that he would ever stand conspicuously amongst his fellow men. "That is the one who died and came back," they would say, and would carry on saying it.

"They talk about a funeral, when the relatives find the boy," she called. "How do the relatives make one?"

"A long time ago we had one for our relatives but I did not see it. I was hunting."

"What about for your... other wife?"

"She did not die. She only went away," Kamili shrugged. He urinated beside the path. "But the *sadet* has told us about the funeral. A house is built for the dead person, and poles raised up covered with flowers, and so many pigs killed that each family gets a haunch, and the *sadet* sings many new songs—ones we never heard before!" He finished peeing, and shrugged again. "But no one dies here."

THE DYING
PARATROOPER

Emanuel Tremier, 1954.

NONE OF them knew the wounded man's name; he must have anticipated, wrongly, that the Viet Minh would capture him, and that a POW would be better off without papers. But his zippered breast pocket did contain a taped-together photograph of a hopeful-looking woman and two gap-toothed kids, and each time Manu dressed the man's wound he'd pass the picture around.

"He'll see those kids again," he assured his men as they lay panting beneath the palms, "and he'll bring *us* to them, too. Birthday parties. The little wife will wear a blue dress, and he'll tell her how we carried him. A kid'll sit on your knee, Schultz!"

And that finally pulled Schultz to his feet. He was, Manu believed, the most sentimental German to ever don the *kepi blanc*.

When the Manu who'd been a forty-four-year-old lieutenant-colonel of the 1st Free French Parachute Regiment had led men over and into Normandy, his uniform had had an identical zippered breast pocket into which, before the jump, he'd secured his glass eye. He thought of the English Channel at 0400 glistening greasily beneath them—could any place be further removed from the tangled mess of a mid-afternoon on the Laotian frontier? Pascal and Schultz called that fight "World War II" and "the previous war" but as far as Manu was concerned every fight was the same.

The wounded man wore the insignia of a corporal of the 1st Foreign Legion Parachute Battalion, but they hardly ever saw that badge for he was kept wrapped in a tarp tied to a branch swaying from the men's shoulders, or it *did* sway as long as they walked on flat open ground which was the case for perhaps one minute of every hour. Otherwise he was being passed over and under logs, across creek-beds, dragged without benefit of ropes up rock faces which the men themselves only scaled by standing on one another's heads. *"Baraka,"* his soldiers said of the wounded man, and whether a man's first language was French, German, Wolof or Arabic he knew this meant the paratrooper was wildly lucky. Only Manu knew that the iodine had already run out and nothing more could be done for the wounded man but to wait for him to die, at which time they'd leave him to the jungle without uttering so much as his name.

They'd carried him for three weeks, ever since the French had surrendered the long, flat valley at Dien bien Phu.

ON MAY 7, upon receiving Colonel Lalande's order to finally attempt a breakout from the trenches of Strongpoint Isabelle after rendering Lieutenant Préaud's tank and their remaining howitzer inoperable, Emanuel Tremier—in his official alias of Sergeant Ferdinand Merde of the 12th Company, 3rd Battalion, 3rd Foreign Legion Infantry Regiment—had led two dozen men between the bomb craters toward what had once been Ban Loi village. After the Viet Minh's mortars opened up, though, only he and four others climbed to their feet. Then they came upon the as-yet uninjured paratrooper and a T'ai tribesmen—a sergeant in the 301st Battalion—silently awaiting the departure of three Viet Minh regulars patrolling the riverbed of the Nam Yum. Manu watched the trio cheerfully unfold their packets of rice; then, rather than attract more of them with unnecessary gunfire, he climbed an overhanging tree and dispatched all three with his knife—he was still well-nourished on tinned pâté, after all—though the third was hard going. Perhaps word had come back to the Viets that the army of the French Union had, after fifty-six days and nights of siege, unequivocally and understandably abandoned Dien bien Phu, their final bastion against the Communist incursion into northern Vietnam, and in celebration the patrol may have relaxed their mealtime vigilance, but in any case Manu was *baraka*. Excepting two specific days in 1918 and 1944, his life in the service had been one of perpetual *baraka*.

On the other side of the riverbed they swelled their ranks with two soldiers of the Moroccan Colonial and two Senegalese in helmets flat as soup bowls. He felt confident they'd make their escape. But on the overlooking ridge Manu's *ad hoc* squad discovered a seventy-five millimetre artillery piece disguised as an inclined tree and guarded by fifty Viet Minh, who, in the resulting firefight, shot the paratrooper through the throat and effectively disembowelled the T'ai tribesman, leaving Manu in sole charge of nine men from four diverse units, none of whom knew the wounded man's name. Yet none hesitated when Manu ordered that the paratrooper be carried on their mosquito-bitten shoulders toward their expected salvation at Muong Sai in Laos, because it was inconceivable that he could survive the afternoon. Each fit man was already overjoyed to be free of the mud-swaddled bunkers at Dien bien Phu.

Manu carried a compass and the conviction that Laos would remain in French hands until the radio carried by Pascal told them otherwise, and until then they would straggle westward as the compass dictated. A corporal had once told Manu there was an iron bridge at Muong Sai and bamboo shoots drying on carpets beside the road.

The communal rations gave out. Green bananas weren't hard to find, and though they set off diarrhea that was at least a change from the nausea of a perpetually empty stomach, though now whenever Manu felt pressure in his gut he couldn't guess whether its ultimate product would be a gas or liquid. He wasn't a chemist.

He assigned a rearguard to shepherd the afflicted and ordered the rest to stagger on, because if they marched only when all nine of the upright men were able they wouldn't have travelled a hundred metres in a day. The men believed cigarettes could cure anything, bowel trouble in particular, and asked him again and again if there were any more, and though he still had three packs Manu insisted he had none. He wanted to be able to pass the Gitanes around if the moment came to accept the inevitable.

One midday he ordered the squad to hunker in the shade when one of the Moroccans, bearded Youssef, hurried up the trail to say that Villier—a chinless Lyonnais of Manu's own company—was squatting in the bushes not too far back, and would the sergeant come see? Manu followed, leaving the men to hum the hated *"La Petite Tonkinoise,"* chew stalks of grass and lick the sweat from their wrists. He and the Moroccan left the trail and waded through the foliage. Yes, there was Villier behind a web of creepers, but he wasn't insensible as Manu had feared—he was spooning gobs of mustard from a tin into his mouth while a bar of chocolate teetered on his knee. The sergeant took Villier by the scruff of the neck and marched him up to the squad, each of whom received a drop of mustard and a fingernail of chocolate—meagre, yes, yet so unexpected as to taste like Christmas Eve. Without result Villier and his pack were searched before Manu kicked him soundly in the ass.

He preferred to trust the men under him. It was well known that men joined the Foreign Legion when all else had failed in their young lives; some had been officially presented the choice between enlistment and a police court. And because Legionnaires seldom inquired after a comrade's history lest they be asked to reveal their own, Manu had never revealed anything as rudimentary as how he came to lose his eye. Thus he ruminated as sword grass gouged his arms. For foot soldiers in a regular wartime army, the days between actions were achingly dull—but at least they had viable objectives, battles to win, lands to reclaim, and a soldier could imagine that once these were achieved he might be that much nearer to home's soft arms and dry socks, and reload his magazine all the more quickly. The Foreign Legion, however, only wanted time. The generals might demand that all hearts be set on Objectives Ten, Eleven and Twelve, but a Legionnaire knew the Legion simply wanted its five years, provided the Legionnaire live that long. Overrun a nation or lose a battle half-asleep, he'd be no nearer home, so why contribute chocolate and mustard to the pile? The five years would stretch before him regardless.

ON MAY 27 hushed talk began that the hopeful-looking woman and gap-toothed kids were not the wounded man's family at all but that he'd rescued them from the bottom of a trench. And on the evening of May 29 the talk ceased being hushed as they slept beneath the wet season's rains for the twenty-second night and Sergeant Merde allowed the still-living paratrooper to remain wrapped in the only tarp, though it was only a tent-half salvaged from the mud of Isabelle. He ordered the men to build a shelter of thorny branches and to shut up, which did nothing to diminish the ongoing debacle of the radio.

In the morning they lapped water from leaves—even in that high country the streams were all of mud—while Pascal, stained-black knees on either side of his face, wound his radio and Manu walked in a criss-cross along the path they'd cut the night before, flattening every poor bush with his rubber heels, whispering *Dien bien Phu Command here, please give your—what, Merde's gang? We have your position now! Pull the brush back so the chopper can set a foot down!* And with the sound of this delusion flickering in his ear—for hadn't Dien bien Phu Command ceased to exist on May 7?—Manu trampled the same insufferable sapling and thorn bush, because nothing in that part of the world would lie down, while Pascal turned his dial to produce each crackle and hiss ever produced by a frying egg until he finally lit on that phantom transceiver playing its record of Josephine Baker singing *"La Petite Tonkinoise"*— they'd now heard it so many times, morning and night for three weeks, that even as they straggled west, Pascal's batteries disconnected and radio silent on his back, they could hear every chord change and rhythm-break buried in the insects' buzzing from every leaf and pebble and blade of grass as well as from every tree and cave and thicket the next valley over and the valley beyond that. Through any twenty-four-hour period they were never the same insects, either, the same *species*, that is, for in the night the noise was X, the morning it was Y, the afternoon was Z, and the evening, the twilight, was most deafening of all as armies of minute bark-boring bugs reproduced the sound of hammers on tin pans. Pascal no longer attempted contact with Muong Sai or with the remnants of Dien bien Phu in the evenings. Even if the incoming signal had been audible over the din, Pascal and Manu agreed that there was no sense wasting voltage on a tinny rendition of *"La Petite Tonkinoise"* when a hemisphere's worth of insects were performing it already.

It was bad enough to have given himself the *nom de guerre* of Merde; he did not wish the men to think it justified. The recruiting sergeant had asked, "Do you wish to become anonymous and change your identity?" and it had been a simple thing for Manu to press his heels together and say, "Merde!"

"What sort of stockings will the wife wear?" Schultz asked.

Under the weight of the wounded man's branch, Drapeau bent so far to the side that his helmet ought to have fallen off, yet he hauled himself over rocks and down the other side. At the instant Isabelle had fallen each man had been in a sufficient state of exhaustion to have been hospitalized in any civilized country, yet three weeks later they tottered on, fortified by water that dripped from cut vines onto their tongues, though during the heaviest of the fighting Dien bien Phu Command had insisted each man receive a half-gallon of liquid daily that the Asiatic heat not strike him dead. And exactly which civilized country was he imagining? Until his arrival in Indochina in 1949 he'd given France the benefit of the doubt. After his first five years' service he might have become a shoemaker or country schoolmaster but he'd re-enlisted as a Legionnaire because it was naive to be anything else. Or perhaps he had been short-sighted; perhaps there were isolated villages in Canada and Argentina where people were *not* casting children onto bonfires.

"A spider like *that*," he warned Aziz, "needs to be brushed off in the direction it's walking."

Drapeau had leeches halfway up his thigh; they swayed like fringes on a cocktail dress. The wounded man was set down, Léopold went on ahead, Drapeau moved to the front of the branch and Sergeant Merde took his turn at the rear—they had little else to carry, with the rations gone. They'd flattened the empty tins to keep the Viet Minh from making bombs out of them, lucky sods that they were, because hadn't Manu's old captain said that only a man with an empty stomach could be shot in the gut and live?

"They give him soft looks," the insects intoned, à la Josephine Baker, "but it's me he likes the best." Such an optimist, that petite Tonkinoise, next she would say to look for the silver lining and keep to the sunny side of the street, those notions Manu's grandmother had insisted upon with every puddle he fell into, every scratch across his St-Lucien brass buttons—even if the veal backed sideways into his stomach so he vomited into Isabelle's apron, his grandmother would tilt her head and tell him that more good than bad really did arise from such a thing, for didn't it demonstrate, in its small way, that God's world was richer than any mind had capacity to comprehend? She was not tramping with him into Laos to tell him to look for the silver lining, though, for his Grandma Sabine had been killed at his side on Good Friday, 1916, crushed beneath masonry when a German shell fired from the cannon Big Bertha travelled one hundred kilometres to strike Saint-Gervais during evening service. Dust in his eyes, he'd cast slabs of stonework aside until he'd come upon her blue-veined hand somehow still clutching a hymnal page—and, damn it, what hymn had it been?

On night guard in Mascara he'd driven himself mad trying to remember which hymn, then he'd done it again while inspecting sentries between the moonless train tracks and the Hanoi barracks. The sort of thing a kid would be annoyed by, trying to remember if he had *ever* known a certain thing, but a man of forty-seven and then of fifty-two ought to have said *feh* and not cared a damn. The Legion was regressing him. It didn't seem likely he could grow any *older*—in '46 he'd been the only recruit in his class without acne, and when he'd strode like another de Gaulle to the recruiting sergeant's table the poor man, rather than quite properly rejecting him, had saluted.

HE CHEWED a poppy flower, its meagre liquid saturating his tongue for less time than it took his eyelid to blink back the *meng*. He and Pascal stood submerged in elephant grass, a breeding ground for the same microscopic insects that had burrowed into the reprobate Villier's little toe so that it had stretched like a balloon and burst. Manu and Pascal took turns striking with their machetes, *cuk, cuk,* then shuffling forward, grass heaped to their waists, Pascal's blood running down his forearm. He stopped now to suck at the side of his thumb. On April 30, while they'd still been hunkered down at Dien bien Phu, every Foreign Legion regiment had celebrated Camerone—which for a Legionnaire is as good as Christmas—and the major had recited the immortal story of sixty-five Legionnaires in the burnt shell of a farmhouse holding off two thousand Mexicans, licking their own wounds to blunt their thirst. Was Pascal doing that now? And what password had Manu given the men he'd sent back up the trail to forestall any rear attack?

One of the Senegalese, Léopold, black as an oiled road, carried the radio in back of them, while behind *him* the Moroccans waited beneath a flowering tree. Deep lines ran down the face of Aziz, the elder, giving him a look of perpetual melancholy, and though his jaw was black after weeks without a razor he was baby-cheeked compared to teenaged Youssef, who in the space of a month had produced a beard from throat to eyes that rivalled a Biblical prophet's. It caught in creepers. At the end of each day the Moroccans unrolled their striped *djellaba* cloaks and, bundled like infants, fell asleep before anyone else. Pascal closed his bottom lip over his new moustache, shook out the thumb then savagely struck the grass.

"You remember—any hymns?" Manu asked in syncopation with their *cuk, cuk.*

We're at ease, Pascal began to sing,
We're rough and tough!
No ordinary guys.

This was *"Le Boudin,"* "The Blood Sausage," the Legion's anthem. Though with its haphazard pauses it was painful to march to, it served as an admirable work song for men who'd only eaten blades of grass.

For the Belgians, Pascal crooned, *there's none left,*
They're lazy shirkers.

Ah, yes! Manu had given the password "Belgians." With a grin he looked back at Léopold but Léopold lay half-submerged in the fallen stalks. Fainted. Heroism to make a schoolboy gasp. "At Camerone," the major had intoned as they'd gripped their tin mugs and waited for the next 105-millimetre to fall, "Captain Danjou's wooden hand was found amongst the corpses, and now rests in the museum at Sidi Bel Abbès as the Legion's most precious relic." And when the bones of Merde's squad were finally uncovered, he thought, that cement block of a radio would be shipped to Sidi Bel Abbès as a memento of a two-hundred-kilometre trek undertaken solely to save their own skins.

May our pain help us forget death, Pascal finished,
Who never forgets us.

When Manu had first drained a bottle for Camerone in 1946 it had seemed preposterous that the Legion should have gone to war against, of all the people on earth, Mexicans, but that now seemed altogether sensible compared to fighting these shadows called the Viet Minh.

NINE MEN SAT in the crooks of trees. Below them a black-and-yellow spider spun a web between the trunks they'd climbed; the trembling threads made Manu think of the grenades strung to tripwires over every square metre of Tonkin province. A stream trickled below them. Maybe he'd suggested they wait for a deer to drink so he could shoot it with his .32 revolver. But the wounded man lay on the ground, so perhaps they were baiting a tiger, in which case Villier would have to shoot it with his *pistolet mitraillette,* though after his toe had burst Villier's foot had gone septic like nothing Manu had ever seen. Pascal perched one crook up. His eyes were shut and ants crawled over his fingers where they gripped the branch.

"Do you think it will happen?" Manu whispered.

"Will what, sir?"

"Well, why," the sergeant mumbled, "did I have us climb up here?"

"Ambush. You sat down for a drink and said you saw the Viets."

Manu wasn't at all thirsty—of course he'd had a drink!

"Let's climb down."

It was a laborious process, for gravity was stronger than they and breaking a leg just then would have been as bad as stepping on a mine. Drapeau crouched over the wounded man.

"Wrap him up," Manu ordered. "What's the matter—gangrene?"

"That's just it, sir," said Drapeau, "there's no infection to speak of. Out here with the mould and bugs, and no iodine in a week!"

The wounded man hummed, just for a moment. He looked up at Manu then shut his eyes again.

"He's getting stronger," admitted Manu.

"Maybe the air has antiseptic qualities," said Pascal.

But then they all looked at Villier, who cradled in his lap the boot he could no longer wear. His foot smelled like a pig farm.

"These here in the mud are deer tracks, sir, I swear to it," said Aziz.

"Bivouac above the high water," ordered Manu. "There'll be rain again."

A centipede the colour of a boiled lobster clattered out of the leaves, stopping the Moroccans in their tracks.

"It can only kill if it's longer than thirty centimetres," Manu said.

He ordered a stop at a fall of logs that did not appear to be alive with ants. From their earliest days at Sidi Bel Abbès they'd been taught to post a guard, yet after pulling their boots off to reveal toes like white grubs the men all stretched their legs out and fell asleep. The rain started soon after. Manu heard a tree go down, a sharp *crack*, and as he turned over he found the sound of the drops against the tarp extremely comforting.

THE CHURCH AT
ST. AUBIN-SUR-SEULLES

Emanuel Tremier.

THE ANTS woke him before first light; he brushed instinctively at his bad eye, thinking they were nesting there, though they'd only been on his arm. Then he sat up slowly and listened for Viet Minh. Water dripped from the branches onto the half-tent stretched over his head—it had been tied over the place where half the men had already been lying, and the other half looked to have wriggled under in the course of the night. Who'd been carrying a tarp all this time, to only unfold it now?

He watched his eight men sleep. He hadn't called them to 0600 reveille—though without a trumpet, of course, he'd simply barked "Reveille!"—since the third morning, because reveille was the way station between a warm bed and a meal, and he'd failed to provide either. If a spider appeared this morning, though, he might get after it with his knife and have the eight legs to divvy out for breakfast.

Breakfast. For him Linh had learned to make crepes, tiptoeing into a Hanoi bistro to see how the hot pan had to be inverted, because she'd wanted him to stay with her each morning rather than go to the barracks for a croissant and coffee-with-rum before inspection. The other NCOs spoke of their *congaïs* as though they were show dogs—the tricks they performed, their looks, their eyelashes like Daisy Duck—but Manu never spoke of Linh. She had wanted to become pregnant and he'd seen no reason why she shouldn't. He must have been too old, that was all. But one night he'd felt particularly fit and they'd made love a half-dozen times, and afterward he'd lain there like a wrung-out sponge, the oil lamp throwing their shadows up the cheap panelling of the house he'd rented, the moths braining themselves against the blinds.

"I'll tell you what went wrong in the last war," he'd said. "If you want to hear."

"It doesn't have to be tonight."

"I've stopped being sleepy."

She'd sat up on the bed while he'd lit a cigarette for each of them. Her hair had draped her shoulders and her nipples had been flat as bottle caps.

"Germany invaded France in 1940 and stayed there four years. That's the start."

She'd nodded encouragingly. On the kitchen wall she already kept a map of Europe clipped from a textbook.

"But I got away to England and joined what we called the Free French, and we got ready to take the country back again once the English and Americans made their plans to help us."

"When the Japanese were here?"

"That's right. And in the meantime I set up a parachute regiment so that we'd be able to drop straight into Normandy, and I imagined the farmers would come out of their houses with their shotguns and we'd all drive the Germans over the Rhine in an afternoon, no trenches, no artillery hitting Saint-Gervais, nothing."

"And you were in charge of the whole regiment?"

She'd resembled a rabbit, her hands beneath her chin.

"For the better part of that day I was, yes. We dropped thirty kilometres outside Caen with orders to rendezvous with columns coming south from the beaches. And it was terrific after all those years of waiting, after stifling in trenches in the last war, to be running through fields, one village after another, on our way to Caen. Most places we took the Germans by surprise, they hadn't even known an invasion had started, and we captured the few dozen Nazis in each place and the people cheered us. They threw us hams. A kid with his arm in a sling gave me a hatful of candy. We found a row of their tanks parked in the road and we blew them up with pentolite. Just a terrific war."

"But what are 'Nazis'?"

He'd stroked her thigh and considered a seventh time.

"You never heard of them? They were Germans. Not like our boys here, our Germans are the good ones. In one place they'd known we were coming, and *that* was a fight. Shot the last of them in a stable. We were getting happier by the minute. But then we saw that our next village had a pillar of smoke rising over it, that looked bad for whoever lived there, I thought maybe it was an ammunition dump and a shell had hit it, but the map didn't show any ammunition dump. It just said St. Aubin-sur-Seulles.

"We drove some cars over in a hurry and saw two German trucks going out the other way, heading north. Threw a grenade at us, missed, and I thought it was funny that these people would never have to look at Germans again, I made a joke about it. But then there weren't any people in the street until we saw this woman running, hands and face all black. She said that she couldn't get the church doors open and needed help because the Germans had herded everyone in and set it on fire. Even the kids, she said, every kid. She'd watched from an attic. I put her in the car and drove up the hill and we saw that the smoke was coming from an old stone church the same as anywhere. When we came around the corner the doors blew off it like they were made of cardboard."

Linh had put her hand over his heart then, as she often had, her fingers smelling of basil and tobacco and him.

"That's what happens when a fire gets too hot inside. Nazis must've doused the pews with gasoline. But nobody came out, even with the doors gone, and we had to wait a half hour before we could get near it. I ordered the houses searched. The poor woman was tearing her hair out and I told her, you watch, you watch and we'll get them, by Bastille Day there won't be a German alive. Nathalie was her name. She said it didn't make sense because the nearest Resistance was in another town down the line, but it had been easy for the Germans to round everybody up because it was tobacco ration day."

"Nathalie."

He'd looked at his cigarette.

"The dogs came out with their tails between their legs. Sniffing for their masters. The smell was atrocious. I finally decided I'd better have a look and I must have checked my watch three times as I walked across because I was worried about that rendezvous at Caen. I got to the steps and went inside."

He'd stopped, tongue on teeth, listening as he always did for footsteps beyond the window. But there had only been insect drone.

"You don't have to tell it all tonight," Linh had said.

"I was breathing through a handkerchief soaked in vinegar so the smell wasn't bad. But do you know what it looked like in there?"

Linh had just gazed at him.

"Like a department store that had caught fire with the mannequins all piled on top of each other. There were hardly arms or legs on any of them, and the faces had all burnt off. That was next to the doors, but along the walls it was different, there I could at least see whether they'd been men or women and what they'd been doing as they'd died. Mostly parents huddled over their kids, all tangled together. I remember a hand without any fingertips, holding onto a locomotive. I didn't like that, made me imagine the kid picking it out of his dresser drawer before they went to see the friendly Nazis, and then the parents must've been steering the kids around by the shoulders to keep them from getting underfoot. Four *years* I'd been away and I couldn't have come a half hour sooner. And then the worst of it."

"No more tonight," Linh had said. "Another time."

"Around behind the altar I found this little boy's legs. Just the knees down. He was wearing red-and-blue socks, and brown shoes with the soles tacked on. And I heard his voice like a bell ringing beside my ear, he said, "Pa-*paa*," like he was annoyed and expected his dad to do something about it. And I could picture his short pants, his sweater, the hair in his eyes. When I'd been holding that hatful of candy he'd still had those things. I'd told Nathalie all that bullshit about revenge but I realized there could never be enough. We wouldn't be able to kill them enough times. I walked out, past my men, officers, dropped my pack, threw my gun down, walked out of town."

She'd put her forehead against his gnarled hands.

"Darling."

"There might've been other Tremiers before me who set churches alight and shrugged, and maybe a different Emanuel Tremier would've rolled himself a cigarette and sent Hitler a ten-minute curse, but this Emanuel Tremier walked down to the forest and covered himself in leaves."

"That's the one I would've wanted," she'd said.

"He isn't good for much. I found a farm, changed into somebody else's clothes. Every house was deserted, I guess because there'd been the tobacco ration. I lived in one place until the relatives came sniffing around the door, then I slipped out and went to live in another. A lot of trucks drove into St. Aubin-sur-Seulles, Frenchmen, it looked like, there to clean up the mess, but I just wandered around, a civilian. I wound up in that town Nathalie had mentioned and got to whispering in a café and the next day I was with the Resistance, stealing gas out of a truck. They didn't have any reason to trust me, maybe they let me tag along so I'd be the one to get caught, but our captain fell in a ditch and I gutted a couple of Nazis and I think that stood me in good stead."

"Gutted?"

"Sorry, love, I did, yes. I liked our captain. Bresson. Got us American equipment and we followed their columns right into Germany. We got into one town in Bavaria before anybody else, and we knew where the head Nazi for the place lived, the burgomaster, so we ran to the house so we could throw him down the stairs but his servants were already laying him out on the sidewalk. He'd poisoned himself and his whole family, six kids, all dressed in white. They were there on the sidewalk too. I looked at their hands, their little blue mouths, and I said, 'Couldn't they have killed five and left one for me?' And Bresson's nose was running. He was crying too. I'd seen him rip a collaborator's tongue out with his bare hands."

And with that vision in their brains he and Linh had fallen asleep. A month later their gate had been booby-trapped with a grenade, ripping off her arm, and she had died as the neighbours carried her to hospital. It had been well known the *congaïs* were being herded into service of the Viet Minh and she must have resisted or maybe they'd wanted to eliminate a sergeant of the bloodthirsty Legion, but in either case he'd have preferred if they'd shot him behind the ear and let Linh be. *I can do or think nothing but what springs from my love for you,* he'd said that at the funeral as her family had sat with their hands in their laps. He'd told the story of St. Aubin-sur-Seulles just that once, and he would never tell it again.

There had been an Air Force nurse at Dien bien Phu. On the final night she'd been evacuated with her wounded and he'd only had time to watch her C-47 taxi down the strip before the shelling had become too thick and he'd had to look to his men, but once she was airborne what could have stopped her?

The sky pinkened and bats the size of house cats returned to the treetops. Manu discerned a brown shape amongst the leaves and at the same time realized the wounded man was no longer in the tree where they'd set him—his untenanted branch lay on the ground. Manu tipped a scorpion out of his boot and crept from under the tarp.

The brown shape was the paratrooper. He had shot himself through the roof of the mouth with Manu's .32 and the squad wouldn't have to haul him another step.

Manu returned the gun to its holster. Thanks to the rain no blood was in evidence, but the spilled brain matter churned with ants. For weeks the squad had been dragging itself forward without a shot fired, and now one bullet had brought about one death.

The men woke up and gathered around Manu and the dead paratrooper. At some point in the night Schultz's sewing kit had been unrolled and a safety pin extricated to attach the photo of the gap-toothed children to his lapel.

"Good God, what would I have done with my last breath?" asked the German. "Poured myself the longest drink on earth."

"Written a note to your girl," said Drapeau.

"Your mother," suggested Manu.

"Yes, certainly! 'Your eternal loving son.'"

"Think you can raise Muong Sai?" Manu asked Pascal.

"We might be high enough."

But Manu could not bear to listen to Josephine Baker or the frying of eggs just then, nor, he imagined, could the men. As they stumbled down through the trees Manu saw that overnight the stream had doubled in width and that in the middle Villier stood pissing joyously, for when was the last time any of them had had enough to drink to piss in any quantity?

"For Christ's sake, Villier!"

"Soaking the foot, sir." He addressed his superior without slackening flow and with his thin nose upraised. "I reckon we'll drink upstream."

As they shuffled up the bank the other six looked at their commander sideways. In Algeria, in the forts at Mascara or Nouvion, any sergeant of the 3rd Foreign Legion Infantry Regiment would have stretched Villier and beaten him across the solar plexus, or flayed him with a rope's end while he ran with a sack of stones on his back under the Saharan sun—*la pelote*, the pincushion, this last was called. But Sergeant Ferdinand Merde had not kept these remaining eight moving since May 7 to want to kill any of them now. Worse yet, he didn't have a rope.

Aziz caught a frog and immediately shared it with Youssef—it was the colour of mud, which led them to believe it wasn't poisonous. Schultz found grass which he said didn't taste too bad. Manu studied the treetops, for a nestful of eggs would have been just the thing.

"Adrenalin keeps a man going," he told them again. "Adrenalin and water."

Burying the paratrooper would squander their strength. Once the bosses in Hanoi had made their tally and presumed him killed in action, the man's family would at least receive that typewritten pronouncement—*He died for France!*—sure to produce paroxysms of joy even if a Legionnaire had been Hungarian. There'd been a lot of Hungarians. There was nothing worth salvaging on his body—Drapeau had been wearing the paratrooper's boots since May 10. Manu studied for the last time the insignia of the 1st Foreign Legion Parachute Battalion above the dead man's breast pocket and thought of his company landing outside Caen, their parachutes billowing like jellyfish.

"There was a French voice, sir!" cried Pascal.

"Muong Sai?"

"I couldn't say, sir. Static after that, so I disconnected."

"What about '*La Petite Tonkinoise*'?"

He shrugged, and folded the tarp so painstakingly it might have been the tricolour.

Without the wounded man to carry they walked erect as church spires, rifles at their shoulders, full canteens at their hips. Villier marched gamely forward, teeth gritted, upon the crutch Schultz had cut for him. Even if they didn't reach Muong Sai *that* night they would at least have shelter—the tarp was theirs again!

And that afternoon they came upon an actual hut. Low and thatch-roofed, it sat on rickety poles amidst a stand of trembling trees. No smoke rose from it and they saw no sign of recent life, though all around Insect Z flagellated madly.

"Maybe there are no Viet Minh this far west, sir," murmured Drapeau.

"If we're in Laos then there are Pathet Lao. The orders are the same."

"Sir, if it *is* deserted," suggested Pascal, "we might sleep there and not burn it down until morning."

At this prospect the Moroccans' eyes lit up and the Senegalese pressed their fingertips together.

"Who has grenades?" asked Manu.

Three men had strings of them, as he'd known, so it worked out neatly for him to accompany these three up the middle while the six without grenades split into right- and left-hand flanks, each man armed with a trusty bolt-action '49 Saint-Étienne or a '36 Châtellerault. Names like wines. *Two* on the left—Villier, collapsed under a tree, couldn't be relied upon for reconnaissance.

His Legionnaires had been trained exhaustively in detecting Viet Minh tripwires but the Africans had come to Dien bien Phu direct from landing at Saigon so he ought to have told them to drag a twig in front of them. Yes, there was Léopold rising from a crouch behind a stump, showing the thumbs-up. He straightened to the level of the hut's floor, peered in and gave the thumbs-up again.

Beneath its damp thatch the hut smelled like a steam room. Three half-whittled sticks decorated the floor along with a handful of black feathers, and though a fire had at one time burned in the corner Manu found no teacups on hooks, bullet casings, Maoist pamphlets or cheery Confucian wall-hangings—no Viet Minh. How far *had* they come?

The squad caught and ate a large blue-and-yellow lizard; found a tree laden with a dozen hard green bananas; drank from their canteens. Schultz taught the Moroccans to leapfrog—Aziz claiming with a wink that he'd never seen it done—until Pascal hurried down from the gloom.

"Two men speaking French, sir!"

"Did they hear *you*?"

"I couldn't make them understand. One said, 'Helicopter?' then I lost them."

"And *'La Petite Tonkinoise'*?"

"My God, I never did hear it! I didn't realize—"

"What were they talking about when you raised them?"

"Horse racing, sir!"

"We may see something tomorrow," said Manu.

He allocated the hut to the Foreign Legion and told the Africans to stretch out beneath the tarp. And it was an appropriate night to crowd under a roof, too, for at that elevation Manu felt chilled for the first time in three years. The instant he shut his eyes he was peering out again from Isabelle's trenches as it was shelled by night. With each burst of fire across the ground it seemed a genie would appear.

GIRLS,
OLD LADIES

Emanuel Tremier.

THE MEN were talking when he awoke; none seemed to have noticed the black rat peering down from a rafter and wondering how such men could survive without food.

"I can do it straight away," said Pascal. "I'm out in November."

"I'm the next October," said Schultz.

"Then we can do New Year's Eve 1955 at *Les Deux Magots*, and whoever gets there first orders mussels."

"I'm not until '58!" said Drapeau.

"Hand of honour, then, we'll go back *every* year," said Pascal. "Sign up for another five and we'll be there after that."

"What about that, sir?" asked Drapeau. "Can you go for New Year's 1958?"

Villier lay on the corner of the bamboo floor, his hairless chest drawing shallow breaths, tears running down his temples. He'd managed to set his rotten leg outside along the hut's meagre porch, but Manu saw that the skin had already split above the knee and crawled with flies. No one asked Villier his plans for New Year's Eve 1958.

"Who's sentry?" Manu asked.

He ordered Léopold to take the tarp down and prepare it, after a one-day respite, for use as a hammock. He started the rest of the men cleaning their weapons with the cotton cloths that had been gritty and black since Dien bien Phu; after a full night under shelter they chattered happily while wiping spiders' eggs out of their firing chambers.

"But if it isn't the Viet Minh's," Pascal suddenly whispered, "who *does* the place belong to?"

Squatting in the thicket, Schultz was stung twice on the bottom by immense black ants. The resulting purple boils were so painful that he marched without trousers, but it was the subsequent fainting spells that prompted the Moroccans to prop him between them. And Villier was so much heavier than the paratrooper that it took Manu, Drapeau *and* both Senegalese to carry him, leaving Pascal burdened only by his radio and machete. If the Pathet Lao were to fall on them, Manu considered, the squad would need half a minute just to find their rifles, but perhaps the smell of Villier's leg would drive them off long before. Drapeau fell aside to wretch bile.

INSECT Y HAD taken on a certain rhythm and Manu wondered again if it wasn't the sound of welcoming snare drums and coronets played by the soldiers of Muong Sai after spotting his squad through their own array of telescopes. He balanced the branch on the tendons of his shoulder, extricated his compass and saw that due west lay straight ahead.

"What, *down*hill?" joked Aziz. "We have crossed the Alps?"

Yellow birds flew in ellipses above their heads. To their right the jagged cliffs rose higher than ever, ushering the squad into the valley below—a carpet of untouched green. Could a more perfect training ground exist for the Pathet Lao?

"Beautiful," said Léopold, repositioning the branch, and it struck Manu that only a Senegalese could say 'beautiful' so convincingly. But Muong Sai's iron bridge was not in sight, so how many men would he lose crossing yet another valley?

"That's water down there," said Aziz.

At this they felt Villier stir within the tarp—and sure enough, a tear-shaped pendant of blue glistened from the midst of that carpet. They had only to scramble down one shelf of red rock after another to reach it. The heat was nearing its height and the canteens were empty.

"Give me morphine, sir." Villier's nostrils were caked with black snot. "You can spare one for me."

"There isn't even gauze, old man."

No drums were beaten as they descended on their haunches, no buffalo horns blown to alert the countryside. But with only a single outcropping left to navigate the Senegalese-who-was-not-Léopold slipped and cut his thigh open from hip to knee.

"Is it very bad, sir?"

"Deep. Clean the dirt out it might be all right, let's get you into that lake—too high here for crocodiles, don't fret. What's your name?"

"Private First-class Bouna Gassama, sir."

"Have I asked you before?"

"Yes, sir." Bouna grimaced as a trouser-leg tourniquet was pulled tight around his hip. "Many times, sir."

Manu felt strangely compelled to lie down beside the man, and did so. The tops of the evilly buzzing trees dropped closer, near enough to suffocate them both, but in the next moment the trunks stretched a kilometre into the air, their branches mere pinpricks, and then all was well.

"Did I faint?"

"Sir, I believe so," said Pascal.

"Where's that boy? His wound needs bathing."

"I sent them on, sir. I told him if it looked all right to wade in."

"Three-prong advance?"

"Yes, sir. Only four of them are in any shape for action, but I told them to scout it out as best they could."

"Get me up."

They give him soft looks, crooned Insect Y, *but it's me he likes the best.*

Under a tree Aziz stood sentry while Villier lay panting.

"Has he had water?"

"Let me tell you, sir!" Villier said through his teeth. "This foot of mine ought to go in the museum beside Danjou's wooden hand!"

"Yes, wouldn't they make a pair?"

"Give me morphine, sir."

"No, old man."

"We'd have to mummify the foot," Aziz advised.

The surface of the lake was blinding beneath the afternoon sun and Manu tugged his helmet down to his eyes. The long grass swarmed with dragonflies. The trees bent so low that it was difficult to see where exactly the lake began but nonetheless the men had beaten a path through and now stood to their waists in water, splashing it over the backs of their necks or submerging their arms to scrape mildew from between their larval toes. Schultz-of-the-swollen-buttock ran through the shallows toward him raising a din like a steamboat, dangling boots thudding against his chest, but then remembered himself and tiptoed over the flattened rushes that reminded Manu of German tanks he'd seen in Normandy, treads thick with matted corn stalks. Schultz saluted then turned smartly to show the sergeant and Pascal his bare behind, gazing at them expectantly over his shoulder.

"What am I meant to be looking at?" asked Manu.

"The boils are gone, sir!" he whispered. "Remember they had to carry me?"

"Huh! *Baraka*," said Pascal.

"Yes, *baraka*!" Schultz grinned.

Manu waded out. The water was so clear he could watch his callused white feet crossing the rocky bottom. Too clear to be fed by any stream—it had to be a spring. He took a long drink from his helmet, and even mingled with sweat and Vietnamese dirt the water tasted magnificent. He shut his eyes and breathed up his nose, and he suddenly felt he was held together with tendons and muscle again rather than kite string. And though it provided an ideal opportunity for a Pathet Lao sniper to plug a Foreign Legion sergeant through the top of the head, he refilled his helmet and drank again.

"Can you walk all right, Private?"

"Yes, sir." Glistening water dripped from Bouna's ears as he loosened the tourniquet. "Ah, you see? You can still see the place."

"That cut looks a week old."

"Yes, sir—it does, doesn't it?"

He couldn't blame Bouna for smiling.

"If I could eat a chicken," Drapeau said, "I might have it in me to shave!"

Léopold appeared silently amongst the rushes, boots still on, rifle in his hands. He saluted hastily.

"I have reconnoitred the whole way around, sir."

"And?"

"On the other side there are tracks of many people."

Manu strapped his helmet back on.

"Pascal!" he hissed. "Get them out of the water!"

"And there is a path that they travel by," Léopold went on, "though I did not go down. They don't wear shoes and the feet look very small. Not so small as pygmies, you know, but not so big as mine."

The Viet Minh often went barefoot, was it the same for the Pathet Lao? Mao tribes who'd been put to work building highways had migrated as far as possible from existing roads—perhaps *they* lived in the next hollow. Or someone else altogether.

"Routine reconnaissance operation."

"What about Villier, sir?" asked Pascal.

Aziz the sentry joined them and saluted, a weary grin disrupting the lines of his face. He glanced back toward Villier's tree.

"I still see him okay from here, sir. That smell is quite bad."

"Join the others," said Manu. "I'll do what I can."

He unholstered his .32 as he approached Villier. Yes, the stench was fearsome. A battlefield smell. He breathed through his mouth.

"We're off on an operation, old man. Back as quick as lightning. Take this in the meantime, and if a tiger comes along aim at the back of his ear."

Having released the safety, he closed Villier's fingers around the gun and laid it on his chest.

"I need a crutch," Villier whispered.

"Ah, there's this branch. You reach it?"

Manu hurried back toward the spring and his able-bodied men. If there *was* a village he would not even have to think, he would simply follow protocol from the Red River delta: if the squad was *not* fired upon and found no weapons he'd question the inhabitants regarding Communist activity in the area, and just as in the hovels of the Red River he'd be met with shrugs and babble, and whether honest or deceptive babble he wouldn't be able to guess because he only spoke French—with the exception of *baraka*, of course, which had stood him in good stead. Even before asking the way to Muong Sai he would have to question the inhabitants regarding Communist activity. And if the squad *was* fired upon he would simply follow the other protocol: kill the adult males and burn the village to the ground. Thanks to the protocols there were few shades of grey.

And if Vietnamese youngsters hadn't hated the French before, what better way could there be to drive them into the Communists' arms than gunning down their uncles and fathers? If the Germans had never left France in 1871 and still spat upon her pavements to this day, wouldn't he expect the sons of Paris, of Brest, of Aix-en-Provence to throw down their lives for as many generations as necessary until the murderous foreigners were driven out? The same notion had inspired barefoot Viet Minh to drag guns the size of trees up the mountains overlooking Dien bien Phu.

AFTER TEN MINUTES' descent Léopold crouched low beside the path, scrutinizing the crags to their right. The sun was beginning to lower over the treetops, inspiring birds in their hundreds to loop skyward, and Manu dropped to his elbows and wormed to the front of the line.

"*Another* hut, sir," Léopold whispered.

It sat halfway up the slope. A tangle of firewood lay on the porch.

"Should we go up, sir?" whispered Pascal.

"Let's monitor it for more than thirty seconds, shall we?"

"Sir? It's been ten minutes."

Up and down the line the men feigned to *not* stare at him—the two Senegalese looked particularly bewildered. Why in hell did his head feel so heavy?

"Leave it. If there is a village I want to see it before dark."

"What are those under that tree?" asked Schultz.

"Figs," said Aziz.

"Hear that?" asked Drapeau.

The men cocked their heads but Manu heard only Insect Z.

"Down there," Drapeau whispered, nodding down the path. "Chopping wood."

"Would they make an ambush by now, sir?" whispered Bouna.

"More likely they'd booby-trap the trail. Divide in three—you take one wing, Pascal; Schultz, you're on the other. On my sign. Rendezvous here at 1800, or if there *is* a village, wait there. Half an hour. Usual passwords. Watch your step or you'll find your balls in your mouth."

That was how a sergeant was meant to talk! The men wound their watches, batted mosquitoes away and eyed with suspicion each fluttering leaf. A hundred metres down the path the sound of wood-chopping became unmistakable, while a trail forked from the path to climb to their right. Manu signalled the Moroccans to follow him.

Squinting up at the hillside for a glint of metal, a movement, Manu was keenly aware—despite *decades* spent without it—of how his vigilance was compromised by the loss of his eye. Beside him Youssef bit his lip while Aziz kept his eyes wide open and his square teeth bared. Sweat dripped from their noses. Yet their hands looked absolutely steady, fingers light on their triggers, when they ought to have trembled from malnutrition if nothing else. Queer.

A pebble rattled above them and Manu raised a warning finger. The three men proceeded in a collective crouch, their bottoms barely clearing the ground, and as Manu peered around the bush, hardly breathing, a grey face appeared. The black-bristled face of a large pig. It shook its pendulous jowls and ambled forward, gravel crunching beneath its trotters.

"Shush," Manu whispered. "Scat!"

He lifted the butt of his rifle to discourage the animal but it steered around him, keeping its snout to the ground as it shook its generous hips and, by association, its spindly tail.

"No, go away!" whispered Youssef. "Fuck off!"

Tail still wagging, the beast stopped directly behind the sergeant, blinking myopic eyes at his lowered bottom. Manu swivelled on the balls of his feet and attempted to stare the creature down, and at this disappearance of his cherished bottom the pig raised its chin and gave a raspy snort.

"He's waiting for you to shit, sir," murmured Youssef.

"Start back down," whispered Manu. "This is the toilet."

THEY CAME UPON the faintest of paths to their left. Schultz nodded to Pascal who nodded in turn to Drapeau before adjusting the millstone-weight of the radio on his back and stealing silently through the yellow grass and on into the undergrowth. Drapeau wiped his chin, winked magnificently at the Senegalese then crashed after the radio man.

Amongst the trees the path was perceptible only in that it was not choked with creepers. The two men walked with knees bent, heads low. Despite the clanging cicadas they could hear the wood-chopper's *thwack* only a hundred-odd metres ahead. They slid beneath branches, peering ever ahead, eyes clouded with mosquitoes—the ravenous sort as well as the huge, rattle-winged ones that never bit anyone. Roots sought to trip them, ten at a time snaking across the vague path, and not for the first time Drapeau felt the Indochinese jungle was too big for him and the trail unworkably small, as though he'd pulled on his kid brother's pants. Ahead the bright gaps between trees became wider—a clearing? Drapeau sniffed for any fragment of smoke but smelled only the thousand diverse biological parts that made up the humus of the forest floor, as well as a smear of his own blood thanks to a mosquito that had gone up his nose. No smoke equalled no cooking and probably no people, unless the meal of choice in this particular back-of-beyond was lemonade and day-old crème caramel, his personal favourite since the age of three.

The radio man hunkered down behind a bush crowded with wizened red berries and Drapeau peered between its branches. He nearly swallowed his tongue. In the clearing stood two hunched figures he assumed to be apes, maybe the sort that jammed sticks into anthills and slurped up the ants like honey, he'd seen pictures of that sort, but after six beats of his heart he realized they were men, filthy-black men of the Lao mountains, no taller than his own Sylvie who would have had the baby by then whether he'd left home or not, nothing could have stopped that so what difference did it make what *he* had done? He recognized them as human the moment the bigger one lifted a heavy knife and lopped a dead branch in two and threw the pieces into a basket. The little one lifted a bow from the tall grass and fired above his head so quickly Drapeau hadn't had time to see whether there'd been an arrow or not—but there must have been because a second later a green bird with a shaft through its breast fell between the figures. Pascal was making signs.

"What?" Drapeau whispered in his ear.

"The *village* is on the other side. See that smoke? So we go around."

Drapeau looked unambiguously at his rifle. Pascal shook his head.

"For all we know," he whispered, over-mouthing the words for emphasis, "there could be a *tank* down there."

Drapeau blinked away mosquitoes, peering between the leaves as the taller jungle-man raised his knife. The bird's head flew over his shoulder on a jet of blood.

"See you on the other side," Drapeau finally whispered.

He went left, Pascal right. There was no vestige of a path, and though sweat ran down Drapeau's face in sheets he decided the canteen would make too much noise, so he let it dangle and straddled a rotted log. The whole thing seemed ridiculous—how long could men survive on as little food as they'd had? They weren't just *men*, though, but Legionnaires. How many nights had they slept at Dien bien Phu with Viet shells knocking them out of bed? Two months' worth, that was all. He could tell Sylvie about that, she could talk about birthing the baby—enough war stories to last them a lifetime.

For the Belgians, there's none left, he sang into the roof of his mouth, *They're lazy shirkers.*

Why exactly had he and Pascal separated? He hadn't understood that. He squeezed between two black tree trunks, each running with sap, then from the tree against his back he heard a *thud* distinct as a hammer-blow and thought that one of the green birds had run head-first into it. But the next thing Drapeau realized, even before nausea surged into his fingertips, was that he couldn't move from where he stood. Couldn't draw a decent breath. And that from his ribcage, just below his right armpit, a shaft of wood protruded—an arrow? He couldn't breathe and needed to vomit but worse yet was being stuck fast where the sap smelled of the medicine he'd spat out when he was a kid. He lurched forward, away from the tree, but only shifted himself a hair's-breadth along the shaft of the arrow. The nausea was going to drop his knees out from under him.

Leaves crackled. The filthy-black boy from the clearing set a foot on the parade ground, his bow strung with yet another arrow. His eyes, set far apart on his face, were open very wide, his mouth pinched so tightly—he resembled an owl costumed as a filthy boy, overwhelmed by the sight of this bullock trapped in his kid brother's pants.

Then, without stirring a leaf, he disappeared.

If he'd been able to lean forward, Drapeau considered, he would have set his head against the tree and slept. He felt drained as an overturned cider bottle.

"Belgians," he sang into the roof of his mouth.

BOUNA, LÉOPOLD and Schultz gripped their rifles and rolled sideways off the path, their canteens and cartridge belts clanking like tin cans tied to a dog. The grass was blessedly high and hid them far better than the shallow trenches at Dien bien Phu had. For what was coming up the path? Voices, and a vague wooden knocking—it might have been a cadre of Pathet Loa, it might have cattle wearing bells. Such a lovely twilight, Léopold thought, it would be a pity to tear it apart with these guns.

The sight that climbed the hill was the stuff of fairy tales, and when it finally chattered past he let out a long breath of relief that, despite their exhaustion, neither he nor Bouna nor Schultz had tightened a trigger out of sheer anxiety. For three dark young women had passed, empty buckets over their shoulders, long hair twisted past their waists, two smiling at their silent bare feet as the third told a story that seemed to involve a great deal of hiccuping. Wearing meagre woven loincloths, each had displayed, below her small round breasts, the sculpted mid-section that Léopold so prized. Bouna might have been disappointed at the lack of fat behinds, but probably not—and thank goodness Villier was dying in his tarp, as he certainly would have voted for raping them.

Schultz sat up in the long grass, his mind finally distracted from the gap-toothed kids' mother—he wore an expression like he'd just seen a trio of nude girls.

"Would they make an ambush by now?" whispered Bouna.

They straightened their helmets and crept down the path. The path levelled and Léopold was so intent on the source of those tendrils of smoke, just a hundred metres ahead, that he didn't notice the intersecting path until a line of women appeared out of the bush two strides to his left. Older than the bucket girls but equally naked, on their backs the women wore baskets of wood suspended from bands across their foreheads, leaving them too stooped to even see the men. But the soldiers could not turn this to their advantage, for there was no cover in which to roll. Instead Léopold stood very straight. If a machine gunner *was* present he would have to be uncommonly skilled to mow them down and leave these women untouched.

"Ladies," Léopold said.

"Ladies, good evening," Schultz said at his shoulder.

The first in the line straightened stiffly, lifting the band to the top of her head to peer up at them from beneath tufts of grey hair. She was missing a good many teeth. The other women's staring faces appeared behind her with choreography straight from a nightclub, two on the right, two on the left, one with a baby on her back and a load of corn in her arms, another with lighter skin than the others. None scrambled to lob grenades or even cried out.

The first woman bent backwards so that her basket of wood lay upright at Léopold's feet, then the woman herself knelt beside it.

"*Kuliginta,*" she murmured. "*Shin, shin, kuliginta.*"

"*Kuliginta,*" the others repeated, coming forward with their baskets.

Léopold took a step back.

"They're giving us wood?" said Schultz.

Like bushbucks, Bouna thought, they haven't yet learned to be skittish.

"Mon-monsieur?" asked the lighter-skinned woman. "Monsieur?"

Léopold looked at her more closely: she spoke French as though her mouth was full of water, yet she had what might have been a European nose as well as breasts less pendulous than the others' but hips a little wider—she would have to keep well ahead of Bouna! The woman gestured up the darkening path.

"*Lélah-lélah pré?*"

"We are Legionnaires of the 3rd Infantry Regiment," Léopold intoned.

She stared, rapt, at their equipment: each pouch, cartridge and sheathed knife. The other women murmured. The toothless one rose quickly, the load of wood strapped to her back once more; she had evidently changed her mind about their being spirits. By Léopold's watch it was already 1745.

"Are there Pathet Lao?" Schultz asked sternly.

"Lao?" asked the white woman. She moved her tongue across her lip—she seemed to relish the word like a taste in her mouth. "Sisavang? The king?"

"Did she say 'king'?" asked Léopold.

Bouna smiled giddily. "Where is there a king?"

"How do you come to be here?" asked Schultz.

The white woman conferred excitedly with the other wood-bearers in their *shush-kush* tongue; with the baskets on their backs they resembled a conference of hedgehogs. The men stared at the diverse breasts, of course, yet Schultz realized that much of the thrill of seeing a naked woman must stem from the knowledge that you've been allowed what others have been denied—if a woman was *always* naked it wasn't quite the same. Though breasts were still breasts!

"*Telinga*," muttered the baby's mother. "*Lélah-lélah telinga?*"

"*Telinga?*" The white woman turned on the Legionnaires. "*Telinga?*" She moved fingertips to her lips, eyebrows raised, then frowned dramatically and stared at the ground. Then looked up with a quicksilver smile. "Eat!" she cried, gesturing to her mouth again. "Eat, eat? *Telinga?*"

"Yes, Madame," said Bouna. "We *will* eat."

"We have time," said Schultz.

THE WHITE WOMAN

Emanuel Tremier.

THE LUMINOUS hands of his watch said it was one minute until 1800. Manu watched the silhouettes descend the path, shadows overlapping shadows now, and tried to make out what they were saying.

"*Sangan kutu, sangan kutu!*"

Neither French nor Vietnamese, and he did not know Lao. For all he knew it was Burmese and they'd stumbled a hundred kilometres too far into a British hill station.

Three women slipped past, chattering gaily, wet buckets across their shoulders.

Then Manu was in the path, signalling to Aziz and Youssef. Sudden darkness had changed his priorities—the squad had gone too long without beds, without a meal. He could hear the buckets sloshing ahead and below him, then saw rocks to climb down, and beyond the rocks the village spread before him: a half-dozen houses on stilts, cooking fires glimmering like so many fireflies through bamboo walls. He heard atonal singing, then an old man coughed, and two or three children let loose playful shrieks. A Pathet Lao village might have sounded just the same at 1800 but if these were Communists there'd have already been gunfire. He let his rubber soles find their way down the first rock and after a minute he reached the bottom. Above him a stone rattled and a Moroccan whispered a curse. An aggrieved chicken flapped its wings nearby.

"Is that you, sir?" asked Bouna's voice at his hip.

"Josephine," whispered Manu.

"Baker," said Bouna. "Schultz is arranging supper, sir. We had a look—they're like cavemen, is what Schultz said. No gas stoves. One woman speaks French, she might *be* French except that she's not wearing any clothes."

"Went to school in a town." Saliva ran from the roof of Manu's mouth at the notion of a cooked meal. "Might know the way to Muong Sai. Has Pascal come down?"

"Yes, sir, but not the young fellow. They separated."

"Down now, Private?" asked Manu. "All in one piece?"

"Bent my fingers back," said Aziz.

"The second house on the right," advised Bouna—wherever he crouched, he was quite impossible to see. "Have them send me out a plate of something, sir."

With the Moroccans behind him Manu strode between the houses. The darkness churned with figures creeping down ladders and into the path. It didn't seem to be the supper hour at all—children jogged on either side of them.

"*Boos!*" they shouted.

"Dinner," countered Manu.

"*Lélah-lélah boos!*"

It was quite unlike the Algerian hinterland, where every gaze was suspicious, the door of each mud *mechta* shut and barred—which only demonstrated how little these people knew of the French. Fires crackled simultaneously in the houses and he wondered how a wooden village kept from going up in flames. A cluster of shoulder-high figures milled in the path and Manu thought he recognized the voices of the water-bearers—perhaps the villagers were gathering for their share.

"Josephine!" Schultz called down from a doorway, his left side illuminated by the yellow fire within.

"Baker," called Manu, and the dark crowd parted for him. "Sentry down the far end?"

"Bouna. There's a fine lady here, sir, who's killed half-a-dozen chickens for us."

Manu's hands found the ladder and he climbed, waiting for the chiselled log to snap beneath him until he realized he'd done little else in 1954 but lose weight like a punctured sandbag.

"Bend low, sir," said Schultz. "Aziz, old boy, wait a moment!"

The place—or was it the people?—had a pungent wet-dog smell that immediately reminded him of Eugène's gangly old spaniel, Bayard. Besides Schultz the tiny house had three occupants: a leathery old crone pulverizing delicacies with mortar and pestle, Pascal inspecting his radio in the corner and a second woman vigorously plucking chickens with her back to them.

"Madame," Schultz called in French, "I present our chief, Sergeant Ferdinand Merde, a gentleman of the first order in spite of the name."

The young woman glanced over her shoulder at Manu and feigned a smile. Her hair looked very black and her skin very white, especially compared to the crone, and the planes of her face, Manu realized, were just like those of his mother as she'd sat up in bed beside her electric lamp. In fact, if she'd had a new dress and a scrub, this woman might have resembled his mother *exactly*—and he realized the very obvious truth that, despite the many hundreds of places that he'd searched for her in the past four decades, he'd never looked for his mother *here*, wherever this was. He saw her eyebrows, that downcast smile, and felt sick like he'd swallowed a litre of water. She'd risen and was stepping toward him now, picking something from her finger, while he was meant to remain calm and unruffled!

"She may be a countrywoman of yours, sir," Schultz droned on. "Or maybe she's Portuguese and learned French off a matchbook cover."

"Ah, Monsieur," she was asking him. "*Shin nai ban? Lélah-lélah paituco—*"

He held his arms out to the woman. The rifle on his back felt heavy enough to drag him to the floor, its strap a garrotte against his neck, but he held his arms out to the woman—to her grey eyes, the freckles across her nose, her long neck like a dancer's.

"Oh?" she asked.

He managed to shuffle a heavy boot across the bamboo slats and place a hand on the back of her head, her black hair dry as straw, then another hand on her bare back, hot from the flames, then to pull her to the sodden breast of his uniform.

The old crone leapt to her feet, fists in the air, and the flickering fire filled with castanets. Pascal stood up in the corner, the thatch gouging the back of his head.

"Sir?"

Manu was fifty-four years old, one-eyed, an orphan, and here was his mother. She smelled like Bayard the spaniel. In an official report this would seem a pipe dream, he reasoned, and indeed in ten minutes it might seem a pipe dream, but what reason did he have to doubt his senses?

"It's my mother," Manu said into her hair.

"No, sir," Pascal said softly. "It isn't."

Nonetheless the woman kept her eyes squeezed shut, cheek pressed hard against the strap of his canteen.

"Evidently she knows him," murmured Schultz.

She extricated herself, grasped Manu's hand, loudly kissed his knuckles, then stroked his cheek so that he would forever after cherish the reek of raw chicken. She squinted up at him conspiratorially, then pressed against him once more with the wiry strength of a Turk he'd once wrestled.

"Nico," she murmured. *"D'bai kama."*

"Ah." Schultz shrugged comically at the old woman. "Doesn't know him."

Why should she say his *father*'s name? Manu wondered. Yet she *had* said his father's name, it could not be coincidence, so besides the bare fact of her existence there was nothing else he should have been surprised by. He did not wish to let go of her but needed badly to sit down.

"But is Nico your *real* name, sir?" asked Pascal.

"It's Emanuel," said the sergeant.

"Manu?" the woman asked, wide-eyed. *"Brah kama?* Manu *didiki?"*

She squinted up at him again, hands still against his chest. He inhaled that acrid meat smell. Was it possible his mother had been this short? Through the flickering light he watched the old crone flail her arms as if afflicted with chorea.

"WHAT NOW, *is that one your father?"* Pak cried, seizing Sisil by the shoulders to pull her toward the unplucked chickens. *"First they must eat the meal, come!"*

But the tall old man held Sisil's wrist!

"But what are you doing here?" he asked.

"Sir?" said Pascal.

Manu's fingers relaxed and Adélie knelt to resume her task, briefly giving her son the old tight-lipped smile. Even as he dropped onto his bottom, shaking the house, his eyes never left her.

"Kamili must greet them before you speak another word," Pak said as she sprinkled the broken peppers over the rice, *"and you may never touch the men, never, no matter how far your family has travelled. My family came to see me here so I remember. How far have the black ones come?"*

"The old one says he is my son from where I was before."

"That boy you talked about? Why does he look like that now?"

Adélie threw down the last chicken, its guts still in her hand, and stared across the room at Old Manu. The other soldiers sat beside him now, murmuring, no different than the times that Bonheur and the others had smoked cigars with Nicolas. Now there was dinner to serve; thinking could come later.

"We'll just bivouac further down the trail—not too far, sir," said Schultz. "Leave the sentries to collect Drapeau when—"

"No, no. Too long without beds." Manu stared across the hut without blinking. "Remind me in the morning to collect what's left of Villier."

He untied his boots' brittle laces. He could not guess whether she would still be there when he looked up.

"I agree, sir, that it might be best to camp elsewhere," said Pascal.

Through the floating flecks of ash and *meng* the two Legionnaires-First Class watched the white woman bring her cleaver down with a thud. Her breasts swayed unabashedly and smoke

313

lodged in the backs of their throats, providing timely distraction from the tang of the sergeant's feet.

"Say, my old man died at Stalingrad," Schultz yawned in Pascal's ear. "Might be he's in the hut next door."

"In Hanoi we caught this deserter," Manu murmured. "Put him against the wall, fired over his head and he fainted. Just to give him a scare. Brought him around and he kept looking at his hands. He said, 'This is how they look when you're dead.' So it's all relative, do you see what I mean?"

"Sergeant!" Aziz called through the wall. "Civilians want to bring weapons in."

"Firearms?"

Kamili and Gani climbed into the hut with their bows on their backs and arms full of firewood. Kamili stacked his branches and eyed the new arrivals soberly. He tugged curls of hair behind his ears.

"The old one is—is my father," said Sisil.

"They should not have come in without me," said Kamili. *"You told a story that your father was dead."*

"There he is."

Kamili stroked his ribs with his fingertips.

"The noi ban is getting the jar and colours ready." He brushed a spider from Gani's arm. *"This one shot a deer but couldn't find it."*

Kamili had a new pot of poison in the rafters that the *sadet* had not blessed yet—otherwise that deer of Gani's wouldn't have run one step!

"We could have used a deer!" said Pak, arraying chickens over the hissing coals. *"Her relatives are three different colours!"*

"I want the children to dance," said Sisil. *"Where is Uroh?"*

"Drinking her water," said Gani.

"I will arrange them." Sisil got up and threw her mass of hair over her shoulder. *"Under the fig tree?"*

But Kamili was already creeping after Gani to see the tools the men had brought.

314

SCHULTZ AND PASCAL lifted their rifles across their knees.

"You needn't lay an ambush in here," said Manu.

"The boy might hurt himself, sir," said Schultz.

Manu watched his mother back down the ladder. Should he follow? No, he'd already frightened her enough, and if this was a dream he'd soon be elsewhere.

Pascal shifted himself so that they might not interfere with the radio.

"Hello, chaps," said Schultz. "Speak French?"

The two natives crouched on either side of him.

"*Lélah boos stu'ung?*" asked the little wiry man. "*Wijah?*"

"What's your name?" Schultz grinned at the boy. "*Apa nama?*"

"What'd you say?" asked Pascal.

"That's Malay. Cute kid, isn't he? Looks like a kitty-cat with those eyes!"

"He could chew through your neck."

The boy didn't crouch on the floor, Manu thought, so much as hover over it. Would he have fared better in a barricaded church than those children in sweaters and shorts? He might've swung up to the belfry and flown away.

The native man pressed his fingertip against the front sight of the rifle and the Legionnaires sat up straight. Manu noticed then that the wiry hunter held a cleaver in the other hand—shouldn't he have noticed that long before?

"*Pisau,*" the boy whispered through his front teeth. "*Pisau tom.*"

Kamili rapped the cleaver against the gun's barrel, *tang tang tang!* If it *was* a sort of shovel he had to test the iron—maybe it could help Sisil with planting.

But then the old man snatched it away!

Gani leapt to his feet, sucking in his breath—*soh!*—which Kamili agreed was appropriate. He reached to take the shovel back but the old man curled around it like the thing was his beloved and the other big men jumped up, holding *their* shovels in the air like they meant to spear him. In his own mother's house!

"Moleh!" Kamili pointed to the door—they could learn to be civil in someone else's hut! He slapped the floor with the flat of his hand. *"Oruma mako kama!"*

Pascal still held the rifle to his shoulder. He watched the jungle man flail about and imagined the array of red holes that with so little effort could burst across his chest.

"Sir?" he asked.

Gani gave the Legionnaires his most withering look. He sucked in another *soh!*

"Sit," said Manu. "It's nearly dinnertime. Here." He unfolded the waterproof pouch and produced the three blue packs of Gitanes. "I can smoke something else when the time comes."

"No, you can't mean it," said Pascal. "Really, sir?"

He flicked his lighter and lit his first cigarette in a month—his longest abstinence since he was eight. Though it seemed a shame, with Drapeau still—

"Api!" Kamili leapt back, eyes big as fists.

"Take this down to Aziz and Youssef." Manu handed a pack to Schultz. "Tell them after we eat they'll go on sentry and the password changes to 'Mother Bigoudis' unless it's Drapeau coming in."

The cat-faced boy concentrated like a mathematician while he puffed his Gitane, until the old crone set him to work shuttling banana leaves, groaning with rice and meat, all around the hut and down the ladder. Tobacco ash drifted majestically onto the food; he would've looked at home dishing soup in the finest bistro.

Two more old women climbed up and sat with the hostess. Grease dripped from Manu's elbows into his lap, and when he'd sucked the chicken bones clean he wiped his fingers on the thatch ceiling.

"Tell me straight now, Pascal. Did I *dream up* that woman with the lovely brows?"

HE HAD ALWAYS believed that if she *had* sailed away it was to somewhere that they spoke French, and with her tuberculosis it would only make *sense*—if such a thing entered into it—to sail to somewhere warm, which ruled out Québec. As a boy of ten he'd written letters asking after her to the administrators of all such places, and after the first war he'd served in the colonies in North Africa, West Africa, Polynesia, Tonkin, asking after Adélie Tremier in the hill stations and oases. He'd spent his furloughs reading entry lists and hospital records. There had been very few Tremiers abroad in the world but that fact made little difference, and then he'd realized that he might hunt for Adélie Lissner as well and began to read the same columns again. Then in '35 Messageries Maritimes had unearthed a lot of misplaced passenger lists. He'd taken his leave in Marseilles and discovered unequivocally that she'd sailed aboard the *Salazie*. He had bawled right there at the records counter because it was the first evidence he'd encountered that she'd still been alive two days after creeping from the house. He'd been transferred back to Indo-China, expecting to find her on the dock at Saigon. He'd left their family portrait with the Immigration Department. He had not looked for her grave. Never. He had volunteered for operations where administrators and the postal service had never penetrated, and in '38 had proposed to ferret out partisans in Cambodia and Laos but was called home to man the Maginot Line. For years he'd nearly convinced himself that he'd been dragging himself around those backwaters for no reason, none at all. But he saw now that it wasn't so, there had been a reason. If this was all make-believe he would wait until someone kindly informed him of the fact.

AS SHE SLID down Pak's ladder, Sisil decided she'd show Manu that really no time had passed at all. But then she was reminded of that evening she herself was presented to the community, for here were all of the villagers crouched on the path, sipping their nightly water and staring up at the house to await the next turn of events—*then* she remembered the business of the tops and the Farandole, and she gritted her teeth against the trouble that was sure to come. Would she be better off to not believe it was Manu?

If she could arrive at the village, why shouldn't he? There was no logic in disbelieving.

"*Sisil!*" called the voices all around her. "*Didn't Kamili colour his face?*"

Silhouettes of soldiers sat in the *noi ban*'s doorway. Every time those newcomers spoke she could only comprehend a word or two though she felt sure she ought to understand it all, just as she believed when she was a girl that she ought to understand the dog. How could she explain to Manu that their water would stop his skin from looking so old, and his eye so strange? For surely he was a young man in the throes of some affliction—*visage*, that was the word for face, but eye?

"*Sisil!*" someone called. "*They can't find berries!*"

"*Not in the dark!*" cried someone else.

She would have to remember enough words to convince him that she'd been planning a second trip through the swamp and that in just a few weeks she'd have been on her way back to him again. Why had she even left his side just now? To find those things that would make him recognize her. And to help Sisil recognize Adélie.

A grunt—she'd stepped on Uroh's father's hand! She recognized his enormous ears. He thrust his poor fingers into his mouth.

"*Wijah, where is Uroh? We must give a dance.*"

"*I am here,*" Uroh called from the black thicket.

"*There can be no dance until we colour our faces,*" said Wijah. "*For men to welcome other men as we look now—they would laugh at us!*"

"*No one painted their face to welcome me,*" said Sisil.

"*The sadet is here now. And these are men.*"

Twigs snapped.

"*Why does Uroh hide back there?*" asked Sisil.

"*She says the men are spirits.*"

"*No,*" the girl shouted, "*if they are men then we are spirits!*"

"*No, no, no. They are the relatives from the story.*" Wijah sucked his fingers then spat distractedly into the grass. "*They've only come to find the dead boy by the spring.*"

"IF I HADN'T seen you *both* I'd say it was beyond belief!" Pascal gestured magnanimously with his Gitane, for after weeks of jungle the hut was equal in his eyes to a brass-and-linen restaurant. "But for argument's sake, sir, how's she so well-preserved? Frozen in an iceberg?"

Kamili and Gani still squatted on their haunches, studying the mysterious shovels and squinting at the white men whenever a particular syllable sounded familiar. Pak had left for the *noi ban*'s.

"She'd had tuberculosis more than a year the last I saw her. I remember she took me to a puppet show, of all things, before she went away."

"Some combination of the TB and this climate?" Pascal suggested.

"Nah," said Schultz, "in China they drop dead by the million."

"She ought to have *stayed* home," Manu said. "Dr. Koch had the cure the moment he discovered the bacilli, that's fact, but the Germans withheld it. That's their nature."

"That's not true, sir!" said Schultz. "There never—"

"Mademoiselle!" Aziz said beyond the wall. "Good evening!"

"Ah," Adélie replied from somewhere outside. "Eve-ning—*sangan*?"

She appeared in the doorway looking as pleased as when she'd first brought Manu a box of pastels. She wore a black hat that sagged like an omelette down the side of her head and a ruinous charcoal shawl about her shoulders, pleated as though it had once been a skirt. Her clothes smelled spitefully of damp. Manu climbed to his feet. Kamili picked something from his tongue.

"*Brah kama!*" She knelt, tugging the corners of the shawl to cover her breasts, then lifted the hat reverentially as though it were adorned with birds of paradise and orchids. "Re . . . member?" she suddenly asked. "*Ch'nam?* The, the . . . Luxembourg?"

Remembering was like reaching into a fountain and pulling the coins out one by one—and when had she ever thought about *fountains*? Gani crouched beside her and she lay the hat across his back so he resembled a turtle.

"Hen-ri-ette?" she suddenly asked. *"Dindah kama?"*

"Henriette, really? You remember her?" Manu's voice sounded as deep as her father's. "The old girl went to the morgue every day after you left to see who'd been fished out of the Seine. Then she died of Spanish flu in '18. Came for Friday dinners until I went to St-Lucien—hell, she might've come after that, but—"

"Manu," she said abruptly.

"Maman?" He took her hand and kissed it. "Will you admit I'm dreaming?"

"What?" She bit her lip.

"We never withheld any tuberculosis vaccine!" blurted Schultz.

"Shin delah kama?" asked Kamili.

"Baw," she murmured. *"Kama delah boos."*

The hunter rose and threw a log on the fire.

"Luxembourg," she repeated, then held out her hand for a cigarette.

Pascal gave her his.

"Sadet delah moleh!" The wiry hunter waved his bow, berating them in his staccato voice. *"Delah moleh!"*

"Shin moleh," Adélie replied. *He* could go if he wished, but she would see the *sadet* later. *"Kama moleh nih!"*

He inhaled in frustration—*soh!*—threw his quiver down, picked it up again and went down the ladder. The omelette flopped to the floor as Gani leapt up to patter after his father. Adélie threw the sorry hat over her head and tugged it down to her eyes.

"Who is that lanky fellow, Madame?" asked Pascal.

Adélie puffed methodically on the cigarette. She looked like a scarecrow on its mid-afternoon break.

"Kamili," she said, guessing correctly at the question.

"Sir?" Aziz called from outside. "Up the hill they're having a sort of party, sir. That's how it looks."

"I can go up, sir," said Pascal. "I'd like to see it."

"Sir," said Aziz. "There's some whisky in the house next door. A big jug."

Schultz jerked forward. "Sir?"

320

"Whoever's not sentry can drink." Manu stretched, vertebrae cracking, and yawned into his fist. "You two are on at 0200 and nobody fires a shot no matter how hilarious they feel. There's a stockade at Muong Sai."

Schultz was already down the ladder.

"I heard it, I heard!" Aziz said from below. "We can—"

"Speaking personally," said Pascal, climbing to his feet. "I'm not sure I haven't been drunk since sometime this afternoon. We'll wake up and this place will have vanished. *Baraka*, isn't it?"

"Tried the radio?" asked Manu.

"Sir?" Pascal paused, ducking his head in the doorway. "Want me try it now?"

"No." The house creaked as Manu settled on his elbows. "In the morning."

Then Adélie couldn't hear any of her villagers, only soldiers laughing on the path. Pak's hut held only herself and this drowsy giant her Manu had turned into. And the floor needed sweeping.

Manu said, "Can you remember what we were singing when the ceiling fell on Grandma Sabine?"

The wrinkles that Nicolas had displayed whenever he wished to be taken seriously now lined her son's forehead. On his sunburnt, grey-bearded soldier's face. She wanted to tell him that he shouldn't have been pining for his mother, if he had been, he ought to have been pining for *grandchildren*.

"Can you remember what the hymn was?" he insisted.

"*Yeut, yeut,*" she murmured. "Slow."

He took a long pull from his canteen and, despite the murky depths he drank from, the water still tasted fresh as a crack in the rocks

"*Me'ek,*" she said. "Your." She swallowed. "Eye? *Me'ek shin?*"

"This? It's *glass*." He put a fingertip to the socket. "Want me to take it out?"

She threw out her hands to stop him.

"Remember Eugène from around the corner?" he smiled. "We went up to the front together in the *First* World War."

"Eugène?"

"Cut in half by the Germans' first barrage. Two lieutenants out of St-Lucien—"

"St-*Lucien*?"

"Two of us against the Kaiser. I was first out of the trench but a line of barbed wire got caught under my helmet and before I could get free the troopers pulled themselves up by the stuff on either side of me. One of the points went straight in."

"Oh!"

"That's right. That juice in your eye is hotter than you'd think."

She knelt beside him to peer at where his left eye had been. In the glass she saw her own reflection. She brought her hand beside the eye and tapped it with her nail. Even the lids seemed dead, though the lashes of the other eye blinked madly.

"What do you do here?" he asked suddenly.

"Here?" She pulled the shawl tight again. "We... plant? *Buas.* Rice."

"And what have you taught them?" he yawned.

"Oh? Nothing," she managed to say. "Nothing."

And she curled on her side like a cat. Her son massaged one of his rancid feet, put his hand on his gun for a moment, then massaged his other foot. She wanted to tell him that she'd taught the women to make yellow and black dyes from saffron and cinders and that she'd started them weaving on a loom but they hadn't cared for it; these villagers didn't mind subtle changes provided they were stretched out over a thousand years. But perhaps if he was still in the village the next day, if the Light of the Morning hadn't wrested him from her, she would tell Manu how these people had found the spring and hadn't grown older, not even the baby on Me'ek's back who still wasn't big enough to be named.

Manu gasped and she saw in the dwindling light that tears were running down his cheeks. Even the side with the glass eye. She moved beside him and made him lie back so his head was cradled in her lap. The bones of his emaciated shoulders dug into her shins like knots of firewood. He exhaled. He closed his eyes.

"Hush," she said, reaching for more coins from that fountain. "Hush your boots."

She stroked his hair, then kissed his forehead. He folded his hands over his belly as she went on stroking his hair. She wanted to tell him that from the moment he'd embraced her she'd known he was taking her away to die, and that it was all right. But he was asleep by then, his head twitching in her lap.

AFTER SHE LEFT her son snoring Adélie had to walk to the clearing in the dark, which wasn't difficult after the routine of years though there was no trace of a moon and no glimmer of light in the clearing—Kamili had let the fire die. But when she swung herself up the ladder she discerned him sitting up on the mat, black against the blackness.

"Will he take you away tomorrow?" her husband asked.

She stripped off her skirt and lay down next to him.

"Who?" she asked. "My father?"

"You should go with him," said Kamili.

Her heart gave a hard beat. He was right—she did want to go. Not only to be with Manu, which was reason enough, but to leave the village far behind. To see the world the Germans had nearly destroyed with their cannons and bayonets.

"Why do you say that?" she asked.

"I know that the old man is your son. When my mother's family came to see us long ago *they* were old too. My own cousin was an old, old man."

"Why aren't those people here? Didn't they drink the water?"

"They died in a fight."

"The water didn't help them?"

"The spring cannot keep a man with his throat slashed alive any more than it could a deer ripped apart by tigers."

She ran her fingertip down the inside of his arm, which was their signal. In the darkness his hands found her bare hips, and she spread her legs.

"Why do you say I should go?" she asked again.

BARAKA RUNS
OUT VERY SUDDENLY

Emanuel Tremier.

AT FIRST light Manu was awakened by the reassuring sound of the chickens fussing beneath him. As a long-legged spider crawled across the intricate shadows in the thatch he remembered that Villier and Drapeau were still unaccounted for. The muzzle of his rifle was pressed beneath his arm and his pack was his pillow.

He checked that his eye was in before sitting up. In the corner Pascal lay curled, snoring softly, around his radio. On the other side of the hearth what appeared to be a woman—presumably their leathery hostess—lay in a ball.

Outside a diffuse greyness brightened the sky. He rose and bent nearly double to slouch out the door and stand at the top of the ladder. A boy was passing lithely along the path and gnawing the end of his thumb until his large eyes turned up to see Manu. Then he vanished from sight.

Chickens fretted beneath the huts, the odd pig voiced its displeasure, and over the distant trees nets of black birds moved back and forth, pulling the net in, releasing it. This had always been the hour for Insect X, but that phase of their operation was over now. Rather than *"La Petite Tonkinoise," "Le Boudin"* resonated in Manu's head.

A long phlegmy groan emitted from the hut next door. Though most of the squad was likely asleep there he knew it couldn't be any of his men—he knew their noises well. Then more coughs surged from the surrounding huts, along with the grudging crackle of new cooking fires. Hadn't Pascal's duty begun at 0200? He would have to walk up the path and see who'd stood in for him. But he suddenly needed to sit. An old woman appeared in front of the hut opposite; she hung a basket down her back, picked up her machete, took two steps then immediately turned back to clutch her ladder. She coughed painfully, high in her chest, then briefly turned wild eyes on Manu before clawing her way back up to the hut.

A cigarette would get him on his feet, he felt sure, but—unbelievable to his morning-after self—he had given away all three packs. The man next door groaned again. The floor creaked behind Manu, and Pascal stood behind him.

"I'll try the radio now, sir," he said. "It's warming up."

"Dark in there."

"I could work it blindfolded. Have you seen the woman?"

"Where should we look for Drapeau?"

"At that fig tree. And I'll take some men up for Villier."

The floor creaked again, then the insistent sizzle as the radio came to life before falling quiet as Pascal put in the earpiece. The sun crept over the rim of the crags behind Manu, illuminating the valley in orange. Far to his left rose a peak shaped like a tooth.

The village came to life: hunters loped up the path with frail-looking bows in their hands, quivers dangling at their waists; tiny dark boys and girls crept down the ladders of their houses and up those of their neighbours; a trio of half-naked matrons hurried to climb the ladder next door. A nursing battalion?

In the hut behind him the old woman keened like a creaking door.

"Who's on sentry?" Manu called into the darkness.

"Schultz is uphill, sir. Youssef's down. Doesn't drink, of course, so I took his tonight. Couldn't have stayed on my feet."

"Was Schultz any better?"

"He has that Teutonic constitution."

Manu's mother stood at the bottom of the ladder, her bosom draped with some sort of sacking, her legs slick with dew.

"Good morning," she said. "How did you sleep?"

She'd lain awake for hours, practicing.

"All right, but I still don't feel too good."

Adélie climbed the ladder and sat beside him. She set her small sunburnt foot beside his—the callused foot of the child whose curls had once brought nursemaids to tears.

"Will you stay?" she asked.

"I may. Send the men on and stay here myself."

She touched his bearded cheek with the back of her hand.

"Excuse me, sir!" Léopold jogged up the path, barefoot, untucked. "There's trouble with the man in that house where we slept!"

"Too much drink," said Manu.

"Pak?" his mother called over her shoulder.

One of the matrons reappeared on the porch next door, shouting as though the house were on fire, and villagers appeared from all directions—only a few dozen, but as they darted about it seemed to Manu there must be hundreds. Bouna and Aziz slid from the house, rifle-straps rattling, bleary-eyed.

"He is *rahat*," said Adélie, rising. "Our, um, our headman is . . . sick."

"What are they doing for him? I might have a quinine—"

"But no one can be sick here! *Baw!* Pak?"

"You three run up to that lake," Manu ordered, "and bring Villier down."

The villagers had mobilized too—men dug a hole in front of the headman's house as two big fellows hurried up with a post. Naked boys sprinted off to each point of the compass while adults shouted after them.

"Sir?" Pascal called. "I might have something."

But Manu was already following Adélie through the crowd.

"*Rahat?*" the villagers said sharply in their ears. "*Boos-boos rahat!*"

Mother and son climbed the headman's ladder until they could see the *noi ban* himself on his face in a shaft of light, bottom in the air, pushing himself toward a brass dipper beaded with water. His tongue protruded and clumps of white hair drifted across the floor. Adélie hurried to the old man's side, helping him to sit, his head against her shoulder. She lifted the dipper to his lips and with a sigh he grasped the handle.

"*Our good water,*" she told him, "*will make you well.*"

With a spasmodic gesture he dashed the contents into the corner. The matrons came in again—where had they gone?—and helped the *noi ban* to his mat. Blood trickled from his mouth.

"*Get Ama!*" Adélie cradled the dipper in her arms. "*Run and get Pak! They will know how to mend him!*"

"*They are bad too,*" the matrons cried, stroking the old man's wrists. "*We have been to them.*"

A young woman hurried up the ladder; to clear the way Manu jumped from the doorway to the ground and nearly turned his ankle. He felt dizzy as a weather vane—why had they smoked every last cigarette? A single Gitane might have settled him.

"Sir?" Pascal called through the bamboo wall.

"*What is it,* Me'ek?" Adélie asked the new arrival.

"*Is the sadet here?*"

"*He is coming.*"

"*The baby will not wake up. He is breathing, but...*"

Manu struggled up the ladder into Pak's hut and found the old woman sitting on the hearth with her head in her hands while Pascal, shaking like a leaf, stood over the radio.

"They request confirmation, sir! Christ, hope the batteries—"

Manu took up the little microphone.

"Sergeant Merde speaking, 12th Company, 3rd Battalion, 3rd Foreign Legion Infantry Regiment. Go ahead. Hello?"

"This is Muong Sai airstrip, Sergeant," said the voice—a French voice, from Marseilles, by the accent!—"What is your position?" it asked.

"Difficult to say exactly," stammered Manu. "Northern part of Laos, I believe. Do you—do you know a tall mountain shaped like a tooth?"

"Like a tooth? You mean Pa Na?"

"I don't know. We came west from Dien bien Phu."

"Let me—yes, that's about right. What is your position to the mountain?"

"North. Fifteen or twenty kilometres north."

"Can you send up a flare in sixty minutes' time?"

"We have no flares."

"Can you light a fire? A significant fire?"

Kneeling beside her bucket, the old woman sipped from cupped hands only to spit the water out.

"We will light a fire," said Manu.

"And Sergeant, try to—"

The voice cut out. There was not even a hiss. Manu pulled a long face.

"Let the batteries rest, sir," said Pascal. "Try in an hour."

"*Boi rahat,*" the old woman croaked without raising her head. "*Boos-boos rahat.*"

"Doesn't matter now," said Manu, lurching across the hut. His watch read 0630. "We need to cut a helicopter pad."

He was nearly knocked over by Gani, the cat-eyed boy, running up the path with a dead crow spread across his chest. Its wings fluttered as though they'd both take flight.

The posthole in front of the headman's was now a metre deep. Adélie hurried out of the crowd, laced her fingers through Manu's and clutched his hand against her hip as though anxious he not wander off.

A man took the bird from Gani and beheaded it with a stroke of his chopper. They lashed the slender head to the top of the post then shouldered the wood until it stood erect in the hole. They stomped earth down around it. The bird's blind eyes, alive only with ecstatic flies, gazed across the thatch roofs, keeping watch for any more malevolent spirits that might stumble upon the village after leaving it unmolested so many years. One of the matrons appeared on the porch and everyone spoke at once.

"Our *noi ban* ... is almost dead," Adélie explained. "*Ligi-ligi.* Teeth fall out."

In another hut a woman started to wail. Heads suddenly turned amongst the throng and strident voices raised, for someone was descending the path.

"Sir, she's not *well* up here!" called Pascal.

"Maman," the sergeant blurted, "in one hour we have to—"

"Here," said Adélie calmly. "Here is our *sadet*."

Manu recognized Schultz's broad face, his free arm swinging jauntily, before he even noticed the figure at the German's side: the long-haired *sadet*, apparently, hurrying with teeth bared and a machete in his hand. Sunlight gleamed off his potbelly.

"He's a bit worked up, sir!" called Schultz. "Thought I'd better—"

"Pascal!" Manu shouted, letting go his mother's hand. "Get out here!"

The crowd backed away from the two newcomers—children giggling, tugging at each other's arms—as the *sadet* spoke shrilly, waving the great knife overhead, his jaw thrusting like an eel's. Pathet Lao, thought Manu.

"No, no!" gasped Adélie. "In our, our spring, there is a dead man!"

Manu pictured gangrenous Villier floating upon the clear water.

"So what is going to happen?"

"He says he—"

Then the *sadet* swung the machete at Schultz's temple, burying the blade halfway into his head. The German's mouth twisted into half a smile and he dropped like a felled pine. While Manu groped in his empty holster it occurred to Adélie, perversely, that a chicken would have at least flapped its wings.

The *sadet* knelt to retrieve his knife, the crowd shouting and surging, until blood burst in three places from the magician's chest and he fell on his back with one leg twisted beneath him. The villagers dropped to their bellies with their hands over their ears to ward off the otherworldly noise. Over his shoulder Manu glimpsed Pascal crouched on the ladder, rifle still raised, and only then did the sergeant remember that he'd given the .32 pistol to Villier.

Puddles of blood shimmered around Schultz's body. The black handle of the machete stood perpendicular to the ground like the headman's pole—the pole with a *crow's head*, of all abhorrent things, lashed to its top. The sergeant took his '49 Saint-Étienne from Pascal.

"Tell them all to go up into the house," Manu told his mother.

"What . . . what are you going to do?"

"I don't know."

She stepped forward and began to speak softly, helping children to their feet, then cajoling the women to stand. One by one the villagers climbed the ladder. A long-armed man leapt up, spear in hand, but Pascal fired a shot into the sky and the man threw the weapon down. Manu glanced at his watch—0635. His paperwork would be simpler if he could report Schultz as having died at Dien bien Phu. They'd have buried him there in parachute silk.

"Sir?" The sentry Youssef saluted at Manu's side, though his eyes, of course, fell on the corpses.

"Disarm anyone who comes in sight," the sergeant ordered. "Even a kid with a slingshot."

"How long, uh—how long do they stay in there?" asked Adélie.

"Tell those three men to dig a hole for the soldier," said Manu. "Those three."

"*Yeut, yeut*, child. What about our *sadet*?" she asked.

"He can rot."

Adélie led the men to a spot behind the house, and with bare hands they began to dig. When they glanced up she saw no bitterness in their eyes—she saw no expression at all. It would take fifty years for them to digest the events of the previous half-hour.

"We ought to bury him ourselves, sir," Pascal said from the ladder.

"That's true," the sergeant nodded. "But I want our eyes on these people."

"I must check on Pak," Adélie told her son as she regained the path.

"Sisil?" called Uroh from the headman's doorway.

"Sisil!" called Gani.

The children's noses ran. Such a chill ran down Adélie's spine that her teeth clacked together.

"*It will be all right*," she told them.

She crept up Pak's ladder but did not find the old woman on her mat.

"Shh," said Kamili from the corner.

He sat with his arms around his mother, the back of her grey head against his chest. Adélie knelt. Pak breathed as though her throat were full of seed pods. Kamili's large eyes did not blink.

"The water is poison," he whispered.

"The *sadet* told us." Adélie felt tears welling. "A dead man in the spring."

"It is a white man. His arms are out like a vulture."

Pak's eyes flickered open. She licked her blue lips.

"You whites are a bad crop," she said.

Kamili pressed his mouth against his mother's scalp. Adélie rubbed her wrist.

"Is the *sadet* down on the ground?" he asked.

"He is dead."

"His magic could not beat them?"

Adélie stood and bent low under the roof to kiss Kamili hard on the mouth. She kissed him long enough to breathe in and out three times, then sat on her heels. He held his mother tight again.

"Will you fight them?" she asked.

"There is no one to bless the *wourali*, and the men are bigger than deer."

She did not remind him that an unpoisoned arrow might also kill a soldier. He slipped an arm beneath his mother's knees and began to rock her.

"They have made a poison," he said. "The spirits have abandoned this place."

"Only the old people and babies are sick."

Kamili pressed his lips to his mother's brow.

"Blood came out of my nose," he said flatly. "Where is Gani?"

"He's well. He is with the *noi ban*."

"If we ran far enough into the forest we could find another spring."

"Which way will you go?" she asked.

"East. Will you come?"

Adélie climbed to her feet.

"I will stay with my little boy," she said, and ducked through the doorway.

From the *noi ban*'s hut a dozen villagers gazed out like sheep in the back of a butcher's wagon. The *sadet*'s fly-crusted mouth had slid open to reveal his peg-shaped teeth. Manu sat with his rifle across his lap; his face was white as putty.

"What are you going to do?" she asked again.

He glanced at his watch.

"In ten minutes we'll start for that fig tree. We have to light a fire for the helicopter and hope my knees don't drop out from under me. I must have the flu."

"A hel-i-copter?"

"Like an aeroplane. Has a propeller on the top so it can come down, pick us up, fly us away. It'll be the noisiest thing you've ever heard."

"It has a steam engine."

"Something like that," he smiled. "Where's a place that's flat and open?"

"Our... our rice fields." She pointed southwest.

"Too far." He squinted at the distance. "Maybe they'll see a spot from the air."

"They've finished digging, sir," said Pascal. "Can't be very deep."

"Just get him buried."

Unseen women began to keen inside the headman's house.

"What are they saying now?"

"A... a baby." Adélie wiped her nose on the back of her arm. "A baby died."

Leaning on his rifle, Manu climbed to his feet, then followed Pascal behind the house to the long hole in the red earth. Behind them the three wide-eyed men carried Schultz's body, his head lolling so that the machete's handle drew a drunken line in the dirt. They breathed through their teeth as though the limbs they gripped might spring to life at any moment.

"Can't we pull out the knife, sir?" asked Pascal.

"Don't touch it," said Manu. "Who knows what that son of a bitch had on his hands."

The men lay Schultz in the hole, criss-crossed with roots and scurrying insects, and turned the corpse's head so that the handle lay flush with the ground.

"Wait a minute," said Manu, and though the men didn't understand they obligingly backed away. Kneeling amongst the beetles, he retrieved the photo of the hopeful-looking woman and gap-toothed kids from a blood-spattered breast pocket.

"With my compliments." Manu wiped it off with the side of his hand and passed the picture up to Pascal. "Tell the folks you've settled down."

Pascal swallowed hard. "Much appreciated, sir."

They stood at attention as the three villagers threw clods of dirt over Schultz. Of all the men killed under Manu's command, Schultz was the first to be buried without a chaplain—what in Hell had all those chaplains ever said?

"Our Lord," Manu murmured, "please look after our friend now. His *baraka* ran out very suddenly. Amen."

"Amen," said Pascal, helmet to his chest.

Manu looked at his watch—0700. Youssef stood sentry in front of the headman's hut, and in the heat of the morning his beard had begun to steam.

"Any sign of Aziz?"

"No, sir."

Manu stopped beside his mother and fought hard not to vomit.

"Maman," he said, "I understand that you may wish to stay here with your stepchildren, but putting my own wishes to one side I must inform you that in view of possible Communist incursions it is my duty to return any and all French nationals to Union-controlled territory. Will you comply?"

She nodded, almost to herself, and began to tie her hair in a knot.

"Tell them they can come out of there," he said. "But that they're not to step beyond the houses today. If they do they'll regret it."

She climbed the headman's ladder and spoke quietly. Youssef batted at a bee. Pascal struggled down from Pak's hut with the radio on his back.

"That fellow who smoked our cigarettes is up there, sir."

"Armed?"

Adélie trotted over to her son and again took his hand, exactly as if they were in the Luxembourg Gardens and the year was 1904. Though his hand was now large and clammy as a black-pit herring.

"I can't think of what to set on fire," he told her.

As the villagers crept down the ladder the newfound poison demonstrated its versatility: men had lost thick handfuls of hair; Me'ek, groping toward her own hut, looked to have become paralyzed down one side; matrons staunched bleeding noses; and Uroh, in her father's arms, looked like a dried husk of herself—smaller, with flaking skin. Whose arm could Adélie take, when each of them needed her? They stood on the path as though they'd never seen the village before.

"Three funerals," Lemek murmured. "The *sadet* would have sung."

"She must drink water to get well!" Uroh's mother sobbed, passing a hand across the girl's cracked forehead.

"Not today," advised Adélie. "It might be better tomorrow. You must stay in the village now. If the water is bad you must all run into the forest."

"Which way?" they asked.

"East," said Adélie.

They shuffled toward their huts or squatted beneath Ama's house. The gravediggers climbed their ladders, followed by drowsy-looking children, while Uroh's vacant-eyed parents carried her home. Then Adélie was left with only Gani before her. He wiped his wet nose in the crook of his arm.

"Will you come back after you go away?" he asked.

"Go into your grandmother's," she said. "They're waiting."

Yellow mucus pooled in the corners of his eyes.

"Be a good boy," said Adélie.

She flew up the headman's ladder, and the women genuflecting beside the shrivelled body did not so much as raise their eyes. She retrieved her eight-sided dipper.

A taste like burnt bacon had filled Manu's mouth. He watched Ama's sons puzzle over the *sadet*'s shattered breast, and as they stuck their fingers deep in the bullet-holes he felt his knees begin to buckle. To steel himself he pulled his boot back and kicked the corpse across the face, opening a square gash in its cheek.

"Son of a bitch," he said, then started up the hill.

It was inexcusable! Adélie's first reaction was to reach for the hairbrush to spank his bottom, as though the intervening years had simply never happened and they were in his room even now. She saw vividly the light filtering through his windowpane and the boughs of the trees outside, as though they were standing with their bare toes sinking into the white rug even as she watched his filthy trousered behind hurry up the hill ahead of her. He was slightly bowlegged, as his father had always been, and with so many straps and belts swaying between his behind and her eyes that she couldn't have found a clear spot to spank. She thought all of this to keep from thinking of Uroh, who would only dance the Farandole now if someone dragged her.

"Was the radio *really* Muong Sai?" asked Youssef.

Some object thudded through the air over their heads, and though it had sounded nothing like a helicopter the soldiers frantically turned their heads. A heavy-winged black bird alighted on a high branch and swayed there, peering down at the village.

"Vulture," Manu murmured.

"Vulture," the men agreed.

Manu leaned his hands on his knees and spat a ball of mucus into the bush.

"You are too ill to travel," she told him.

"You ought to know, Maman."

As they climbed, tatters of mist dissipated on the hillsides. Beneath the fig tree they found Bouna, Aziz and Léopold panting on their backs.

"What's delayed you men?" asked Manu, dropping onto his behind.

"Excuse me, sir," said Aziz. "Have you ever carried a drowned man?"

Manu followed the Moroccan's gaze up the path to where a single boot-clad leg protruded from the bushes.

"Not for years," answered the sergeant.

"Where's Drapeau?" asked Pascal.

The Africans climbed to their feet and peered into the trees.

"I could find the place we went in, sir," offered Pascal. "It was dark, but—"

"I'm sorry," said Manu. The hands of his watch read 0725. "Denied. Who knows the rotor diameter of a good-sized helicopter?"

"Sir, it might land at this spot," said Youssef , fingers in his beard, "if we could remove this tree."

Adélie stared down the hill to where the path disappeared behind a banana palm. She held the dipper to her chest. It smelled of church candles. Tall ones. No one appeared on the path.

"Ten metres, sir?" said Bouna.

"Sir, do you mean to say," asked Léopold, "that a helicopter is *coming*?"

"If it weren't for the tree there'd be plenty of clearance." Pascal paced across the circle of well-trod dirt. "Fifteen metres at least. Look, here's where he killed the piglet in the ceremony. Here's where he burnt the shavings."

"Was the fire . . . very big?" asked Adélie.

"I thought so, Madame. Everyone seemed pleased."

"Yes," she said. "That means good luck."

"Shall we go down and requisition saws, sir?" asked Léopold.

Manu's teeth began to chatter—the damnedest thing!

"Who's got grenades?" he asked.

With the folding spades from their packs the men set to work digging a cavity beneath the fig tree. Bouna had left his at Dien bien Phu, so his task was to keep a weather eye for scorpions scurrying amongst the roots. Manu lay beside the path.

"Set a rock under the charge so the impact goes into the tree."

Adélie set her son's head in her lap. She stroked his brow with grimy fingers.

"Not so far underneath," he said. "I don't want the thing to fly straight up! Come on. One minute."

"Should we start the fire, sir?" asked Pascal. "They might already be in sight."

The men tilted their heads. All that could be heard was a monotone cooing and rattling bamboo. To the south shapes like eyelashes circled low in the sky—more black birds.

"Set that shack on fire," said Manu, jerking his chin toward the lonely hut of the previous afternoon.

"That," said Adélie, "is the *sadet*'s house."

"All the better."

Pascal hurried up the slope; with its thatch roof overhanging split-bamboo walls, the house looked as flammable as a haystack in high summer.

"There is magic there," said Adélie. "From . . . where they were before."

Pascal tugged out a handful of thatch and held his lighter to it.

"Damnit!" he called. "I'm out!"

Aziz tested his own lighter, then dashed up the hill. Through half-closed lids Manu watched the two soldiers confer over the handful of thatch, which they threw down disgustedly before heaping lengths of spindly firewood in the doorway. The lighter's blue flame swayed.

"Zero minutes," said Manu.

"Nothing will light, sir!" shouted Pascal. "It's asbestos!"

"We can spare one grenade."

Aziz produced one, pulled the pin and lobbed the grenade onto the roof as the men skittered down the slope and dove for the ground. Manu pulled his mother's head down and pressed his hands over her ears—were there grenades in her day?—and when the blast came it was like a genie clapping gigantic hands together. One of the *sadet*'s bamboo walls tumbled end-over-end down the hill and the remains of the roof blazed with an orange flame half a metre high, now a whole metre—Manu feared the place might burn to the ground before fulfilling its purpose. He twisted his head in his mother's lap to watch Léopold wedge a red stone under the exposed roots.

"What now, sir?" asked Pascal, dusting himself off.

"Straighten the pins. Feed a creeper through that'll go from there to here, get the radio out of harm's way and pray to God it's the last time we have to use a fucking creeper for anything at all."

"Manu!"

"Sorry, Maman, I'm woozy as hell. They're clustered all right? Get them flush against the wood. *Now* what's the matter?"

"A few centipedes, sir," said Youssef. "It's all right now."

"Help me across, Maman. We don't want to get murdered by a lot of toothpicks."

"Ready, sir!"

"Defensive positions!" the sergeant shouted from inside the thicket.

Black crickets leapt in alarm as the men dove for the bush like rabbits into a warren—the Viet Minh themselves couldn't have done it better, though they'd have hidden with a patriotic song in their hearts. Pascal tugged the length of sap-dripping creeper, and before they heard so much as the tinkling of pins the genie brought a tremendous pair of cymbals together and filled the air with smoke and splinters. Adélie and the six men lay face down in the beetle-infested grass as the surrounding trees whipped backwards.

As the last of the pebbles and wood chips *rat-a-tatted* to the ground the little party found the morning that much brighter, for the fig tree, its trunk pulverized, had collapsed into the jungle. An untidy clearing faced the sky. Adélie resisted shrieking at the sight. She set her teeth together and seized Manu's arm.

He smiled. "I ought to have been an engineer!"

"Ah, sir, look here," said Bouna. "We didn't get Villier out of the way."

Manu, pulled to his feet by his wiry mother, parted his lips but said nothing as he heard the *wup-wup* of a helicopter. The men shielded their eyes and Aziz, his sad-dog face bisected by a grin, pointed to a shimmering dot approaching from the south.

"There!"

Léopold admired the shattered tree.

"Much of a hole under there?" asked Manu.

"A very good hole, sir."

"Throw Villier in and cover him. Pascal?"

"Sir?"

"You have ninety seconds to find Drapeau. We won't wait."

Pascal slid the radio from his back. Adélie narrowed her eyes to watch him disappear down the empty trail—for in her heart she'd wanted one or two specific villagers to have followed her—then turned her gaze toward the *sadet*'s flaming hut, momentarily forgotten during the Miracle of the Exploding Tree. Only the porch was recognizable, and she looked for meaningful shapes in the merrily gusting smoke. If not for Manu at her side she would have thought she was watching the end of everything.

Her son watched Bouna and Léopold's pink gums as they grinned at the sky.

"Go bury Villier," he ordered.

He did *not* watch his men carry the corpse across the clearing, but a moment later glanced over to see a purple leg, well-chewed during its bath, protruding from the hole. The men held their breath as they shovelled. Manu felt it symbolic, somehow, a Frenchman buried beneath a shattered Asiatic tree—but he couldn't say of what, exactly.

"Say some words, sir?" asked Léopold.

Manu shook his head, so with helmet in hands Aziz spoke over the grave. The insects' grating was overpowered by the din of the approaching helicopter; it was near enough now that they could count its four wheels. Pascal jogged back up the trail, his eyes on his toe-caps, a long scratch across his cheek.

"I am thirsty," said Adélie.

"Who's got water from yesterday?" asked Manu.

His own canteen was underneath him, but each of the men still had a little. She drank from Pascal's.

"What will you order in the camp?" Bouna asked. "Rum for me."

"Brandy," said Léopold.

"Wine," said Aziz.

"Coffee," said Youssef.

"Cognac," said Pascal. His red eyes still scanned the bush.

"Don't get your hopes up," said Manu. "It might just be wine from concentrate."

"I," Adélie announced, "want coffee."

Though the pilot had obviously seen their beacon the men waved their arms and leapt as though they meant to fly up and save the helicopter the trouble of landing, while in the grass Adélie sat with her legs folded beneath her, sobbing as though she were staggering once more through her parents' empty house. The helicopter dropped like a kestrel and Manu wrapped his long arm around her shoulders and tried to think of something that might comfort her.

"That's a Sikorsky S-55," he said.

She squinted up at the numbers on its bottom but couldn't be bothered to read them. Amongst the interminable forest this portable iron works was an abomination.

Manu watched his men slap each other's backs, Youssef nearly knocking Aziz flat, then dust and leaves and pebbles and sawdust lifted from the ground as though the world had been inverted. Like a crepe pan. The helicopter set down in the clearing they'd made, its back wheels followed by the front, a real Sikorsky S-55 painted with tricolour insignias, so long and tall that the goggled crewmen seemed to wave down from atop a diesel locomotive. Goggled Frenchmen. Since the worst days of *"La Petite Tonkinoise"* Manu had given up imagining that such people even existed. But if his *mother* existed, for God's sake, why shouldn't a nation of forty-two million? The double doors below the cockpit slid open, revealing a third airman beckoning to them while his yellow scarf snapped like a regimental banner. As one body, Manu's men bent low and scrambled forward, knuckles and rifle-butts scraping the ground though the blades spun two storeys above their heads. His mother did not stir; she kept her chin pressed to her chest, her splayed hands shielding her face from debris.

"Can you make it?" he yelled in her ear.

She nodded *yes-yes*, *yes-yes*, and he realized, amidst that tempest of red sand and bark, that she was no longer sobbing but smiling so broadly into the back of her wrist that it might have been her birthday. She cupped her hand over his ear.

"Is it really you?" she shouted.

He gave a half-smile before tipping forward on his knees and vomiting. He wiped his mouth, then retched again; the veins bulged purple from his neck. Adélie rubbed his back reassuringly, and over his heaving shoulders saw Gani and Kamili step from the woods onto the path that led to the spring. She barely recognized Gani, who flew up the path as if shot from a bow, but Kamili, a long bundle draped over his shoulder, stood to gaze at her through the dust. He still resembled a bust of Caesar. She realized it must be his mother he carried over his shoulder. Grit stung her eye and when she looked again her husband was gone.

"Time for us!" coughed Manu, a rope of drool dangling from his chin.

Hand in hand they climbed into the helicopter's belly. The squad sat in a cluster on the steel floor while the man in the scarf held a rail and grinned down at them all. He inspected Adélie without changing expression.

"Civilian, sergeant?" he shouted.

"Yes!"

The vibrations inside the aircraft were tremendous—anything not riveted down rattled like dice—so that as the man in the scarf crashed the doors together Manu took his glass eye from its socket and slipped it into his pocket. His five men suddenly looked quite nauseated; perhaps they were not good flyers. The man in the yellow scarf produced a bottle of rum and Manu eyed it anxiously—he needed to know that Bouna would have the first mouthful.

The Sikorsky lurched skyward and his teeth knocked against his knee.

Ten metres above the ground, now twenty, and Adélie immediately felt cold. The only window was set high in one of the doors, so she grasped the rail and stood on tiptoes. She hoped to see Kamili loping along, with Pak once more on her feet. Adélie pressed her cheek against the damp glass but only saw treetops and red crags rising at random. Surely they were over the village *now*, full of her friends grieving beneath their neat roofs—but then the helicopter shifted so she nearly fell backward and all she saw was a line of smoke against a blue sky.

"Madame!" shouted the man in the scarf.

He helped her to sit beside her son, though the trembling floor was the coldest thing she'd ever touched.

"I—I only," she shouted, "I only went there so I could come back to you!"

Her son looked pale as chalk.

AN UNEXPECTED
ARRIVAL

Pierre Lazarie, 1954.

DRIVING INTO town from the airport I wished desperately that Saigon were not so flat, that I might look down from on high at the twinkling lights of Cho Lon and rue Catinat and the river and imagine that it were all spread out for my benefit, a bachelor's playground, in the very moment that my companion of a decade took wing for the other side of the world. There'd been every reason for Georgette to go: by leaving Saigon she'd avoid being murdered at random by a Viet Minh grenade, and, once in Paris, she'd almost certainly meet a fellow with greater powers of concentration than I regarding matters of the heart. As the attendant had embossed her ticket she'd told me, "Love is misfortune," in a tone in which a child might be taught the alphabet, as though I'd never experienced the emotion for myself. And in regards to Georgette it was possible I never had.

I parked in the theatre square, perhaps rashly, considering the four years' worth of bloodstains on its pavement, and went into the Continental. But the tables were full of couples we'd known all our lives, so with a nod to Old Nguyen I went across to the Rex and found a deserted corner of the bar. I remember sucking lemon halves with absolute gaiety. Then I drove home to find that the servants had vacated the place, as arranged, though Binh had been good enough to leave a light on. I would eat in cafés now, and send my shirts out, and sweep up the gecko droppings myself. And, perhaps more importantly, following Renard's diatribe, I would no longer be sleeping under the same roof as "morally ambiguous" Vietnamese. Though after eighty years of French mismanagement they could have their ambiguity with my blessing.

In the morning I took the back entrance to avoid the madman Le Port and in my office found, of all people upon the face of the earth, Dubois himself sitting in the same chair he'd occupied in Frémont's day, though Immigration had moved beside the river, of course, and we were now the High Commission. Ten years had passed; he was stout and very bald now with a rubber-grower's sunburnt hands. We shook, and he had a grip like a gorilla's.

—As I was coming into town, he announced, I realized you two are about the only ones still here!

I moved behind my desk, grateful to be on familiar footing for what might prove an awkward exchange.

—She's gone back to France, I said. I put her on the plane last night.

—No! Georgette? She loved the place too much!

He shook his head, quite mystified. Ten years after she'd spat in his face and slammed his leg in the car door, he evidently still cared more for her than I had ever done.

—Old Georgette, he said.

I pushed the cigars toward him and lit one myself.

—Know anyone who'll buy a plantation? he asked.

—Get one of these Americans tight enough and he'll meet your price with what's in his back pocket. I imagine you've lost your workforce to conscription.

—Ten thousand trees and no one to tap them.

—Kept any girls in your employ?

—That's none of your damn business.

He sucked at the cigar peevishly, but once it was smouldering he tossed the match into my ashtray with a wink. His eyes were nests of wrinkles.

—Got two of them waiting at the hotel.

—I don't blame you, I smiled thinly. And as much as I joke about Americans we wouldn't be able to cross the street without them nowadays. Seems that when we set out to destroy our industries we put our back into it.

—Cabinet back home ought to decide if it wants a war or an economy!

—And now that we've *lost* the war, I said, we have exactly neither.

—Dien bien Phu's made it official, has it?

His laughter betrayed a timbre of exhaustion. I contemplated his double chin with some relief, for he'd better resembled a skeleton the last time I'd seen him. But even behind that massive desk I found I couldn't parrot my usual speech regarding the cyclical nature of both economic downturns and right- or left-wing sympathies on the part of the public—I had *stolen* his wife, after all, in as bald a manner as the man's own head!

—Do relax, he said. I didn't even have a boy to send for cigars, so this really is tremendous. I've read my fill of year-old newspapers this last while, I can tell you.

—You always were a stalwart for the antique papers.

—Talking of antiques, why should you still keep that ragged picture on your desk? What was the name again—Fornier?

I slid the letters from the *Signature required* tray and reached for my pen.

—Tremier, I told him. I will nose around for prospective buyers for you.

Dubois took the hint and hoisted himself up; the arms of the chair managed to withstand the load.

—Free this evening? he asked.

—No, I'm afraid. The junior Frémont has his masquerade tonight. A month ahead of schedule—he doesn't believe anyone will be left in town by July 14!

—Is *that* why it's tonight? He muttered it was for Bastille Day but I thought better of asking.

—Oh, will you be there too? I asked.

—As of half an hour ago. What will you go as?

Binh's wife had sewn our costumes months earlier—Georgette was to have gone as a harem girl. I grimaced down at the Statement to the Press I was about to sign.

—A genie, I said.

—Wonderful, Dubois called from the door. I'll go as a bottle.

THE GENIE was a common character in Vietnamese village ceremonies, though he bore little resemblance to Aladdin's better-known servant, and I'd been well aware of this fact from my student days but hadn't thought to ask Lan which she would be making. Consequently the Frémonts' doorman gave entrance to an imposing figure in black turban, knee-length black cloak, a perfectly round white mask with narrow eyeholes and a pasted-on black beard, and fantastic gold slippers with pointed toes. Lan was not a shoemaker, after all, so I'd had those made in town.

—Save us! cried Frémont, in the guise of a masked d'Artagnan with a sunburnt, peeling nose. It's the messenger of death!

He was the younger Frémont, of course; his father had died in 1944 under the Japanese administration.

—On the contrary, kind sir, I announced. I'm here to chase the evil ones away!

—And go they will, with a face like that! Who's under there, is that Signac?

—Show me to the drinks and you'll find out.

I couldn't imbibe with the disc in front of my face so I swung it to the back of my head, took a champagne and circled the aromatic buffet tables. With the exception of the wines and string quartet, Frémont had gone native in his hospitality: platters of mincemeat and basil, pigeon breast and transparent fish, steaming tureens of beef *pho*, even jars of rice whisky presented as though they were the very latest thing.

—Well, next year, I heard him say, we might meet at *Les Deux Magots*!

Then a woman laughed amongst the dancing pairs, a tray of glasses crashed to the floor and an elderly man costumed as a samurai threw a lit cigarette in the air and caught it in his mouth. Dubois, dressed unconvincingly as a bell-bottomed sailor, saluted me from his temple with an expertly assembled *cha gio* roll.

—Who's the caterer? he winked. Might have been your old favourite Le Loi!

—Lord almighty, man, you have a mind like a steel trap.

—Not at all! I've just had unlimited time to reflect on what came before.

His smile looked painfully wide. He moved even closer.

—Le Loi never did get a book out of me, I stammered. I might try a different tack and describe how the Ming Chinese felt at being the defeated power of 1428, as we've had some insight into that.

My Sorbonne fantasy reappeared then as it so often did: from the windows of our dismal student lounge, beams of sunlight shone through my tumbler of wine. "Verdant spring passes quickly," someone was saying, "and man ages rapidly like a bamboo shoot."

—I mustn't stay long, said Dubois. My girls are waiting.

He was shouldered aside by Frémont himself, searching out anyone with a sword that they might duel.

—How do you manage all these native servants? I asked him.

—You mean how can I trust 'em? Don't spread it around, but we pay 'em fully *half* the European wage. There's no such thing as a well-compensated Communist!

I danced with several heavily perspiring women. Was I eating enough with Georgette out of the country? they asked. Was I *really* the first Vietnamese genie to count time to Strauss, and wasn't it awful how they played us for fools at the negotiations in Geneva?

Even at seventy-five Madame Frémont was lightest on her feet, bar none.

—I took the train out of Hué a few days ago, she whispered, and I'm sure I spotted your friend Marguerite on the platform!

Marguerite. I still gaped with astonishment at the memory of her parading into my hemisphere so that Masson could ask me for a job. "Love is misfortune!" I ought to have shouted at him.

—Is that where she and Aldo ended up? I'd assumed she was too preoccupied with a pipe to step out of doors.

—True, Madame Frémont smiled, she's not so nice and chubby as she used to be!

As the strings subsided the tuxedoed valet appeared at my elbow.

—Telephone for you, sir. The caller is a Monsieur Le Port.

—What, now?

—There is a line in the study, sir.

A browning photo of Frémont *père* smiled from the desk.

—What is it now, Le Port?

—Just trying to wrap things up here, sir, before I come in Monday and begin again. Not sure how this mildewy thing came to me—the note says "P. Lazarie" and "1936" but that couldn't be you, could it? Wait, what's *this* stamp? "1909." How old *are* you, anyway?

I'd fired him once already but the only applicants for his job had been convicts, so we'd had to bring him back. Though scores of Vietnamese had been eminently qualified.

—What file's this? Is it 1909, Le Port, or 1936?

—Here's another clerk's name—"H. LeDallic." You know him?

Even in that stifling room a chill ran up the back of my neck.

—It says "LeDallic"? I asked. Really?

—Well, is it your file, sir, or isn't it? I want to go home now.

—You haven't told me the applicant's name! I shouted.

—Hold on, I dropped it.

I heard him shuffling papers, each integral, no doubt, to the continued existence of the French Union.

—Here, it says "Adélie Tremier." You know her?

Through the doorway I watched Frémont stalk across the foyer, the tip of his scabbard rattling against the marble floor. He peered in at me, tilted his head, then went away with a whirl of cape.

—Renard put you up to this, I said into the receiver. Put him on the line.

—What?

I found only a finger of champagne in the bottom of the flute.

—Lazarie? he asked.

—Tell me succinctly, I said, why this was on your desk.

—I *have* told you! This woman flew in the day before yesterday from a hospital up in Vientiane, and now the Army wants confirmation of who she is. "Immediate confirmation." Took two days for the kid to run her file down. Shall I have him skinned?

Dubois the sailor appeared, arm-in-arm with the musketeer Frémont, and the two began to waltz for my benefit. Dubois led.

—Keep her there, I said.

—She hasn't been *here*, she's at Doumer Hospital! They said she has a son who—

THE RAIN HAD resumed and the wipers cast a translucent smear across the windscreen. I'd planned to have them replaced, of course, but had been too distracted of late to see that plan to fruition—had been too distracted, some might say, since January 1936. Since my return from the Mekong all those many years before, I'd been telling myself that if Henri's death had come as a shock to everyone then Adélie Tremier's, if ever confirmed, would go down as one of the most *expected* in human history. I had not left Saigon since, of course, in pursuit of Adélie or for any other reason.

How old would she be now? She was ten years older than my mother, I hadn't forgotten that, so therefore she'd been born in 1880 and was seventy-four years old. I imagined the subject of that beloved photograph as a leathery cadaver, with hair like a dandelion gone to seed—and what about the illness which had almost killed her? As I very nearly ran a pony cart off the road—my golden slippers making me lead-footed—I began to wholly doubt if it would be the same woman at all.

On its sidestreet near Ben Thanh Market, the Doumer had served as a hospital for underprivileged locals before being unceremoniously seconded by the Foreign Legion to serve the appalling number of casualties being flown down from Tonkin. Its door was continuously guarded and windows grated against grenades, but at half-past nine in the evening it was such a hive of activity, as bandaged men were hoisted in and out of trucks, that I marched quite unhindered into the foyer. Eyes peeled for that dandelion-headed woman, as though she'd be expecting me, I very nearly knocked down a white girl standing just inside the door.

—You must excuse me, I said. Were you going out, Miss?

—Oh, no! Not just yet.

She spoke with a certain harshness as though French were not her first language. Her dark hair in an oblong bun, she wore a khaki Air Force mechanic's uniform with a waist tapered by safety pins and with trouser cuffs folded halfway to her knee. *I* at least had had the foresight, speaking of costumes, to leave my mask and turban in the car.

I held the door open but she continued gazing out at the night. Moths flew in. The tilt of her head and carriage of her shoulders were painfully familiar to me. Even the space between eye and eyebrow. Weakness shot up my arms like a serum and I let the door clack shut. I took up her hand, all the time imagining LeDallic berating yet another example of my gross delusion in the line of duty and threatening to brain me with a saucepan.

—Madame . . . Tremier? I said.

She didn't withdraw her hand but merely stared up at me, her delicate mouth hanging open; her every feature looked just as it ought to have done, despite the years and the cast-off uniform.

—I am she, the woman said.

Then I found that my knees were quite unable to support me, as behind her the black windows suddenly expanded to gigantic proportions.

—Please help! I heard her call. He's fainted.

The clattering typewriter and ringing telephones sounded impossibly distant. A pair of soldiers hauled me from the sticky tiles to an iron bench. I brushed tobacco from my cheek—but where'd she gone? Ah, beside me, gripping my clammy hand with fingers of steel. She smelled of sandalwood and loamy soil, and the skin I glimpsed beneath her collar was brown as café crème.

By now my imaginary Henri had thrown down his saucepan and uncorked a Paternina Gran Reserva out of sheer exasperation—if we'd found her in 1936 would I have collapsed then, or had I been felled by the toll of years? She lifted her chin and released my sorry hand, smoothing down the legs of her uniform as a bearded doctor hurried over. He held my head steady to peer into my right eye, then the left.

—I'll see if a bed's available.

—No, I said. I'm here visiting a patient.

I had no need for the 1905 portrait to see that Adélie's nostrils and spare lips were quite unchanged and it crossed my mind—quite without a reason—that I'd have no use for that picture ever again.

A native nurse appeared with a wheelchair, and the same two soldiers slandered me under their breath—and who could blame them?—as they set me down within its creaking frame. Then I was left with Adélie. She leaned on her knees, that ellipse of hair falling against her neck, and tilted her head to examine me as though I were a caged rodent in an alley.

—I've come to speak to you, I explained, on behalf of the High Commission, Madame. If you'd prefer to go somewhere less antiseptic, my car—

—Come up and see Manu, she said.

I was required to show my papers to military security—and quite rightly, considering my robe and pointed slippers—then she rolled me, her rubber sandals slapping with aplomb, into the elevator. My heart beat like a bird's as I watched her wait stiffly at the pimply operator's side. The muscles in her jaw tightened and she clenched the handrail. Evidently elevators were not her element.

We started down the third-floor corridor; voices bellowed from a room on the left.

—"Covered in glory," that's what the headline'll read! "Covered in glory."

—"The Secret Saviour of Dien bien Phu!"

A flash bulb burst the instant we reached the doorway and I felt strong enough then to climb out of the chair, and I chanced to place a hand upon the back of Madame Tremier's lean arm. Three grey-suited men from *Le Courrier Saigonnais* filled all of the space in the room not occupied by the bed or a pair of steel chairs, while Captain Tremier himself, of the triangular brows and glass eye, leaned against the drawn blinds and gripped the windowsill as though he were balanced on a precipice. A saline drip fed into the back of his wrist. His stubbly hair was snow-white, wattles of skin dangled below his chin, and the best his face could offer the newspaper camera was the deep lines of a perpetual frown. It had been fifty years since our last meeting, to judge by the changes in him.

—No, gentlemen, he murmured. Please.

—Though we'll have to write "Sergeant Ferdinand" more often than not. You know, "Merde" isn't the sort of thing you can print in the paper a hundred times a day!

—Could you move that eye so it looks this way? asked the photographer.

—Come! insisted Adélie. You must lie down before you fall down!

She knocked the men aside like ten-pins as she crossed and took Tremier by his pyjama'd arm. He obligingly slumped against her. From their chatter I deduced he was a veteran of the cataclysm at Dien bien Phu.

—Aha! cried the reporters. Didn't the little nurse mention a long-lost daughter? And what brings *you* here, Lazarie? Friend of the family?

—Only to express the thanks of a grateful government, I said.

—Photo shaking hands?

—And can you explain the get-up, Lazarie?

—No, to both queries.

Tremier heaved his long legs onto the bed and his pretty young mother—however counterintuitive that might seem—pulled the blanket over his large bare feet.

—Any last quotes? asked the reporters.

The patient studied the bed rail. He scratched his forehead absently.

—Only that, with the men who made up my squad still fighting for her, France can feel nothing but the greatest pride.

—Aha! the reporters said. Timeless.

—Timely!

—Did you throw your weight around, Lazarie, to get him in his own room?

—Half the wounded who came south have been shipped to Massachusetts, said the photographer. Cleared this place out!

—The United States?

—Sure, the United States!

—"Through these gallant exploits, the hard-bitten Sergeant Ferdinand has covered not only himself but the entire Legion in glory."

Taking their hats from the stand, the *Courrier Saigonnais* men departed. I stepped forward to shake Tremier's hand but the young woman was so occupied in arranging his pillows that I felt I'd be underfoot, and took a seat beneath the humming light bulb. "I've accomplished the impossible," I wanted to tell him. "Here is your mother, long dead of tuberculosis." The girl seized his stubbly head and kissed his temple a dozen times, *pa-pa-pa-pa-pa-pa-pa*. As he lay back on the pillow she wiped his brow with a damp cloth—she struck me as a woman with a great many younger siblings.

—How do you feel, Tremier? I asked.

He lifted his hand to waggle the fingers; evidently the intra-venous bothered him.

—Never better, he said. The name is Merde.

—How do you like the accommodation?

—It seems very modern! said Adélie.

A sigh shuddered out of Tremier and he lay his hand on the sheet.

—I nearly told them, he murmured, that each time the Mer-curochrome ran out up at Dien bien Phu the men would pray for maggots in their bandages. The only sure way to clean out rot.

I crossed one genie's leg over the other in what I felt a very meaningful gesture.

—My name is Pierre Lazarie. We've met once before, Sergeant, but you were introduced as Captain Tremier. I was asked at that time to find your mother.

He lifted triangular brows to study me.

—I gave you that picture of all of us, he recalled. You were the youngster.

—I've come along to update your mother's file.

—Where's the picture?

—On my desk. I'm Adjutant to the High Commissioner.

—Go and get it.

—It will be in your hands tomorrow. And this woman they said was your daughter looks remarkably like the woman in that picture.

—When we arrived at Muong Sai, Adélie said, we were in a terrible state. We couldn't think what else to say.

Tremier squeezed his mother's hand. He managed a sheepish smile.

—Monsieur Lazarie set to work looking for you when I first came out to Hanoi. 1936.

—Did he? she asked. That must have been extremely frustrating. *I* couldn't have found me, and I knew where to look.

—And though it pains me to ask, Madame, have you managed to maintain your youthful sheen through diet and exercise?

—Nothing so involved as that, she said. Monsieur Laramie—

—Lazarie! I said. Pierre!

My jaw dropped open—how could she not have known my name?

—Monsieur *Lazarie*, have you really been hunting for me since 1936?

—Yes, ah, the dry season of '36. We believed you'd—yes, and it is you, ah—

—Excuse me?

—We had reason to believe you'd reached Luang-Prabang—

—Oh, but I did!

She spoke as though I'd asked whether she'd seen *Diabolique* on rue Pellerin.

—Ah, I said. Nevertheless, my partner and I met with one difficulty after another. He was killed and the search called off.

—That horrible fat man? asked Tremier. What happened to him?

—Don't concern yourselves. Merely an accident.

Which did LeDallic a disservice, of course.

—If he knew me before, Adélie told her son, perhaps I'll tell the whole story.

—I may doze off, he replied.

—But your water's nearly empty—mustn't get thirsty!

She extricated a battered canteen from the locker, detached the saline bag with practiced hands then stepped lithely toward the corridor. And though the doorway was half her height again she clearly *stooped* as she passed through it, as though she feared hitting her head. And why the canteen?

—So, I said. You were at Dien bien Phu?

Tremier folded his thin arms across his chest.

—I've been anywhere a Frenchman has fired a shot in anger, sir. I could be a schoolboy's textbook. When Maman's not chattering in my ear I've been telling myself that we're quite unlike the Nazis because when *our* operations take us through villages we tend to leave the children alive, but by God! If we're comparing ourselves to Nazis then we may have a problem!

This was more than I could follow; I listened for footfalls from the corridor.

—Yet how can either of us be certain this is your mother? I asked. Just for argument's sake.

He studied me again from beneath those historic brows.

—Because she *looks* exactly like her. You have the picture.

—Yes, I said, but this friend of ours looks as Adélie Tremier did *fifty years* ago. Which to my mind must prove that she is not the same woman.

—Tell me another theory if you must. I may doze.

I glanced again at the empty doorway.

—What if this young woman appeared up in Laos and some old-timer told her she was the spitting image of that Tremier woman who'd come through forty years before, and then when our friend ran into you she saw her opportunity?

—Asinine. How could a stranger have known the names of my mother's cronies and that she'd wanted me to attend the École des Beaux-Arts when I was nine?

I folded my arms across the bed rail.

—But what if your mother had lived up there for ages, might *still* be alive in Luang-Prabang, age seventy-four, and our old-timer introduced them based on their resemblance? And this younger version sucked up information like a sponge.

—And then lay in ambush for me in a village so far removed it hadn't seen a visitor of any kind, white or otherwise, in fifty years. And *recognized* me, though any picture she might've seen would've shown a kid. I've puzzled this out. She knew me though I haven't used the name Tremier since 1944. Asinine. If you're sure she's an adventuress then go to the supply counter and arrest her.

—Well, in truth, I told him, I saw immediately it was your mother.

I swung a slipper jauntily.

—What's your prognosis? I asked.

—Huh. Malaria, they tell me. Or cholera. Though I haven't had fever. And a dozen blood tests have come back negative, as far as they're telling us. I know better.

He shut his eyes.

—How do you mean? I asked.

—If she can carry on *living* in all defiance of science, why shouldn't—

—It was that sweet orderly! Adélie trumpeted. I told him we might have a long night so could he bring us in a little coffee, and do you know what he said? He might have a croissant or *two*, can you imagine?

Ducking through the doorway with a shade more subtlety, she strode to the IV stand and hung up a fresh bag, though it had an identical notch in its side. She reattached the tube, kissed the back of Tremier's hand, then returned the canteen to the locker. On anyone else her quasi-military costume would've been laughable. She took her seat, wrapped her arms around the sergeant's forearm and swept a hair back from her cheek.

—So, she said. My escapade.

Suffice to say the young woman once more confirmed that she was the same Madame Tremier whom LeDallic and I had hunted for, that she *had* been on a quest for life eternal as we'd been told, or at least for a remedy for tuberculosis, and that, departing Luang-Prabang in late 1909 or early 1910, she'd *succeeded* in finding immortality's apparent source in a mountain spring in the Lao hinterland, and for the subsequent forty-five years had lived in an adjacent village, taken a husband, raised crops and, as I could see for myself, not aged a day. The spring had lately lost its power, though, after a gangrenous Legionnaire drowned himself in it, which sadly only confirmed her tribe's superstitions, as in her early days she'd narrowly avoided being executed after sullying its shallows with a wooden waterwheel. Suffice to say, if its subject had not been sitting in front of me I wouldn't have believed a word of it—does a human being not age rapidly, after all, like a bamboo shoot?

—But if it was an *underground* spring, I suggested, couldn't there be an unpolluted outlet somewhere else?

Tremier at last opened his eyes.

—Hadn't thought of that, he murmured.

—Can't you confirm its location?

—North of Pa Na, he said.

—What, the mountain in Laos? All of China is north of Pa Na!

—The helicopter men at Muong Sai will have a record, said Adélie.

—The airstrip? I asked. The Pathet Lao attacked it last, what, Wednesday—mortar attack, base burnt to the ground. Not a scrap left.

At this they sat studying each other as though deciding upon an aperitif. Adélie kissed the back of Tremier's hand. What paths had these two trod in their time? What place did I possibly have alongside them?

—It occurs to me, I said, that for the purposes of my paperwork I ought to see some irrefutable proof of your identity. Have you held on to a passport? Some letters?

She stretched her tawny arms, then went to the window. She peered between the slats of the blinds and I wondered if our Saigon even resembled that of 1909.

—Only proof, I'm afraid, determines whether a story becomes history or a novel.

—In the hotel room I have an eight-sided brass dipper given me directly from the hands of Sisavang Vong.

—Well, old Sisavang, for one, *is* alive, but sadly beyond the state where he might confirm one fact versus another.

Tremier began to snore raggedly and Adélie took a broom from the corner and began to sweep, immediately raising a cloud of dust.

—I can't sit still! she whispered. By this time of night we'd be in bed, certainly, but during the day I'd be weaving, chopping, pounding, gutting the dinner. Not one moment for sitting and fretting, which was certainly preferable.

I lifted my feet that she might sweep beneath them.

—One story we tell, she said quietly, is that when the Creator made all the nations in the world he asked them to receive the marks they would each write with—alphabets, I suppose—and to bring something to write on. Some brought wood and stone, but our people brought a deer-skin. They took their marks back to the village and sat down to decide what they would write but the dogs ate up the deer-skin, so ever since, sir, the only proof of anything is if someone says it's so. Half the time we know a story isn't true but we remember it right along with the others, which taken all together make the world more interesting, wouldn't you say? So what harm can it do to write in your file that I came down from hills age seventy-four? You needn't take a photograph!

—It's *her*, said Tremier without opening his eyes. Any other woman would've given me some peace.

As Adélie tipped out her dustpan, a stooped orderly in white tunic backed through the door, pulling a cart laden with steaming cups of coffee, a plate of croissants and dainty balls of butter. I'd never had a chance to eat at the party and my mouth watered at the sight.

—None left in *our* kitchen, Madame. They drove these over from the barracks!

—*Asala? Alla!* Adélie cried.

—What did you say? I asked.

—Why, what did I—oh, that was village talk! I'm just happy the coffee's hot.

She bustled about with our plates and cups. Tremier took one sip and set his coffee down. At a glacial pace the orderly rolled his cart toward the door. I pulled my croissant in half, found this a chore as it was hopelessly stale, but buttered it nonetheless. Adélie stirred her coffee, contemplating her own pastry.

—For all those years I didn't want for anything but my little boy and what we have here now. To dip a croissant in milky coffee and watch the droplets bead, then pull out all the insides and stuff them in my mouth.

She took it in both hands and slowly tore it in two, but it did not flake the way a croissant ought to. She sniffed it. Then with furrowed brow she walked to the corner and dropped the two halves into the wastepaper basket.

—I'll wait until the bakeries open, she murmured.

The orderly hurried out. Like Georgette, injured pride had lent him wings.

—Maman, said Tremier, I should've asked those newspaper idiots the state of fair Indo-China since things went to shit. These doctors are tight-lipped bastards.

I nearly leapt from my chair—since fainting on arrival, I'd hardly been useful.

—Well, I said, there's a conference in Geneva just now trying to decide what's to *become* of fair Indo-China. We're there, of course, Russia, Britain, a few others, even the Viet Minh—are you sure you have the stomach for this?

Tremier watched the ceiling.

—Nothing's been ratified, I went on, but ever since England let India go without a fight we don't seem to garner much sympathy. My guess is that they'll divide Vietnam at the 17th Parallel, give the north to the Communists and let us keep the south—let Bo Dai keep the south, I ought to say—but then there's pressure to unify the country again in a year or two and hold elections to decide whether the man in the paddy field wants Bo Dai or Ho Chi Minh in charge, but I can't see that happening. They'll never hold an election in the south. Bo Dai could never win. At which point the north will have to march south, election or not, because most of the rice is down here. The revenge of the Trinh over the Nguyen is how I see it, three hundred years after the fact!

—Why wouldn't Bo Dai win? Tremier grimaced. He looks okay.

—Ho Chi Minh has railed after autonomy since before he was expelled from high school and now he sits at the head of twelve million people who've backed him every step of the way, while Bo Dai is the insipid president, as *appointed* by us, and insipid hereditary emperor before that. In the meantime the Americans, from the sound of it, plan to show every Communist the error of his ways by dropping money on him out of an aeroplane. Haven't we done stupendous work? If the Khmer kings wait until the end of days as emasculate trees, I can little wonder what will become of us!

Neither was listening. While his mother collected dishes Tremier straightened up on his elbows.

—You know, I would've chucked her whole story, he said, if I hadn't seen for myself how that lake went to work. Fixed up the men better than a whole street of hospitals!

—Ah! I smiled. And that was a new one on you?

—Except for one time. First came out to Tonkin. We bivouacked by an old temple. We needed sticks to stand the tents up so this corporal climbed a tree and started hacking them down. The priest came out and said, "Stop"—he spoke French—"stop," he said, "that's the sacred tree." The corporal yelled something back at him and the priest just bowed and went inside. Ten seconds later I watched the corporal fall out of the tree. Broke his eye socket.

But before we could discuss the notion of coincidence Adélie countered with a tale describing the origins of her once-enchanted pond: in order to provide for weary travellers, simply put, it sprang from the mouth of a murdered boy.

—You see? she concluded. For every horror there is a wonder!

—Though some might argue that the opposite is true, I said.

—No, no, murmured the sergeant. Maman's here next to me, and where's the accompanying horror? There's none.

I nodded amiably at his sunken cheeks, the saline drip, the bedpan on the floor.

—Oh, love will see a person through any amount of misfortune, she murmured. Despite continents and centuries.

Which was certainly a change from the "Love is misfortune" mantra I'd been enamoured with. Elbows on the blanket, she gazed rapturously at her son, whose lone eye stared at the fly-specked ceiling.

—But do you think, Manu, that if they go far enough into the forest they'll find another spring like that?

The ringing of bicycle bells drifted up from the street. He spoke, though his lips hardly moved.

—I've told you. There's nothing like that in the world anymore, Maman. Since you've been away I've seen what the world is.

She smiled across at me as if to say, *Isn't he wonderful?* Then she took a handkerchief from her pocket, set it on the blanket, carefully unfolded it—as though she were merely familiar with handkerchiefs but had never used one—then with great deliberation wiped the perspiration from either side of her neck. I jogged my slipper on the end of my foot and felt hollow-boned exhaustion envelop me.

—Will I find you here tomorrow? I asked.

—Certainly we'll be here. Oh, and you've been such a dear, I must ask—

—Yes?

—Manu will be dying to know—what are you dressed as?

I DROVE HOME through the many-puddled streets. I twisted my pillow until four o'clock in the morning and then, because I couldn't bring myself to creep into the High Commission to retrieve the photograph, I sketched her face upon the tablecloth again and again.

AN UNEXPECTED
DEPARTURE

Pierre Lazarie.

'D JUST begun opening letters when Le Port opened my door without a word, allowing Dubois to make straight for the cigar box. He slipped five into various pockets. He'd evidently been out all night as he still wore his costume.

—I was reminiscing about the old days, he said, and your man asked if I'd ever heard of this Madame Tremier who disappeared into the jungle twenty years ago! So I—

—Forty-five years, as he knows very well. I went over to Doumer to see her.

Dubois collapsed in the chair and turned the photograph toward him—Adélie's hair still lifted by that gust of wind.

—Succulent! he hissed.

—Funny how no one mentions the husband and son sitting with her.

—But what's she like? Preserved in a jar?

I realized that of all the Immigration Department men who might appreciate her story none but Dubois, the potato-cheeked sailor, was still living—as though time had scooped us like peppercorns into the palm of its hand and scattered us quite at random onto a side plate—so without preamble I summarized the tale she'd told.

—And "took a husband," did she? I admire that turn of phrase! When can I have a look at her?

I threw down my pen—why had I come into the office at all? Habit, just the same as my ten years with Georgette.

—Let's take my car, I said. We can see whether Tremier's shown any improvement, though he went in the Foreign Legion so it's a different name—didn't you see this morning's piece on the courageous Sergeant Merde who walked his platoon across Laos? That's the same Captain Tremier who sat in this office!

—This morning's paper is years too recent for me.

We strode down the corridor until he paused outside Albin's office, which of course had once been his.

—"Sergeant Merde of the Foreign Legion," he murmured. Wish I'd thought of that, instead of a goddamn plantation! Do you know what I'll ask? "When life is everlasting," I'll ask her, "is it possible the situation might degenerate into perpetual orgy?"

I took him by a navy-blue sleeve.

—You *can't* see her, I said. You need a bath rather too badly.

I drove lazily up rue La Grandière, grinning to myself as if this time she really would be waiting for me in the foyer. As the bowler hats and drums and horns of a Chinese funeral passed I considered that perpetual orgy is likely more enjoyable in the imagination than in practice.

I parked the car and sauntered around the corner; beneath the shade trees, smiling natives bicycled along the sun-dappled pavement. A white woman was crossing, quite hatless, to my side of the street. Her white gown revealed a substantial amount of ankle but even more impressive was the sheer quantity of black hair falling down her back and cascading in ringlets down her bosom while framing, achingly, her long and exquisite neck. She walked haltingly, chin in the air as though a footman had just helped her down from a coach. Then as her eyes fell on me and a smile formed at the corners of her mouth I realized it was Adélie herself, her gait hampered by an impossibly large pair of shoes.

—I thought that I must have had the wrong idea about coffee! she called. But then I came outside and found a café, and I realized that the hospital's coffee is atrocious!

—I could file a report, I said feebly.

—I've been three times this morning! Have you ever seen so many natives in white shirts? When did they start to wear white shirts? Aren't the cars *quiet* as they go by? They sound like zithers! And I must say that *you* are looking very well, Monsieur Lazarie!

She offered her bare arm and I took it without hesitation— *pounced* on it, more accurately. The Legionnaire on guard saluted as we climbed the steps.

—Do you realize, she went on, that it's only thanks to paved streets and tiled floors that we're able to wear white at all? We'd be covered in dirt otherwise—yet another thing that makes a city palatable. Oh, and electric lights. And water from a tap!

The elevator boy's expression betrayed less emotion than the panelling.

—How old are you? she asked.

—Forty-one, I said.

—That's not *so* old. My husband was older than me when I was married.

Her first husband had been five years her senior, I knew that from her file, and her fellow up in the village? A thousand? She scratched her wrist as the glare of the second floor went past, and I imagined the pressure of those brown arms around my waist. The flies banging against the ceiling possessed enough insight to see that if she did turn to me it would only be out of heartache for her ailing child, her desecrated home, and that whenever *my* natural time expired, in six months or fifty years, to bring her still more grief, there'd be some other lop-eared fool for her, then another, *ad infinitum*. Though none would wait as long as I had—eighteen years! All this between the second and third floors as I studied the line of her jaw framed against her hair. She smiled.

—I realize that in a hundred years I may be stripped of everything except this sorry life, she said, but give me a cup of coffee as black as tar and I will not grumble. I may reach for the sugar when I'm at my lowest, but I will never grumble.

The boy slid back the iron gate. I thought of tipping him, of course, but refrained lest he saw my fumbling through my wallet as an opportunity to slice my belly open.

—I ought to have asked how your son is feeling! I said in the corridor.

—He sleeps. Asked for a pencil this morning. Perhaps he's drawn something.

—It occurred to me that you might be filling his intravenous from that canteen.

—That was our last good water! He filled it himself.

—Then it ought to be doing him a world of good! I said.

—No. If he recovered he'd be sent to kill more people.

—How much is left?

—There isn't any.

She went ahead of me into his room, lowering her head only slightly. A panorama of moss-specked roof tiles crowded the window.

—Aha! she cried. You *are* awake, you urchin!

Tremier lay with his good eye half-open, reading a telegram. They'd taken out the IV, though his pyjamas hung off him like badly pasted wallpaper.

—What's that? she asked. One of your friends has written?

He folded it in half and set it on the blanket.

—Answer to a wire. A nurse I wanted to locate. Not good news.

—A girl from this hospital?

—I knew her up north. Good morning, Lazarie. Have you come after proof?

I took the remaining chair as nonchalantly as possible, glad to be in a suit and tie.

—Only to see if you're feeling all right.

—It feels like something's leaking out of me.

—They jabbed you again, said his mother. You didn't bat an eye.

—Have you read the article on your exploits, Sergeant Merde?

His mother clicked her tongue, went to the window and lowered the blinds. Her son had fallen back to sleep with the telegram still between his fingers. I smoothed down my necktie.

—But what will happen to *you*, I asked, now that the water's run out?

—Oh, I haven't had a drop since Muong Sai!

She resumed her seat and I shifted mine closer to hers, then for several minutes we sat watching Tremier. His unshaven neck looked impossibly thin.

—I'd wanted him to be a painter, did you know that? I would have sold myself to the gypsies for him to have become a painter. Fifty-four years old now, he could have had a retrospective. Think of the gallery walls covered with his paintings, the catalogues. Imagine for a moment the world in which Emanuel Tremier is a painter.

The orderly shuffled in and handed her a metal bowl containing one egg.

—Ah, thank you! Raw this time? Thank you. And might you have a razor and things, that I might shave my father?

The man nodded vaguely. I wondered how many children he had at home and what the Communists taught them at midnight meetings.

—You'll have to bear with me, she said. This may take a few minutes.

Swaying, she held the egg overhead on the tips of her thumb and forefinger. I was more than happy to sit and watch whatever in God's name she was doing.

—Will it be 417? she murmured. Will it be 416?

She carried on reciting numbers until the egg suddenly cracked in her hand. She deftly caught the contents in the bowl.

—Good, he'll be all right for today. Apparently it will be a patient in 409. I hope he needn't suffer.

A foul smell drifted in from the corridor as the meal carts rolled past. I was meant to lunch with Renard yet I didn't stir. Madame Tremier leapt to her feet, though.

—I'll take advantage of you, Lazarie! she said. Sit with him for twenty minutes while I try the café on the next block!

In truth I was not happy to oblige, for the room's pickle-brine odour was worse than usual. With the increase in Viet Minh attacks I'd spent enough time at bedsides to envision an article, "The Diverse Aromas of Hospital Rooms in Saigon and Environs." The patient rubbed his empty socket with the flat of his hand.

—Wheel me to the elevator, he yawned, and we'll wait for her together.

The orderly located a chair and we were soon on our way down the corridor.

—They can say what they like, Tremier muttered. I wasn't made to lie in bed.

—Why, what have the doctors decided?

—This last one said it's anemia. I ought to have four and a half million platelets or some goddamn thing.

—How many *do* you have?

—One and a half.

I leaned over him to press the call button. His breath was atrocious. The same elevator boy was on duty, so I said nothing as we descended. In the foyer a doctor nodded to Tremier, then a whole cluster of soldiers.

—You're very popular, I said.

—Just *baraka*, he replied bafflingly. Patch of sun over there. Let me walk.

Large grated windows looked onto the street; the mid-morning sun threw geometric shadows across the linoleum.

—Do you *want* to walk?

—No, he admitted.

I opened a pack of Gitanes as we gazed outside. He took one without a word. On the street an Army truck loaded a patient and shuddered away, then a line of Legionnaires paraded up the sidewalk, arms swinging high and wide, each man slightly ridiculous in his cylindrical white *kepi* and sensible khakis hampered by huge red epaulettes. Tremier sat straight as a flagpole as they passed. Alongside a native girl pushing a perambulator, two women with shoulder-poles strode past, their baskets piled with white bouquets. Tremier snatched at a lethargic fly. A pair of doctors trotted up the steps and the sentry slid out of their way.

Then Tremier leapt suddenly to his feet, lurched out the open door and down the steps. On the sidewalk three Vietnamese youth stood around an open satchel. One lifted something—it might have been a piece of fruit—just as Tremier threw his arms around the trio and *collapsed* on them, as though to protect the boys, but there was immediately a loud bang and an orange flash enveloped all four.

I had lived in Saigon long enough to recognize an exploding grenade and so threw myself to the linoleum, expecting shrapnel to rain against the window. None came. I leapt up again. I may have been first on the scene, though it's difficult to recall now. Tremier lay face-down with his arms around two of the boys, their heads twisted, bellies mangled, in a veritable lake of dark blood. A tamarind tree stood some metres away and the third boy was attempting to drag himself up its diminutive iron fence. He had lost a foot. The Legionnaires surrounded him and I had the impression he was being seized by circus ringmasters.

The native girl, who'd been nearest bystander to the explosion, sat hunched behind the overturned perambulator with the yowling baby in her lap. Neither showed sign of injury. One of the shoulder-pole women crouched hatless in the street, collecting their strewn flowers, while the other crawled across to stroke the girl's arm. The child was Vietnamese, I was surprised to see, for ninety-nine times out of a hundred a native girl pushing a perambulator in Saigon is governess to a European family. She opened her blouse to offer the child her breast and the street lapsed into what seemed like silence—despite shouting from all sides and the shrieks of the one-footed Viet Minh—to be replaced a moment later by the yowl of police sirens.

Tremier's right hand lay across a dead boy's torn shirt. The hand, in repose, of a sergeant of the Foreign Legion: brown, slightly liver-spotted, gummy with gauze where the IV had been attached, and though long hands they were remarkably thin. They better resembled a potter's hands than a soldier's. I wondered whether he was really the exclusive property of his mother and the Foreign Legion or if he had a wife somewhere, children. His face was no longer a human being's, so my eyes rested instead on the shredded leg of his blue pyjamas until a white plastic sheet was thrown over the dead men.

—Viet Minh assassination cell, a policeman announced.

I allowed myself to be herded back along with the rest of the crowd. I might have shown my credentials and stayed with Tremier, but he was no longer Tremier.

The policemen set the perambulator on its wheels.

I backed onto the toes of the woman behind me, apologized, and saw blood spattered on the hem of my trousers. I had witnessed a battle, and no mistake. No cannon had been fired, no rifles so much as raised, but it had been warfare as deliberate as any action fought by Le Loi or de Gaulle. As an atom bomb left the victor no spoils I felt sure that all future wars would be fought one sidestreet-grenade at a time—certainly the uniformed soldier was a thing of the past, for what could he be but a target?

—Was it an accident with a car?

Madame Tremier gripped my sleeve, her black eyes peering over the myriad shoulders. I took her hand, slipped an arm around her waist, and steered her forward toward the policeman. I might have been more tactful but I can't imagine how.

—An attack, I said. And your boy has been badly hurt. Very badly hurt.

I felt her draw up.

—He's in his room!

—No, I said. No, he's here.

I no longer steered her; she seemed to drift above the pavement, and the policeman lowered his white baton and stepped aside. The mutilated Viet Minh youths had already been loaded onto stretchers, leaving only Manu's bare feet protruding from beneath the sheet.

—That isn't Manu.

—Don't look. It wouldn't do to remember him as he is under there.

She crouched beside his bare, pathetic feet. Her features— grey pouches under her eyes, cheeks, the corners of her mouth— hinted at how a septuagenarian face ought to have looked. She breathed shallowly, twisting her lower lip between her fingers.

—They're his feet. God, they're ugly!

She lifted one and kissed its cracked, leathery heel. Then dropped it. Then set fingertips to the pavement to steady herself.

—A car did this? she asked.

—He saw a grenade and ran out to stop them.

—But the fool couldn't *walk*!

Two hospital orderlies touched her shoulder and she backed away that they might set down their stretcher. They lifted Tremier aboard, sheet and all, then rushed up the steps as though something might still be done for him. At the door they passed a line of Legionnaires with their *kepis* to their chests. I looked back at Adélie—her tearless, chalk-white face, the hem of her dress stained red—just as she raced past, barefoot and noiseless, across the pavement and up the steps. She was inside the hospital by the time I'd taken two strides. I heard a crash of metal. Men shouted from the foyer and from their voices I imagined the Viet Minh had made another attempt.

A rifle stock stopped my passage through the door but in truth no one's eyes were on me; they were fastened on Adélie. The stretcher lay overturned. Encircled by soldiers and orderlies she sat on the floor, cradling Tremier's head to her chest. She stroked his hair, lifted his hand to kiss the knuckles and I saw that her chest was slick with gore. Even the soldiers could only stand and wipe the backs of their necks. A Vietnamese boy waited at her back with a mop and bucket.

—His daughter, someone announced.

—Let me through, I said.

But even then I could only hover over her as she pressed the dead man to her like a—well, as a mother would her child. As some mothers might hold a child.

—Madame, one nurse said, we must . . .

—You see, Madame, said a doctor, it's, it's . . .

I crouched and put my arms around her, my shoes sliding on the wet tiles. I pressed my forehead to her wet ear, held her shoulder to my chest. Each gulp of air tasted of blood, and if I hadn't truly been in love with her in the years before we'd met, I was in love with her in that moment.

370

—Okay, I whispered. Okay. It doesn't help him. You see it doesn't help?

She jerked away as though to drag him to a dark corner, but I held her fast. The muscles in her back shifted against me like machinery.

—Mademoiselle, please, said a ragged voice. A little dignity.

A gaunt Foreign Legion medic gripped a clipboard, a smouldering cigarette between his fingers.

—I assume you can hear me, Mademoiselle, so I ask that you let us do our jobs. He is property of the French government until such time as we choose to release him. Security of the facility must be maintained before anyone else gets killed.

I relinquished my grip that she might look up at the man but instead she slumped sideways against me, her cheek against my shirt front.

—By which I mean come back tomorrow, the medic said.

Eyes pressed shut, she let her son's head slide to her lap, and the orderlies immediately spirited the corpse onto their stretcher, threw the sheet over him and hurried across the foyer. The medic was already in hushed conversation with a yawning nurse. My last glimpse of Emanuel Tremier was of his white feet passing between the elevator's grated doors into shadow.

Legionnaires offered hands to help us up, but I remained on the floor with my arms around Adélie. I didn't care how long we sat there.

—I must tell Kamili, she whispered.

SHE'D BOUGHT two dresses that morning, as luck would have it—and if there still was such a thing—so after being allowed to shower on the second floor she changed into the fresh one. I threw away my jacket. Fortunately my shirt was not badly spattered.

We tottered outside. Beneath the tamarind tree a native police inspector, pen in hand, interviewed the girl with the perambulator, and when she nodded toward me he asked for my story of the attack followed by a reiteration of my story. While I spoke I watched Adélie walk the few steps—once more in her shoes, and awkward as a colt—to the ashen-faced young mother. I couldn't hear what was said but after a moment Adélie produced a handkerchief, wiped the girl's eyes, then kissed her forehead. She was hardly recognizable as the Adélie I'd pulled from the hospital floor, and I wondered how many Adélies there'd already been and how many there were yet to be. The girl lifted her sleeping child into the sunshine and placed it in Madame Tremier's arms, and though it raised its hands in alarm Adélie tucked its head under her chin and swayed confidently.

Cyclists steered nonchalantly around a conical-hatted street cleaner sweeping blood into the gutter. Adélie kissed the child before placing it once more in the girl's arms and walking back to me, her heels clattering dully against the pavement. I repeated my particulars, then led her to my car.

From force of habit I drove toward the Continental. At rue Pellerin I stopped for a policeman's raised hand and Adélie opened the passenger door and stepped down into the street, much to my alarm, only to open the rear door and drag herself onto the back seat. The officer raised his eyebrows and slammed both doors shut.

When I peered behind me she had pulled her knees against her chest and the blanket from the floor over her head. I couldn't hear her, for I used the horn more liberally than usual as we navigated the intersections. The city, the day, the entire year were too shrill, too hot, too utterly baffling. I was struck with the conviction that every native astride a 1927 motorcycle was hell-bent on killing himself and everyone around him.

I parked on rue Catinat and sat with my feet in the street. A great many men in canary-yellow suits walked past. I thought them asinine. I gave Adélie a handkerchief from the glove box.

—Whatever happens next, she murmured, I must have rice whisky.

Old Nguyen still sat behind the bar at the Continental, propped on a stool beside the ports and sherries; LeDallic's ambition for him, regarding Nijinsky and the League of Nations, was now impossible as both institutions were no more. Nguyen's inane grandson now poured the drinks, Nguyen the Much Younger.

—We've missed your lady wife!

I ordered my usual red, and for my friend a tumbler of rice whisky.

—Distilled in Hanoi, isn't it? I asked. How long before the brand isn't available?

—Oh, Monsieur Lazarie! said the bartender. There is nothing to worry about!

Wide-eyed, Adélie sat at my usual table in what had always been Georgette's chair, taking in the other diners and their flashing cutlery. A group of pimply young men wagged their ties at each other as they stole glances in her direction.

Without a word we drained our glasses. The waiter came. I asked for more drinks and ordered the *plat du jour*.

—Do you have croissants? Madame Tremier asked.

—Certainly, Madame.

—Fresh this minute?

—From earlier this morning.

—I'll have rice.

—*Only* rice, Madame?

—And some chicken. Don't cook it very much.

At one time the balconies would have been crowded with new arrivals, spellbound by the spectacle of the rapturous East, but now they stood empty.

—If you'd prefer to go elsewhere, I said, maybe to put your head down—

—Call the waiter back. I want coffee.

Old Nguyen himself poured the coffee at the bar then set the white cup in its saucer. Madame Tremier only stared as it was set in front of her.

—But if he *had* been a painter, she finally said, the baby and those women would be dead now. Have you heard of World War I?

—Have I? It killed a quarter of the men in France.

—He lost his eye there.

A bearded man laughed uproariously on the other side of the courtyard. The elderly couple beside us bent over their cassoulet.

—I mean to go to the Island of Khône as soon as possible, she said, to examine a road that ought to have been built, oh, somewhere. Across the river from it. I won't be able to eat that food when it comes.

—The houses on Khône are all blue and white, I said.

—Oh? Perhaps we ought to go together.

Anticipating afternoon rain, young waiters unfurled blue canopies above our heads. All new staff.

—I could sleep right under this table, said Adélie.

As she let her head hang forward, her bare shoulders looked thin as a bird plucked clean. She lifted heavy lids and blinked at me.

—Heaven is here on earth, somebody once told me that, can you believe it? They said we only had to look for it.

—Oh?

—When I was a child of six I didn't believe it!

—But what about this place you've come from?

—There? No. The *real* heaven wouldn't have crashed down so easily. Not so . . . delicate. Or so muddy.

—Then we must savour heaven when we find it, I said gravely.

She slid her saucer to one side and lay her cheek on her hands. Then she sprang to her feet, looked down at me, breathing through her mouth, her hair hanging like dark foliage. She sat once more. Her fingertips pressed to her brow seemed to be all that kept her upright.

—He couldn't have suffered, I said, if it's any consol—

—I just remembered Uroh, she said.

She inhaled desperately a dozen times, collected herself, frowned at me, then unfolded the red napkin and blew her nose.

—I have lived most of my life, she said, with someone else in my mind, like a carrot in front of a donkey—do you know what I mean by that?

—I can imagine, yes.

—Before we stir from this table, she said, you must eat whatever's on your plate.

—I seldom eat much.

—I don't doubt that, your wrists are thinner than mine!

We lay them against each other between the bud vase and empty glasses. I believe, in my defence, that my wrist *was* thicker than hers, though the jutting bones bespoke a man who did not look after himself.

—We'll have to linger, at any rate, I said. This time of year it rains all afternoon. Now I must ask so as to avoid any confusion: are you *really* Adélie Tremier?

—That man's waving to you, she said.

Sure enough, Old Nguyen stood in front of the bar—it had been years since I'd seen the hems of his trousers!—twisting a knotted hand in front of his chest. I rose to my feet. He jerked his head toward the lobby then shuffled in that direction with the speed of an agitated beetle. I realized that his white cutaway jacket was the last in the room, as all of those young waiters had vanished—or evacuated, to be precise. Those morally ambiguous waiters.

—Lazarie? asked Adélie. What does he—

Around us smiling customers lit their pipes, loosened their ties, signed chits with a flourish. I took her arm and pulled her to her feet.

We would run from the place, certainly, but first we would describe to our fellow patrons, through tightening throats, what was likely to happen, what was *going* to happen, and they would listen dumbfounded, their cutlery in their hands—no one had ever fled the Continental in Henri's day, after all, and those left behind would very shortly pay the price of that luxury. Pay very dearly. Adélie would tug white-lipped at my sleeve, and with her village in ruin, her hard-fought spring debased, I would wonder as we began to run if she might ever find a place in this latest version of the world where she might sit idly or where women did not kneel by the roadside in tears. But we would cross the red tile of the courtyard, rush down that carpeted corridor, cross the venerable wooden floor of that lobby, pass through those celebrated doors—and this writing testifies that we *did* pass—into the silence of the still-sun-dappled street. Our fingers intertwined.

ACKNOWLEDGEMENTS

M ANY, MANY thanks to the Canada Council for the Arts for financial support during the writing of this book.

Thanks to Anne McDermid and staff for being Adélie's initial backers and to Chris Labonté at Douglas & McIntyre for his passion for this book and its world. Thanks to Barbara Berson for her exhaustive edit, empathetic suggestions and for saving the book from being a shadow of itself. Thanks to Rick Maddocks for early feedback, Kerri Thompson for Luang-Prabang stuff, Edward Buckingham for French-language legwork, and Gillian Duncan-Vandermeirsch and Karen Handford for prospective names.

Many authors' works contributed peripherally to this novel, but a handful of books were invaluable: *A Legionnaire's Journey* by Leslie Aparvary, *In Laos and Siam* by Marthe Bassenne, *Indo-China and its Primitive People* by Henry Baudesson, *The White Death* by Thomas Dormandy, *Hell in a Very Small Place* by Bernard Fall, *A Dragon Apparent* by Norman Lewis, *Before the Revolution* by Ngô Viñh Long, and *France, Fin de Siècle* by Eugen Weber. I'm also indebted to Cornell University's astonishing *Southeast Asia Visions* website as well as to the fiction of Colette, Marguerite Duras, Graham Greene and Émile Zola. Roux's story of the magic lake is adapted from "The Enchanted Mountain" in *Laos Folklore of Northern Siam* by Katherine

Neville Fleeson, the recipe for Wourali poison is adapted from Charles Waterton's *Wanderings in South America*, and Adélie's farewell note is paraphrased from a letter written by John Keats to Fanny Brawne.

I'm especially grateful to Mr. La, my guide west of the Pak Ou in northern Laos.

Many thanks to the Advents, Collises, Handfords, MacArthurs, Schroeders and Suttons, and especially to Nicole, Jimmy and Finn for feeding me and taking me for walks and keeping my heart filled right up.

LINCOLN CLARKES

Adam Lewis Schroeder was born in British Columbia, completed a master's degree in Creative Writing at UBC and has since travelled extensively. He is the author of the story collection *Kingdom of Monkeys,* a Danuta Gleed Award finalist, and the novel *Empress of Asia,* nominated for the Amazon.ca/*Books in Canada* First Novel award and the B.C. Book Prizes' Ethel Wilson Fiction Prize. His story "This Is Not the End My Friend" appears in *Darwin's Bastards: Astounding Tales from Tomorrow.* He lives in Penticton, British Columbia.